THE VOLCANO DAUGHTERS

the VOLCANO DAUGHTERS

Gina María Balibrera

PANTHEON BOOKS
New York

All rights reserved. Published in the United States by Pantheon Books, a division of Penguin Random House LLC, New York, and distributed in Canada by Penguin Random House Canada Limited, Toronto.

Pantheon Books and colophon are registered trademarks of Penguin Random House LLC.

A portion of this work appeared, in different form, in *The Wandering Song: Central American Writing in the United States,* edited by Leticia Hernández-Linares, Rubén Martínez, and Héctor Tobar (San Fernando: Tia Chucha Press, 2017).

Library of Congress Cataloging-in-Publication Data
Name: Balibrera, Gina María, author.
Title: The volcano daughters : a novel / Gina María Balibrera.
Description: New York : Pantheon Books, 2024.
Identifiers: LCCN 2023030465 (print) | LCCN 2023030466 (ebook) |
ISBN 9780593317235 (hardcover) | ISBN 9780593317242 (ebook)
Subjects: LCGFT: Novels.
Classification: LCC PS3602.A59549 V65 2024 (print) |
LCC PS3602.A59549 (ebook) | DDC 813/.6—dc23/eng/20230908
LC record available at https://lccn.loc.gov/2023030465
LC ebook record available at https://lccn.loc.gov/2023030466

www.pantheonbooks.com

Jacket illustration by Eleni Debo
Jacket design by Jenny Carrow

Printed in the United States of America

FIRST EDITION

2 4 6 8 9 7 5 3 1

For my family

It appears to be a typical banana republic,
except, of course, that it does not export bananas.
—THOMAS P. ANDERSON, *MATANZA*

The only way for the . . . people to survive is to inhabit Xibalba
without letting themselves be overwhelmed by its lords.
—*POPOL VUH*

SELECTED CHARACTERS

Las Fantasmas, Our Narrators
Lourdes, daughter of Rosario, archivist, cachimbona
María, daughter of Rosario, younger sister of Lourdes, painter
Cora, daughter of Alba, who studies soil and sky
Lucía, daughter of Yoli, chelita who builds her own púchica loom

Las Mamis
Rosario, mother of Lourdes and María
Yoli, mother of Lucía
Alba, mother of Cora
Socorrito, mother of Graciela and Consuelo

Las Hermanas
Graciela, daughter of Socorrito, taken from her mother to serve as El Gran Pendejo's oracle, memorious
Consuelo, daughter of Socorrito, younger sister of Graciela, taken from her mother to be a consolation to Perlita, a sculptor
The great-grandmothers, who worked indigo and braced their backs against la ceiba to weave stories

Some Men
El Gran Pendejo, the General, descendant of the volcanoes, who kills thirty thousand Black and Indigenous people in 1932. El Gran Pendejo describes himself as god to the archbishop.
El patrón, a lesser pendejo. He runs the finca on the volcano where Graciela, Consuelo, and Las Fantasmas are born, and where their mothers work.
Germán, the father of Consuelo and Graciela, childhood friend of El Gran Pendejo
Patrick Brannon, the gringo who loses his mind when he comes to tame the sea, who brings the railroad and all colors of tontería
Phillip, Patrick's cousin, a hobby spiritualist who lives in Manhattan
Señor Domínguez, father of Lourdes and María, who lives in San Francisco's Richmond District with his recognized family
Héctor, Cora's man. He wouldn't describe himself as a Bolshevik, though others might.
Luis, Consuelo's painting teacher and her eventual boyfriend
The aviator, a writer, artist, and philanderer, eventually Consuelo's husband. Big baby.
León, one of those fufurufo idiots who puffs up his chest and plays at all sorts of things. ¿Cómo se dice la Lucía? Ah, sí, el fuccboi.
Felix, who creates the kingdom of rocks near Oppède le Vieux for artists seeking refuge during the Occupation of France. Consuelo's eventual lover.
Tommy, chronicler of our national unhappiness, dear young man
Los Mild Detectives, a pair of Hollywood cops, no less menacing for all their bumbling
El Scooter, the wet-eyed trout of trouts, tender, verbose, inarticulate, elastic-bodied

Women of the Capital
Perlita, the widow of Germán
Ninfa, grandmother, hyperrealistic artist, housekeeper for the Estate, former nursemaid to Perlita
La Claudia, daughter of Brannon, poet
Lidia, housekeeper to El Gran Pendejo
Las Rositas, a group of teenagers, children of the landowning class ensconced in comfortable rebellion, whose vow to make art or be art is writ in blood

En Los Yunais
Madame Belova, self-declared master, charismatic dilettante
Lindita Domínguez, wealthy finca wife, amiguita of Perlita
Rosie Swan, Hollywood star, güerita with a false name

Las Comadres de San Francisco
Josefina, who listens to ghosts
Silvia, who feeds her people
Clara, who brings the light
Miyuki, who runs a teahouse in Japantown
Salvador, el hijito de Graciela

The Creatures, Chimerical or Otherwise
El duende, naughty little guy, always serenading death. Lorca has been searching for him. Ya lo sabes. In this book, he tap-dances all up and down our mortal coil.
The ocelot, pet of Perlita's, both adored and neglected
La Siguanaba, a mother punished for her desire. Her child is lost to her, and she returns beside water to lure men to their death. Sometimes also known as La Cigua.
La Chasca, a princess punished for her desire. She drowns herself after her lover dies and returns with the full moon to bless fishermen.
Blood Woman, who defied her father, touched death's head, and made a heart of tree sap and smoke, before escaping to perform miracles in another world
The birds, who gather in the ceiba, marking the days' hours, always listening, the owls who carry Blood Woman from one realm into another, los torogoces who carry a thread in their beaks through time, the cackling ravens above and around us
La Prudencia Ayala, poet, loca, presidential candidate, fruit vendor, oracle, not a figment of our imagination, but mythical all the same
Los cadejos, the magic dogs of the volcano. One is a terrible omen, the other your savior.
The buffalo of Golden Gate Park, destroyed in herds while this land was devoured piece by piece. Some of the descendants remain here, perched on the edge of this world, where the sun sets. Vamos a la vuelta de toro toro-gil.
Popol Vuh, the living, breathing book of the people

The Writer
La Yinita, mestiza, bien educada, un poco nervous, yo

THE VOLCANO DAUGHTERS

PROLOGUE

HERE WE ARE. ALL IS STILL.

Cuando vos vas, yo ya vengo. We begin at la púchica root of the world.

Before we were made, the animals chattered. Jaguars spat the bones. Monkeys howled, volcanoes howled, the stars howled, cold and enormous. Someone listened and chose to destroy them, miren que, with a pair of large and ordinary hands. And after, those large hands that had made the beasts felt only emptiness. They itched to create something that could also create, beings that could carry life's bright-blue thread through years and years, and so they rooted for just the right materials.

Poco a poco, new beings took shape. But the first, the mud creations were deemed soft and senseless; then the wood creations, bloodless and deformed. They were all cast away.

But maíz was tender, supple, fertile—talon of a wandering bird, a feather's iridescence, a hard flake of jade, blood, milk, gold, gota a gota, formed a mano, a mano, a mano—then, slowly, we children de Cuzcatlán became too.

And us? There are four of us here in these pages. We are Lourdes, María, Cora, Lucía.

We cipotas were born of our mothers in a high, igneous sliver between the forest and the sea.

You see, before the massacre that killed us, we lived. We survived earthquakes and mudslides, the eruption of our volcano, Izalco. In the mountainside town where we all died (abandoned to rot, para más joder, piled like husks and leaves in a felled forest), our mothers had listened to radio piped in from the capital and smoked hand-rolled cigarettes in the coffee fields and never washed the black dirt from under their nails. We were in many ways like our mothers, even as we fought them, ignored them, hid from them, lied to them to run into the forest to kiss boys. (Except María—she kissed mostly girls.) What else could we do? The world was changing, everyone kept saying, but where was there for us volcano daughters to go?

Graciela was our friend. Like us, she was left for dead. But somehow she didn't die in the massacre, as we did. Our cherita Graciela and her wannabe-chelita sister, Consuelo—when our souls discovered that they both had lived, pues, we hitched a ride on their life threads, followed along with them for the rest of their days.

Our own life threads, severed by our deaths, whip in the wind with our carcajadas. You've heard our carcajadas, our cackling laughter—it carries with it the stories of our mothers and grandmothers, the stories of ourselves. There are parrots in the field, and we're always listening, siempre, a la vez. Sometimes we speak as one. Sometimes the wind scatters us apart, each a different seed. An eternal part of us remained after the massacre, the part that you hear, the voice telling you this story from all directions. We are gathering the threads of our lives, finding the words to write a new book of the people, to make our world. Miren que, the word makes the world.

Because you know what we've learned? Every myth, every story, has at least two versions. The growing of indigo and coffee, the movies and their magicians, the railroad tracing its long legs across our land like un pulpo, the story of a disgraced mother, a dictator, a nation's beauties, a weeping woman beside water, a prophet. These mythic figures shift shapes, depending upon who tells their story and who listens.

Some morons say that we don't exist, that we all disappeared in the massacre. But we live, seeded through the hills. Long ago we built temples to Ix Chel, goddess of the moon, of the earth, of war, of birth. She taught us how to weave, and we fell beneath her trance until the threads were taken from our hands. We are older than your sense of time. You pass us on the street. You squint into a mirror at home, painting your face to resemble ours. We stand on sunset rooftops shaking out your linens, and we take a long bus ride home. We teach your children in school; we take your temperature; we run for mayor of a bullshit town and they want to kill us for it. You sing our songs. You study our movements. We plan to outlive you. And we are here, telling you this cuentito.

Vamos a la vuelta. We all have work to do. Lourdes is putting everything in order, rewriting the Archives; María is charming whomever she pleases and slipping them a knife in case they need it; Corita is walking a field of bone-rich soil; Lucía is making sense of the dilution of skin. We are dead but we sing, we cackle, we lose our shit, we tell you exactly what we think, we don't always agree, we do not tap-dance—more on that later. Trust us when we take your hands. We'll bend time to tell you about nuestra hermana Graciela and that fucking warlock who held her captive. We'll chase her sister, that silly güerita Consuelo, around the world. Consuelo, we adore her too, the idiot.

And oye, la Yina. Let's not forget her. She's the one putting our words on this page for you. We're talking to you right now, Yina. Mind if we call you that? It's what guanacos call Las Ginas, those cheap plastic flip-flops—but we wouldn't expect you to know that, pocha. Yes, yes, you're Salvi too, you've done your research, chele, you're muy educada. You're helping us tell our story. But fíjate: don't get carried away with la poesía, ¿me entiendes? Don't forget to listen. These words are ours, these stories ours.

And so now: All is silent and waiting. All is silent and calm. Listen to us. It begins.

PART I

∞

1914-1932, with a Brief Stop in the 1880s

1

OUR MOTHERS CARRIED US ON THEIR BACKS UNTIL WE kicked in the noontime heat. In the afternoons, they untied us, babies all born in the same season, and let us crawl beneath the ceiba tree as they worked. In those early days, before we could walk, before María was born, las faldas of the ceiba were high and wide enough to contain us. We ate earthworms and licked the ceiba's bark. We waved at the birds and sprouted teeth while our mothers took turns running over from the coffee fields to count that we were all still there, quickly pointing at each of us as they did. Lourdes, Cora, Lucía, Graciela. They took turns making sure that none of us were choking or hungry or covered in shit. They took turns nursing us, two at once to save time. They took turns, patting all of our little bellies, rubbing our backs, wiping caca from our fat little butts with a rag, rocking us to sleep and setting us down again between the skirts of the roots. We were safe.

During the rainy months, in the late afternoons, our mothers piled us together like sacks of yucca inside the sorting room. We napped as rain soaked the roof, awakened the smell of the building's history—the sharp stink of last year's cherry harvest, the bitterness of indigo. In that room we crawled over one another's baby legs and patted one another's cheeks, not knowing where one of us began and another ended. In that room, we took our first tumbling steps. María was born in the rainy season, and then we were five: Lourdes, María, Cora, Lucía, and Graciela.

Later, when we were older, we went to the nuns, who dressed us, who taught us to read and write, who cared for us during the day while our mothers worked. The nuns dressed us from bins that arrived from abroad. We had our own clothes, refajos that our grandmothers had made, long woven skirts, tops with the smallest embroidered starflowers lining an open collar, but these became nightgowns in favor of the pastel dresses from the nuns, ruffled dresses that rapidly grew too short for our growing legs, too tight around our bellies, dresses with puffed sleeves made of tulle, lace, and starched cotton. On our feet we wore soft leather sandals like our mothers—we called them caites—but María always kicked hers off, said she ran so fast they burned her heels.

Somewhere on the volcano there were men, driving carts, working beside our mothers, guiding animals uphill, but we rarely spoke with them, nor did we sense or mourn their absence from our daily lives. We took turns imagining our fathers because we thought an understanding of who they were might unravel the mystery of who we were. It didn't. We were of our mothers.

Our mothers talked to us about the fathers of our friends more than they talked about our own. But from their chambre, we pieced together some stories. Graciela's father was much older and had once lived here. His name was Germán and he was a colono—he'd risen in the ranks at the finca until he'd owned his own plot of land. At the time he had chosen Socorrito, Graciela's mother, Germán was the most powerful man on the finca after the old patrón. He pursued her, leaving her gifts that were entirely impractical for the life that she lived, but told a story about who he was becoming, and the kind of life that he might offer her—silk stockings, a perfume oil that smelled of lavender, a velvet hat with a little net, a purse made of glittering beads.

As a boy, he'd met a gringo railroad man who drank special water—water in all sorts of colors—that he said made him more powerful, allowed him to listen to the dead and control the future. This crazy gringo was rich and promised Germán he'd purify his soul with that special water, with his potions of color and light. He swore that he could raise Germán out of his circumstances, out of the colonato that bound him to labor on the coffee finca on the mountain. Germán, fatherless, poor, had listened to the gringo, who promised him a future in the railroad he was building to bring the coffee crop to the coast, and who sent him abroad to study economics in Switzerland. His coursework and experience in the shadow of the Alps eventually proved irrelevant to his later position in the capital as the oracle of that fulano, el warlock, but afforded him a refined sense and understanding of the improbable.

The gringo, Brannon was his name, was obsessed with colors—thought some healed, some gave vitality. And when he saw Socorrito, whom he knew Germán liked, he encouraged the match, for, as we understand now, the color of her skin, fairer than any of our mothers', was exactly what he was after.

Transmission. Stories all have masters who control how they're told and to whom. Thanks to the rich gringo, Germán had become a master. And as a teenager, he transmitted the gringo's stories to his best friend, a man we came to know as el generalísimo, the púchica warlock, El Gran Pendejo. They were boys together, you see. El Gran Pendejo was from the volcanoes too, though later he did everything he could to erase that history, believed this bullshit from the gringo could help him do it, could help him erase any trace of where he came from, to separate our stories from his own.

By the time that Socorrito's first pregnancy, with Graciela's older sister, Consuelo, had begun to show, Germán had already left the finca to live in the capital. The General was rising in the ranks there and found Germán a post as his spiritual adviser. Soon, Germán married in the capital as well. Socorrito hoped that even though Germán had left her, she might still have rights to his land, but while he had been freed from el colonato, she was fixed in place.

Then, when Consuelo was four, a man, a thug from the capital, came to our village and took Consuelo from her mother's arms, after knocking Socorrito unconscious.

He left a note on the ground, which Socorrito discovered when she awoke, and considered destroying its fine seal, its delicate paper, its blot of indigo ink, in the fury of her rage and grief. Instead, reasoning that this was perhaps the only way she might find her daughter, she brought the paper directly to the gringa nuns to decipher for her, moving through her thick pain like a sleepwalker, because Socorrito could not read the lavish penstrokes of her child's father.

German had Consuelo and he intended to keep her in the capital. You see, this new wife of Germán's was barren and Consuelo was to be a gift for this barren woman, who yearned to be a mother. She would be una consolación; she would live up to her name.

In the capital, Consuelo would receive an education. She would live there not as a servant, but as a daughter. She would not be made to work; she'd already been removed from el colonato, which we'd all been born into, which our mothers and grandmothers had been born into. El colonato, which tethered us to the finca, where we would work until we died. Instead, Consuelo would become "civilized"—that was the word Germán used in the letter. And when she was an adult, she could choose to leave the capital and return to the volcano, if she so wanted.

This was all written on the piece of paper that Socorrito had received. Sister Iris had slowed over the word "civilized" as she read.

After that Socorrito slept with the paper—the promise, she called it—under her head. This small scrap may have been the only thing tethering her to the earth, now that her daughter was gone.

Our mothers comforted her with laughter, when it became clear that their anger and sorrow would not return Socorrito's daughter to her. *Civilized,* they scoffed. "With that pelo colocho, nearly as colocho as mine?" Rosario made this same joke every time, gesturing at her own curly hair. Colocho, pero colocho. Rosario was Black, tiny, and striking, with golden-brown eyes. She was delicately vain about her beauty, reminding us of a small lioness. She strutted before the other women when they gathered to bathe in the river on hot days, her short feet wide and soft as paws, gems of water dripping from her hair as she stretched her arms in the sun. We, her daughters María and Lourdes, our skin went lighter on a gradient—Lourdes's a deep, warm brown, and then María, de piel canela.

We imagined Consuelo more pale still, como una chelita, but with pelo colocho that some indita in the capital was forced to press flat every day with an iron, or else shove under a hat. She'd be like the characters in those books that the nuns had given us, about orphans in ruffly pinafores in old-timey England—a girl who would never want to return to the volcano.

Even after Consuelo was taken, Germán returned to the volcanoes now and then, but Socorrito was never again invited to stay on his land. Still, he found time to impregnate her, this time with Graciela, and this time without love, without tenderness, without gifts. Socorrito had hoped that by offering herself to him again, she could convince him to bring Consuelo home and stay. But at the end of each visit he returned to the capital and left her behind.

Over and over, throughout our childhoods, our mothers let slip that Graciela's father was not only still alive, but living in the capital, as the General's second-in-command. According to our mothers, Germán was his most trusted adviser. The General made no decisions without consulting him first. But on the radio, the General, baboso that he was, announced that he alone was the one who ruled the tides, who told Izalco when to erupt, who shaped the moon. He talked about the coffee harvest as if he'd picked every last cherry himself, as if he'd invented the railroad that carried the beans to port and out of the country, where they were transformed into fantastic amounts of money that we never saw. He spoke of the great ships at port from Los Yunais as his Very Good Friends. ("My Very Good Friend Los Estados Unidos enters the harbor of La Libertad on this blessed day!") We thought he was a clown. He really believed these things—that he had the power to control our whole universe; it was the same tontería that the gringo Brannon had talked about, that if he surrounded himself with red curtains and bathed in turquoise water, he'd be invincible. He may have heard the stories secondhand from Germán, but this fulano had swallowed more of the gringo's crazy water than his friend. When he came on the radio to announce a new victory—how he manipulated the weather, how he could perceive the world's radiant vibrations by pissing and shitting, which he deemed sensory activities, like seeing and hearing, how he used that wisdom to shape the price of an automobile—our laughter smothered his rejoicing.

Men. They made us laugh then.

Cora's father, meanwhile, was a mystery to us for many years; we thought maybe he was a stranger we sometimes saw driving a cart through town. But then María heard her mother, Rosario, talking about el patrón as though it were him. We howled at that idea. Corita was too sweet, too smart, to have that bolo for a father.

Lucía's father, light as she was, must have been visiting on business from Los Estados, but we never heard much about him.

And unlike the rest of us, Lourdes and María had been claimed, in a slight way at least, by their father. He was a rich and ordinary man whose parents owned the finca and the land that we worked on, a coffee man who lived in the north, in some place called California, with a chele wife and twin daughters who had just begun to walk. He came to the village twice a year, in October and April, before the harvest and after. With his shoes sinking into the mud. With his long black car's nose pointed always away from the volcano. Las hermanas had been told never to call him Papá—always El Señor Domínguez—but when they were alone, they couldn't help themselves.

The closest we came to him was María's christening. He brought blankets and a stuffed rabbit for María and a porcelain doll with blue glass eyes that opened and shut for Lourdes, and he stood in the back of the church while the visiting priest anointed María's little head before dipping it into the fount. After the ceremony, while everyone slowly filed out of the church, he slipped out too, and drove back to the capital without saying goodbye. Their mami said, "He paid for everything, the lace dress, the tiny shoes. I'm not going to make him pretend." After that he grew distant again; even when he was in the village, his eyes looked through us. He and his brother owned the point that our world turned on, but he didn't change the shape of our lives. We were distant moons to him.

In those years, though, we were safe. Our mothers protected us. What had happened to Consuelo was an old story, and since then, our mothers had encircled us with joyful ferocity. What had happened to Consuelo could never happen again.

2

WE MUST HAVE BEEN NINE, MARÍA SEVEN, WHEN THE MAN arrived looking for Graciela. We saw him at the end of the day, after school. He'd arrived in a shiny car and wore slick black shoes; he could be from nowhere but the capital. He saw Graciela start down the path for home and followed her, so we did too. But he was faster. When Graciela noticed the man, she began to run. We kept close behind her, racing through the trees. We saw her dash into her shack and shut the door behind her. The man from the capital wasn't far off; we could see the sweat soaking through his linen shirt. We threw rocks onto the path, to let him know we were there, watching him. He did not slow.

He pounded on the door of Graciela's house, screaming her name; a vein bulged in his neck. We threw the rest of our rocks at his back until our pockets were empty. He pounded harder and then kicked the door open. We crept forward on our haunches through the green, surrounding him in a half-moon. Graciela was not inside the shack.

"Where's your friend?" he asked. His eyes looked nowhere.

"Are you her papi?" Lourdes called out, still partially hidden in the trees. Because who else could this man be?

But he laughed shrilly, cruelly. "Do I look like a viejito indio to you?" he said.

Offended, Lourdes threw another rock, but it missed him, broke into a dull clump beside his foot. María, taking her sister's cue, spat.

"She's not here!" Lourdes yelled. Then a little softer, with joy: "You son of a bitch." Hijueputa, hijueputa. We'd heard it on our mothers' lips, heard it from el patrón, when he sat drinking his aguardiente on the patio with the other coffee men. We'd been waiting for just the right moment to say it ourselves.

"Little witches," the man said, looking at none of us. He reached into his jacket pocket. We were hoping for a gun, like the one the patrón carried in his waistband. But instead of a gun the man took out a square piece of pink paper. He squinted and tacked it to the door.

Lourdes pushed her little sister out from behind the mango tree that was hiding her, and María ran to the door, reached for the paper, and crumpled it in her fist with an urgent sense of duty. She turned and smiled, first at Lourdes, then at the man. The man picked her up by the back of her dress and threw her against the tree. She kicked a long thin leg and cursed in the words we'd taught her, spitting out the susto. She'd be fine.

Lourdes grabbed the machete from her hip and lunged at the man. The blade glanced the side of his palm and drew blood immediately.

"I'll have your mothers killed," he said, the ogre in every fairy tale we knew. But then he ran away from us down the path, so we laughed at his threat. We watched until he became small and dark, a moving shadow. When we could no longer see him slipping down the side of the volcano in his shiny, muddy shoes, the misty air seemed to exhale, dusk settling around us.

Graciela came out from behind the shack, appeared beside us.

"My mami told me to hide behind the woodpile if any strangers ever came looking for me," she told us. "He thought it was witchcraft," she said, smiling. "You all were bien brave. Cachimbonas." A grandmother spider shone in her hair. Cora gathered it onto her finger and brought it to the ground.

Later, we asked Lourdes why she hadn't killed the man with her machete. She explained that she'd just been trying to teach him a lesson. If Graciela knew why the man had come, she didn't tell us. And we didn't tell our mothers about any of it until after the letter had come.

. . .

Maybe a week later, at the end of her day in the fields, Socorrito found el patrón waiting for her, the white air pinkening around him. On the rare days he scaled the rutted paths in the hills, he carried a walking stick and pulled rubber boots on over his usual linen trousers, which made them puff out at the knees. Socorrito approached him with caution, steadying her caites on the steep lines of the volcano's face. The basket of coffee, her day's work, swayed to a balance on top of her head. El patrón acknowledged it with a point of his lips.

Socorrito had never been alone with el patrón. She squared her shoulders and met his dusty yellow eyes with her black ones. He was known for his sloppiness in the late afternoons. While his wife, the bitch of la finca, gathered with her friends on the shaded porch, he drank alone and wandered lecherously around the village, looking for women. A decade ago he'd fathered Cora in this way, forgetting, or pretending to forget, that he even knew Alba's name as her belly swelled in the weeks that followed. But if he tried anything with her now, Socorrito would be ready. Socorrito was fast, and by this time of day, he was drunk enough to stumble if he tried to chase her. If she needed to, she could knee him in los huevos—a real feat if she could keep the basket of cherries on her head while she did! She grinned at the thought. Izalco hissed.

El patrón handed Socorrito an envelope, the seal of which had been torn already, by a mother-of-pearl-inlaid letter opener, clasped daggerlike by his wife. The thick yellow paper slid out of the envelope and into Socorrito's palm. A telegram.

"It's from the capital," he said.

Socorrito's cheeks flushed and she felt a tightness in her throat; her vision went watery. The basket at her crown rocked and settled. She gave a curt nod, as though she'd been expecting this, but she hadn't. Coffee girls don't receive telegrams from the capital. She'd never even learned to read. She'd have to ask one of us to help her but knew it couldn't be Graciela. What happened to Consuelo had taught her that news from the capital was almost certainly dangerous for her, for her daughter. Socorrito thanked el patrón and hurried home, unable to catch her breath.

That evening she knocked on the door of Lourdes and María's shack, and Rosario, their mother, came to the door and invited her inside. Rosario offered Graciela's mother the cigarette she had rolled behind her ear, but Socorrito shook her head no. She was disheveled and breathing hard. Rosario pulled her inside. Lourdes and María watched from the stove as the mothers talked, heard Socorrito tell Rosario that she could feel two hands tightening around her neck, pulling her underwater. Rosario took her arm and brought her to a seat on the floor.

Finally, Socorrito called Lourdes over. She put her arm around the girl and nodded to Rosario. Lourdes shrugged her shoulders and winked at María, who sat staring out the window. María's arm was tied with a rag where the man from the capital had broken it. She'd told her mother that she'd fallen out of a tree.

Socorrito and Lourdes stepped outside the dirt-packed shack. Birds shrieked across the sky; the workers continued their path home.

"Read this to me," said Socorrito, handing Lourdes an envelope that was torn around its edges. Those gringa nuns had taught us volcano daughters to read, but rarely did our mothers make use of our knowledge.

Lourdes opened the telegram:

THE FATHER OF YOUR CHILDREN IS DEAD. BRING YOUNGER DAUGHTER TO THE CAPITAL TO PAY HER RESPECTS. GO HOME WITH BOTH.

There were two train tickets in the envelope too.

Lourdes looked up at Socorrito. "Do they mean both your daughters? Why does Graciela need to pay her respects to someone she's never even met?"

Socorrito nodded and squeezed Lourdes's little shoulder. She looked lost. She frowned into the setting sun, her eyes blank. "The important thing is that I'll be there too," she said. "And I'll return home with both of them."

"Are you afraid?" Lourdes asked her.

Socorrito shook her head, but in truth, she was. Her next move had been plotted for her, but she didn't trust it. It was too easy. She suspected that the letters and the tickets were a trick, a cruel one. Consuelo was not yet an adult, not yet the age when Socorrito had been promised her daughter would be free of the colonato. And la promesa—the education, the travel, everything on that fancy thin paper that Socorrito kept beneath her pillow—all that could be a lie. Maybe they wanted Graciela now too, and Socorrito would be left alone, her only comfort the idea that her daughters would have a future she never could have given them.

She had no choice; she had to go. If this was all a trick, it was still the only crack of light through which she might see Consuelo again. She would go to the capital with Graciela. She would bring the disintegrating paper that contained la promesa and she would fight if she had to. And if she was very lucky, she'd return with both her daughters. She smiled at the thought, then let out a laugh, and another, and another.

"You've got some ghosts in your head." That's what Lourdes used to say to us if we cracked, if we couldn't stop laughing or crying. She'd hold our index fingers in her dirty little fists. "Let them dance, shake them out." She'd push us gently to the ground, where we'd writhe like worms.

Socorrito's crazy carcajadas had turned to sobs, her head full of ghosts, when Graciela arrived at the house, looking for her. She came to her mother's side and rubbed her back without a word.

"We have to go pay respects to your father," Socorrito said. "And we're going to bring your sister home. They may fight me, but I'll fight back."

Graciela, then: Did she smile, for a moment? If she did, the smile left her face immediately, and when we looked at her, she seemed concerned only with steadying her mother. There was a small part of her, a part that shamed her, that thrilled at this news, at meeting her sister, exchanging her refajo for one of the round skirts we'd seen the bitch of la finca and her friends from the city wearing, about going to the capital. Dancing lessons! Maybe she'd get to take dancing lessons.

She'd never say that to her mother, though. Instead she reassured her that they'd win the fight, that they'd bring Consuelo home. She wondered aloud with us, if it were true, as our mamis had always hoped it was, that Consuelo would be able to free us of el colonato too, like a magic trick. If she came back, they said, we could all live together on the volcano, working only for ourselves. To have their own land—that was the dream our mamis held most fiercely.

We didn't remember Consuelo; she'd been taken before we were born. Graciela would sometimes mention her, though, and while she didn't remember her sister either, had never met her, we knew that she'd always believed that one day Consuelo would return to the volcano. Her mother had promised that she would find her in the capital and bring her back. And maybe that moment had come now. But if we're being honest, we'd always wondered why Consuelo would come back. We didn't know why anyone would leave a fufurufa life in the capital to come work on the volcano, if they had a choice.

Our lives were wound up in the lives of las hermanas Graciela y Consuelo; we knew it even then.

La cherita Graciela. We remember a child like us: fatherless, with skinny legs and scabbed knees, long, heavy hair, torn dresses, and caites on her feet, two rabbitlike new teeth, jagged edges, black rainforest dirt rubbed deep into her elbows and knees. We adored her, burned with the wild, jealous love of young girls. We pushed in line outside the chapel to share a pew with Graciela; we crowded her in the fields, offering tastes of candy we'd stolen to impress her. We took turns braiding her long, sticky hair. She remembered everything: every song, every story, every joke. She sang to us, verses she remembered our grandmothers singing when we were tiny. She listened to all of our dreams and wrote them down in a notebook, connecting their threads to trace constellations uniting us. In the evenings, she told us stories until we fell asleep, reciting each line as if she were reading from the musty chapter books in the small library at school. These were books she'd read once and never forgotten. She'd memorize every detail, even without understanding their meaning. In our country, we have a word for this. *Guayabear:* to remember, por el chacalele.

These days, Lourdes haunts a library where she reads books by these hijueputa professor types, who all have something to say about our friend Graciela. They claim that Graciela was a saint, that when she went to the capital, she blessed the warlock's hold on our cafecito economy and inspired his visions of our future with her cosmic mestiza beauty. He wanted to put her face on coins, you see, an emblem of la raza cósmica. But he never got to that; the massacre came first.

They say that Graciela's skin was the perfect dilution of Indian and enough European to erase the Black. That's how it goes: gota a gota, a mano, a mano, ya lo sabes. An old story: la raza cósmica meant that, to a certain breed of capital-dwelling Ladino, Graciela was perceived as possessing that hardy, inextinguishable spark of ancient magic that they were so drawn to, even as they wanted to rid the place of its darkest people. Because that was the thing with Graciela, what made her so desirable to them, those hijueputas: her hair could be tamed into smooth waves and pinned back, her fingernails filed and painted, her locution trained so as to be impeccable. She was as light as her mother and could wear a hat in the dry season so as not to fall into the darkness of her earlier line. And her children would be lighter still, perhaps with ojos claros. La raza cósmica, púchica vos—what good was it to us?

Graciela was the future, these professor types write in the púchica books Lourdes can't stop reading. Por la gran puta, then why did the General and his men try to kill her? Why did they kill us, we who were un poco lighter, un poco darker, and each of us beautiful? According to those hijueputa professor types, we were cosmic too. We were cosmic, yes, but still too india. Our babies, if we had been able to have them, would have been of broken color.

Once, Lucía saw all this laid out in a single painting. Lucía la güerita had been given a practical penance for some pecado none of us can remember. She never got hit. (Lourdes, with her darker complexion, she got hit.) Instead, the nuns sent Lucía to sharpen a box of pencils in the church basement, which was piled with junk and storage. She found the painting down there, propped on a desk that someone had carved el dia-blo into with a little knife. The painting looked like a family tree, un árbol de la vida, but this one was a story of falling: up or down. She didn't know it then, but there were hundreds of versions of this painting all over our land—another cosita brought over with the conquistadores—vamos a la vuelta. They told the story of the real colors that the General and all those hijueputa types were so obsessed with.

They began with simple blood: Spaniard, Black, Indian, albino. You could call them the primary colors. And from the different ways they could be mixed together, Lucía counted sixteen possible combinations of family, and each baby was given a name: the Mestizo, the Wolf, the Mulatto, the Castizo. These were the babies of "broken color," and so were the ones that followed them: the Criollo, the Morisco, and the Chino Cambujo, Cimarrón. Lucía read the names aloud, stumbled over them: Albarazado, Barcino, Jíbaro, Zambaigo, Calpamulato.

And then their babies: Jump Backward. Turn Around. Floating in Midair. Coyote. I Don't Understand You.

At the bottom of the painting, with no frame to contain them, were the Barbarous Indians, different from the ones pictured in the squares above. These Indians were pockmarked and bony, chasing sickly horses across the landscape. These Indians had no family.

The thing was, the painting made no sense. Lucía found her own face, her black eyes, skin light as flor de izote, all over the painting—her moth-er's too. According to its system, María and Lourdes should share the same box, but Lucía found the shades of their skin from the top of the painting to the bottom. She found Lourdes's long rizos. Consuelo and Lucía shared a shade. Graciela was two, maybe three or four, of the babies with broken color. Cora's mother was not who she should be. But who knows who her father was. El Gran Pendejo's aim was to bring us all back to the lady with the giant powdered wig and smashed chichis at the top of the tree. According to the painting's logic, she was more beautiful than all of the faces beneath her. Her son was not beautiful to our eyes, but his daughter, mixed with a mother of broken color, who was supposed to contribute vigor to the family line, was pretty. We knew girls who looked like her.

Lucía touched the painting as she looked. Her greasy living finger left shadows on each of the sixteen squares. The nuns had tried to hide this ugly fucking painting from us as a kindness, but over the years we saw versions of it everywhere, and we memorized it, por el chacalele.

3

THE NEXT DAY, SOCORRITO PULLED GRACIELA OUT OF SCHOOL; she told the nuns that they were going to the capital to pay their respects to her daughter's dead father's family. She bleached Graciela's First Communion dress, which just barely still fit her, and gave her a pair of white patent-leather shoes with a wide strap and bronze buckle that Sister Iris had found and stored in a box in the church basement, beside the sacramental wine, saving them for an occasion such as this.

Before they left, we went with our mothers to say goodbye. We cipotas settled on the floor to play and whisper with Graciela, while our mamis laid out food, grabbed one another's arms, and let loose carcajada after carcajada, their wide embrace encircling us. We had a favorite song in those days, by La Güerita del Norte: "Arráncame la Vida." Tear this heart out. Rip my life out by the roots. La llevaba en el alma. Yoli, Lucía's mother, fiddled with the dial when it came on the radio, filling the room with La Güerita's wail, with our wails.

Graciela had packed a bag with her toothbrush and a refajo, embroidered with stars and roses by her great-grandmother. We remember our mothers wearing refajos when we were small, the ones our grandmothers had taught them to weave by tying their looms to a ceiba, harnessing sky in the indigo-blue thread. But by the time we were old enough to learn, our mothers were too calaceadas, too exhausted in their bones, to teach us. One day we will, they said, again and again, until we no longer showed any interest in the delicate patterns on their long skirts.

When Socorrito saw Graciela's bag, she protested. "You won't need a change of clothes!" she said. "We aren't staying long. You'll pay your respects, we'll get your sister, and then we'll come right back." She had that crazy, vacant look in her eyes again. Socorrito needed Graciela to believe every word she said that night.

But Graciela rolled up the refajo and her toothbrush anyway and folded them both into the waistband of her First Communion dress. She didn't want to be stuck with dirty teeth in an uncomfortable dress. And she wasn't really convinced that they would be staying only one day. Socorrito had taken on a forced optimism that Graciela didn't trust. She was afraid of what they might find in her dead father's home—his body? The fight her mother had mentioned?—and had lain awake at night, biting the inside of her cheek, tearing off the skin around her fingernails. That evening, as they prepared to go, she leaned against us, glassy-eyed, dizzy with exhaustion.

We watched Socorrito pull her hair back from her face. The nuns had lent her a dress too. It was too wide for her, and she smoothed the fabric against her thighs. Blurred pale-blue flowers bloomed over her ass. She studied the sharp edge of her cheekbones and grinned into the mirror. She purred like a cat. We cipotas, gathered together, cooed like birds in recognition of Socorrito's beauty, her thick, liquid hair. We strutted and laughed, flipped our own hair, though only Graciela's was as thick and liquid as her mother's.

Socorrito was prepared to do anything to bring Consuelo home. Our mothers laughed—maybe the rich, barren wife in the capital wanted to fist-fight an india. The wife in the capital would be güerita, of course. Like the blue-eyed seraphim on our prayer cards. Tall, in a white gown that didn't trap dirt.

Socorrito spun around and landed a fake punch on Alba's round shoulder. "See, I can fight!" she said. Alba grabbed her machete and swung it in a playful ellipse above her head, howling. Rosario slapped Socorrito's ass. Yoli cackled and screamed.

"But hopefully I won't need to," Socorrito said. "It's all written here." She patted la promesa, which was tucked into the top of her dress between her tetas.

Imagine them, our mothers. Imagine us, circling them on the floor, our bare feet dusty and safe. And Socorrito, all the while, imagining one more, Consuelo. What bayunquería we would have had all together.

"Imagine this." Socorrito had been saying it all night.

"Imagine I bring Consuelo back and she's able to take us all out of el colonato," she said. "Maybe her father left us some money so we can all get some land together, on the other side of the volcano." That optimism, again. We wanted to believe it. Graciela lay her head in Lucía's lap. Cora braided her river of hair as we listened to our mothers' dream, as we had all our lives.

Our mamis often talked with us about a new home, up on the other side of the volcano. They dreamed of buying some land, growing their own food. And the patrón? What would he do? Our mothers dared those Ladino fuckers to uproot their imagined life.

Sometimes, when they had a day off, we'd all hike over to the other side of the volcano, through the densest part of the forest. There was a clearing we returned to, which Rosario had found years ago. This would be a good place for a milpa, they told us. Miren que, all that water from the stream. We could build our houses here, in this little valley, facing one another. Alba would dig into the soil and sprinkle it with her fingertips, dancing it from one hand to the other so we all could see. Miren que, how rich and fertile this soil is—we could have an orchard here. Yoli would tell Alba to start flirting with a strong man on his way up the colonato ladder, someone with a wide, strong back who could get us started on the building, or at least carry the materials in his cart. Alba would cackle, and then whisper to Yoli, thinking we couldn't hear her, telling her to just go fuck that guy herself.

Socorrito looked up at the volcano now, up toward that imagined home that existed beyond our vision. "Maybe we'll be there soon," she said, and our mothers cheered, cackling now about something else entirely.

Moments later Socorrito and Graciela would walk down the hill to the train station. We embraced them, gathering them to us, smelling the fufurufo lavender perfume on Socorrito's neck (a gift from Graciela's father, years and years ago), breathing in Graciela's long hair, its scent of Ivory soap, blackened tortillas, and copal, rubbing their backs before they descended.

Bring us something back, something good, we called after Graciela, and we let ourselves believe for just a little bit longer that she really would return with her sister and change our lives forever.

4

BY THE TIME THEY'D ARRIVED AT THE STATION, HANDED OVER their tickets, and found their seats on the train, evening was settling thickly into the sky, and Graciela noticed that Socorrito finally seemed tired. The train had no way of navigating around the volcanic ranges that spanned the distance between Izalco and the capital except with a slow, winding climb to each peak, followed by a queasy descent. Socorrito held Graciela's wrist as they sat, which embarrassed the girl. She was too old for that, just as she was too old to be wearing her First Communion dress. And yet, feeling that shame birthed a sadness within her that she couldn't make sense of. She twitched, just for a moment.

She watched the path of the railroad tracks out the window, the trembling side of rock that once flowed smooth and hot. The train, it seemed, should have run out of road, the tracks slipped and fallen into the wild below, dozens of times already. But at the last possible moment, again and again, it curved, looped around wide swathes of mountain, descended in noisy, sloppy circles. She felt an urgent need to keep her eyes open. She told herself that if she stayed awake, the train would remain on smooth tracks. The earth would not crumble beneath her. She would meet her sister. They would return to Izalco. But if she fell asleep, the train would slip, lose its hold on the volcano's rough side, and tumble through the air. Her stomach rose and tightened at the thought. Socorrito squeezed her wrist again. Graciela bit the inside of her cheek, the smooth skin comforting between her teeth. But her eyelids were heavy, and she began to nod. As Izalco faded behind them with the sunset, Graciela finally slept, better than she had in days.

She awoke to an urgent tapping sound. The train window beside her head was still black, and her mami snored. Then, a scrape and a spark, and a light bloomed against the glass. A perfectly formed miniature man, a tiny duende, appeared floating outside the window, holding a match. He sneered at Graciela and held the fiery torch to the glass to show her the sea, cresting wild and angry.

Graciela shook her mother's shoulder, but Socorrito did not wake. She snapped her fingers, flicking the glass in front of the little man, who glared with a tiny menace. Dropping his matchstick, he began to fly backward, out of Graciela's sight.

Duendes usually mean no real harm. They bring mischief and disorder, shattering glass in an empty room, or rummaging around in a drawer and hiding your socks. This one, though, sneered, eerily human. That may have been why he frightened her.

When Graciela woke again it was light out and her mami was straightening her dress, telling her not to raise her arms over her head. The sleeves pulled around her arms and through her chest; the dress would split down the sides if she moved the wrong way. The train had stopped. The sharpness had returned to Socorrito's eyes. She took Graciela's hand, and on this first morning in the capital, Graciela was grateful instead of ashamed to be held by her mother in this way. Socorrito guided her down the narrow aisle and into the thick, bright air of the city around them.

The marketplace beside the train station seemed to snake all the way up the mountain, a procession of gray tents filled with fruit, cookware, gutted fish fanned out on enormous blocks of ice, men weaving in circles, promising to sharpen knives better than all the other men promising the same service. Here, the sky was vivid, blooming humid and blue. Socorrito seemed alert and competent here, as though she'd been many times before, though as far as Graciela knew, this place was as new to her mother as it was to her.

She walked Graciela to the edge of the platform and asked a conductor for directions. The man began drawing a map in the air and the duende's hateful face appeared in the space between them, only for an instant. Graciela blinked him away until he faded into sunspots.

A long black car, polished like a mirror, pulled up alongside them and began to honk. Socorrito pulled Graciela out of the road. The car honked again and then the chauffeur stepped out. He called Graciela by a longer name than she'd ever known that she had—here, suddenly, she was not just her mother's, but her father's too. She looked to her mother to confirm that it was really hers; Socorrito nodded. Her dead father had claimed her.

The chauffeur wore white gloves and a cap with leather trim. He bowed, and Graciela caught a flicker of terror in her mami's face before she turned to her and smiled softly. The conductor walked away, and the chauffeur lifted Graciela into the backseat of the car. Socorrito crawled in after. The engine vibrated, and her mami shook her head—disbelief? Pleasure?—as viejas pressed against the windows, pushing their carts, screaming about mangoes and jicama, scattering when the car began to move, taking Graciela and Socorrito with it, deeper into the capital. They passed a man selling plastic bundles of hard tamarind candy from a cart in the center of the road, and a restaurant with a sad-looking man in a red-splattered apron squatting out front. A pretty woman walked alone with an ice cream cone, its rose-petal brightness threatening to melt into her gloves. Couples strolled the grassy promenade in front of a marble palace, the women shielding their pale faces with creamy lace parasols, the men with waxed mustaches and narrow-brimmed hats, walking for the pleasure of it.

"The presidential palace," the driver said, pointing to the marble, columned building that commanded the entire facing street. Graciela had seen a postcard of this building, taped to the wall of our classroom. The palace had looked like an enormous wedding cake there. Here, its façade was dirtier, and somehow larger.

"Have you been to the capital before?" the driver asked, maneuvering the car out of the main square and up into the hills. Mamá shook her head, her mouth a straight line. As the car ascended, the houses became larger and more hidden behind gates and palms and long, curving driveways. Graciela searched for glimpses of the lives inside those mysterious windows; she grew nauseated with the effort.

After forty minutes or so, the driver slowed in front of a tall iron fence woven with bougainvillea and hibiscus. He stepped out of the car to unlock and pull open its wide, heavy gates, then got back in, grinning, and they drove into the Estate. Just inside stood a fountain full of stone angels, and beyond that, a tile path that wound through a garden. Jacaranda flowers dripped brilliant violet over the grass, thorny roses and birds-of-paradise shone like spears along the borders of the dew-wet garden. Ahead of the car was a hilltop mansion larger even than la finca house, four stories tall, with balconies at every window, roses spilling over soft white walls.

The driver helped Graciela and Socorrito out of the car, and they followed him up the tile path, lined here with fruit trees—mangoes, avocados, passion fruit, all of it too ripe, bending the branches into a fragrant canopy over Graciela's and Socorrito's heads. The air here was brighter than on the volcano, overwhelming Graciela's vision, and its heat was harsher on the skin. And the noises of the city below—delivery trucks, horses, competing radios, and vendors pushing their carts—wafted up through the hills and settled into the breeze, a hum.

Marble staircase, white marble floor slick as glass, an enormous mirror carved with demons, of black, iron-hard wood, an outdoor courtyard, a golden cage filled with hundreds of birds.

An old woman in black appeared at the door, introduced herself as Ninfa. She extended her hand to Graciela, who wondered if the black was for mourning. *Is this viejita my father's wife?* She was comforted by the thought, by the familiarity of this woman; Ninfa's hand was warm, and, like Graciela and her mother, she was india. Graciela looked to her mother's face for confirmation. Socorrito's frozen smile had softened in Ninfa's presence, but her eyes scanned the room for understanding.

"Gracias, maitra," she said.

The woman in black led them into an even larger room, and it was then that Graciela understood that Ninfa was wearing a uniform. Two nenas a few years older than Graciela, inditas also, wore black dresses identical to Ninfa's, and carried trays with pitchers of ice water across the shining floor. An ocelot bucked on its chain, and Graciela jumped.

A woman, güerita, sat on a chaise, with her long legs folded beside her. She ate unhurriedly from a platter of cut fruit that seemed to float in midair on a table made of glass.

Ninfa cleared her throat in a bid for the attention of the lady of the house, and Graciela understood that this was the widow. Her dead father's wife rose to greet them.

Socorrito took in her breath at the woman's height. Perlita had shoulders like old mountains and a face bronzed like a mask. She wore her hair on top of her head, wrapped loosely in a white silk turban. Graciela noted her easy bones and plush skin, which at the time we all mistook for a halo of vague divinity, but during her time in the capital, Graciela grew accustomed to this halo, the glowing skin of the very rich.

"Consuelo, get in here," Perlita called out of the side of her red mouth, extending her arms for a brief embrace of her guests.

Graciela's sister scrambled into the room like a fawn. She was tall and thin in white lace, and despite what our mothers had told us, she wasn't really a child. Or she was a girl pretending to be an adult. Her face was delicate and fine, but she had surprisingly long limbs, suggesting a resemblance to Perlita, which could not be, because la güerita was not her mother. She smiled and dipped into a ridiculous curtsy.

Socorrito, who had been silent until now, ran to Consuelo and grabbed her. She began to sob on Consuelo's narrow teenage shoulder. Graciela noted the older girl's terror at this outpouring of emotion and went to intervene.

"You're my sister?" Graciela embraced Consuelo, wrapping her arms around their mother too.

We saw it then: Graciela's beetle-shiny eyes in Consuelo's narrow, moon-colored face, Socorrito's wide india nose in both. Socorrito's daughters. We watched Graciela watch Consuelo. A polite smile played on our friend's face. But Consuelo went red, with anger or embarrassment. She stiffened in Graciela's and Socorrito's arms. For a moment, Graciela was hurt, confused, afraid she'd done something wrong.

"Graciela, your father's eldest daughter," Perlita said with a strange crispness, looking nowhere at all. "Your sister, Consuelo." Consuelo blinked fiercely.

"Hello, Mami," Consuelo finally said. Socorrito whimpered, her arms still wrapped around both daughters. Inside of the hug, Graciela felt Consuelo's body soften again.

"Mis hijitas," Socorrito said.

"We're all together now!" Graciela said, wanting to trust her mother's optimism. She felt Consuelo nod against her back.

"You must be exhausted from your journey," Perlita said to Socorrito, hovering just behind her, jutting her chin urgently at Ninfa. She tapped her nails on the back of Consuelo's head and, on command, the girl extracted herself from her mother's and sister's arms.

Ninfa's face brightened. She took Socorrito by the arm, pulling her away from her daughters, and led her up the marble staircase. Socorrito resisted at first, but when it was clear she couldn't free herself of the older woman, did her best to put a reassuring smile on her face as she climbed the stairs.

Watching her mother go, Graciela felt a slow wave of panic wash over her. Perlita urged her to sit and make herself comfortable on the chaise, to have some fruit.

"It was so nice to meet you," Graciela said, swallowing a cube of papaya, and then a perfectly round grape. The grape's sour explosion was a revelation.

Perlita did not respond, but stared plainly at Graciela's face, studying it for clues.

I suppose we should be on our way, Graciela tried to work up the courage to say.

Are you packed and ready to leave with us, Consuelo? Graciela wanted to say but did not.

Consuelo, meanwhile, perched on the arm of the chaise and refused Perlita's offer of fruit.

Ninfa returned a few minutes later for Graciela, and took her upstairs to a shining bathroom, where she'd drawn hot water into a porcelain tub.

A bath? Why? Graciela wanted to say, but something in the air of this place shut her up.

Ninfa scrubbed village dirt off Graciela's small knees, and washed her hair, massaging her head. Graciela was too tired to squirm in the water, shy as she felt in her nakedness.

After the bath Ninfa wrapped her in a towel that felt like a blanket. She said La Doña had brought it back from a trip to Europe. She sat Graciela in front of a mirror—her cheeks were pink now—and spent a long time combing out her hair, cursing only a little bit, then she braided it and wrapped the braid behind Graciela's head, tying it with a ribbon. Graciela studied her face in the mirror, as Perlita had stared at it earlier. With her hair pulled back tightly, each of her features was emphasized, the depth of her eyes, the slope of her nose, the width of her mouth, the brown of her skin, all on display. Bien chula. Graciela admired herself freely.

Ninfa took her by the hand and led her out of the room, down a long hallway, and, with another key, opened a high door and brought her inside. A vanity with three mirrors was set up opposite the bed, and a wide window opened to a wrought-iron balcony overlooking a garden. "This one is yours," she said. "You'll rest now. There's clothing in the wardrobe for when you wake up. But first, you must rest. I'll fetch you for dinner if you're still asleep."

Exhausted as she was, as beautiful as the featherbed was, Graciela's heart thrummed, her eyes hungry for this new place. But what about her mother? Graciela felt she should go looking for Socorrito, that they should gather Consuelo and leave the Estate before the day's last train. But she couldn't resist her own curiosity.

She got up to explore the contents of the room, slipping her feet into a pair of velvet slippers set on a leopard-skin rug beside the bed. Graciela opened the wide windows to the balcony and studied the courtyard below: a green square holding two marble fountains, and an avocado tree and several papaya trees planted in a circle, at the center of which was the golden birdcage. The white curtains ballooned into the bedroom as Graciela stood on the balcony in the silk robe, looking out. After a moment she came back into the room and shut the glass doors carefully, crossing the room to an ebony wardrobe.

Inside she found a light-blue dress with yellow smocking and a full skirt. She pulled the dress over her head and spent some time fussing with the buttons, which were embroidered to look like yellow sunflowers.

Beside the wardrobe, hanging from a trio of hooks on the wall, was an oval mirror. She looked again. Long, wet black hair in braids, shiny beetle eyes, and this strange dress. It was a beautiful face. Was her father in this face? Was there a trace of him somewhere inside the Estate? Graciela cracked open the door and found the hallway dark and silent. She crept downstairs.

A large glass door on the first floor of the mansion led out to the courtyard. From outside, the workings of all four floors of the house were visible through large picture windows. The birdcage, she realized now, was as wide as the shack where she and her mother lived. She saw the familiar forms of the birds she knew from home, preening and cooing, flying in polite circles, napping. Corita had taught us their names. The torogoces, clock-birds, twitched their flared blue tails in time, green parrots hung upside down, indigo hummingbirds trilled.

The glossy marble fountains on either side of the cage misted the air, and Graciela found a seat at the lip of the east-facing one. She slipped her toes out of her left velvet slipper to trace her skin against the smooth coolness of the tiles that paved the ground and listened to the sound of the rich people's water, water that moved for beauty's sake alone. Graciela followed a gentle humming noise to the other side of the fountain and found on its edge a dead crow, lying breast up, its feathers glossy and iridescent, insects swarming its sticky dead joints. The ocelot, loose now from its chain and wandering the grounds, sniffed and circled Graciela and the dead bird. She hadn't realized the cat was outside, watching. For a long moment, Graciela was trapped in that circle, the ocelot's golden eyes fixed on her. Graciela could not move. She heard Ninfa calling her name from inside the house. The spell shattered, and Graciela ran back inside.

Ninfa settled Socorrito and Graciela in the dining room before Consuelo and Perlita arrived for the evening meal.

"Where have you been?" Graciela whispered to her mother, who was seated at the other end of a long table. "Why are we staying for dinner? Why were you up there taking a nap when we could have been leaving?"

The late afternoon seemed like an eerie dream, and now she was awake, alert, suspicious. The barren, rich wife was icy and frightening, like the Victorian schoolmarms she'd read about. Ninfa's eyes looked dead, sparking to life only when Perlita summoned her. ¡Puya! And her sister, Consuelo—did she even care that she'd met her hermanita and seen her mother for the first time in ten years? What was wrong with her? And she certainly didn't seem like she was about to leave this pesadilla behind and live on the side of a volcano. Even the furniture in this place made Graciela uneasy. The dark wood of the table had legs carved with demonic faces; there were porcelain figurines of dead-eyed shepherds and sobbing clowns. Inside, the house smelled of a curse.

"We should leave, now," Graciela told her mother softly, remembering Socorrito's steadiness from the night before and trying to conjure her fight. "Let's just go." She wanted her mother to take her by the hand and run out the door, before anyone could offer them any more velvet slippers or featherbeds.

"Oye," Socorrito said. "Stay calm. We'll wait for Consuelo." Socorrito spoke as though half-asleep. Graciela couldn't understand why she was going along with this. She seemed out of her mind.

She was. Upstairs, Ninfa had urged Socorrito into the bath, to calm her. After the shock of seeing Consuelo and then being torn away from both girls had faded a little, Socorrito had felt comforted by the older woman, who brought her bath salts and towels, and a warm robe afterward. She'd fallen asleep, sedated by a tea of herbs that Perlita had asked Ninfa to make for the occasion. Now, Socorrito, unaware that she'd been drugged, felt not quite rested, but had been lulled into a state of relaxation that seemed, to Graciela, entirely inappropriate for the situation. The sharpness in her mother's eyes that she'd seen that morning, just a few hours earlier, navigating at the train station—that competency was gone. She was mysteriously calm, this woman, smiling blissfully, stupidly, like that púchica porcelain clown.

"That's the important thing," Socorrito said to Graciela, slurring her words. "We simply hold up our part of the bargain. We stay calm. We don't lose our shit. They made a promise."

Consuelo arrived just then in her white lace dress and found her place at the table. Her face was red and splotchy—she'd been crying, and it was clear she was ashamed—but she had powdered her wide nose and forehead with floury makeup too light for her skin, rough patches of acne buckling beneath, and had painted her lips and lower eyelids a startling fuchsia. She wore an enormous pendant, a hairy brown spider suspended in resin, on a velvet shoelace tied around her neck. Graciela suppressed a giggle and smiled perhaps too forcefully. Socorrito covered her older daughter's hand with her own.

"Consuelo, are you ready to go home?" Graciela finally asked.

Her sister didn't answer.

Consuelo knew, of course, that she would not go to the volcano tonight, that she likely would never see her mother again after this dinner. Her fuchsia-rimmed eyes were filling with tears, and if she were forced to speak, they'd spill over. If she could leave this place, this table, she would. Though she had no desire to return to the volcanoes—wherever that was—with a mother she barely remembered, away from the solace she had carved out here in the capital with her friends. She grimaced at her new little sister and let their mother pat her hand, that infuriating, empty, clown grin plastered on her face again. Graciela held their mother by her other wrist, her face flashing with fear.

The first course, a soup, was finally served, and Graciela's desire to return home was overcome by her hunger. She was ravenous—aside from the grapes that she'd had earlier, neither she nor Socorrito had eaten since before their journey the night before. The abundance was irresistible—

after the soup came medallions of beef, vegetables in a thick sauce, bread with butter. Consuelo ate beautifully—tiny, deft movements of a delicately grasped knife and fork, not a noise or dropped morsel, but a slight shaking in her hands throughout that looked to us like electricity sparking inside a bulb. Graciela watched Consuelo, tried modeling her movements after her sister's elegant, trembling ones, but she quickly lost her grip on her knife and it clattered to the floor.

Perlita chuckled and raised her glass.

"I'd like to take this opportunity to thank you both for coming and paying respects to Germán. Graciela, I know he wished he could have known you in life, and I'm sure he would be proud that you have inherited his role."

Graciela's stomach dropped at the sound of her name in Perlita's mouth.

"You must be mistaken," Socorrito said, the strange, serene expression still on her face. "Graciela has no plans to stay here. We're going home after dinner."

"We're going home," Graciela repeated.

"Ay, no. You see, Graciela is home now," Perlita said. Socorrito shook her head, but her serene expression remained. Slowly, like a bored actress, Perlita continued, her eyes glazed and staring off somewhere beyond the door to the kitchen. "You'll be going home tonight, but Graciela won't be returning with you." Perlita smiled, her teeth purpled with wine. "Neither of them will be."

Graciela nudged her sister under the table with the toe of her new velvet slipper, but Consuelo didn't make a sound, or even acknowledge her sister. Why didn't she say anything, this useless teenager? Graciela's heart kicked like a rabbit.

"Graciela has a job to do here," Perlita droned on.

Graciela, Perlita explained, would take over her dead father's position at the palace as the General's adviser. She would give the General the confident insight that he required to lead our great nation into the prosperity of the new age, as prophesied by the Great Economists, by the ministries of education and military, and by the holy wisdom embodied in the Society of Sacred Letters and Objects, to raise our people from out of the darkness from which they came.

Remember that: *out of the darkness from which they came.*

Graciela looked to her mother, bewildered. *This güera has lost her mind,* she said with her eyes.

"Stay calm," Socorrito said aloud to Graciela, and then she turned to face Perlita. "Graciela is a child," Socorrito said. "She has no business advising a General." There was a strain in her voice—she struggled to speak clearly through the sedative.

Graciela turned Perlita's palabras over in her mind, trying to make sense of them and what they asked of her: the Society of Sacred Letters and Objects. She loved the sound of these words. She did not understand their meaning.

"The General believed," Perlita said, as though Socorrito had said nothing, "that my husband possessed a sacred mind, a mind capable of helping him to sculpt the future of the nation. And he believes that Graciela has inherited her father's sacred mind." Perlita turned to Consuelo, pointed her lips, derision in her eyes. "Clearly that one didn't." Consuelo scowled, la tarántula clacking against her flat chest.

"What the hell is she talking about?" Socorrito whispered furiously to Graciela.

"I have no idea," Graciela said loud enough for the table to hear. She didn't understand why her mother was frozen. They needed to get out of this place—it was clear their time for escape was running out, if they hadn't missed it already.

Perlita kept on, ignoring them entirely, talking about the thrust of the nation's will, its desire for transubstantiation—not just *transformation,* you see, but *transubstantiation.* She stumbled over the word, as though she did not understand how it had appeared in her mouth.

The nuns had taught us about transubstantiation. It meant from bread into body. But the way Perlita used it, it sounded like something larger, something that would change every single person in our small nation.

Perlita finally paused in her speech to address Socorrito with a red fingernail, sure of herself once more: "There is no higher honor than to sit at the General's right hand," she said.

Graciela pinched herself. She must be dreaming again. She looked around the room for an exit, a window to jump out of. She could grab one of those fufurufo porcelain figurines—the crying clown looked heavy enough—and shatter the window. She and her mother could jump to the ground below and run as fast as they could. And Consuelo? Puya, forget her, she was lost in a trance.

"No." Socorrito spat out the word, the anger in her throat louder now, the haze around her seeming to lift. "I was promised both of my children." She was trembling, encachimbada, pero púchica encachimbada. Graciela had heard the purr of her mother's anger, but never this full-throated roar.

Socorrito pulled the paper, la puta promesa, from her dress and presented it to Perlita, who laughed. Graciela met Consuelo's eyes. Her older sister was shaking, toying with her spider necklace to soothe herself. Graciela looked away, surging with shame and rage.

"Indiada, pero indiada," Perlita said, smacking her lips. "Don't you understand? Can't you see that I'm extending a very gracious favor to you?" Perlita shoved her elbows onto the table. She snatched the paper from Socorrito's hand, balled it in her fist, threw it on the ground, and spat on the floor. Socorrito grasped for the ball of paper, as though its words, which had never meant anything, could restore her life.

"Give me my children!" Socorrito screamed.

Graciela tried to grab her mother's hand, pull her away from the desmadre table. Where was the fucking porcelain clown? Break the window, and then they would jump. La púchica Consuelo could follow them or not. But then the maids crowded into the room, each cloaked in a heavy silence, and the driver from earlier came running. They circled the table, blocking the exits.

Perlita glared at Socorrito's sputtering, screaming mouth, as if her eyes could rearrange the other woman's teeth.

Always when we need a knife we come up empty-handed. Had Socorrito worn her own clothes, she would have had something. But in this púchica dress from the nuns, she had nothing. She seized a butter knife. She lunged at Perlita; Graciela screamed. The chauffeur grabbed Socorrito from behind and shook her until she dropped the knife. He pinned her hands behind her and started to pull her toward the door. Socorrito tried to reach for her daughters, but their faces were slipping away. Two maids held Graciela as she wailed. She thrashed and kicked in the maids' arms, screaming for her mother, as they shoved her in a closet and locked the door.

Socorrito wondered, as she was dragged up the stairs, if this was the same man who had knocked her unconscious so many years before. His roughness felt familiar.

Consuelo put her head down on the table and made her body small. She waited it out. She cried for her mother, for her new little sister, for herself. She lifted her head to see where the room had settled. The hired nenitas ran out the back door of the Estate. Consuelo wondered if Ninfa had managed to pay them. Above, her mother's screams, the heavy footfalls of the chauffeur. Perlita had left the room, her tacones clicking as she paced the halls. In the mess, Ninfa had forgotten to feed the ocelot, and she trilled menacingly from her chain in the courtyard. Consuelo took a breath and walked out of the Estate's open back door, quickening to a run now. She ran down the winding hills of the colonia and into the shimmering lights of the capital, humid air catching in her throat, her tears freshening her garish lipstick as she ran, away from the strangers who were her family, to meet her friends.

Upstairs in the room where Graciela had rested, Socorrito rammed her elbow against the balcony window until it shattered. But the time for her escape had run out; her girls were gone. Ninfa came into the room with the sedative that Perlita had instructed her to give Socorrito—not the tea this time, but the kind meant for a púchica horse—but when she saw the blood, and Socorrito still pinned down by the chauffeur, she began tearing at the bedsheet fabric with her teeth and bandaging the other woman's wound. Socorrito reached up and pulled the old woman's hair. Ninfa hadn't wanted to administer the sedative. In fact, at this point in the evening, Ninfa glanced at the broken window and considered jumping out of it herself. She was too old for this. Enough of this crazy rica and her jodida schemes and endless drama. She stanched the blood. Old as she was, Ninfa was still strong.

She pointed her lips at the chauffeur and he pulled Socorrito's lower jaw open. She dropped in the big fucking pill and the man clamped Socorrito's mouth shut.

When Perlita appeared in the room an hour later, she found Ninfa crying, standing over Socorrito's body. She motioned for Ninfa to be dismissed, and the older woman complied. Perlita inspected Socorrito to be sure she was unconscious; she was smoking, letting the ash fall on Socorrito's borrowed dress. When she was certain that Socorrito would sleep for several hours, Perlita summoned the chauffeur again. He carried the woman like a child, laid her down in the backseat of the long, shiny car, and drove her through the night to the volcanoes.

After Socorrito had been taken from the capital and Perlita had gone off to bed, Ninfa gathered herself and set to work cleaning the ruin downstairs. The hired nenitas had fled when the fighting began. She'd need to find and hire new ones quickly, to have them trained and ready to serve the General at dinner just a few days later. It wouldn't be hard. Everyone needed work now.

She could hear Graciela snoring fitfully on the other side of the locked closet door. She patted her key ring. The key to this particular door was missing. Perlita must have taken it to lock the girl in. Ninfa told herself that if only she had the key, she would open the door and carry the girl outside and into the capital, carry her as far as she could into the night. The fantasy soothed the film of thick guilt she felt over her participation in what had just happened. But the truth was, if the old woman had wanted to get the keys, she could have.

Why didn't she?

Because she would lose the job that fed her children and grandchildren.

But she could find another job, couldn't she?

And that was it. It wasn't just the job. There were Perlita's entangle-ments with that warlock, the General, which Graciela was now helplessly entangled in. It was whatever retaliations he would devise against her that frightened Ninfa more than the loss of her family's income. She'd heard things. People disappeared.

Consuelo, meanwhile, was nowhere. She must have run out. Ninfa was quite aware that Consuelo crept out of the Estate like a cat to meet that art teacher of hers. She didn't blame her. What would it take for Ninfa to leave too? She wasn't a teenager. If only she had a harder heart. She'd practically raised Perlita after her mother died giving birth to her. And Perlita. Perlita was crazy. She was vicious, conniving, and cruel, but somehow still, Ninfa loved her, remembered her as a thin, fussy child, absolved her now as she would have absolved that child.

Ninfa turned from the closet door. It was time to clear the dining table, set the dishes to soak in a tub of soapy water. The rest could wait until morning.

That night, before bed, Perlita unwound her turban in the mirror. It was made from imported silk, and its jewel was a real emerald from Bogotá. Let loose, her hair was long and black and fell to the middle of her back. She flipped her head upside down to brush it from the roots to the ends. We have to admit, she was beautiful.

It was one thing, Perlita often said, to politely entertain the fashions of the times, but it was quite another to do what Consuelo did—to deco-rate herself like a fortune teller. Perlita had known all along that she could not give up Consuelo, her consolation, whose face she had studied for years, whose indiada nose she admired and despised in turns. For ten years Perlita had told Consuelo that she'd better listen carefully. Listen to how to behave like a civilized person. Could una india be remade, "moth-ered," as it were, into another class? But Consuelo was something of a failed experiment. Despite the education Perlita had provided, the tutor-ing, the art lessons, she was hopelessly indiada. Pura india. In certain light, Perlita thought Consuelo's face wretched. And lately, all Perlita could see of her was her dark makeup, the mystical jewelry, the gawky stoop of her shoulders mismatched with thick thighs, the hair she let frizz around her face, her acne.

But. All was not lost. If the General would accept the offering of Consuelo as a bride, or a favorite mistress, Perlita would be in his good favor forever. And now Graciela had arrived to tip the balance further her way. A bride and an oracle—Perlita had secured a fortune for herself, turned her dead husband's cheating into gold. But Perlita would have to throw away all of Consuelo's tacky costume jewelry and marketplace rags first. At fourteen, she was still just a child, but soon would come time for her to stop playing in costumes. Perlita didn't believe any of the nonsense that the General claimed to, that garbage about colored water and séances, the transubstantiation of the nation. She knew it was fashionable in those days, that in Los Yunais, in Europe, there were gringos all over who were trying to talk to ghosts. Ridiculous. But she knew better than to deny a man like him what he wanted. That would only hurt her. With her husband dead, her dead parents' fortune dwindling, economic oracles all around the world predicting a global crash—it was essential that she use the bastard daughters to her advantage.

Perlita told herself that she simply cared too much—feeling annoyance, disgust, tenderness, the desire to brush Consuelo's hair, when she should feel nothing. This vision she had of her own abundant kindness soothed any guilt she might have had for twisting the promise that she'd made to Socorrito. Las hermanas were Perlita's property.

And as for Socorrito: "A kindness to bring her all the way back to her muddy little village. Other women in my position would have just disposed of her, after the trouble she caused, the threats," Perlita said aloud to the four walls of her bedroom, stilling the chatter of her mind. The silk lay on the floor beside her open window, silvered by a beam of moonlight, rippling like our river. La luna llena es una mujer. And so Perlita slept soundly.

5

SOCORRITO WOKE THE NEXT MORNING, ALONE IN THE FOREST, lying on her back. She rubbed her eyes and found the moon, swollen like a golden bruise above her. Her tongue was rough and dry as a cat's and her caites were missing.

Two shoes, both daughters, gone.

When she tried to stand, her stomach flipped and she fell to her knees. She made her way to the water, where she vomited until she could no longer hold herself up. She rested her cheek on a stone and wailed like Siguanaba, the ghost whose child had been stolen from her as punishment for trying to fool the powerful. Nothing belongs to you, our mothers used to tell us.

Socorrito lay in the cool mud and listened to the water. She watched the yellow moonlight flicker on its surface. If this was the river, then she was a half day's walk from the village. The river held her wails; Siguanaba's cries rose from the water's depths, rippled on the surface.

Siguanaba, the woman with the head of a horse and the heart of a traitor, who lay in the dark beside rivers, letting her long hair fool anyone who saw her into thinking she was beautiful. Siguanaba, sitting beside the water, brushing out her hair with a fury, as though she could undo the tangle she'd made of her life. Siguanaba, howling for her children as Socorrito howled for hers. Was she the kind of woman who's most beautiful the first time you see her, but becomes a little bit uglier each time after? (You notice only her crooked teeth, the band of loose skin around her waist; you wonder who gave her that bruise on her cheek.) Socorrito patted her belly, the tender bruise on her cheek, felt her mouth, as if touching these parts of herself might help her to understand where she was.

Socorrito wondered if Perlita's people had left her for dead. Was she dead? It was hard to know. Some say Siguanaba died running headlong into a ravine trying to escape her grief. And who wouldn't? Mujeres, madres, hijas, Malinches, mestizas, todas Siguanabas. Socorrito entered the water to her waist and listened for the pack of cadejos to encircle her with their howls, hoping the water would either drown her or guide her home.

6

LAS VIEJAS, OUR GREAT-GRANDMOTHERS, USED TO SAY THAT our ancestors grew from the ceiba tree, and sometimes we cipotas return to its great webbed foot, awakening in our decrepit bodies beneath a canopy of dozing birds.

Another bright-blue thread. La púchica root of the ancient world also begins here. Pluck this one from the ether; we'll trace it.

Our great-grandmothers were the last of the age of indigo. They reeked of piss no matter how much they washed, no matter how long they outlived the crop that had poisoned them. Coffee came in during their youth, but the indigo had already seeped into their brains, their wombs, and the smell of it lived for generations in the wooden beams of the sorting room, eventually mixing with the stench of rotten red coffee berries softening from their stones, heaped high enough to warp a body.

Our ancestors grew xiquilite, the plant from which indigo is processed, in small plots, on land that belonged to them, moving them over the seasons so as not to destroy the soil, cultivating xiquilite alongside zapotes, delicate red beans, maíz, and potatoes, balancing the soil, nourishing themselves with beauty and food. They grew xiquilite as medicine. And they wove with cotton threads dyed in its color, tying one strap of the loom around their lower backs, just above las nalgas, and the other strap around a tree, anchoring them to the earth. They soaked thread in indigo, and then embroidered their woven pik'bil gauze with it, cloth for their nobility. Back then, the color was holy. Indigo shining in their refajos, they felt as beautiful as the sky. They painted the walls of their temples with it. And used in that way, cultivated in that way, indigo caused our ancestors no harm.

But in the time of our great-grandmothers, indigo had lost all of its holiness, and the land no longer belonged to them. By their time, our people no longer wore indigo, and that bright blue had become poison. Our great-grandmothers were forced to perform the miracle of multiplying their efforts, gringos imagining them as machines in order to ship our royal blue around the world. It was this enormous volume of indigo, the complete immersion in its acrid stench, the relentlessness of the indigo, that destroyed their bodies and devastated the soil.

They worked in the wooden storing room. Three enormous vats filled it then: one of dark water, a pile of stones beside it; another of water, full of large, muddy flakes; the last brimming with our great-grandmothers' piss and the piss of the forty other women working beside them. Some beat the waters of the second vat with a splintery oar, the waters changing color before our eyes: from a rancid gold, to green, to an impossible aquamarine, to a still-stranger lavender, which deepened into a blue-violet shimmering like a beetle's back.

Some women reached into the vats and pounded the pulp with stones, their arms thrashing beneath the surface of the waters. Some fished for garbage, pulling up ceiba leaves, pebbles, a clot of menstrual blood, human hair. Some crouched on the floor, using their machetes to cut muddy bricks of iridescent blue into squares the size of a baby's palm. The best pieces of indigo were named after the throat of a dove because of the way they caught the light. These pieces were harder, lighter than the other indigo.

Our great-grandmothers' hands, up to the elbow, radiated a deep violet-blue. Stiff, thick fingers, burned bloody to the quicks, ocher shadows where the nails should be, the same golden glow in their faces. This radiance was jaundice, the poison doing its work on their bodies. At night, some of the women fell asleep coughing blood into their mats. They complained of headaches and dropped into dead faints, blaming the heat. Their men found them dead: one girl sprawled lifeless on the floor on one of the sacred mornings Izalco deigned to erupt, pulmonary blood darkening her mat; one girl collapsed dead at the Festival of the Black Virgin in Juayúa; one girl went missing for a week and was found broken, at the bottom of a well. Hers was one of the saddest stories. They say she suffered visions, hallucinations, momentary paralysis, days of blindness.

But somehow, despite it all, our great-grandmothers lived.

Later, when the indigo market slowed, and the railroad was complete, our great-grandmothers were made to plant coffee. Hoping coffee would be better, easier on their bodies, they planted the seeds during the dry season, rows of dusty, pale dirt mounds like infant graves. The plants came up yellowish, and deepened to a sick green. Our great-grandmothers packed tobacco into the sides of their mouths, spat it into the fields as they worked. The ceiba birds roosted in their ancient tree, leaving and returning like clockwork, just as they did decades later, when we worked those same fields.

Our great-grandmothers' words dried up before we were born, but the building where they made indigo, where they sorted coffee berries, still stands today. Our mothers worked there too, and then we did as well, worked inside those same splintered walls. But it's only now that we have died that we can hear when the purple-fingered viejas call to us.

Oye, listen.

In the final days of indigo, an Irishman came to the edge of our world. He was calculating how he could multiply his wealth, how the sea might be of service to him. His stomach jolted a little at the thought; the sea had always frightened him. Others described him as a titan of industry, but often, he felt just like a little boy, adrift and solitary. We see him now as a frightened, pious white man, like all the others. The Atlantic he had known was the color of slate, hungry and freezing cold. But the sea of delicate blue in front of him seemed somehow wilder in its convulsive beauty. Patrick Brannon vowed to tame this wild place, to harness the sea.

You see, long before El Gran Pendejo, before coffee, before our great-grandmothers lost their minds, we had ejidos, our own pieces of land, land that we planted as we liked and held in common. We grew what we needed to eat. But the communal land that had shrunk with indigo disappeared altogether with coffee. Our fruit trees were pulled from the ground, the roots shredded and burned, along with the milpa of maíz. Lines around our farms were redrawn by an invisible hand until suddenly nothing belonged to us.

In Patrick's care, under arrangements with the ruling class of our country, with the money bags in Los Yunais, the land shifted quickly and then slowly. Coffee needed space to grow and process, and years to mature.

So Patrick needed a railroad to slice through our fractured land, to carry the coffee to the sea and beyond. He built the railroad for decades, piece by piece, each one gifted in exchange for debt or favors or promises, in our country and abroad. Of course he built it with an invisible hand. Other bodies broke carrying the lumber and laying the ties.

Dark-skinned men built Patrick's railroad. And for a hundred years after those dark-skinned men built the railroad, the people of our country claimed that they had not existed, had never existed. In newer paintings of caste and color, Black people occupied fewer and fewer squares, until soon there were no places for our people to call themselves Black— the word was removed from the census entirely. Ask Rosario, la mami of Lourdes and María, and she'd say she was Black. But "mestiza" was what the patrón wrote in his records of the workers on his finca. Rosario could speak the words aloud, but unless they were written, they did not count.

The word makes the world.

But Patrick, who had redrawn the contours of our land to harness the sea, was afraid. Since the onset of the railroad project, for weeks and then months, he had been plagued by nightmares. They all followed the same pattern: A woman undid her hair beside a river, let it fall thick as a blanket, as Patrick reached for her, aching with desire. Her skin was oddly cool, and as he touched her, he noticed a fat maggot crawling through her hair. She turned to face him, and where there should have been eyes were bleeding wounds. He woke up screaming most early mornings, sometimes punching the wall beside his bed. Falling back asleep was often impossible, and he walked the streets to the rutted footpaths, ascending the volcano until the soft green light of early morning arrived. He was terribly lonely in our country. Not to mention that everything to do with the railroad was late. The materials were impossible to find, the price of wood rose sharply each day. And the money. He had no more of it, had gone flat-out broke. He felt like a professional beggar as he made the rounds, seeking funds, a clown in a dingy top hat, imploring sensible people into his traveling circus's flapping tent.

On one of those sleepless mornings, he sat outside el comedor, watching la maitra prepare to open for the day. She threw a bucket of soapy water on the concrete and scrubbed.

She'd seen him before, this wild-eyed baboso. He stank. She poured another bucket of water beneath the barstools where he sat trembling, splashing him a little. Her own son, Germán, was chopping firewood behind el comedor for the stove. La maitra peered around at the back of the building. Twelve years old and still impressionable. She'd keep him away from babosos. He was a good boy.

Germán, me entiendes—this is el papi de la Consuelo y la Graciela.

"You're not well," she said to Patrick.

He nodded weakly. It was true. The relief Patrick felt in that moment, to be seen by another person, to be spoken to so sharply! He often felt that he walked through a country of ghosts. Or perhaps he was the ghost. The people here—natives, he called them—looked right through him. He rubbed the dream from his eyes, feeling the skin of his graying face. His flesh was real, clammy, mortal.

"Deliver us from evil," he said, mouthing the end of the Lord's Prayer.

"Why don't you sleep?" she asked. "Every morning you get here before I do."

"I can't sleep," Patrick said. He lit a cigarette, and before la maitra could say another word, he told her about his nightmare.

La maitra listened patiently as she scrubbed down the walkway in front of her family comedor, smirking out the side of her mouth. La maitra was nearly certain that she'd heard about this man, his name circled by the stink-hungry flies of chambre, the kind of gossip that sometimes is the key to our very survival. When Patrick had finished telling the story of the woman by the water with the dead eyes, la maitra opened her mouth to speak, but una carcajada escaped instead. Yes, she'd heard about this man; her niece had told her stories about him. What had her niece overheard in the market—something about this gringo bloodying noses in a rage, throwing women like furniture. Pathetic. He was a skinny little man, but these gringos drank until they were saturated with it. She laughed. Patrick's eyes went glassy and la maitra's carcajadas got louder as we laughed with her. We laugh because we know, and la maitra knew, that the woman from Patrick's dream is La Cigua. We know her. And we knew exactly why she'd chosen to torment this man.

"Are you married?" la maitra asked Patrick. He shook his head. But la maitra was onto something. Patrick was betrothed to a woman, the niece of one of his father's business associates in New York, a woman with a long, lovely white neck and no chin to speak of.

"Not sure, huh," la maitra said to Patrick, grinning as she inspected his very soul, comparing the man she saw with the rumors that swirled around him. "How many whores did you see this week?"

Brannon reddened in blotches from his throat to his forehead. "It's just that . . ." Patrick whispered to la maitra. "It's just that I'm so lonely," he said, compelled to answer la maitra because of this loneliness. She was the first person he'd talked to in days. He felt an intimacy with this woman, about whom he knew nothing.

The dark air between them, it was conspiratorial. When she laughed at him, which was often, he was wracked by punishing shame. But he hungered for that shame—it reminded him that he was real, that his flesh began and ended in his body. He was not the diffuse light on the milpa. He was not the torogoz, or the nauseating sea, cresting.

"Is that why you hit them?" la maitra asked. "Your loneliness? I've heard about you, you know."

It was true. Patrick felt as though his head were being held underwater. He saw his reflection in la maitra's pupils. He was pathetic. He was real, a simple, fleshy man, and he was pathetic. He did beat the women.

He'd happened upon three of them in a corridor laughing at him, and something about the sharp tones of their laughter and their defiant beauty unlocked a rage in him.

Patrick lay down on the soapy concrete, ashamed and exhausted.

"Until you stop this, the nightmares will continue. Or else someone's going to put an end to all of your days and nights," la maitra said. "Buzo," she said. "La Cigua—that's the woman in your pesadillas. She knows how to find men like you." La maitra spoke freely because she knew that he'd never strike her, despite her scolding, her laughter. He struck the others because they were young and beautiful, because their laughter wounded him more deeply, because he felt large and immortal in their presence.

Siguanaba changes, depending on who's talking about her. This one, La Cigua, the one haunting Brannon, is imagined by men like him as proof that we're all Malinches, traitors, ugly at heart. Later, when he asked the railroad men he had hired, whom he hadn't yet paid, about La Cigua, each gave a slightly different version of the same story. You find her on a moonless night, one said, bathing naked in a river. Another said she's washing linens in the river, in a flimsy dress. They all agreed that she has long, beautiful hair, hair so thick and shiny that you can't help but touch it, bury your face in its scent. But then La Cigua has you, and she turns to reveal the head of a horse, or eyes like knives, or a rotting skull. If you don't die by fright, you're driven mad, or you drown.

But we know who she really is. La Cigua is a woman made monstrous by her grief for her stolen child. She frightens dangerous men in order to protect herself from their harm.

An unfaithful man, drawn to death by water, or to madness— Brannon recognized himself in the stories. He did feel he was going mad. His accounts were drained. He had no prospects for finishing this rail- road, and no means of paying for what he had already built.

All that day, and all through the following night, dark and wet like the mouth of a dog, la maitra's carcajadas remained with him, pulsing like lightning in his sleepless mind, filling him with bright shame. He had to get out of this place. The next morning he sent a telegram to his father asking him to wire money for a ticket to New York City. BUSINESS IS GOING WELL, he wrote. MUST SECURE THE DEAL IN NYC AND SEE LEISE.

Leise was the name of his fiancée; he had no intention of seeing her at all.

Patrick arrived in New York pale and defeated. The thought of begging a robber baron whom he'd once met at a party thrown by his father to fund the part of the railroad that kissed the lip of our shore sickened him, but the plan was all that stayed him from throwing himself off the side of the ship during the journey. He was failing spectacularly in the lurid, wet tropics. But in New York he might yet recover the business and cure his madness.

He stayed with his cousin Phillip in the city, and for a week after his arrival convalesced, staring out the window at the gray, industrious city as though the steel and glass could absorb his delusions. But his nightmares continued. La Cigua was ravenous in New York. She swallowed his tongue and clawed out his eyes. He dreamt that she was there with him, outside of his bedroom window. She stood in the snow, lit by the moon. When he approached her, he felt only warmth and tenderness. But her teeth were made of rusted wire, and she dove to devour his legs. Brannon awoke screaming each night, until he finally decided to dispense with sleep altogether. He paced the halls until dawn instead.

During the day, Patrick didn't leave the house very often because of his asthma. Phillip, too, stayed inside the brownstone, behind long velvet curtains, cloaked in a brocade robe. Phillip was an excellent companion and confessor for Patrick in this regard. Patrick had sworn him to secrecy on a number of matters: *Don't tell anyone I'm here, especially Leise! You must not tell my father I've made a ruin of things. It's a temporary matter, I assure you! You must not tell anyone I've gone mad. Again: I assure you that it's a temporary matter!*

Phillip saw no one, would tell no one. He grinned like a cat. "I wouldn't dream of betraying you," he said. He was wan and frail, but voluble, with wet, red lips. Beneath his robe he wore an ankh, an amulet of the ancient Egyptians. Phillip's ankh was small, decorative, relevant to the fashions of his small, erudite circles. It signaled to others that he was a discerning reader of esoteric texts, that he housed an eclectic collection of anthropological artifacts, conversation pieces, and fragile souvenirs in his brownstone. Phillip didn't believe his cousin was mad; rather, he floated the idea that Patrick might simply be possessed by a tropical demon.

"Ghosts, you see, they become trapped," Phillip said.

(Please excuse our carcajadas. Qué onda, Phillip. ¡Simón!)

"From what I've read, it's really just a matter of coaxing them out. Helping them to emerge into their own state of being."

He believed he knew of someone who could help his cousin. He had read of a Madame Sophia Belova, a woman who saw spirits like the ones that troubled his cousin, and could banish them. She'd ministered to the souls of presidents and kings the world over.

"She seems really very ordinary, in my opinion," Phillip said, tempering his initial enthusiasm in the case that this Belova woman was a charlatan. Himself, he preferred more ornate, theatrical displays of intellect, and his voracious mind recognized no master. But this woman had been a great help to many, and she seemed particularly popular among world leaders, great men of industry, those types. She was in town now, he noted, the end of a United States tour. They could go to her public lecture, if Patrick wanted.

"She seems concerned with decent, broad things," Phillip said. "Nothing too specific, you know—a bit of Eastern mysticism, a bit of the occult, a bit of looking at a leaf cell under a microscope and then marveling at its wholeness. 'There is no religion higher than truth'—that's one of hers, I think. Nothing too deep. But comforting, which is, I gather, what you need right now."

Phillip gathered correctly. His digs at Belova only amplified her intrigue for his cousin. A woman who could cleanly remove the terrors from Patrick's mind, leaving him newly whole—nothing could be more appealing to his broken brain. Like an oligarch, like an extraordinary man, he would be remade with this woman's help.

So Phillip took Patrick to see Madame Belova. Her face was difficult to make out on the stage, but her body appeared tall and broad behind the wooden podium, commanding. Patrick wasn't typically attracted to large, pale women, and she seemed a bit older too. But her voice! Belova held a nightingale in her throat, and when she began speaking, Patrick surprised himself by conjuring a flash of a daydream of fucking her. A certain vibration in the voice emitted a pulsing frequency that seemed to pour light into the center of his body.

All colors become one, she said. All religions, all races. All become one. She spoke of cosmic duty, of a single point of truth that transcends all planes, of transcending this plane for a higher one, of listening to the spirits that come to us, begging for us merely to listen to them.

And Patrick listened. His heart thrummed. He felt ecstasy and unease. He sat breathless, clutching the armrest fiercely. He bit his lip to break the trance. He didn't usually go in for this kind of thing. Aching with both adrenaline and acute shame, he glanced at Phillip, who'd tucked his chin into his cravat and begun faintly to snore.

The curtain fell and Patrick surged with resolve. He needed to meet this woman in person. He made for the aisle in order to run to the stage. Only a few minutes in her presence, face-to-face, and he was certain that his mind would be restored. The demons would be tamed and take leave of him. One of her handlers, an owlish man in thick glasses, appeared in a gap between the curtains, and declared that Madame was exhausted, that she would not be taking questions this evening. Patrick felt Phillip nudge him in the back with his walking stick, and they filed out of the lecture hall.

Outside, it had begun to snow, and Phillip reached to wipe his cousin's face with his handkerchief; Patrick realized then that he'd been weeping. He tongued a fresh wound on the inside of his cheek.

"Something has happened to me," Patrick said. "Some kind of—what is it—primordial chaos?" More tears streaked his cheeks. Snow gathered on his eyelashes.

"Mmmmhmm," Phillip mumbled beside him.

"I sound like a lunatic," Brannon said, without the conviction to emit even the smallest chuckle to disavow his tears. Something had swelled and erupted inside of him during Belova's talk, leaving a grasping feeling around his solar plexus like a hungry mouth. He didn't want the feeling to become smaller. The great men knew what it was to tame demons. He would tame the dark women who haunted him with the force of his own bright vitality. There is no religion higher than the truth, Belova had said. He would devote himself therein.

Phillip's red lips trembled briefly, victorious. His interest in all of this was, of course, primarily intellectual. It was all a bit vague, this talk of oneness. But it seemed—how to put it—culturally relevant. Vague, yes, but perhaps vague enough to be lasting. Durable. Interesting, with respect to the social order, what might be done with the darker races, now that emancipation was here. There was a tidiness to some of these ideas, not a caste system, exactly, but a useful stratification.

He was surprised, pleased, even, that his cousin, typically so material, so taciturn, had been so moved. He'd been lonely out there in the tropics, it seemed, terribly lonely. The way he screamed at night, darting like a mouse around the apartment, barely eating. And the jungle had been as terrible for his constitution as his mind—certainly this was a tropical madness that consumed his cousin—Phillip had never seen Patrick so thin, so pale. They resembled each other more closely now than they ever had as children.

LOURDES: Achis, Yina, you're sounding like a fucking mestiza Henry James.

MARÍA: ¡Ma ve, Lourdes! Who the fuck are you talking about, Henry James?

LOURDES: Henry James, cherita, come on! "Tropical madness"! "So taciturn." Ma ve, Yina.

CORA: Lourdes, have some patience. These are old white men. La Yina is using the words that make their world.

LOURDES: I'm not saying I hate it. I like it! It's cozy—como se dice—"exotic." Just that La Yina is sounding like these fucking gringos when she's telling this part of the story, the same way she did when she started talking about the jodida furniture in the Estate, the púchica dark wardrobe, those porcelain clowns, all those otros bolados.

LUCÍA: Ay, you clowns. You missed the point. Did you hear them talking about that single point of truth, how all races become one? That's the shit El Gran Pendejo went on about. The endpoint of all races is one race. That's mestizaje, that cosmic-race shit. But all you can talk about is púchica Henry James.

In the days that followed, Brannon became fixated on the ideas he'd heard Belova talk about, convinced that she'd be able to help guide him to his single point of truth. To erase the narrow monotheism he had clung to like a crutch—maybe that was the cause of his failures! His neuroticism, his business mismanagement, his fearful desire for small, dark women who despised him, and the shame that followed—he wanted to erase it all with that singular light. Perhaps he needed something larger, more capacious. A bright light that would cut through his body, mind, and soul like a blade. He was a man of large ideas, wasn't he?

Phillip had an idea of where Belova might be staying, and Patrick spent his days walking in tortured circles, orbiting the street. An ordinary-looking hotel, painted that newish shade of gray, to house a spiritual savior. His madness had spiked during this New York winter with the proximity of Belova. He was unable to sleep for more than a couple of hours at a time. For three days, Patrick went and knocked on the door. He never heard a reply.

On the third day, when he returned to the brownstone, Phillip greeted him with a telegram, reminding his cousin of the other reason he'd come to New York—the railroad and the robber baron, who had conceded to a meeting. Patrick's father had known the robber baron for years, and he had sent a note.

At Phillip's urging, Patrick bathed for the first time in a week and dressed himself in clean clothing. As he walked to the meeting, he recited his pitch. He'd begin with a description of the soil—he'd carried a small cloth bag of the stuff with him here. He'd throw it casually on the robber baron's desk and let its fertile blackness spill onto the man's papers. He'd have to spit on it before entering the building—it'd gone a bit stale. He'd emphasize the dividends the robber baron would reap, in indigo, and most of all, in coffee. The market's demand was booming, and he'd be a fool not to have a hand in loading freight with the stuff. The fertile, volcano-rich land, jungle-thick, was lying in wait. Hardwood to be logged as well. And the women were beautiful, he'd tell him. They were lighter than Caribbeans, and more delicate.

But by the time he'd climbed the stairs to the offices where the meeting was to be held, Patrick was sweating, clammy, breathless again. When he entered the office, he was no longer certain that he knew how to tell this story. A gray vein pulsed in his forehead and he threw his overcoat over the back of the robber baron's door with more force than he was accustomed to using in a business setting. The old man registered no alarm.

Patrick huffed and tossed the limp pouch of dirt, frosty from his walk in the cold air, into the space between them. The old man flinched and brought up a liver-spotted hand to guard his face. The pouch landed on its side and emitted a mild fart, puffing grainy soil over the old man's papers. Suddenly crestfallen, flush with shame, Patrick apologized. The vigor left his body as he stooped to sweep dirt off of the robber baron's papers, and attempted to steer the conversation toward his aim, the railroad.

Despite Patrick's performance, the rich old man remained unconvinced of the value of the enterprise.

"Why build a railroad around one of those damn islands?" he said.

"Isn't it small enough that you can just walk right across it? I'll carry the coffee myself!"

CORA: Ay, it's not so terrible to be small! Besides, the volcanoes make us bigger.

LOURDES: What's that line from Roque Dalton: "Is there anyone who isn't fed up with your smallness?" At least he says it with ternura.

MARÍA: Lourdes. Pendejado Roque Dalton, this big fucking man. Me da churria. Puya, hermana, you're quoting a man so small he cheated on his wife with a thirteen-year-old. Talk about smallness. A decent poet, but it must be fucking said. Just one of the many reasons I don't fuck men. Even as a ghost.

LUCÍA: École, María. Ay, vamos. Back to gringolandia. Vamos a la vuelta.

Patrick didn't push the matter, didn't clarify that the country wasn't an island, but a jewel on the Pacific side of the isthmus. A spiral pattern in a knothole of the wood paneling a few feet above the robber baron's desk commanded his attention. Since his nightmares had begun, Patrick had not let his eyes linger on shapes like this—they swallowed his soul, ravenous as the void in La Cigua's face. Now, though, he could not look away. Patrick let the spiraling wood pull his mind inside its smooth whorls. Around and around he went, deeper and deeper, until he found a soft, inviting quiet.

Eventually, the robber baron barked a hoarse cough; spittle foamed in the corner of his mouth. Patrick glanced at the old man across the desk, dusted his knees as he stood, and left the dark office, forgetting even to extend his hand to thank the old man for his time. Patrick left the building thinking only of Belova, comforting himself with the certainty that if he could just see her face, his nightmares would vanish, his accounts would stabilize, and the slowness of this enterprise wouldn't really matter.

He walked three miles to the ordinary building where Phillip believed

Belova was staying. When he arrived he found that he was too disgusted with himself to stand there knocking again. He tasted his stale breath. Though he'd bathed in preparation for his meeting, he'd barely slept or eaten in days, cowering in the shadows of Phillip's brownstone. If Belova opened the door this time, he'd probably collapse. He was pathetic. He craved a good scolding from la maitra. Head swimming, Brannon staggered back to his cousin's home, hoping to escape his notice when he returned.

Days of silence from the robber baron followed, until the solitary discomfort prompted Patrick to combine his impulsiveness and his resources and extend his trip. He telegrammed his father again, who wired more money. He'd follow Belova's ship to London, where she was scheduled to give another round of lectures. He'd meet her on lands closer to his own true home. As for the railroad, he had plenty of contacts he could pursue there. His father's circle in London had been much more enthusiastic about the tropics than the rich old man in New York. He told himself he was traveling for business.

Patrick wasted no time after his arrival in London. The next morning, he stood in the driving rain, ear pressed to Belova's door. His heart seized at the sound of the voice again.

"Let the cowboy in," she said. A benediction. The door fell open, and in the threshold Patrick beheld an empress. Her crystal-blue eyes, hard and alert and rimmed in kohl, seemed to tug at him like a magnet. Her jowls were caked with rouge and silver hair fuzzed around her face.

"Welcome, cowboy," the empress purred, and brushed his shoulders with both of her hands. She removed his sopping overcoat and threw it on the floor.

Curious, he thought to himself, as he felt his earthly being transformed into some kind of clay, molded by Belova's hands. No longer pathetic, he was ruthless, lionhearted, capable. Patrick was remade.

He knelt to kiss her hands, and she swatted at him playfully with a folded newspaper. She brought him to a sitting room, where she gave him a cursory examination.

She listened to his heart with her head pressed against his chest. She struck his knees with a soup spoon and tutted at his slow reflexes. The idea was to move toward cosmic improvement. Belova believed her teachings might better the human race through accelerated evolution.

"Where do your people come from?" Belova asked Brannon. She stuck fingers in both of his ears and nodded his head for him. "In the future," she said, "all different people will become one, faster, brighter, lighter. It's our responsibility to transmit this knowledge, pass it down through the ages. The wisdom we have now will transform all those who come in the future."

LUCÍA: Are you hearing this shit? *All different people will become one.* Miren que, it's like that ugly casta painting, Spanish blood dripping down through the ages, *transforming* us until we've disappeared? Am I crazy?

CORA: You're not crazy.

MARÍA: You're not fucking crazy.

LOURDES: You're crazy, girl, but, puya, you're also right.

"Rheumy eyes," Belova said. She coaxed him to eat a raw turnip, sliced paper-thin and arranged in the shape of a fan on a plate. Patrick's lip quivered as he told her about his dreams. The empress held a crystal on a shining chain above his head and measured the circumference of the circles it spun, holding her breath. Suddenly, Patrick was exhausted. He fought the urge to lay his head in Belova's lap, until she invited him to do exactly that.

"I know you," said Belova. Again, her voice was the open door, leading to a warm darkness his spirit craved. His body pulsed; the infrastructure of a boomtown was electrifying inside of him. Patrick's railroad sparked and rumbled; enchanted, he dozed on the pillow of dusty velvet skirts and crinolines.

When Patrick awoke, the empress Belova gave him a ruby ring. It fit his finger perfectly.

"You need fresh blood. And more of it," she said. "You lack vigor!

That's why the ruby." And then she sent him away. He was to return after three days.

Three days and two railroad meetings later, he returned to Belova's door, as promised, wearing the jewel on the ring finger of his soft right hand. His blood bore a vigorous metallic charge. He felt like a boy. Belova inspected his eyes by holding a match up to them. She ordered him to open his mouth and she inserted her nose, sniffed his breath.

"Better," she said. "And the nightmares?"

"Vanished," Patrick said. "I'm positively rosy," he said. "Aren't I?"

Belova nodded curtly and presented him with a manuscript of her teachings. This time, she allowed him to kiss her hand before sending him away.

Patrick remained in London another fortnight, awaiting news about the railroad, having promised he'd now leave Belova to her work. The New York robber baron's letter declining Patrick's offer came via telegram. It didn't matter; the Englishmen wanted in, as did a San Francisco company he'd talked with months ago, Prescott, Scott & Co. They'd provide the equipment, the locomotives, and the rolling stock. They'd complete the line's final twenty kilometers, taking it all the way to the sea. Patrick's railroad was funded. The nightmares had faded. He would return to our country a cowboy and finish the thing.

On the deck of the ship, he sat reading Belova's manuscript. He was no longer afraid of our sea. Its pale blue, a mirror to the sky, spoke to him in Belova's voice. In her language of colors the entire ocean promised divine ascendance. This deep, rich blue—the color of abundance, a triumph. The color of transformation. Red, of course, was vitality, vigor—the ruby ring. And white—white was the color of heaven, a pure heart that contained within it all colors, all light.

Patrick returned to el comedor to thank la maitra for guiding him on his path to transcendence with her scorn, though when she'd scolded him months ago, neither of them knew what a gift her derision would be. She smiled slyly at this idiot.

"I am pure now," he told her. "Your laughter purified me with utter rage. I died and returned. I no longer touch the stuff," he said, pointing with his lips, like one of us, at the dusty bottle of aguardiente la maitra kept on a shelf in the comedor. "I won't ever again."

"I simply have the best plato típico in town," she said, knowing the story of La Cigua had terrified him. For the sake of the women he'd harmed, she was happy he'd stopped drinking himself baboso and violent. He and his pendejada railroad, the railroad that had destroyed her dead husband's small plot of remaining land, could go right to hell.

She still believed him to be a drunk. Now he was just drunk on these foolish ideas. But over the years, Patrick revealed himself to be kind enough, a regular customer. He brought gifts for her family during the holidays. La maitra's son, older now, was no longer forbidden from speaking to the idiot gringo. As the railroad was built, Patrick imparted his wisdom to young Germán, who would one day become the absent father of our Graciela.

And Germán, of course, shared this knowledge in turn with his friend El Gran Pendejo, when he was but El Bichitito. Coffee's rise accelerated, and Patrick found both young men good jobs at the finca, loading beans onto freight cars that carried the gold to the sea, where they were shipped, alongside the conquistadores' Royal Road, up the Pacific Coast to San Francisco.

After the railroad, Patrick founded the Society of Sacred Letters and Objects in the capital, a sort of artists' salon, a roundtable for discussing the possibilities of his ideas, threading them into music, culture, poetry, even politics. Its members adopted sobriety as well, in the spirit of purity. Patrick married a woman from our country, whose mother's mother had known our mothers' mothers. A daughter was born, and he identified the child as a poet, immediately. We would come to know her as La Claudia; she was a friend of Consuelo's, an older girl she looked up to. You'll meet her later. La Claudia, though her father called her Maggie. She was mestizaje's promise incarnate. Dark hair, fair skin: a cosmic child.

What happened next had long been ordained in our ancient stories: a ferocious battle for order and stability took place, one dependent on magic. And the magic here took many shapes: words made law, the voices of the dead channeled through a young girl, a painting that charted the destiny of skin, a railroad that traversed nations along an old royal road, an ocean of ancient tears, and fertile, verdant land fed by igneous rock. Our lives destroyed, our bones the harvest of a fragile ego. Our souls wrapped around these threads.

7

GRACIELA AWOKE WITH A START THE MORNING AFTER SHE'D arrived at the Estate. She was still in the closet; Perlita unlocked the door and pulled it open. Socorrito was nowhere, and Graciela screamed as if trying to shake her mind loose from a nightmare. "I want to go home. I want my mother."

Perlita exhaled smoke in the child's direction and shrugged her satin shoulders. She fixed her eyes somewhere beyond Graciela's body.

"Here you are," Perlita said, moving her cigarette around in a wide circle. "You're very lucky to be here. Here, you'll live like a princess," she said. "We'll feed you, dress you, even take you with us to the country, abroad. Do you know how many children would die for all this? A touch more gratitude would be politic."

Perlita considered Graciela's face, lifting the girl's chin with a long finger. She was pretty, dark. Her mother's sharp cheekbones would arrive within a few years, sooner if Perlita fed her less.

"You're rather smart, aren't you?" she continued.

Graciela was silent. She bit down on Perlita's finger as hard as she could.

Perlita sighed. "Indiada." She tsked. "We'll teach you here. Don't worry, cherita," she said, as blood flooded the bed of her fingernail.

"Don't worry," she said again. "You'll make the General look brilliant. You know, he loves tiny Indians," Perlita said.

Graciela was stunned, listening but not understanding. Indiada. She wondered if she was more or less indiada than Consuelo, according to Perlita. The inside of her arm was approximately the same color as Consuelo's. Consuelo had black eyes like ours, with flecks of gold in them. But Consuelo also had different clothing, a short, wavy haircut, and wore a hat to shield her skin from the sun when she stepped outside, even for a moment.

"It's a good thing you're already so sharp," Perlita said. "You won't be going to school anymore. We've tried that with your sister—Consuelo. She wasn't made for it." Perlita pointed her lips with displeasure. She knew there would be no fight from Graciela—she could see the fight fading from the child already. Graciela had arrived tired, uncomfortable, and dirty in that cheap, too-small dress. She'd never slept in a proper bed, had a proper bath. Anything would feel like luxury to her, Perlita was sure.

And Graciela was tired. Her eyes and throat were raw from crying. She didn't know what this crazy güerita meant, that Consuelo wasn't made for school. Was Consuelo stupid or something? In school, the nuns had talked about "mercy"—blessed are the merciful, mercy as a gift, mercy that saves another from a terrible fate. As she was beginning to understand it, Graciela and Consuelo were both at Perlita's mercy. Consuelo had had more time to figure it out, how to live inside this mercy. Graciela would have to ask her how to do it.

"And besides which," Perlita said, "you'll have plenty of things to do here. Ninfa is getting older and needs help. She'll teach you everything. She's infinitely patient, a paragon in her field."

(Puya, chelitas are always calling inditas patient.)

Perlita sighed, looked from the ceiling to the door. The rain began, and she smiled out the window at the drenched bougainvillea tapping at the glass.

"Come here," Perlita commanded. Graciela stepped forward and remained perfectly still, allowing herself to be embraced by Perlita's thick and surprisingly firm arms. She smelled of lavender perfume, the very same one Socorrito had worn. Graciela closed her eyes, savoring her mother's smell. Upset as she was, she felt ashamed for biting the woman's finger.

Perlita took Graciela's face in both of her hands again, jolting the girl to alertness. She studied Perlita's face as Perlita studied hers. The woman had a long, thin nose, a sharp chin, and wide eyes, light brown. Her brows were painted in extravagant, broad arcs, a line feathering upward between them into the powdery landscape of her forehead, a crack in dry-season dirt.

"Such a beautiful child," Perlita said, her red mouth curling like a hook. "Let's have some breakfast now." Graciela, starving, accepted this.

She followed Perlita back to the hideous goblin table, where Consuelo sat before a feast of pastries, fruit, and cheeses. She wore the lace dress from the night before, rumpled and stained with the fuchsia lipstick, which was hideously smeared all over her small chin. Graciela tried to catch her eye but Consuelo looked beyond her sister, grabbed a pastel de jocote and scrambled out of the dining room, the spider swinging. Upstairs, a door slammed. Graciela wondered what she had done to make her sister despise her.

After breakfast, Graciela was sent to Ninfa's quarters, a room set off the back of the kitchen. Ninfa greeted her warmly, inviting her to sit on her lumpy bed, while she traced an outline of the Estate's rooms in pencil on a large piece of brown packing paper.

Ninfa could draw faces that looked like photographs. Her grandchildren had rows of portraits she'd drawn of them each year for their birthdays tacked onto the adobe wall of their home. Three grandsons and a granddaughter between her two daughters in the village, all in the same little house. The youngest, Ysa, was three, the eldest, Ramón, nearly twelve. She went home to them one weekend per month and slept in between her daughters.

Ninfa stuck the tip of her tongue out while she concentrated, shading the edges of the dining room.

"Okay, vaya, pues," she began. "These rooms will be mine," Ninfa said, ticking off Consuelo's bedroom, the dining room, and the great room that opened to the courtyard with the cage of birds. "And you'll take these"—Ninfa tapped the kitchen, the bathroom, Graciela's bedroom, and Perlita's bedroom. "And the stairs," Ninfa said. "My back can't take them anymore." Ninfa marked the edges of the rooms with closets and windowsills, casually drawing each one to scale. "You'll get the big closets and windows to clean. Help an old lady." Ninfa grinned. "We mop every other day, all of it. And I dust and sweep every day, each room. Laundry twice a week—I'll take the clothing, you'll take the linens."

Graciela nodded. Ninfa's room smelled of copalito and rain.

"Will you help me?" Ninfa smiled as she asked this question that had only one answer.

"Of course I will," Graciela said. "But you must help me—please tell me where my mother is. I need you to bring me to her. And if she's dead, I need you to bring me to whoever killed her so I can kill them." This last part Graciela nearly growled.

Ninfa's eyes changed when Graciela asked about Socorrito. Her irises went blank, hard black, like igneous stones. The lines of her face, which made her appear twice as old as Graciela's mami, seemed to lift and vanish. A trick she had perfected after years of service in the Estate.

Perlita had told Ninfa that she'd be fired on the spot if she discussed Socorrito with either Graciela or Consuelo. Despite her blank face, Ninfa would not lie to these children, not even on behalf of Perlita.

"Let the child forget her," Perlita had said when Consuelo was first brought here, and then again the night before, after Socorrito had been hauled away. "It's the kindest thing." Ninfa remembered how Perlita had wailed as a child whenever her mother's death was mentioned. Perhaps she really did believe that not mentioning Socorrito to her children was the kindest thing they could do.

Maybe because she'd been so young when she'd come to the Estate, Consuelo had stopped asking about her mother years ago. But Graciela, she knew, wouldn't let go so easily.

And as Graciela stared at Ninfa, she began to detect a flame moving behind the older woman's eyes, the breath puffing her nostrils, her blank face beginning to tremble with emotion, a statue coming to life.

"Your mami is alive," Ninfa said. "I wouldn't keep that from you."

"Then help me find her," Graciela said.

"I wish I could," Ninfa said. "But I can't." The girl began to cry. "I promise you, though, that you will be happy here. You'll have more than you ever dreamed."

More of what? Graciela wondered. Whatever more was, she didn't want it. All she wanted was her mother and her home, and to be with us, and she did not understand why she'd been ripped out of her life by the roots, transplanted in this place that seemed barely to want her.

That afternoon Graciela found Consuelo sitting cross-legged in the center of the kitchen floor, sucking on a mango pit. Sticky gold strung from the corner of her lips. Consuelo nodded when Graciela came inside, her eyes holding her in the room. She spit out the mango pit. It skidded across the tiles and picked up dust beneath a low glass-topped table.

"There's more over there, if you want one," Consuelo said, raising her little chin in the direction of the fruit basket on the dining table.

Graciela took one, and the wet little knife beside it, and collapsed noisily on the floor beside Consuelo. She studied her sister. Soon, Consuelo's mysterious resting face would become familiar: practiced, cool, and arid, a sand-polished stone upon which the world's small outbursts registered as errors. Now, though, Graciela understood Consuelo's flat expression to mean that she fucking despised her, and Graciela, utterly alone beside her sister, put her head on her knees and cried.

"I don't understand why you won't talk to me," she wailed. "You're my sister. Why are you being such a mean, stuck-up ice cube?"

Graciela felt the oval tips of Consuelo's nails on her back. Her sister rubbed small circles, and with her other hand wrapped long, fruit-sticky fingers around Graciela's wrist.

"Listen, hermanita," she said after a few minutes. "I have to go to my painting lesson. But I'm not an ice cube. I'm a goddess carved of white marble. The *Venus de Milo*!" Consuelo stood up. "And I don't hate you. I promise. Listen, sppp!" Consuelo waited a beat, while Graciela lifted her face from her knees to look at her sister.

"Luis isn't just my teacher. He's my lover." Consuelo wiggled her eyebrows, her nostrils flaring by accident. "Don't tell anyone, okay?"

Graciela shrugged, feigned a lack of interest, but truly, she was impressed. "I promise," she said, grateful that her big sister had confided in her, surprised by how strange the girl was. Now Consuelo squeezed Graciela's wrist too hard, pleading for Graciela's total attention with bulging eyes.

"Well . . ." Consuelo paused. "That's not actually quite true."

"I'm listening," Graciela said, using the knife to peel the mango's skin with a dexterity that Consuelo found impressive. Her own hands never stopped shaking.

"He's not really my lover. I just really like him. Luis. I wish he were my lover," Consuelo said. "I'm only fourteen and I've never even kissed anyone. But still, don't tell Perlita I said anything, not anything about him! I promise this time, it's the truth."

"Fine," Graciela said. "I don't care. I'm just glad you don't hate me." Graciela brought the fruit to her mouth. Consuelo curtsied and ran out of the room, very late now for her painting lesson.

When Graciela had finished the fruit, she spat the pit out into her hand and wiped the blade clean of mango juice in the folds of her skirt, slipping the pit and the knife into the pocket of her dress. *Hermanita.* She repeated the word to herself, testing it aloud. Consuelo, this skittish güerita, was her sister. Graciela fingered the blade and was grateful. A sister and a knife—she felt a little safer, having both in this strange place.

That night she lay in the beautiful featherbed, the first time she'd ever slept alone in a room, and out the window she saw the roofs of the rich laid out beneath the house. She hadn't noticed the broken glass of the window earlier, glinting like jagged teeth in an open jaw.

She slept that night with the knife beneath her pillow, cool as a piece of moon.

. . .

In the days that followed, Consuelo claimed Graciela, like a doll, like a charm. She sat beside Graciela at dinner, hugged Graciela good night, entered Graciela's bedroom unceremoniously and took a nap on her bed. Consuelo was certainly no wise elder, silly as she was, but Graciela received the warmth of her company and even her most boring stories with appreciation. She was terrible at French, hopeless. Her best friend, La Violeta, was also sort of her worst enemy, too fufurufa for her own good, but nice enough. Her art teacher and desired lover, Luis, Graciela learned, was three years older than Consuelo, a first-year student at Bellas Artes.

"Luis is the kind of artist who can do anything he wants to—paint, draw figures, sculpt—he's a genius! And he's a communist!" Consuelo said. Graciela had never heard the word.

"A communist? Is that when a person only eats fruit?" Graciela asked.

"No, you idiot!" Consuelo said. "A communist is like a university student with a beard. Who wears rough, wrinkly pants. He's from some little village like you are—"

"You are too!" Graciela interrupted. Consuelo flicked her ruby nails in the air in front of her face, eyelids fluttering.

"Anyway," she said, "he's from some tiny village, and he's mestizo on his mami's side too. But he won this drawing contest a few years ago, and so he got to come here to the capital and enroll in the university."

"Wait, does that mean that I'm a communist?" Graciela said. "That we're communists because we're from the village and our mami is mestiza?"

"Do I have a púchica beard?" Consuelo said. Graciela screamed a laugh. The floor bucked and groaned. Downstairs, Ninfa banged on the ceiling with a broom handle to shut them up. (Perlita had a headache and could not be disturbed.)

LOURDES: Those days, according to certain hijueseismilputas, anyone who wasn't a rich Ladino was a communist. After the massacre, many of the men who were still left on the volcano

stopped wearing those white pants—they didn't want to be
called communists.

CORA: Indio first, communist second. Sometimes you were a communist just because of your indio face.

LOURDES: But the pants were a giveaway too. You were indio, anyway,
but weren't trying to hide, so also you must be a communist.

CORA: You can't put on a pair of fucking pants and become an indio
or a communist. And you don't stop being an indio or a communist when you take them off. But of course that's how it
was.

LUCÍA: But it was different in the city, no? In the capital communists
could be chelitos. But if they wore a beard and studied at the
university, maybe weren't especially devout, didn't associate
with the terratenientes—communist. Or if they preferred
poetry to business—boom, communist. A communist
would be in favor of free elections, of letting women vote.
Maybe they have friends who are men who have sex with
men, and they don't try to kill them when they find out. Or
they know women who have sex with women and they don't
give a shit.

MARÍA: Boom, communists, every single one of you. You can thank
me for that.

Laughing on the floor of Graciela's room, all Consuelo really knew
was that Luis at least looked like a communist and that Perlita would
never approve of him for that. She told Graciela that Perlita had begun to
declare her a "failed experiment" only after their father had died. ("Murdered," Consuelo said with certainty one day, though she would say
nothing more when Graciela begged her to tell her how, or why.)

Consuelo told Graciela how, during the viewing of the body, Perlita
would enter the living room, where the casket stood open, and sigh
heavily. "Hopeless," she'd say, staring at Consuelo.

"It's only that she misses your father," Ninfa had said to comfort her,
but Consuelo knew that it wasn't that. Before Germán had died, Perlita

had called Consuelo stupid a few times. That was one thing. But after he died, Perlita seethed, told Consuelo that she was an absolute waste of good money, indiada through and through, indiada with no hope of bettering herself.

"That prieta skin, so ugly," Perlita had said to Consuelo once when she was twelve, about a hired nenita who was two or three shades lighter than Consuelo. Or, "Those art lessons aren't cheap! The indita better learn some things." Consuelo had sensed then that Perlita was trying to hurt her sideways, so that any time Consuelo reacted with tears or fire, she could claim innocence, polite surprise. But now Perlita no longer had to throw her punches at a slant. She could look Consuelo right in the face and grimace. "Darker and darker every year," she'd say. "All the money I've spent, an absolute waste."

But Consuelo, at least, would get to complete her education. Perlita would fulfill her promise to Germán, if only to keep up appearances.

Graciela thought that this was terribly unfair. "Why don't I get to go to school?" she said. "You're the failed experiment!"

"Ah," Consuelo said. "You see, I may be stupid, but my father insisted on school for me." Consuelo talked about their parents this way—never "our," but "my" father, "my" mother. "With you, indiada as you are, even more than me, and with my father gone, there's no reason for her even to bother with sending you to school."

"Are there at least books here that I can read?" Graciela murmured into Consuelo's ankles.

Consuelo laughed. "You know how to read?"

"Of course I do," Graciela said. "I was the best reader in my class."

Consuelo took a matchbox Luis had given her and two long cigarettes from the box on her lap and offered Graciela one. She took the cigarette, thinking of the ones her mother rolled by hand and smoked in the fields while she worked, of the few puffs she'd shared with us after school in the forest, once we were a little older.

"Do all little girls smoke where you're from?" Consuelo asked. Consuelo was not the best reader in her class. And Consuelo was barely fourteen, still a nenita herself.

"I thought we were from the same place," Graciela said. Consuelo struck the match, lit Graciela's, then her own. They breathed in together, holding the fire in their lungs.

"Did you ever miss her? Our mami?" Graciela asked.

"I'm not sure I even remembered her, really," Consuelo said, though in truth, she had missed Socorrito, whom she remembered as gold filigree, bright against the village's misty greens and black rock. Consuelo held the memory of being small, her body wrapped securely against her mother's warm back, like paper worn thin from folding and unfolding.

Graciela rested her head on Consuelo's bony ankles. Rain all morning, and now the sun pooled in the little bits of glass jutting from the broken window's sill, framing their bodies in light.

"So, who was our father, then?" Graciela asked. Talk of their mother was too painful. "What did he do for the General?"

Consuelo became fire. "Don't you believe a thing they tell you here! He wasn't just some adviser! He told the General what he wanted to hear and brought him any sick thing he wanted and was there to be killed when someone had to die."

"What do you mean, somebody had to die? I thought they were friends," Graciela said.

"You know what they say," Consuelo said, getting up and throwing her cigarette off the balcony. "Best friends make the best enemies."

Puya, the drama of this one. The truth is, Consuelo had no idea what had happened to her father, if he had betrayed the General before his death, or even how he had died. Perlita had told her nothing, so she'd made up her own mind. But she wasn't entirely wrong. The General didn't murder Germán. Not exactly. He just gave him terrible advice.

Germán had increasingly become concerned by how his old friend interpreted the wisdom of colors, the search for unified truth. And he wasn't afraid of telling his old friend that he thought his ideas about what it really meant to ascend out of darkness into light were, at best, delusional.

"What's next?" he said one afternoon, in a meeting of the General's advisers. "You'll drink bleach to lighten your skin? Murder a village of prietas? You know that your lineage might be traced back there. Back where we both come from."

Germán barely recognized the General sometimes. Once he'd believed in Vitalismo, that providing a vital minimum amount of food, clean water, clothing—no more than the minimum, you see, so as not to enrage the terratenientes—would encourage the illiterate indios to strive toward god, the purifying tonic of labor, and abstinence from liquor, and that one day, together, lighter, they would all arrive at some national utopia. But lately, the General's vision had become even more demented. He claimed that all indios were communists, that they had to be tamed, neutered, their balls cut off, in order to rise into the light. Whether this fixation on balls was rhetorical or not, no one dared to ask. The General had brown skin himself, his advisers noted, had Indian blood as well. All he wanted, they gravely misunderstood, was to better his people.

But that was exactly not how the General wanted to be perceived, and he took Germán's words, the way his old friend had exposed their origins, as ridicule.

The next week, at a large dinner, the General raised his glass to deliver the meeting's prefatory epigram.

"I dedicate this to Consuelo, the daughter of my oldest friend: The petals of your lips are fine, but no rose your legs entwine!" he said, the medals on his chest clattering, his cheeks shiny with retaliation.

Germán told him that, decorated or not, next in line for the presidency or not, he'd decapitate the General if he so much as looked at his daughter again. Consuelo was barely twelve years old then.

He smiled when he said it, but everyone at the table had gone silent. To them, Germán was the one who had crossed a line, not the General. Everyone knew his daughter was una indita prieta.

Later, when the room had emptied, Germán apologized for speaking out of turn. The General pretended to forgive him, praising his audacity. And Germán, afraid for his life, tacitly accepted the General's empty words. The General, who had, for several years now, been less of a longtime friend and more like a crazy, violent uncle whose favor meant the pause of debt and the security of a decent life for Germán and his family.

Germán obliged the General, listening patiently as he steered the conversation to one of his favorite topics, offering medical advice to Germán.

Since childhood, Germán had suffered violent convulsions. They erased whole days from his life, and he would awaken from them weak, with froth on his lips.

When he'd arrived in the capital as an adult, the General had paid for him to visit the Ministry of Health, where he was diagnosed with epilepsy and treated first with Benzedrine and then Luminal to ease the severity of his spells.

But recently—perhaps since the men had begun to disagree—the General voiced his own ideas about Germán's condition more forcefully.

The diagnosis of epilepsy had always been to Germán a distastefully feminine one—neurosis, lunacy. But his old friend suggested that the seizures brought him closer to the divine.

"See what you can discover when you remove that veil and touch what's behind it. Enter the spell," the General would say. He believed that medicine of any kind was a weak man's response to spiritual failure. The seizures were an attempt at communication from the invisible forces—he was sure of it. Why wouldn't Germán listen?

Luminal made Germán sleepy and impotent (though he knew better than to share that side effect with the General, who would have seized upon Germán's impotence with unbridled glee), but while it didn't halt the seizures altogether, it did reduce their frequency and their intensity.

"See what it's like without the medication," the General said. "What about your own innate vitality?" At the word *vitality*, Germán bit the inside of his lip. He was not prepared to discuss his vitality with the General, who would only delight in tormenting his huevos at the next Society gathering.

"See," the General said, noting Germán's discomfort. "These drugs are a crutch! And they're probably just fueling your nervousness in order to snare you."

Germán considered the General's persistence. Tan chute he was, more meddlesome than an old woman! Germán had already converted his diet to a meatless one, at the General's behest. It was simpler this way; Germán spent nearly every meal in the General's presence anyway. It shut him up.

So why not stop taking the medication for a few weeks? Why not take some jodido enema of purple water, just to prove the General wrong, to shut him up for a while? And, on a break from the Luminal, maybe, just maybe, he could get it up again for more than a handful of minutes. So, telling no one but the General—not his wife, not his doctor— Germán quit his medicine.

One late afternoon in the palace, not long after, the General stepped away from his game of chess with Germán to take a piss.

Returning down the hallway, the General heard a thrashing. Like when the jabalí would break free of the fence and root around in the trash when he and Germán had been boys en el campo. They'd be sent out to scare them away, screaming, throwing rocks. And then they'd spend the next day repairing the fence together. "Vamos a la vuelta, del toro torojil," he hummed.

When the General entered the room, he found the pieces of the game rolling over the floor but the thrashing had stopped. Germán was still, facedown on the board. The spell was over. The General had seen his friend seize before, but he always returned afterward. He thumped him on the back.

"Tell me what you see!" the General demanded. Germán's back was stiff, and the General kept his hand there, waiting for Germán's breath to arrive beneath it.

Later, the General wept when the coroner collected Germán's body. *Impossible,* he said to himself. *How could the invisible doctors have failed him? Have failed me?*

Eventually, though, he accepted his friend's death as an omen that pertained only to him. His wisdom had failed Germán, but that had happened for a perfectly good reason. His youth was buried, held by no living memory but his own. At the Society now, he had no one to scold him, to tell him to be reasonable. Now the General was truly free.

To Perlita, the General said only that Germán had finally reached behind the veil, that he had achieved enlightenment. "You'll see him again," he promised. Perlita scowled at him, incredulous with hatred. The haughty bitch.

And that was the true story of what happened to Germán; neither Graciela nor Consuelo would ever hear it.

At the Estate, Graciela often wasn't sure what to make of Consuelo's theatrics, but she adored her, had endless patience for her whims and rages. Consuelo seemed frail and vulnerable, with her gawky limbs, her peeling skin, her stuttering and tremors, her lying, and her nervous laughter. Graciela felt herself sturdier, wiser, and she wanted to protect her older sister. And she felt safer herself when she made herself a home in the tight space carved out by Consuelo's loneliness. They were both left, in their own way, with their uncertainty, but they were left, now, together. Graciela studied her sister's face, steadying her as she listened to her sister's theories of friendship and betrayal.

Soon, she knew, they'd be called downstairs. That evening the General was coming to dinner and they would be presented before him like gifts. He'd pass his eyes over Consuelo, the familiar one, tired, yet to be chosen. And he'd see Graciela, the new one, for the first time.

8

Y EARS LATER, AFTER EVERYTHING, GRACIELA WOULD CURSE
herself for not leaving that afternoon, before meeting the General,
before falling under his power. Why hadn't she, in the minutes before
Ninfa called their names to hurry up and get dressed and ready, before
the General arrived in his car, before her work at the palace began the
following day, grabbed her sister's hand and run? Despite the inevitable
protests from her silly sister—that she wasn't going anywhere without
first saying goodbye to Luis, without first gathering her velvet pouches
full of dried rose petals and stolen cigarettes, her tarot cards, her púchica
spider necklace—they would have run.

Where? Back to the volcano? To us? Somewhere else? Los Yunais?
Mexico City? Paris, France? Either way, in 1932, we cipotas would still
be dead.

Ninfa shouted up the stairs. The girls stood and went to get dressed
in the clothing that Perlita had chosen for the occasion: matching gray
flannel dresses, with shiny black buttons up the backs. They fastened
each other up before heading downstairs.

Graciela, Consuelo, Perlita, and Ninfa stood in front of the house, along
the wall of fruit trees, heads bowed, as the General's car arrived. The
driver came around to the side of the car facing the Estate and held open
the door. The General, broad and ursine, emerged, raising his right hand
in a stiff greeting, a mass of hair atop his head, rich, black, waxy cherub's

curls. The driver removed a white satin cloak that tied in the front with gold braid from the General's wide shoulders, revealing a white suit that glowed bright in the setting sun, the jacket cluttered with ribbons and medals that clinked as he strolled across the front gardens of the Estate to where Graciela, Consuelo, Perlita, and Ninfa stood waiting.

The General made his way down the line, giving his hand to be kissed. Closer now, he was stout, smaller than he appeared by the car. The top of Perlita's turban rose higher than the top of his head. He had a large, sorrowful face, a hairline that hung low over his forehead, wide eyebrows like caterpillars, tiny black eyes, and a thick knob of a nose. His face, lined and ashy brown, was much older than his hair.

Looking at him, Graciela could see that beyond the pompous hair, his nonsense about color and souls, this bayunco of demanding his stubby little hands be kissed by children, there radiated something large and sinister about this man, some insatiable want, as though in his chest he held a hungry, swirling magnet.

LUCÍA: Like a plump little vampire, in that silky cape!

When the General came to Graciela, at the end of the line, he fell to his knees with a wrong-sounding thump. Perlita gasped and brought the back of her wrist to her forehead. Ninfa stared straight ahead. Before Graciela's feet, the General's shoulders rocked up and down. Consuelo turned to her sister for an instant to flutter her eyelids. She smirked, but Graciela could see that Consuelo was frightened, and beside her, Graciela was too. Consuelo made a practice of edging herself into laughter when she was afraid, rationalizing that if she could laugh in the face of fear, that meant she was safe. Graciela, young as she was, knew it was often safer to shut up.

The General pressed his mustache against the white patent-leather strap at the top of Graciela's right foot, and kissed, and kissed again, making tiny squeaking sounds, like a finca mouse. He kissed her right foot a dozen or so times, and then moved on to her left. It tickled, and Graciela bit her finger to hide her laughter.

"Smile," Perlita hissed at Graciela from down the line. So she did, and the General began to weep.

Consuelo squealed, unable to contain herself. "Oh là là!" she whispered, feral in her throat. Perlita dug her sharp elbow into Consuelo's side. Susto rose in Graciela's chest, binding her throat like a hand.

"Your pearls, your pearls!" the General moaned. He took a handkerchief from the pocket of his satin jacket. The General blew his nose with dignity. "Ah, they're already lost to us!"

"Your teeth," Ninfa said. "Where did you lose them?"

"At home, before," Graciela said. At their first wiggle, Lourdes had insisted on the extraction of Graciela's front two teeth, by tying twine around both of them, wrapping the cord around the handle of the door to la finca's storage, and then slamming the door shut.

Now the General removed a white glove and handed it behind his back to Ninfa. Gently, he pried open Graciela's jaw, and, using his thumb, pressed her tongue to the roof of her mouth. With the pad of his forefinger, the General patted each of Graciela's teeth, counting beneath his breath. Black hairs sprouted from the whorls of his liver-spotted ears. He pressed against one of Graciela's fang-sharp bottom teeth, and rocked it back and forth, loosening it from the roots. Graciela swallowed, her tongue still pinned.

"Please assure me when the next pearls fall, that you will catch them?" the General said. Ninfa murmured a vow. The General waited a cautious beat and slowly removed his hand from Graciela's mouth. Her tongue fell clumsily back in its place, and she tasted a trickle of salty blood springing from the tooth the General had manipulated. Ninfa vanished to the kitchen and returned holding a sloshing bowl of water, a linen cloth draped over her arm, just like in Mass.

The General bathed and dried his hand, replaced his glove. He righted Graciela's jaw; she hadn't realized she'd left her mouth hanging open. With his hands on Graciela's cheeks, her peripheral vision disappeared; the Estate, the cicadas and birds, the bitten roses, the ocelot—they were all gone. For a few moments Graciela forgot that anyone else in the world existed besides the two of them. She hated him, and she wasn't exactly sure why, her throat simmering with bitterness as she looked at him.

The General lowered both his hands to the tops of her shoulders and gazed into her face, bliss spreading over his own. His cheeks were no longer wet with tears, but huge, old, and radiant. The evening air was very quiet. Graciela held her breath, entering this new life, in a silent sacrament.

"At last," the General whispered. His eyes fastened a light onto hers. "At last. My oracle! My precious, precious oracle! At last you are home." *Oracle.* Graciela knew that word. There was a woman in the village who called herself an oracle for extra pisto. She had her nieto howl behind a curtain as she rolled her eyes and held her hands above an overturned salad bowl and tried to stir up village chambre. ("Beware of the woman with the ojos verdes como una serpiente—she's charmed your man!") Everyone knew she was a joke.

The General roared with laughter, and, with a drop in her stomach, Graciela fell back into the world of objects. The ocelot stretched and yawned. The General's face went purple, and his roar commanded the others to join in with polite giggles. Graciela waited until she heard Consuelo's fake laugh before she contributed her own.

"You're home, my darling. At last, at last! How I see him in you! In every fiber!" the General said.

Perlita gave a signal to Ninfa, pointing her lips toward the door, and everyone proceeded inside for dinner. The General rested his paw on top of Graciela's head and hummed contentedly. Graciela hated his hand on her head, the easy control he had over her. Consuelo, just in front of her, reached for her hand. She held it until they sat down to eat.

At the table, Consuelo shook like a match again, but without a smirk, her movie star eyes large and glossy. Ninfa shook out the napkin beneath Graciela's wrist, dropped it into her lap, and returned to the kitchen to order the first course be brought to the dining room.

The meal was deployed by the troupe of little girls hired for the occasion. They filed out of the kitchen in starched uniforms, immaculate and easy, with heavy trays of soup held like air. In the kitchen doorway the next procession of girls stood waiting, bearing trays of meat. They stared at Graciela but looked away quickly when she stared back.

The General sat at the head of the table and lifted his glass of plain water.

"To the past, to the present, to the future. Three rings: one of gold, one of silver, one of bronze. All of which are linked in you, my oracle," he said, then turned and winked at Graciela. "And tomorrow we begin our big project. I hope you are ready. Together we'll work to transform our pulgarcito. Dar a luz—to give birth, right? It will be hard work. But together we will give birth to light. We will make our nation real."

Real? What did he mean, make our country real? It was real.

"Aurora borealis," the General continued, his glass still raised. "Would you call the sudden flashes of the aurora borealis, the northern lights, a 'reality,' though they are as real as can be while you look at them? Certainly not; it is the cause that produces them. They are but a passing illusion." He dabbed at his mouth modestly. "I've never seen the northern lights—have you?" he asked Graciela.

Terrified, baffled, she shook her head no.

"But surely you can imagine them, if I tell you about them well enough, can't you?" the General asked.

She understood then that this was a lesson, at which she'd always excelled. She nodded fervently.

"As long as you have some imagination, some depth, you'll have no problem at all," the General said. "Consider their uncanny glow with me: gold, purple, bright, impossible blue! Shining out against the black of an Arctic night!" He closed his eyes and began to whisper: "They are just an illusion! They hold no heat of their own! They dance at the whim of an invisible hand!"

Eso. He was nuts, not a cookie left in his head, but in that room, at that table, he charged the air with electricity, and Graciela felt as though she'd die if she responded incorrectly. Consuelo's nonsense about best friends becoming best enemies tugged on her. What had her father done wrong? If she could find the right words now, say them like a spell, she might ensure her safety, and Consuelo's. Perlita bore into Graciela's eyes with her own, as though the girl were the most wretched of idiots. Consuelo fluttered her eyelashes with spite, but her hands began shaking, rattling the table setting. Perlita kicked her.

The General clenched both fists over the white lace tablecloth.

"Imagine harnessing their energy, that wild cause!" the General was begging her now, and Graciela understood what she had to do.

"I see them. I see the lights," she said, knowing she'd pass the General's test.

"Good," he said. And as though an angel had joined them, a calm gathered around the table.

The first course was served. The General's soup was different from everyone else's caldo de pollo, a bright, mysterious green. He was a vegetarian. *To eat any animal is worse than to kill a man,* he liked to say. *A man reincarnates, while an animal dies forever.* After our deaths, whenever he'd recite that line, we'd cackle in his ears. Scream like four Ciguas. We wouldn't let him sleep through a whole night of his life after that.

The bowl was placed before him, and El Gran Pendejo patted his chest. The chauffeur, who'd been posted near the front door, scrambled to his side. From the pocket of his vest the chauffeur drew out a long chain with a crystal sparkling at its end and held it over the General's green soup. The crystal winked and rocked three or four times. The General nodded, and the chauffeur returned to his post guarding the door. The General brought the bowl to his lips and slurped, greening his mustache. When the soup was cleared and replaced by the second course, the chauffeur reappeared beside him, dangled the crystal perfunctorily over the General's plate. Instead of beef, he had curtido—a mountain of vinegar-soaked cabbage, carrots, and caraway seeds—and a handful of yuca frita, garnished with a sprig of loroco. Campesino food, assembled for a monarch. The crystal winked again.

Graciela ate until her plate was clean, then watched everyone else as they chewed and swallowed and nodded and chatted. She folded her palms and stretched her arms out above her plate, bony brown elbows and square little hands over a smooth white moon. *In every fiber,* the General had said. He saw the trace of her father in every fiber of her. The fibers of her skin and her soul—what did the General mean? What did he see? Graciela unlatched her fingers and turned over her hands; she looked and looked, hoping to find him.

9

THE FOLLOWING MORNING, GRACIELA WAS COLLECTED BY THE General's chauffeur and driven to the presidential palace in the main plaza. The driver's name was José. She sat in the back, watching his hands on the wheel, the nape of his thick neck, stubbled with short hair. She hadn't heard him speak the night before when the General had come to dinner. But now, as the car descended into the center of town, José glanced back at her frequently, pointing out scenes in the street—a clown cleaning windshields, a wailing woman pushing a cart of breakfast tamales, her smile broad and gappy. The rising sun filled the car's window, dazzling Graciela.

When they arrived at the palace, José slowed the car to the curb and got out to open the heavy door for Graciela. The sidewalk was already thick with bodies pushing carts of sliced fruit; a couple of copper-faced bolos passing a cigarette back and forth on the ground; men whose hair was wet with pomade, cologne ripening in the early-morning heat; women carving a path, guiding their children through the crowd with their hands on their small heads. Graciela ached at the sight of these mothers, wondered where they were taking their children. But there was the marble palace in front of her; she darted through the bodies and noise to find the stairs, climbing them two at a time, her borrowed dress ruffling in the dusty wind. At the top of the stairs, a slight woman with a severe haircut and pale eyes stood behind the heavy glass-and-marble door. With some effort, she pushed it open, and gave Graciela her dry hand. She said she was Lidia, and she led Graciela through an empty foyer and into the quiet of a dark room. Graciela began to give her name, but Lidia waved her words away with her hand.

"I know all about you," the woman said.

"Is this where he lives?" Graciela asked. Lidia did not answer.

Graciela tried again: "Doesn't the president live in the presidential palace?"

Lidia turned back, gave Graciela a sharp look. "No one has seen him in years."

Later Consuelo confirmed: the president was a joke, lived with his wife in a mansion in Guatemala and avoided ever setting foot back here. Everyone called him El Wimpy Guy. "I think Perlita used to know him, maybe. Diocuarde, Wimpy Guy, wherever you are."

The room where Lidia left Graciela was paneled in a dark hardwood, and a deep-red carpet embellished with golden medallions was layered over a thick, forest-green rug. The walls held tall bookcases, and red velvet drapes insulated the space from the light and sound of the world outside. The air was stuffy and unclean, smelled of old smoke and greasy, dead skin. Graciela wanted to return to the noise and light of outside, but there was the General, sitting, with his eyes closed, at the head of a long, polished table.

She found her place at the other end of the table and sat to face him.

"Good morning," she said, but the General was silent. Maybe he slept this way each night, upright in a chair, dressed and prepared to enter battle.

Ninfa had told her that the man was strange, and the night before, she had told Graciela that he was stranger even than he had appeared to be at dinner. "Be careful, eh."

Graciela asked Ninfa if it was true what Consuelo had said, about the General murdering their father, and the old woman had just clucked her tongue. "No. Never. He's strange, but he's harmless as a lizard." She knew the truth was somewhere between the two—harmless as a crazy lizard and murderer—but was afraid she'd already said too much. She didn't want to frighten the girl.

"But what should I do when I get there?" Graciela had asked.

"He wants you to listen to him, and to give him advice," Ninfa said. "Nothing more. He believes in signs and spirits. Just play with him, as your father did. Let him come up with stories and then go along with them. But be careful. He's a man like any other."

Graciela thought that sounded like taking care of a younger child, like when we used to watch María, before she was old enough to join us in our games. We listened to her cries and cleaned her bottom, patted her back, held her sticky hands and walked her to the ceiba so she could touch the bark or point at a bird. This is what Graciela's father had done for the General? Certainly there was something about this job that Graciela didn't yet understand.

Graciela could tell now, by the way that the General peeked through his eyelids, how his breathing remained slow and regular, that he was feigning sleep. Thick nostrils pulled air in, and his exhale ruffled the bottom of his broom-straw mustache.

"We'll begin at once," the General said, without opening his eyes. "Recitations of the wisdom."

"Good morning," Graciela said again.

He nodded. "We'll begin at the end of life and how we arrive beyond death. Death is not the enemy. Anyone who tells you that is stupid." He opened his eyes with a start. "Are you ready?"

Graciela wasn't ready, but she knew she had no choice in this stale, dark room. "Yes," she said.

"While the records of important events are often obliterated from our memory, not the most trifling action of our lives can disappear from the soul's memory. It is an ever-present reality on the plane, which lies outside our conceptions of space and time."

He said it twice, then raised his forefinger in the air and pointed at her. She held a photograph of the words inside her mind. She took the words on her tongue.

"While the records of important events are often obliterated from our memory, not the most trifling action of our lives can disappear from the soul's memory. It is an ever-present reality on the plane, which lies outside our conceptions of space and time."

At Graciela's recitation, the General raised his eyebrows and nodded, puffing up his lips. "This must seem very difficult to you, very confusing," he said. It did, of course it did, but Graciela was afraid to agree. "What do you think this means?" he asked.

"Do you have to die in order to find the records of the soul's memory?" Graciela asked.

The General grimaced. He didn't like it when she responded with a question instead of an answer, but she was new, so he forgave her quickly. In the beginning of their days together, he was patient. He treated her like the child she was, speaking to her in gentle tones he used for no one else.

"This is less important than what it means to weave the veil of the future," the General said. The disappointment in his voice made Graciela shudder.

"We weave the veil of the future through this ever-present reality. Truth exists beyond death. Death does not end life," he said.

Graciela had heard a version of this in school with the nuns—death after life. She'd never really believed the story in the literal sense—the rock being rolled back, the bread transforming not into blessed bread, but into the flesh itself. But there was a familiarity to it she found comforting. She could accept this first story of life after death.

"After death we gather all that we remember, and we create the future that we deserve and desire," he said. "¿Me entiendes?"

"Yes," Graciela said.

MARÍA: Who knows, maybe there's something to it all, the soul's infinite memory, exploring reality outside of space and time. I mean, look at us. We're your púchica ghost storytellers, after all.

LOURDES: Yeah, but when he talks about weaving the veil of the future, he's not talking about weaving on our great-grandmothers' backstrap looms.

LUCÍA: He didn't want to weave cloth; he wanted to weave skin, lighter and lighter. Graciela's face was his idea of the past, just like ours were, but her skin he could imagine in the future, blending with time. But Graciela didn't understand any of that, of course. Not yet.

LOURDES: Smart as she was, how could she? It was buried in all that nonsense—it's like when you buy food por la calle because you're starving, and it's covered with salsitas and cremas to hide how tough the meat is, how flavorless and charred it really tastes.

The General inclined his head and spoke slowly. "What we are doing now is creating the veil. We have the technical power to channel the electricity of human capacity. You might help me with this, by listening, by guiding. Together, we might create a beautiful machine, a powerful machine!"

The General told Graciela about the transubstantiation of souls, how they break into thousands of pieces and move quietly over the earth. That the whole earth is connected by pieces of this wisdom, that we must be strong, ruthless, even, to protect them. In Germany, for instance, there was a very strong man, vigorous, unafraid, dedicated to this cause. He would rise in power soon, the General said, sure as the sun. He held the pieces to reclaim the purity of his nation. And in Italy too, there was a wise man, also very strong, who had the power to reinvigorate, renew, remake his country as one unified people. The General believed that Graciela would help him join in their efforts; she would reveal the fate of our country. She was his counsel of souls.

"Close your eyes," he said. Graciela obeyed. More than any of us, she wanted to be good. "Watch each soul burst into brightness, each dark soul emerge into light," the General said. "Like thousands of tiny lightbulbs." Graciela nodded, her eyes still closed, her mind still unsure of what was going on, trying to imagine collecting bright souls for the General.

MARÍA: Whose souls are they collecting?
LOURDES: Our souls, stupid.
LUCÍA: Our souls, bursting into brightness. Our dark souls becoming light.
CORA: Puya, of course. Púchica fascistas.

With that, the rhythms of Graciela's days in the capital took shape. On days when she wasn't working at the palace, she worked alongside Ninfa. She'd meet the older woman in her quarters early in the morning, while it was still dark. Ninfa roused the stove for breakfast, while Graciela swept the kitchen, stairs, and foyer. Ninfa pulled back the curtains and entered the courtyard, where she removed the shitty newspapers from the birdcage and replaced them with fresh ones, refilled the seed, and fed the dogs and the ocelot their breakfast.

Inside, Graciela dusted and polished—the púchica porcelain clown, a large glass bowl that held several speckled marble eggs, the table and the backs of each chair. She climbed a ladder to the demonic mirror, cleaned the enormous curves of its ebony frame, all while Ninfa scoured the floors with hot soap.

They ate lunch together, whatever was left over after Perlita and Consuelo had eaten. Graciela wouldn't realize how tired she was until Ninfa reminded her to sit. They often ate in silence. Afterward, if Perlita was resting, and if Ninfa assessed that they'd accomplished enough work by this midpoint of the day, she'd make café de olla for her and Graciela to share. They'd take it out to the courtyard and relax together. Ninfa would tell Graciela about her children and grandchildren in the campo, her nieces and nephews. And Graciela would tell Ninfa about the General, and la viejita would cackle until the birds swooped up from their cage in a panic.

In the afternoons, Ninfa and Graciela worked together, scrubbing linens and then taking them outside to dry on a line in the courtyard. By the time they began preparing for dinner, Graciela's hands would be shaking.

Nothing escaped Ninfa's notice. "You miss your mother, don't you?"

Graciela nodded. She did. She missed Socorrito and she missed us; the missing had settled into a deep ache inside of her, and her hands ached from the work. But beyond those aches she felt something more frantic too, a fear she couldn't articulate even when Ninfa asked. Graciela wouldn't have been able to tell anyone why she was so scared. And while her hands eventually calmed, the fear remained. Something that hadn't yet happened haunted her.

Sometimes, as they began the morning's work, Perlita would appear in a white silk bathrobe with a loopy *P* embroidered in gold thread over her left breast. Perlita would wink at her, and then flutter out of the room, with her tacita of café cremoso. Her hair was always pulled back in her blue satin turban, done up as it had been the night before, her cheeks powdery crests, long black eyebrows raised to emphatic points in the center of her forehead, implying hilarity or delight or terror. Her face shone; we could study her movements all day without ever growing bored, or truly understanding the parts that made her whole.

On palace days, Graciela joined Perlita for café in the mornings. Since she'd begun her work there, Perlita had softened toward her. She was quick to smile, warm and charming, kind to Ninfa and the hired nenitas. She praised Graciela for how quickly she was learning the proper way to scrub a bathtub or mop a curving staircase of marble. She laughed loudly and took an afternoon nap in the sitting room, her red mouth open and purring, ankles loose and tender. She hosted weekly prayer circles at the Estate and emerged from reciting the rosary with a loftiness in her eyes. She opened ten cans of sardines at a time to let the chained ocelot gorge, giggling when the cat licked the oil from her fingers. She wasn't terrible, Graciela thought. She was almost always rather fun, beautiful to observe, humming a cumbia as she floated through the Estate in her white silks, generous and fair. All the fire and severity of Graciela's first days here—it must have been an act, a way of cleanly setting up the rules of the place.

After breakfast, Graciela would be driven to the palace, and would either be taken immediately to the General or spend her morning in the library with the refuge of books she'd finally found. Consuelo had given Graciela a notebook that had a gold sheen on the edge of its pages—she'd stolen it from a shop in town, but she told her little sister it was her gift to her because she could no longer go to school. Graciela took the notebook with her each day to the library.

"I hear that you know how to read and write very, very well," the General said once, during the morning's first rain. Graciela had slept poorly the night before with nightmares, waking to watch Consuelo crawling in the window after spending the night out with her friends. That morning the General had taken Graciela to the palace library, a room cloaked in more maroon velvet, like the bedroom of a dying queen, and he told her that as long as she was working for him, she was welcome to read every book there, that the room contained a copy of every volume published in the history of the world. "It's all here," he said.

LOURDES: Of course that isn't true. There are no complete libraries, and the General's, in particular, contained only books on the occult, some crap about white marble statues, and what had been left behind by previous administrations.

Our stories are always missing from libraries like this.

CORA: But Graciela found what she needed. She pulled back the curtains that protected the fragile paper and leather from the tropical sun—timidly, then, in the years that followed, with daily hunger. She read *Grimms' Fairy Tales,* dreamt of the stepsisters' eyes pecked blind by birds for years, read about Hans Christian Andersen's lonely creatures, drowned mermaids and siblings flung miserably apart.

LOURDES: She read Charles Dickens and his orphans' morals; and, simón, Henry púchica James, who told her how the world might be built, piece by piece; and Russians—Tolstoy, Dostoyevsky, Pushkin's stories about games of luck and fate and bears chasing girls through the snowy forest.

MARÍA: Snow, can you believe that she longed for snow? Graciela wanted a snowy forest to get lost in. ¡Frijolito!

LUCÍA: When she finished these books, she read others—the ones the General suggested to her, about unending lives and classical lines of beauty. She read the manuscript that Brannon had brought over as a young man, decades before, and learned about the language of colors, séances, and speaking angels. Sometimes they bored her, and sometimes they frightened her with questions about our smallness. *Who are we in a cosmic perspective? Where are we in the invisible realm?* the books seemed to plead, and Graciela had no answers.

CORA: In order to appear as if he weren't an uncultured pig, El Gran Pendejo funded a literary journal with the poets of the Society of Sacred Letters and Objects, and he offered its pages to Graciela, saying, "These are the illuminated souls of our homeland who anoint and consecrate my visions with their ink."

LUCÍA: Inside were idiotic poems about dreamy women the color of mud whose greatest joy was working beneath the sun. Graciela laughed when she read them, knowing no women so simple, knowing how much her mother's body ached, how angry and unsimple she was. But, still, sometimes she copied a passage in the gilded notebook word for word, so that she could carry its tiny world with her.

MARÍA: "Ideas sculpt the nation," the General said. And here he was, sculpting Graciela's mind, sculpting all our lives like clay. His ideas jodidas.

In the afternoons, Graciela sat and watched the General take his bath, cerulean-colored soapy bubbles obscuring the mysteries of his body. The tub was long enough at one end for Graciela to sit on the edge and stretch out her legs, and the General urged her to make herself comfortable, to stay until it was time for him to emerge from the healing waters. His immodesty made her nervous, but she was there to learn the proper meanings of color, so she did her best to push that fear inside of her.

He held up a handful of bubbles and blew them out of his palm into the air. "The turquoise ray of self-regeneration!" he said, grinning. A servant appeared with a crystal jug of hot water, the blue and green dyes marbling against the container's glass; steam fogged the mirrors.

What does any of this mean? you wonder. What is the "turquoise ray of self-regeneration"? We cannot presume to understand all the workings of this man's pendejada mind, but, being fantasmas, we have some púchica insight.

The General, following in the footsteps of Patrick Brannon, claimed to have ideas about color and its power to heal, to contain knowledge, or to be a pathway to cosmic truths. Striations of blue could be our universe; a brushstroke of pink might be another. White held every color, and thus its power was immeasurably vast.

Artists, in particular, loved this way of thinking about color; it seemed to confirm something intuitive that they'd been at work on since the moment they were conscious of seeing the world. But this talk of color also appealed to people like the General, who thought that the shortcut to bettering the nation's race, ascending the tower of skin tones in those casta paintings, might be found in an alchemy of diluted science and faith.

After a day at the palace, Graciela would imagine her brain unspooling out of her ear, would yearn for the solace of forgetting, which was something her precious, solitary mind could not do. When she got back to the Estate, she and Consuelo would sprawl in the late sunlight that pooled in the middle of Graciela's floor, like a pair of cats, until it was time for Consuelo to go see Luis. Before she left, Consuelo would fuss and fuss with her clothes. She'd try on four different lace bras for Graciela, demanding to know which one made her nipples appear the rosiest, just in case today was the day he saw them. When Graciela chose the gray one with a silk ribbon, Consuelo huffed; in her youth, Graciela was mistaken. Consuelo demanded to borrow the white cotton refajo that Graciela wore, which Graciela had tucked into the waistband of her First Communion dress when she came to the capital. On Consuelo's body, the weave stretched and pulled across her hips.

The fabric, a cotton gauze, had taken their great-grandmother six months to weave on her backstrap loom. Consuelo said she could remember their great-grandmother, though she'd only been three when she'd died. By the time Graciela and the rest of us were born, Consuelo was gone, and our great-grandmother was long dead, but she'd left the refajo for Graciela.

Half-naked now, as Consuelo examined herself in the refajo, Graciela was suddenly shy and turned her bare body to face the wall. She was mostly silent in those days. She bit her fingernails to their quicks. She still had nightmares. In some, she was both La Siguanaba and the monstrous woman's youngest child, drowning beneath the waves, pushed under by her mother's hand. She tried to reassure herself, remind herself that these stories weren't real, that they were only dreams, that the longing she felt for her mother, for us, would fade with time. But still she was haunted, by the past and by a future she couldn't yet know.

Sometimes, in the first few weeks that she spent in the palace, usually in the mornings, Graciela felt steady enough to ask the General questions of her own.

"How did you meet my father?"

"Who was he?"

"What did he do for you?"

"How long will I be here?"

"When can I go home?"

The General almost never answered in the moment, just closed his eyes and held up a hand. But in the evenings, before Graciela was collected and taken back to the Estate, and she and the General stood in the foyer together, he'd pat her head and tell her about her father, tell her that he'd been his very best friend, the only person he could trust. Sometimes he would cry, medals trembling on his thick chest.

"How does it feel to finally be home?" the General asked one night in those early weeks, before his bear body swallowed Graciela's sparrow heart in a sudden embrace. She didn't answer the question but turned it over in her mind.

Consuelo had managed to pretend this was her home. Maybe, for her own peace, she should too. Maybe it was time to stop asking questions, she considered, to respond with gratitude the next time the General asked how it felt to be here.

"Let me spoil you," he'd say. "Let me keep you safe and happy."

Sometimes the General wept. "It's so sad you never knew your papá before he died. He thought about you a lot. He was planning a trip out to the volcanoes to look for you, you know. He wanted to bring you home."

Home—maybe someday she'd really feel that this place was that. What else could she do but learn her way forward, forget the past that tugged at her, forget us, forget her mother, sleep through the terrors that broke through her dreams like lightning in a black sky?

Because what if Graciela appeared ungrateful? What if she disappointed him? She knew already: He'd kill her. He'd have her killed.

"If ever you leave me, my sweetheart . . ." he'd say, letting his words trail into quiet, closing his eyes for a minute or two, and then opening them with a start: "If you ever betray my trust, these precious secrets, mi cariña, well, I wouldn't have a choice!" And then he'd laugh, as if he were joking, though anyone could see he was not.

Sometimes, with his right hand, he'd mime a pair of flayed scissors, aiming to stab both eyes out at once, put the flat of his left hand to the bridge of his nose too late, fall backward in his chair, his tongue lolling out of the side of his mouth like a dog's.

Sometimes he was more serious. "I've had to be rid of my enemies, cheap men bought for a few pieces of gold. But you're the best man I've ever had," he said. "Remember how I saved you from the certainty of early death. From malnutrition. I saved your beautiful mind from rot. Do you know how precious you are to me?"

From the window of the library, Graciela had seen women, in widow's black lace, pounding on the door of the palace, until their knuckles ran with blood. She'd remember then the words that Consuelo used for him: *liar, murderer.* Lidia would order Graciela to lie down beneath the long oval table until the angry mourners left. She never opened the door.

Men disappeared. Anyone could disappear.

Graciela knew that she was terrified of the General. But in his presence, somehow, she transmuted that fear into blank and fecund curiosity. She knew her only defense, her only way of saving herself, was to play the part he wanted her to play.

10

O NE MORNING, A FEW MONTHS AFTER GRACIELA HAD AR-
rived, the General took her by the hand and walked her outside. In the trees surrounding the plaza, birds sat on branches, spreading
their delicate bones and displaying the iridescence of their feathers as
they warmed in the sun. A man's high voice called out—he had newspapers, gum, candy, cigarettes. A couple sat by the fountain laughing into
each other's ears. The bright and constant world beat on, steady as a
heart.

The General marched her across the plaza along a precise diagonal
line to a municipal building—the Ministry of Health. They entered the
building, and he greeted the crisp pair of women at the front desk with a
nod, led Graciela to the stairs. They went down, descending into the
bowels of the building, through a series of dull hallways, to an ordinary
door that seemed identical to all the other office spaces in the hall. There
was a small plaque on the door that read: THE SOCIETY OF SACRED
LETTERS AND OBJECTS. MEET BIMONTHLY.

Inside that room one might forget they were in the tropics. The opulence of the office of the Society of Sacred Letters and Objects was similar to the plush baroque opulence of the palace, but the Society evoked a
darkness that was both potent and sleepy. The walls had all been painted
a thick black. A large oval table in the room's center was draped in a
woven black cloth that shimmered with gold threads and was surrounded

by at least fifteen upholstered chairs, their ornate armrests painted in gold leaf. And a lacquered desk pushed against the far wall displayed a pair of tarnished candelabras. The room was stuffy, hard to breathe in.

"It's really dark in here," Graciela said, widening her eyes to see. The General nodded and walked the circumference of the room, seeming to light the space with his large body. He was dressed that day all in white silk.

The room had no windows at all; it was lit instead by a pair of frosted green glass lamps affixed to the wall in ornate bronze sconces. Beneath one was a casta painting, just like the one that Lucía had found rotting in the church basement. This one had faded with age, its frame coated with a layer of oily grime from the smoke and dust conjured by the ceremonies held during the Society's meetings. The General struck a match and lit the green-glass candelabras and their wax dripped furiously; incense flared a gray halo, and unctions simmered on the wide copper plate in the corner—Graciela saw the room aglow in her mind with a vividness that startled her.

She coughed. "It's nice," she said, uncertain if these were the words that the General expected of her.

"It's a humble room, but it's here that we make mountains tremble," he said. "Here we gather to stretch the fabric of our reality," he said, striking another match. "Look inside the flame and tell me the colors that you see," he whispered, holding the light between them.

"Red, orange, yellow, green, blue, violet," Graciela said, looking beyond the flame as her eyes adjusted to the dim room.

"Good," the General said, extinguishing the fire between two broad fingers. Another one of his little tests. It was important to him that Graciela recognize the full spectrum of color contained in one bright light, and she had learned to recite them at his slightest command.

"White contains every ray," he said, after putting out the match.

"So why didn't you leave the walls white?" Graciela asked.

"We ascend out of darkness into light," he said, habitually, absent-mindedly, like a man crossing himself while entering a church. Graciela nodded and repeated the General's words, a smile of faithlessness on her lips, obscured by the midday darkness of the room.

"That light is inside of you," the General said. "Though you may not see it yet. And it is inside of me." He raised the sleeve of his crisp shirt to reveal his inner wrist, the skin a lighter shade than his face or the top of his hands. The bluish veins reminded Graciela of worms throbbing beneath an upturned stone. She nodded to subdue whatever impulse of his might come next.

"I wanted you to see all this before we meet here with the others next week," the General said. "Do you have any questions for me?"

Graciela knew, from talking with Consuelo, that her father had once sat in this room. He had been here as the General's adviser until something in the teachings had pulled them apart and they had begun to argue. The General had banished Germán from the meetings. And then, according to Consuelo, he had killed him.

"Where did my father sit, when he was here?" Graciela asked, a trickle of alarm dripping into her bloodstream. But the General's face did not flash with anger or violence, as she feared it would. He smiled.

"Your father!" the General said. It was as if he were relieved of something. "Your father sat here, right beside me." He indicated his own seat, at the center of one of the oval table's long sides, facing the room's door, and the chair to the right of it with a luxurious caress. "And this is where you will sit as well."

Graciela examined the wear of the velvet on her father's chair.

"You'll serve as my medium, cherita. Your father, brilliant as he was, did not have your vision, and could only advise me on simple matters. A brilliant adviser, a trusted adviser, but . . . His daughter has exceeded him already."

How? Graciela nearly wondered aloud. How had she exceeded her father already? What had she done? She had listened and closed her eyes when he told her to. She had confirmed some of the General's ideas about the aurora borealis, out of politeness. She had memorized his speeches and preferred replies. But that was all.

Just then came three knocks at the door. The General opened it and retrieved a large plate of cakes from the floor. Graciela heard high heels clattering down the hallway at speed.

"Poppyseed!" the General declared. He settled the plate of cakes onto the table. "Please have some," he urged Graciela. "They know better than to bother us when the Society meets. But they never fail to deliver. These are from the panadería on the corner—La Victoria. Excellent." Graciela spotted her favorite, a little cake made with ripened jocote. She reached for it.

"Who are they?" Graciela asked, shoving a cake sprinkled with ajonjolí into her mouth. She hadn't realized how hungry she was until the miraculous appearance of these cakes.

"Oh, las nenitas at the front desk—Ministry of Health or Education, or something," the General said. Crumbs scattered from his bigotes onto the dreary carpet of the Society of Sacred Letters and Objects.

Graciela considered the secretaries. Perhaps the Society—the incense and candles and black-and-gold tablecloth, the dangling crystal pendulum, all of it—was just part of a game of pretend. She wondered if the people around the General merely indulged him as they would a child. If doing so was what kept them safe.

Because, oye. The magic wasn't the problem here. We all knew magic then, and, simón, we know it now. Before we became these fantastic cackling ghosts we knew the unordinary world. Lourdes and María's great-grandmother had been a healer, through her days in indigo and afterward. We won't tell her secrets here, but we know them, por el chacalele. And we watched our mothers draw circles of protection around us; we listened when they told us their grandmothers had sent them messages in a dream, or when they told us that crows carried warnings in their carcajadas.

But our unordinary world was not like the General's, this makebelieve built of sinister magic that he seemed to have invented in order to bend others to the shape of his will. And, indeed, Graciela understood then that in order to survive this place, that was exactly what she would need to do, bend to the General's will, to pretend. This was her job, and she tried to reason that if she did her job, she would be spared from whatever harm he was capable of inflicting. Because it didn't matter that his magic was fake. What mattered was that he could force others to believe in it.

The General led Graciela out of the maze, tracing a different path through the drab hallways than they had taken to arrive at the Society of Sacred Letters and Objects. There were no windows set into the office doors in these strange hallways, no one to be glimpsed inside of them, carrying out the bureaucratic duties of the ministry. Graciela detected an itch of mold tickling her throat as the General hurried them along to an exit at the back of the building. Graciela stepped into the day's sheer brightness. She shivered, followed the General back to the palace, his back a broad shadow, occasionally eclipsing the sun.

"They leave a cake at the door?" Consuelo exclaimed when Graciela told her that evening about the Society. "Oh là là."

"But what exactly do you do in the palace, at this Society?" she asked. "Besides eat cake?" They lay head-to-head on the parquet floor of Graciela's room in the late-afternoon sun.

"I tell him stories," Graciela said.

"You tell him what he wants to hear?" Consuelo said.

"I listen carefully," Graciela said. "And then I make something up, if I can."

It was the best way she knew to explain it. He told her things—that he could cure any disease, for instance; the problem was he just didn't know exactly how yet. He was waiting for the invisible doctors to reveal their wisdom. He was waiting for his oracle to guide him. She nodded, told him that she believed in his powers, and when smallpox overwhelmed the capital, he had consulted Graciela.

"What is to be done?" he asked. He was shaken, deeply concerned about the fate of the people. But his question was also a test, she knew, and she summoned what she could of his language of colors to answer him. She suggested that he string colored lights around the plaza, a healing tone of blue, a vigorous red, a high, sharp yellow as a mind-tonic.

He rubbed his hands together and declared that one day, when Graciela was older, a feast day would be named after him. A statue of El Gran Pendejo would be commissioned by the archbishop, a magnificent sculpture of imported Roman marble, and it would be placed in the center of the National Plaza. As a kindness, he would request a small statue be made in Graciela's likeness, too.

He hired a team of men to climb ladders on a Saturday midday and string cords of colorful glass bulbs through the sky; he hired musicians, held a picnic in the plaza. *My light will render our blood clean and pure,* he said. *I am curing smallpox with these lights.* At the time, listening to him, Graciela wasn't troubled. The lights were beautiful. They didn't seem to harm anyone.

But for weeks before that, it was also true that she'd heard the General pacing the floors of his quarters above the palace library, chanting: *Their blood will clean the streets. My light will awaken this nation. My light will render our blood clean and pure.*

She heard the phrase before falling asleep at night, remembered the duendito who'd appeared in a ball of light on the train to this strange life.

Whenever Graciela told Perlita about what happened with the General, she just rolled her eyes. She dismissed his name with a wave of her hand. "He bores me terribly," she said. Graciela took Perlita's annoyance with the General as a relief; her veiled skepticism of his magic made it less frightening. She brought him up less and less. When she was at the Estate, she did her best to forget the palace entirely.

Sometimes, in the evenings, when Graciela's jobs were done, Perlita would burst into her room. "Spspsp!" she'd say, pointing red lips at her. She'd stuff Graciela's pockets with candy and they'd drive into town, where they'd go to the movies. They'd share a paper bag of popcorn, both of them sending carcajadas into the dark.

Inside the theater, draped in gold and red velvet like the palace, Graciela sat before a screen wide as another life's sky.

There was a blond actress they saw often, Rosie Swan. When she danced and sang, her eyes looked like seafoam caught on wind, her lips like a small animal's beating heart. Perlita said she knew her from the colonia. She'd been an acquaintance of Rosie's mother.

"Really?" Graciela said to Perlita. "She's from here?"

Perlita nodded. "Her mother is Swiss. That's how she got those ojos claros. The hair, though, that's from a bottle."

Rosie Swan was born Leona de la Rosa, and Graciela couldn't believe that she'd given that up just to fit in with the gringos. Cisne Rosita. Pink swan. When she could have stayed the lioness of the roses! What an idiot.

At the movies, nothing was required of Graciela but that she pay attention. A story she had no part in telling unfolded before her. Here Graciela was small and silent in the plush velvet seats, nodding at Mickey Mouse, who seemed somehow familiar. Forgetting herself, she fell for the mouse. She loved the way he danced, the ease and lightness of his movements. He wore tiny patent-leather shoes, gleaming in the animation. Graciela blew him a kiss without thinking too much about it.

A miracle—for a moment, she forgot, forgot that she was motherless, that she might never return home again. The feeling would end with the film, but for now the screen flickered and its heat swirled comfortingly around her with the warmth and buzz of the other bodies in the theater. So many bodies, more than Graciela could count on her fingers. She wasn't alone, and she wasn't herself, and the full weight of her sorrow lifted a little.

The mouse danced on, the grace of his performance a lesson. Beside Graciela, Perlita sobbed quietly into the heel of her hand. Why was she crying? It didn't matter. Graciela knew better by now than to ask her. Perlita was mercury. The mouse tap-danced his tiny feet and leapt into the air as if he had wings, and Graciela's chacalele thrummed. That's how she'd survive, she thought: she'd perform, tap-dance through the capital.

Somehow, in this way, the years passed.

11

THERE'S A STORY THAT'S SURVIVED ON THE TONGUE FOR thousands of years. Es lo nuestro, one we grew up with, that our mothers grew up with, and their mothers before them. It's the story of Blood Woman, who taught us desire, who taught us escape. Without Blood Woman, who tethered sky to earth and soaked the roots with her blood's indelible memory, we would be just dry bones.

Blood Woman's father was Blood Gatherer, lord of the underworld Xibalba, and he forbade his daughter from exploring a garden that contained a miraculous tree. For years she obeyed him, despite her desire for the tree's knowledge, maybe because she was afraid. He had nine willing goons, and at Blood Gatherer's command, they would kill for him. They would kill anyone.

Flying Scab would tear your skin and contaminate your blood. Pus Demon and Jaundice Fiend would poison you from the inside, swelling your limbs and fouling your liver. Bone Lance and Skull Staff would strip your skin from your body, leaving you unrecognizable. Filth Demon and Puncture Fiend would desecrate your corpse with garbage. Y, para más joder, El Wingspan and El Packstrap would kill you on the road if you attempted escape.

So, for years, Blood Woman didn't explore the garden where the tree of knowledge stood. She lay awake, terrified of her own growing desire.

. . .

For years too, Consuelo had done what she was told. She told Perlita that she loved her, and called her Mami, as had been requested of her. She hadn't crawled out the window after dark to kiss her art teacher, Luis, beside the artificial pond in the park down the road. She hadn't shredded her silk stockings with a razor blade in order to look deranged on purpose. Because Perlita threatened that if she defiled herself, she'd be sent to live with the General. And, like Blood Gatherer, El Gran Pendejo had goons.

While he was alive, Germán forbade Perlita from ever making that threat. He knew better than Perlita how dangerous the General was. But now that Germán was dead, every other day Perlita threatened to send Consuelo as a gift to the General. Once, Consuelo painted her lips and outlined her eyes with charcoal, copying Theda Bara's Cleopatra, and Perlita called her a whore and made her swallow a slice of bar soap. Then Consuelo pulled the velvet laces out of her boots and tied them around her neck after reading a Dumas story in her French class about a lady whose head is held on by a ribbon.

"She can't even speak a word of the language," Perlita complained to the French teacher. "I think she's a goddamn idiot. Indiada, pero indiada."

In case you haven't noticed already, Perlita was an unimaginative bitch—always the same insults with her. The French teacher's mouth hung open, and Perlita canceled the remaining courses.

With every insult thrown her way, Consuelo puffed up her lips and slouched, pretending Perlita's words didn't hurt her, even though of course they did. She wished she really could untie the shoelace around her neck and make her head fall off, just to make Perlita shit her pants.

But to Perlita, as far as Consuelo was concerned, all venial sins were mortal too. So Consuelo gave up. She stole the spider pendant from an antique shop in town and strung it onto the shoelace. She stared at herself in the mirror, roaring, purring, hissing. She reasoned that, as Perlita's failed experiment, her best path forward was to one day make an indelible mark on the world as a revolutionary artist—indiada and brilliant, menacing and beautiful, of mysterious origins and surrounded by friends and lovers. And in order to do that she needed to make use of the education Perlita was too proud to cancel altogether. She needed to become undeniably good, a púchica genius.

She knew that Graciela wanted her to go back to Izalco with her. But she also knew that Perlita would never allow Consuelo to free Socorrito and her baby sister from el colonato. And besides which, Socorrito had never loved her. She'd given her up, after all—that was the story that Perlita had fed Consuelo until she believed it in her very core. So why not go somewhere else? Paris, Los Yunais? But first Consuelo needed to attain her genius. She mixed egg into tempera while the rest of the house was asleep and painted until sunrise, or she climbed out the window to meet her friends from art class, craving these meetings like oxygen. No one else understood.

And as it had happened with Blood Woman, Consuelo's desire had become too large to ignore.

Out with her friends at the fountain in the plaza where they always met up, she locked eyes with Luis, her painting teacher. After seeing him, after knowing that he had seen her, she looked away, jerking her head, panicked. She elbowed her friend Maite, pretending that Maite had whispered something scandalous, and threw back her head, cackling.

"What? Do I have something on my face?" Maite said. "Joder, what's wrong with you?" she said when Consuelo didn't reply.

Luis was with some of his university friends, most of them also teachers for rich families like hers. He made his way to her, and Consuelo felt the panic rising. But that night they folded into each other, apart from the friends that they'd each arrived with. They smoked cigarettes and talked until the sky began to fade.

She learned things about Luis that he hadn't revealed in the painting lessons. He was the youngest of his parents' five children. Once he'd wanted to be a lawyer, but the art scholarship had set him on this other path. His parents accepted this change, believing that if he were to become an artist instead of a lawyer, he would become a rich artist, a successful artist, because of his talents. "I still have a few more years before I really disappoint them," he told Consuelo.

They walked together through the lemony light of the plaza, his cheeks red all the while, until they'd made their way back to the Estate.

"I would like to see you again, outside of lessons," Luis said.

"Yes," Consuelo said. And then the desire to flee overcame her, and without another word she began climbing the maquilishuat tree to the window of Graciela's bedroom, cursing herself for being a goddamn idiot as she humped along the branches. *Yes? Yes, and . . . ?*

Luis walked back into the city, charmed, chaste, burning.

The next time Consuelo climbed out the window it was to meet only him.

Some months later, after several more chaste midnights spent with Luis, Consuelo climbed out the window again, this time wearing her sister's refajo and the forbidden velvet shoelace around her neck. Charcoal from eyelid to eyebrows.

We cackle at this Consuelo. This nenita. Our girl was strutting! That night we saw what Graciela adored about her sister—at her best, she was cachimbona, unafraid, fueled by desire. In this outfit, she felt beautiful, despite everything Perlita had ever said about her clothing ("Rags!"), her colocha hair ("¡Desmadre!"), her nose ("¡Indiada!"), her skin ("Híjole, another pimple. Ay, so dark").

And Luis thought she looked good too. Luis had been working with clay he dug from the banks of the Sumpul River in Chalatenango near the Honduran border, where he was from and where his parents still lived. He was working on a series of figurines, each one no taller than his thumb. They were amulets, he said. A break from oil paintings, from all the European bolados that got shoved down his throat at the university. He loved those bolados too, but he was discovering, as he made these amulets, that he loved working with the clay of his home waters, and that the hummingbirds, the cadejos, and the tiny serpents that he shaped in his palm opened up a different secret door inside of him than the paintings did—this was how they talked, breathlessly, about secret doors inside of their souls, about dreaming of certain colors that they had to create as soon as they awoke. He was telling all this to Consuelo, and then he reached for her hand. He slipped a clay figurine into her bony little mitt. A jaguar. He closed his hand around her fingers. She shuddered.

"I like you," Luis said.

"I'm aware of that," Consuelo said, beside herself. "It's obvious. You've desired me from the moment you first laid eyes on me." She grinned at Luis and winked, with her lips puffed out in a way that Perlita said made her look like a tart.

"May I kiss you?" Luis said.

"Please!" Consuelo said. "The moon is full." Consuelo let her blackened eyelids flutter closed and readied herself to be loved eternally. She was Theda Bara, Louise Brooks, Rosie Swan. She was fifteen now, with a funny costume, no mother, and a heart made of fire.

She wanted to kiss Luis, of course, but she was still a girl, silly as fuck, and what she really wanted was to squeeze him and be squeezed by him. She wanted to work the clay of his body into a sacred object. She wanted him to start reciting poetry to her beneath la lunita llena and never stop. Why didn't he call her Mi Cielo? Why hadn't he declared his love for her earlier, upon first sight, the idiot? This grand charade, his acting as though he were merely her art teacher! Merely her pal! Not even a chaste hug after she'd risked her very life to sneak out to meet him! The indignity! He was torturing her, practically making her beg! Why didn't they run away together? Tonight! Why didn't he dive into the fountain and baptize himself in the name of his devotion to her? Ay, what if they swore to each other to keep their affair a secret? What if she made him beg?

Luis kissed Consuelo gently, with trepidation, as though he thought his touch might frighten her. Consuelo seized his hips and pulled him to her, perhaps more vigorously than he could bear. He smiled weakly, embarrassed, then kissed her hands and murmured his devotion.

Luisto, he was a tender young man.

Night after night, they met, growing older, more skillful, more practiced. Consuelo would be giddy and exhausted in the morning, grouchy with her baby sister. With Luis, she forgot her lost mother and dead father. She forgot to worry about what Perlita's contemptuous moods had in store for her, despite knowing that if Perlita found out that Consuelo loved Luis, a university student with communist sympathies, she'd call her a whore and throw her out on the streets. When he looked at her, she became real. With Luis, Consuelo's body transformed into a star; she painted the night sky as its brightness exploded. She plucked the fruit from the Tree of Life, just as Blood Woman had at the beginning of time.

12

WOMEN APPEARED IN THE PALACE LIKE GHOSTS. THE GEN-eral's women escaped silently in the early mornings, running, en guinda. Graciela had trained herself to look away when they flitted by, as if they really were made of vapor. The General was married, Graciela had heard, but she'd never met his wife and she'd seen dozens of these women over the years—pretty, young, dressed for the evening in the morning.

This one wore a tight black skirt and a green silk blouse, darkened with sweat along her back, under her arms, between her massive breasts. Her hair was piled on top of her head, with stiff curls batting her fore-head, glossy and lined. We breathed her in: iron and earth.

Startled by her sharp scent, Graciela asked her about the perfume. She was twelve, almost thirteen now, and Consuelo told her that it was time to pay attention to things like perfume. The woman smiled and scratched her head. Three or four inches of skin along her neck had been torn and creased like delicate paper, and a shaky drip of blood seeped into her green silk collar. The woman pawed through her purse and retrieved a small bottle of perfume.

"Hollywood Jasmine," she said, and, noticing that Graciela was star-ing at her wound, idly brushed the back of one hand against her neck. She brought the hand to the black fabric at her hip, and, like that, the blood was gone. Graciela stood in the hall, long after the woman had left the palace, blinking at the dust motes swimming in the narrow river of light spilling through the heavy open door, sun-blinded and uncertain of anything her eyes told her.

It wasn't long after that Graciela awoke to brownish blood on the insides of both of her thighs. She sat up in bed and filled the pad of her finger with a gem drop of blood, brought her finger to her nose, smelled roses and sweet rust. In the quiet dark of the new morning, Graciela was completely alone and wondered if she was dying, or still dreaming. She peered out her doorway into the hallway and saw that Ninfa was already cleaning the other bedrooms. Consuelo had left for school. Graciela shut the door before Ninfa could see her, went to her bed, and inspected the sheets. There was no hiding the stains. Ninfa would find them in minutes, and this stark fact filled Graciela with dread, as though she'd committed a crime. Without us, she was lost. She faced herself in the vanity mirror, and carefully, as she'd seen Consuelo do a hundred times with lipstick, painted her mouth red.

By the time Ninfa came into the room with her cart to sweep and dust, Graciela had already left, having dressed herself with her heart pounding and run downstairs to the waiting car. She'd hastily buttoned thirty-one of the thirty-two buttons on her dress in the backseat. By the time she arrived at the palace, she was soaked with sweat.

When Lidia greeted her at the door, Graciela took three slow, deep breaths and coughed. She felt her mind was moving slowly. She shivered, then sweated, then ached, without knowing why. She had no idea what to do about the blood and no one to ask but Lidia.

We would have helped, if we could. With a hand on her lower back, we would have said to her, *Hermana, it's perfectly normal.*

But instead, she explained what had happened to the General's housekeeper, who scoffed in return.

"All those books you read, and you've never heard about this? What about your mother? She never talked to you about this sort of thing?" Her sister Consuelo was seventeen now, and could have helped her, she imagined, though Consuelo hoarded this kind of information like a secret.

Lidia led her to a bathroom and helped clean her up, taught her what to do with all that blood. And then she sent her to the library, where Graciela sat alone for the rest of the afternoon. She finished her cafecito, dangled her feet off the chair, tracing her toes along the inlaid flourishes on the marble floor. Graciela's polite smile was always the same: a thing half-broken, on its way to becoming something else.

Later that day, when she went back to the Estate, she stood in front of the bathroom mirror looking for the woman that Lidia said she'd become. All she saw was a gawky child. A gawky child who'd been told by a mad-man that she had phenomenal powers. He told Graciela that the blood flowing through the point of her index finger contained enough wisdom to guide every move he made in his private galaxy. She'd waited for the General's truths about her soul to be made evident in her body. Nothing had revealed itself to her, aside from the way her sadness seemed to break the walls inside her chest when she looked into the sky, saw a heavy, full moon, and imagined her mother asleep in their shack with silver light on her face. A tiny spark began in her belly and told her to pay attention. She did know things: she knew the sadness her great-grandmother had car-ried in her hands, that her mother had carried in her back; she felt that.

If she was half as powerful as they all said she was, she'd have dissolved her body into the wind and carried herself back home. She was tired of telling the General these stories. She wanted nothing more to do with the purity of the nation and wished she could put these pieces of wisdom down. She didn't want to be pure. She wanted to clutch her stomach and bleed, unalone in her bleeding. She wanted her mami.

A mosquito buzzed in her ear, and she shut her eyes, summoning those spirit pieces inside of her. She built a prayer of the words she knew by heart:

Disappear me, Blessed Virgin. Let my soul rise and fall through the ages, unmeasured by the body. Return me to the great chain of mothers, their infinite migrations through the blood, the earth, the birds, the eternally dying stars. In the name of the Father, and of the Son, and of the Holy

Spirit, deliver me from evil, now and at the hour of my death. Tear me out of this life by the roots.

But when she opened her eyes, she hadn't disappeared. She was not home. In the same mirror she saw the same girl standing in the same room, skin wet from the bath. The same mosquito bit her cheek. She slapped at it, and ordinary blood smashed onto her skin. Her front teeth hung over the edge of her bottom lip; her shoulders sagged forward in her nightgown because she held her body without any care.

The train sounded outside the window. She wanted to leave, to find her mother, return to us. She could climb out the window and down the maquilishuat tree, walk to the station in her nightgown, taking the train barefoot over the mountains, disappearing from the capital without a trace. But she knew what would happen: they'd find her and bring her back, and the General and his men would disappear her from the capital, from this earth, without a trace.

She would take the chance. This was not the place she wanted to be a woman. There was nothing she wanted to take with her.

Graciela was halfway down the tree when she heard Consuelo coughing furiously.

"Where do you think you're going?" she called out the window.

"To see our mother," Graciela said. She was cold, afraid, and barefoot. The rag had begun to slip out of her chonis, and she wrapped her legs around the tree.

"I think you'd better stay here with me," Consuelo said. "Where you're wanted." Consuelo coughed again. It was how she controlled the trembling flicker inside of her when she was angry or afraid, or terribly lonely. She didn't like to beg; she coughed like an idiot instead. "Don't you know that she gave you up? She was tired of you. She'd rather take Perlita's money than spend her life raising you. She gave you up."

We watched a wicked light turn on behind Consuelo's eyes. Fear made her cruel.

Graciela shivered, and her heart became a weight. She let herself slide farther down the tree, scraping her inner legs on the bark.

"Wait!" Consuelo said, coughing and pounding her chest. "Congratulations! I saw the sheets soaking in the tub! I didn't get mine until two years ago, because I'm so skinny. We're both women now. Your tetas will be bigger than mine in a month."

Graciela sighed and began climbing back up the tree, more hopeless than ever. She wanted only to sleep.

"Stay here," Consuelo said. Calmer, now that her sister seemed not to be leaving her. "There's nothing for you there. Have you even heard a word from our mother? Do you think she wants to see you?" She didn't wait for an answer. "Listen, I was the same way. Then I didn't see her again until she came here to get rid of you. Stay here, hermanita. You're grown now. We can get into our own trouble."

Graciela dug her fingers into the bark of the tree, driving the splinters beneath her nails for as long as she could bear the pain. Then she climbed back up and through the broken window, into the light where Consuelo waited.

"Por la gran puta," Consuelo said. "Don't do that again. If you're going to run away, you better have a plan, and you better take me with you, and we better be going somewhere that will make us rich and famous!" She had her sister sit at the vanity, and stood behind her, combing out Graciela's hair. It was filled with tiny pink petals from the maquilishuat tree.

"How about Los Yunais?" Consuelo asked. "Hollywood?" She looked up to see Graciela's reaction in the mirror. Graciela practiced the arid stone face that Consuelo modeled so often.

"Let me sleep," Graciela said. "Can you please just go to your room? I won't run away. I don't have the strength to move."

"Can I just stay here?" Consuelo asked, curling her long thin body against Graciela's back. "I promise I'll shut up."

Graciela understood: she had terrified her sister. Because if she'd succeeded in escaping the capital, she would have left Consuelo alone, abandoned, again.

"Fine," she said. "Just shut up and let me sleep."

Consuelo hummed, tapping her long fingers across her silly forehead.

"And no singing, I beg of you," Graciela said. Consuelo stopped humming, but she kept tapping, and as Graciela drifted into sleep she felt each tap as though Consuelo's fingers were inside her own head.

After that Consuelo enveloped Graciela with renewed vigor. The very next night: "Listen, you want to go somewhere? Come with me tonight. You need to have some púchica fun." Consuelo had spent the last thousand nights or so entering Graciela's bedroom to crawl out the broken window into the dark, muttering, "Nothing, nowhere," when Graciela asked what she was doing, where she was going, what she did when she was out there. Graciela grinned like a maniac now to finally be invited to discover nowhere.

"What kind of púchica fun will we have tonight?" she asked.

"Stand around, drink wine. Write poetry. Paint. Smoke. Flirt." By flirt, Consuelo meant flirt with Luis, let him put his hands all over her beneath the dark trees framing the plaza. Later, she tied scarves around her neck to hide the marks his mouth left on her skin, bruises that startled Graciela until Consuelo nervously explained them.

Consuelo sat Graciela at the vanity, held her chin between two fingers, and began painting black half-moons on her eyelids. Graciela breathed in her scent and read aloud the names on the small glass bottles on her dresser: amber, sandalwood, rose, tried to notice each separate smell inside her nose.

"Why moons?" Graciela asked after Consuelo told her she could open her eyes. *La luna es una mujer.*

"They're the thing right now. Like African masks. And hands." Consuelo gestured to her neck. She'd replaced the tiny band of pearls she usually wore with a rosary. Its beads were blackened rose petals that had been dipped in lacquer, and beside the dangling iron crucifix, Consuelo had pinned a tiny golden hand and a tiny brass bell.

She smoothed Graciela's eyebrows as she painted gold around the moons, her fingers like feathers. At seventeen, Consuelo seemed as grown-up to Graciela as one of the General's mistresses. Her acne had cleared, her shoulders had straightened. She even seemed less afraid of Perlita.

"You're done," she said now, turning Graciela around to see her face in the mirror. Graciela smiled with all of her teeth. Candy-apple cheeks, shimmering eyelids, her reflection edible.

Consuelo, one hand dangling out the broken window, let her cigarette ash and spark through the sky as it fell. When she looked into the mirror at a spot of light above Graciela's head and raised her eyebrows, painted thin as wire, she saw her own reflection as a blurred photograph, mouth slightly appalled, forehead raised and commanding, eyes registering errors all over the room, shaking a little. This is how we remember Consuelo. She twitched and sparked like the tip of a wooden matchstick after it had been struck, the moment before it lights up.

Consuelo's friends were painters and poets from the art school who had formed what they called a "collective." Their parents were rich, and the teenagers tore holes in their stockings and painted their faces with sigils and stayed out smoking rose-flavored cigarettes. In the mornings they were attended to by uniformed maids and pressed into fresh clothing, made to comb their hair before breakfast. It was expected that the children who comprised Las Rositas would grow out of this phase, a style that veered disconcertingly close to the style of dissidents and scum: the wide white cotton pants of the Indigenous workers, silk stockings torn like a whore's, the ungodliness of university lecturers. But on the other hand, El Gran Pendejo held séances and sought the counsel of una indita brujita, so perhaps their parents shouldn't have been so worried that their children would be unfairly judged by their appearances. They were rich, after all, bien güeritos, and owned land. The artists they admired most were the ones who regularly showed up at the Society of Sacred Letters and Objects. After all, these artists had to live, and if they behaved in just the right way, the General could be very generous with his funding. Graciela had met some of them, which made her an object of fascination among Consuelo's friends.

The group moved in wet shadows by the fountain across the plaza.

Consuelo pointed her lips toward them as she and Graciela arrived. Las Rositas.

"It's impossible to imagine you as someone who has parents," a boy a bit older than Graciela was saying to the girl sitting on the lip of the fountain, tracing her fingers through the dark water.

"I tend to do whatever I want." The girl sucked on a cigarette and swung her legs. Violeta. She'd spent her sixteenth year studying in Paris. Consuelo had told Graciela that Violeta's parents, who were often at the Estate visiting Perlita, had imagined she'd spend her time in France painting lily pads and bowls of apples, but instead she'd written vulgar poems and posed nude for an old man who called her his muse, his golden child, sometimes his saint.

The apples of Violeta's cheeks gleamed with slick red rouge—a tiny heart painted on each side of her face. She'd embroidered the words NO ME TOQUES on the sleeve of her velvet jacket, along with another pair of hearts.

"This your sister?" the boy asked Consuelo, gesturing toward Graciela behind her.

"La brujita indita," Consuelo said, very proud of herself.

That might be the word you would choose to describe the brown of our faces—we often heard it like this: "No seas india." Sometimes, when we wanted to taste the cruelty ourselves, we said that too. What it meant to us when we were six, seven years old, newly toothless, canela fina as we were the day that they killed us, was this: "Don't be stupid." Later, they killed us for the canela that they saw in our skin, and the word that came to their lips when they saw us then? "India" too.

Graciela pinched her eyes into triangles and glared at Consuelo. Was she so ugly? Was she so stupid?

Consuelo patted her on the head and Graciela shook her off, scowled openly at her sister. The word in Consuelo's mouth had sounded just as it did when Perlita said it, with that hateful creak in the vowels. Graciela turned and said to Violeta, "I like your hearts."

"You do?" Violeta said. "They're something I'm trying out. The idea is to look younger."

"How old are you?" Graciela asked. Consuelo shuffled away to the perimeter of the group, her bell jingling. Out of the corner of her eye Graciela watched her sister chew on her cuticles, glancing darkly over as she talked with Violeta.

"I'm sixteen, but I wish I looked as young as you. It's what my boyfriend prefers. Indias always look like children, even when they're old. I love that." Violeta nodded at Graciela only slightly, and flicked the ash of her cigarette into the fountain. Sparks glowed orange above the dark water, then died.

Consuelo returned, circled anxiously around Graciela's ear. Consuelo the nervous bee, Graciela the flower. "What is it?" Graciela asked.

"I'm sorry I embarrassed you," Consuelo said. She was blushing deep red, as though she were the one who'd been called india in front of everyone. Maybe she was afraid that she would be. They were sisters, after all. Graciela shrugged and accepted her apology.

Luis appeared in the shadows; a smile lit his bearded face. At night, he looked smaller, more relaxed, less of a man and more of a cipote, like the rest of Consuelo's friends. But he was apart from them still—he observed their extravagant gestures with a soft wisp of a smile, careful not to betray any judgment. He nuzzled Consuelo's neck and wrapped his arms around her shoulders. She smiled dreamily back at him; she couldn't help herself.

Together, Luis and Consuelo disappeared into the darker dark of the plaza's perimeter of trees and benches. Graciela, with her moon eyes, stayed beside the fountain with the Rositas, who shyly took their turns asking Graciela about what she did in the palace. What they were most hungry to know was the nature of Graciela's brujería. Why had the General chosen her and not Consuelo? What powers did she have?

"Do you make anything?" a güerita asked. "Poetry, or art, or something?" They all made something.

"Sometimes," Graciela said, not knowing the right thing to say.

"Like what? Are you going to Bellas Artes when you're old enough?"

Graciela shrugged, as she'd seen Consuelo do when she was avoiding saying something.

"We'll see," Graciela said. "I'm a dancer. And a writer." Consuelo had been coaching her.

Instead of saying, "I tell him stories," Consuelo had encouraged Graciela to call herself an artist.

"But I'm a tiny kid," Graciela had protested.

"So what?" Consuelo said. "So am I. But I'm already a painter and a muse."

If Graciela was capable of making the most powerful man in our world shift nature with her stories, she could tell her own too. "Also," Consuelo said, "it's important, with this group, with Las Rositas, that you're capable of making things."

Mostly, though, Graciela wrote silently in her mind without putting words to paper. Something prevented her from writing down the stories that she imagined—maybe it was her mind's habit of keeping, el guaya-bear, a secret pocket of laziness despite her obvious cleverness. She didn't know yet—nor did we—that writing down words makes the world.

She had begun slowly, and only when she was completely alone, to fill the pages of the notebook that Consuelo had given her. She reported on her days, repeating the General's catechisms, describing Perlita's costumes, the way her manner swung between haughty and playful. She wrote about Consuelo, and whom she might have been had she stayed in our village and we'd all grown up together.

Graciela had the notebook with her, but she didn't show anyone the words she'd written, certainly not Las Rositas, who chattered around her like birds beside the fountain. Someone invited Graciela to draw with them, and she nodded.

"You see, we have this pact, this promise," Violeta said. "It's writ in blood." Violeta's deathly seriousness made Graciela laugh.

A woman of twenty-five or so, perched on the other side of the fountain, laughed also, snorting at these dear children. She was Brannon's girl, La Claudia, la hija of the railroad. She worked in the office at Bellas Artes, wrote poetry that angered her father, and was engaged to be married to a man she hated. She enjoyed the way the art students clamored around her, seeking her wisdom, drawn like moths to her rich-girl glow. Consuelo feared and worshipped this woman, who seemed to have a life of glamour, despite having few friends her own age, and who she suspected of once, years ago, fucking Luis.

"What's your pact?" Graciela asked.

"We shall all either make art or be art," La Violeta said, breathless. "You want in?"

Graciela nodded; she felt that she could comply, and perhaps La Violeta would not even force her to draw blood.

They drew with sticks in the claylike dirt of the plaza. A circle, a toilet, a little thumb that spoke foul words, a whistling guanaco, a duende with a huge straw hat. Graciela drew a picture of her mother's face, trying, and failing, to capture the long lines above her eyebrows, the roundness of her cheeks, the hardness of her mother's eyes, which were just like her own. Sometimes Graciela wondered if she would miss her mother less if her brain were capable of forgetting Socorrito's face.

They barely spoke, and somehow, working steadily in the silver moonlight and golden lamplight, responding to one another in the dirt, they constructed a story in pictures.

A light drizzle came and softened the stories to mud. Jorge, the boy who'd been talking with Violeta when they'd arrived, brought out a bottle of sweet wine and handed it to Graciela. She took a long, thirsty swig, and the group cheered for la niña indita. Graciela wiped her mouth and passed the bottle around the circle, then lay down in the mud and waited for Consuelo to return. The moon was full, allowing her to study the faces of Las Rositas, searching for the General's daughters among them.

"I've never had a daughter," the General liked to say, though everyone knew this wasn't true. His daughters were everywhere—the lucky ones in school with Consuelo's friends, the less fortunate in the market selling aguas frescas—each one as broad-browed and stout as he. There were so many of them, all unclaimed.

Consuelo returned from the bushes, stubbed out her cigarette on the black leather sole of her tiny heel, took an orangey-red lipstick out of her pocket, and rubbed the color across the shape of her lips from memory.

She buttoned her black sweater, too warm for the tropics, over a gray lace bra.

One afternoon, about a week earlier, Graciela had sat in the late sunlight watching Consuelo try on different gown and shoe combinations and promenade around Graciela's bedroom before going off to her painting lesson with Luis, pouting into the mirrors and demanding Graciela's praise. When Graciela had told her the truth—that she looked beautiful, but pretty much like the same person in each dress—she'd stomped her foot and called Graciela useless. Then her face crumpled into sudden tears, and she'd hastily apologized and set Graciela's scraps of hair in rollers.

"That was a lie," Consuelo had said. "You're very useful."

"I know," Graciela replied. "That's why I'm here."

At home, Graciela had watched Lourdes make María eat plates of dirt with chopsticks she'd found in la finca house's garbage, force her to do dog tricks on a rope leash, carry her into the yucca cellar in the middle of the night. When María came crying back to bed, Lourdes informed her little sister that she'd been sleepwalking. Was this what older sisters did to younger sisters—remind us of a vaster, wiser world beyond our daily lives, a world that lay transparently over and around our own? As usual, Graciela wanted only to learn; she wanted to learn more of Consuelo's world, to be part of it.

"Ready?" Consuelo asked now, turning to leave the fountain. Graciela nodded and followed her away, back to the Estate, where they scrambled up the same tree they'd climbed down just a few hours earlier and tucked themselves into bed.

13

MUJERES, MADRES, HIJAS, TODAS SIGUANABAS. MALINCHES. Mestizas. But, answer me this: Name the daughter who hasn't disobeyed and thanked herself later for doing just that? What mother hasn't fallen asleep while the frijoles rojos burned the bottom of the pan?

We used to sneak into the woods at night. Once, when María was four, just barely past babyhood, and the rest of us were about six, we went looking for Siguanaba's wounded child, Cipitillo, a boy duende who ate ash and ran on backward feet. We were doing our best to prove to one another that we weren't afraid, but we all were, and at some point Lourdes picked up her baby sister and ran home, leaving Cora, Lucía, and Graciela alone in the dark woods. Someone hissed, *You're next, you're next!* And we cursed Lourdes with all of our best swear words for daring to leave, scanned the trees for a path out and home. We abandoned our plan to find Cipitillo. What would we have done with him when we found him, anyway? Whose idea had this been? A light rain had begun just as we entered the forest and by now it had turned into a downpour. Lightning sliced a ceiba tree in front of us. Dodging the broken branches, we slid into a ravine. When we opened our eyes again, thin morning clouds threaded across the sky. We wondered why we hadn't died.

Spindly, rough branches, tangled and brittle. Above us glowed a pearly white flower, like the moon in a nest. La flor de amate, and its promise of love and wisdom and long life and protection, ours if we could reach its petals, if we could pluck its stem in precisely the correct way. Pick from the wrong part of the stem, bruise a petal, and the devil would appear and destroy us all. Graciela reached for it. The devil appeared like a bloom.

And what about her mother? We saw Socorrito; we knew her life. Perhaps better than her own daughters ever would. For the first few weeks after Graciela had gone, Socorrito couldn't stop talking about the Estate in the capital—the marble stairs, the birdcage, the high fence around everything.

When is she coming back to take you there to live? we asked.

Any day now.

Despite the fact that no letters from Graciela ever came to our town, Socorrito insisted that Lourdes would read them aloud to her, whenever they did. She would call out to Lourdes in the fields, "My little genius, are you going to read to me?"

"I'm nobody's little genius!" Lourdes would shout back, but not as harshly as she might have, had she not ached for Socorrito's misery, ached for Graciela.

After Graciela left, Socorrito was drunk for three years straight. She stumbled in the fields and was useless in the sorting room. One afternoon, María came inside after the haul and found Socorrito there, flat on the ground staring up at the beams.

"Hush, I'm talking with my grandmother!" Socorrito said, barely moving her head from where it lay in the dirt. She whispered feverishly toward the ceiling.

None of us would ever criticize Socorrito for how she was now. Our mothers may have whispered their annoyance, their judgments, but to us, Socorrito was still Graciela's mami. We loved her.

"What does she say, your grandmother?" María asked Socorrito when her whispering halted.

"Nothing," Socorrito said. She spat right into the pile of coffee berries that Lucía had hauled and was now sorting. "She's been dead for years. But if she were here, or listening, or anything at all, well, she wouldn't now, would she?"

María didn't respond, not because she didn't want to comfort Socorrito, but because she barely understood what the woman was saying.

Eventually Socorrito received another envelope from the capital, and we thought it must be a much-awaited letter. But it was just an envelope with money from the Ministry of Health, no word from Graciela at all. Socorrito stayed drunk for two weeks after that, and Cora finally made sense of her words: if her grandmother were here, she wouldn't listen to her, wouldn't even look her in the eye, so angry and ashamed would she be that Socorrito had let both of her daughters be taken to the warlock.

Socorrito waited for more envelopes of pisto. We all did, hoping she'd share the next one with us, which she'd promised she would. But the pisto never came. The next payday el patrón handed her a few extra wooden tokens, useful only for the company store.

Eventually, about three years after Graciela left, Socorrito met an orange-haired missionary from North Carolina who married her. She stopped drinking after that, with the aid of Jesucristo. And with the aid of Walter she no longer had to work. They moved to a big house on the hill above the convent, and we heard from our mamis that Socorrito's gringo planned to take her to the United States. But Socorrito, at least a part of her, was still waiting.

"Wouldn't it be better to stay," Socorrito said, part statement, part question, every time we ran into her in the market or outside of the church. "The three of us, me, Graciela, and El Walter, maybe one more, and just live in the capital in our very own estate, as a family?" Knowing little about these matters, we always nodded in agreement.

Maybe one more, she said, and we knew that she wasn't speaking of the future, another pregnancy, another tiny baby, but of the past. Of Consuelo, the one more who'd come before.

We grew up too, just as Graciela did. Beneath the ceiba, fluff drifted onto Cora's shoulders, and she bled. Lourdes, María, and Lucía bled too. We brought one another atol and steeped hierba buena. We rubbed the small parts of one another's lower backs and took turns combing one another's hair. We laughed with the moon; she was a woman also.

Sister Iris gave María a pair of overalls from the nun's rummage sale de choto; la monja said they were made for her. When María put them on for the first time, they hung loose on her skinny body. How right these railroad stripes felt over her shoulders. She was twelve or so when she got them. Maybe thirteen. She cut her hair even shorter that very day, using kitchen scissors and no mirror, just the feeling of her hair in her hands. Lourdes laughed her ass off when she got home and saw her baby sister.

"It's the real you, María-Malía. You look like a bichito." Lourdes put her arm around her and they both grinned at María's reflection in the mirror.

Cora and Lucía began working together to heal the soil in a plot of land on the other side of the volcano. They clawed at it using a shovel they'd stolen from one of the men's carts, giving it air. They fed it their blood and hair. From the finca store they bought pepper, corn, yucca, potato—and found their seeds to sprinkle into the ground, or in the case of the roots, bury them whole. The idea was to grow our own food, and one day, to bring our lives here, to this milpa on the other side of the volcano.

One day Lucía ran out of the fields and into the forest. We thought she'd gone to meet someone, to mess around a little, so we didn't follow her. Lucía practiced her charm on everyone she met, bien flirtatious. Lonely when she was anywhere without the rest of us. No one told the patrón, and we worked twice as hard to cover for her, filling her basket. She returned that evening with a bundle of sticks wrapped in twine that she'd stolen from the sorting room. Bien bold.

"Miren que," she told us. "I'm making a púchica loom." We laughed so much we couldn't even be annoyed with her. Our great-grandmothers, our grandmothers—they were all long dead. Anyone who could teach us how to build a backstrap loom, how to process the thread and how to weave—there was no one left. But she was determined.

"You've fucking lost your mind," we told her, cackling like ravens.

"And so you ran like your life depended on it, to gather sticks in the forest like some púchica coatimundi?" María asked, choking on her carcajadas.

"Yeah," Lucía says. "I was bored."

We understood. We were all bored. We ran off to the forest every chance we got to escape our boredom. Bored and tired, bored and aching, bored and hopeful, bored and joyful, bored and eager to mess around.

It was there, in the forest, that Cora met Héctor. She liked him enough to learn his name and return to him again and again. He had floppy black hair and brought her flowers. She taught him the names of the birds, and after dark, they'd meet in their spot near a stand of cacao trees.

It wasn't much later that we met Prudencia. She was older than us, old enough to be our mother, though everyone called her a fool because she claimed she could predict the future.

"She's got birds in her head," Lourdes would say of our new friend, and this is one of the reasons we adored her. She and her mother sold fruit on the other side of the volcano. We shared a cup of sliced sour green mango and Prudencia recited a poem that she'd written for us, swaying and singing. Prudencia liked to say she'd make a good king, but would settle for president. She claimed she had a dream about her aunt dying in her sleep, and then she woke up and her Tita Dori was gone. Bien loca, but her poetry wasn't bad. She chattered so much her anciana mother yelled at her to shut up.

"Fíjate, you're going to cut off a hand," she said—Prudencia liked to close her eyes while she sang her poems, the knife its own live animal, chopping the head off of a pineapple.

And our mothers? Calaceadas. Yoli, Alba, and Rosario were collapsing into sleep earlier and more quietly each year. Their backs ached, and the joints of their fingers swelled and curled their fingers into claws. And Socorrito was somewhere else with her gringo—we saw her less and less. We worked more and more. We had to take on what our mothers no longer could do.

·   ·   ·

Vaya, pues.

Graciela had been gone for seven years when the stock market crashed. The price of coffee plummeted. The patrón drank himself nearly to death.

One night the bitch of the finca came running to our row of huts and pounded at Rosario's door—her husband wouldn't wake up and she needed some kind of help. Rosario wasn't happy to be awakened at this hour, especially because the patrón had just slashed her pay—all our pay—and even if he said it was a "temporary matter," we knew better. We all knew that our coffee bean economy was collapsing on itself.

"What do you want me to do?" Rosario asked the bitch as they ran through the dark back to their big house on the hill.

"Hurry up!" she replied.

Rosario clicked her tongue. Cicadas roared.

At the house Rosario got a bucket of cold water and splashed it on the patrón. He was sprawled on the bathroom floor, didn't stir when the water rushed over him like an angry tide.

"Did he hit his head?" Rosario asked the bitch of the finca.

She just nibbled her fingertips and stared dully.

"I'm not a doctor," Rosario said. "Not a medical doctor, not a witch doctor."

"Just do something!" the woman said. "My god, these lazy mulatas."

So Rosario did something. She wound up her arm and, not without some pleasure, she punched el patrón in the jaw. He shouted, and startled awake. The bitch of the finca screamed and reached to grab Rosario by the hair.

"I did it!" Rosario said, triumphant. A stench filled the bathroom as the patrón rose to his elbows.

"He's shit his pants! He's shit his pants!" The bitch of the finca was hysterical. "Get back here and clean up this mess!" she screamed. But Rosario was out the door, running as fast as her sore back would allow.

When the harvest season came, the patrón told us to hold off. We let the coffee berries ripen and fall in the fields; the smell was like rotting meat, like the shit pants of the patrón. The patrón promised to pay after the season was over. We waited. He never paid. *Those shitty pants were just the beginning of our troubles,* Rosario laughed.

One morning, after the harvest season had ended, when they knew he'd be away en Los Yunais, Alba and Yoli threw rocks through the patrón's living room window. They heard the glass shatter, and the bitch of the finca scream and run into the salita as our mothers chased each other back through the forest. They smiled for days after that. They wanted just a taste, a taste of retribution.

Ordinarily, that was the kind of thing that could get them killed. But todo el mundo knew that these were not ordinary times. The air smelled like shit from a season of rot instead of harvest, and no one was getting paid. Their rocks were a warning and a bargain. Pay us before you get worse from us, pendejo. But, still, they knew that they were lucky that no one would suspect two middle-aged indias of vandalizing the patrón's house.

When the patrón returned the next week, he was briefed. He called a meeting of the workers at sunset and demanded to know who had thrown the rocks. He stood on the porch outside his house, the broken window framing his sombrero. He waited in silence. No one stepped forward.

"All right," he said. "I hear your message. You're hungry. You've not been paid. The harvest season was shit." He emptied a bucket into the crowd; the púchica wooden tokens, almost good for nothing, rained down into our outstretched hands.

Our mothers lay down. There wasn't enough work, and they were hardly being paid. They were exhausted, too relieved by a break to share any of their worries with us, and they were hungry. The púchica wooden tokens were not enough—five wooden tokens brought home a stack of tortillas threaded with soft blue mold, some salty queso duro, and a shriveled, too-ripe plátano.

"Look, Lucía—it's your boyfriend." María grabbed the rotten plátano when Lourdes returned from the finca store with her basket. Lucía rolled her eyes, Lourdes rolled her eyes, and Cora grabbed the plátano from María and expertly yanked and squeezed. Its soft cream oozed out with a parade of shiny black hormigas. We applauded.

The only reason we didn't starve was the milpa on the other side of the volcano. From the soil that Cora and Lucía had prepared we harvested corn, frijoles, squash, our own beautiful plátanos. We traded some of that for a whole chicken and eggs from Prudencia's mother. A couple of nights a week Cora cooked for the nuns for a little bit of money and a meal, which she wrapped in her rebozo and brought back to share with the rest of us. And every Sunday we feasted together, a family.

Lourdes started taking charge of the radio in the sorting room, fiddling with the knobs on the dusty machine to find the right song, doing what she could to liven the mood. She wanted to dance, and so she did. That's how she heard that La Prudencia, our friend, La Loca Prudencia Ayala with the birds in her head, was running for president in the upcoming election. Women couldn't even vote then. Especially not afrodescendiente indias like Prudencia. We hadn't been paying any mind to the election—what did it matter to us? Nothing here ever changed. But now, this was something to feel excited about.

The next morning was Sunday, so Lourdes ran to the other side of the volcano to find Prudencia at the market. She didn't stop at the milpa on the way, just showed up empty-handed.

"¡Mi presidente cachimbona!" Lourdes called out to Prudencia. Prudencia was walking circles around her mother's stand, leaning on a cane like a rich old man. Her old mother cussed and spat. It seemed crazy, a dream.

And the radio in the sorting room also contained a secret station, which Lourdes discovered between songs of revenge. The station broadcast news of men our age gathering in the mountains, attending worker meetings. Héctor, Cora's man, began attending the meetings. He heard a speech about women voting in elections, and after that, La Loca Prudencia's bid seemed more possible. He heard another speech about the redistribution of the land. He listened to a man talk about abolishing the wooden tokens in favor of pay, and another who argued that abolishing the token system would be like exchanging a broken shoe for a pile of horseshit. He wanted us instead to refuse to be made to work. Get rid of the fincas, get rid of the colono system entirely. Seize back the land. The man said nothing about slitting the throats of the patrón and his associates, but the crowd was ferocious afterward, a body sparking in the dark.

Héctor told Cora that he was going to the meetings for their children. He wanted their babies to live better. Cora wasn't sure she wanted babies just yet, but she also wasn't worried about Héctor going to the meetings. She brought food to him and the other men. She'd slowly climb the mountain, a bundle on her back—fat tortillas, frijoles rojos, and some pollo tinga that she'd smuggled out of the convent. She had a feeling that the nuns wouldn't care about her stealing food, or even about the meetings on the mountain, but in any case, she always told them that she was going out to watch the birds.

Soon signs appeared in our village, saying that communism was punishable by death. Bolsheviks would be killed on sight. "And how would these killers identify a communist just by looking at them?" we said, smirking. Héctor called himself a worker, anyway, not a Bolshevik. No one we knew used the word *Bolshevik*.

We knew, of course, that the signs that said COMMUNIST really meant INDIO. They meant poor, coffee worker, barbarous. Brown skin, white wrinkly cotton, indios who gathered in groups of three or more. We cackled. Bleeding together as we were, red staining our long cotton skirts. Look at the four of us. Were we Bolsheviks? Were we a communist uprising? The bitch of la finca lay sweating inside; her husband went out whoring for days. None of us were worried.

Later, Cora started going to meetings with Héctor. "There's nothing crazy about them," she told us. "Nothing too wild. Mostly a bunch of men arguing about what a word means. But imagine—if it's true that women could get the vote, we'd overturn el colonato, like that."

Lourdes and Lucía considered joining her next time, but María was busy. Our best chambre was about María. In her overalls and short hair, she'd seduced a woman who lived on the other side of the volcano. She was busy, caressing her lover's face, looking into her eyes, telling her all kinds of things. María was on her way to having her heart broken for the first and only time in her short life. She had no time for meetings.

When desire tips over into taste, there's no going back. Desire tastes sweet. Blood Woman tasted it, like memory, and needed more. We knew how sweet desire tasted too; its sweetness frightened us a little, just as it frightened Blood Woman when she walked deeper into the forest. Desire thrummed her body like an earthquake's aftershock, led her to that forbidden tree.

The skull was waiting for her.

14

AND FOR LAS HERMANAS IN THE CAPITAL, EVERYTHING WAS beginning to change. They were no longer children, and each day they became more aware of the cracks in their world that would shatter all of our lives. But they held off from knowing what the future demanded of them for as long as they could.

But these days, everything was funny to Consuelo. She'd been wound up like a rabbit for so long, so embarrassed sometimes that she couldn't speak, so afraid that she shook. So she'd started laughing. Giggling, sneering, cackling, roaring, sometimes to the confusion of others, but she didn't know what else to do. Perlita called her rude and crazy, ugly and indiada, but Consuelo only laughed more. She could be vicious with Maite and the other Rositas, sprinkling carcajadas on their broken hearts and the flaws in their paintings and poems. But with Luis, after sex, her impulse to laugh was less immediate. She relaxed.

Consuelo lay with Luis in his studio. Outside, bats flew overhead; a monsoon rain was coming.

And tonight Luis was distressed, so Consuelo tried especially hard not to laugh while he told her what had happened. She'd learned that her nervous laughter sometimes bothered him.

One of his teachers had gone missing. He'd gone to a meeting of workers at The Drunken City, an unspectacular café near the university that Consuelo had been to a million times before. Luis suspected that he'd just gone for a coffee and taken a pamphlet on the way out. But the following day the teacher hadn't shown up for class. He'd disappeared, his small apartment ransacked, and the front door left open. The pamphlet from the workers' meeting was found on his desk. Luis had his theories, most of them having to do with someone, a friend or an enemy, an ex-girlfriend maybe, calling the man a Bolshevik.

Luis had no idea if his teacher actually was a Bolshevik. He did wear a beard and a hemp belt, and sometimes that was all that was needed for this sort of accusation to be made. Maybe he'd been watched. In the café, in the classroom, on the street. Maybe whoever was watching him was part of the workers' group, some sort of spy for the government. Whoever had taken him knew where he lived.

That same week, though, a student of his had reported the teacher to the Ministry of Education, saying that he'd made some comment in class about Greek columns being overrated.

Consuelo couldn't help it—she screamed and cackled at this one. "¡Achis! Who on earth would report that? Who on earth would care? ¡Ma ve!" she said.

"Something as simple as this is enough to raise suspicions," Luis said. "Though maybe he said more. Insulted the General to one of his ears at The Drunken City. Something like that. It's hard even to know if it was just one thing. Or if he's being used as an example to the rest of us. If they ever let him go." Luis's voice was heavy and slow.

Ugh. Consuelo bit her lip to keep from saying it aloud. Ugh. She knew she shouldn't laugh, but she hated this Luis. This somber Luis bored her, and though she didn't quite understand it at the time, that boredom was terrifying. She refused it.

No! she wanted to shout in his ear. *I refuse to be bored!* She wanted to pierce through his heaviness, extract that desire nectar, and slurp it up. Dance on his chest. Listen to him breathless, laughing, begging for her. She wanted to watch his eyelids flutter again, to be kissed and licked endlessly.

He rolled over, away from her. "It's so fucking hopeless. I think the General plans to shut down the whole university. Just get rid of everyone and start over with a bunch of Ladino bankers."

To Consuelo, all of Luis's theories sounded ridiculous. This teacher had probably just wanted to escape his own life. Maybe he'd gone to Panamá and was fishing off the Caribbean coast. And really—replace the faculty of Bellas Artes with Ladino bankers? She let loose una carcajada.

Luis ignored her cackle, lost in his own despair.

"I'm going to have to keep an eye on myself and stay out of the General's way," Luis said. "He's not fond of my kind, you know."

"Your kind?" Consuelo said, her tiny eyebrows lifting.

"You know. Campesino parents, artistic aspirations, beard. Technically, those are Bolshevik shoes." He pointed at his scuffed oxfords, stacked one on top of the other, in the corner of the room by the door, tongues flopping out. Though mild, unthreatening, they were ugly shoes, cheaply made.

(Also: anything cheap in those days was Bolshevik. Later, anything campesino would become Bolshevik.)

Consuelo couldn't stand it anymore. She exploded in a fit of giggles.

"Bolshevik shoes, Bolshevik nose, Bolshevik camera, Bolshevik canvas, Bolshevik candy, Bolshevik belly button, Bolshevik suspenders, Bolshevik motorcycle, Bolshevik cowlick, Bolshevik dick!" Consuelo shouted, pointing with delight. "I love your Bolshevik dick! How I love it!"

"Just don't tell the General, or Perlita, for that matter, about my Bolshevik dick," Luis said, rolling back toward her, giving a mild smile. He was trying. Consuelo was young and lovely. She refused to accept the stupid and terrifying reality that Luis lived in. He could hardly blame her.

"Your Bolshevik dick glows red! Communist red! Especially when it's hard—just like a dog!" Consuelo said. This one, tan bayunca.

"Yes," Luis said with patient reverence. "My Bolshevik dick is a humble worker in the struggle, but all hammer, no sickle."

This was too much for Consuelo. She shrieked as if she were being murdered.

It was about this time that Graciela began playing dead on the mornings she was to work for the General. Ninfa would come to rouse her, and

Graciela, full of dread, would cross her arms over her chest. She'd seen the pose in a movie—a beautiful ghost laying herself down in an Egyptian tomb. Ninfa would tickle Graciela under the chin and pinch her arm, and she'd pretend to startle awake.

"I'm sick," Graciela said. "I'm feeling faint. I've been throwing up out the window all night." Slowly, miming tremendous effort, Ninfa pointed her lips across the room.

"The car will be here in fifteen minutes." Ninfa lifted Graciela's pillow, and removed her from beneath the blanket, and suddenly Graciela would find herself on the floor, Ninfa stretching the sheets tight over her mattress. The bathtub filled, the room steamed, and as Graciela sank into the water, she collected her thoughts well enough to announce that she was afraid if she went to the palace that morning she would poison the General with her illness and make him so sick that he might die. Ninfa scrubbed Graciela's back with the same even force she applied to filthy guanábanas, and said, her face smooth as a plate, "If only." For an instant her mouth cracked open in a smile. Graciela was the only one in the Estate who saw this smile of Ninfa's. To the others her face was always blank.

Emboldened by Ninfa's smile, Graciela would ask, "Do you want the General to die?" But Ninfa's eyes were shut again.

"Did you have another nightmare?" she asked Graciela.

She would shake her head no and answer yes, knowing that no matter what she told Ninfa, in moments, she'd be headed to the palace.

But on the days that Graciela stayed at the Estate to clean with Ninfa, la viejita would stir piloncillo and canela into the mud pot to make their café de olla.

"What does he say to you?" Ninfa would ask.

Graciela would recite the catechisms: the blood, the waters, the light. It was all so stupid, wasn't it?

"Achis." Ninfa would roll her eyes. "The same old shit. Nothing new!" What did la vieja expect?

Ninfa grinned. "He thinks you're his oracle—why don't you do something useful? Tell him to increase my daughters' wages. Tell him that he should shave his bigotes. Tell him his mother is from the same village I'm from. Tell him to replace those wooden tokens with colones."

But even as she laughed, rolled her eyes, Graciela knew that Ninfa was scared of the General too.

"He's like all men, ¿me entiendes? You see the women coming and going at all hours. Better for you not to be left alone with him. Try to get him to take you to that Society. Better for you to be surrounded by his baboso friends."

Graciela would shrug, embarrassed, but Ninfa just continued.

"Don't let him touch your body," she'd say. "Don't let him lock you inside those rooms. Always find the door with your eyes and be sure you can open it. Or a window."

"I'll be careful," Graciela said, wanting nothing more than to stop talking about this.

"You know, you're a very smart girl. You're a brave girl. And you have the chance to make a lot of people's lives better. He's an impressionable man, mija. You can guide him. Just tell him to do the right things, mija. Tell him to stop being such a pendejada fool, kissing the royal nalgas of all these rich coffee Ladinos."

Graciela smiled at la vieja, wanting to make her happy, but Ninfa didn't smile back. She extended her palm to Graciela across the table, held the girl's hands in her own, which were still warm from the tacita de barro, closed her eyes, and muttered a prayer of protection. And then, too quiet for Graciela to hear, something else, a secret prayer only she ever knew.

The next day, Graciela carried that protection with her into the rooms of the palace, let it remind her of her power, let it buoy her toward bravery.

When the General called for her, Graciela told him new stories, the ones she knew he longed to hear. She told him that if he increased the wages of the workers, his lifespan would increase by one minute for every woman blessed by his generosity, that they would repay him with their devotion. She stroked his vanity, telling him that at home her mother prayed to his image, which she'd torn from a newspaper and taped inside a niche.

This was a lie, of course, but still he needed more. "Were there velitas? And a cross?"

Graciela nodded solemnly. "A vase of holy water too," she said. "No—forgive me—una tacita de barro," she said, editing herself. "The water was blessed by the bishop when he came to the village."

The General nodded. Graciela didn't know if he believed her, but she vowed to keep trying. (She was too late.)

In the afternoon the General sat in the president's upstairs bathtub and asked the usual questions. Easy questions, if you had them memorized, as she did:

Will the General be president?
Is it better to kill a man or an ant? And why?
Can one measure the worth of the soul?
What is the first stage of the soul's transmigration?

"Yes, the General will be president."

"It is a greater crime to kill an ant than a man, for when a man dies, he is reincarnated, while an ant dies forever."

"Yes, one can measure the worth of the soul. The soul, unattached to the body, makes witness to the process of repeated births on earth, by which method a soul grows by experiences, life after life, slowly growing, thereby into wisdom and strength and beauty."

"The first stage of the soul's transmigration occurs when the body is shed. The soul, bound to the brotherhood of souls, rises and falls in age, unmeasured by the body."

The General grinned like a baby as Graciela responded.

"And you see, then, the cosmic patterning?" he continued. "How it all shifts after I assume the presidency? How I am to be the one to collect the wisdom, the beauty, the strength of all of those bright souls? I am the one who will purify our nation, birth it into a new era of supremacy. Like a great mountain born beneath the sea?"

Graciela nodded.

"And really, cherita, there's nothing to be afraid of. Bodies are shed. There's nothing unnatural about that. Bodies die. Perfectly normal." The General paused here, settling into the bath. Graciela found the window with her eyes. She could try to leave again. Maybe tonight. Maybe with Consuelo, who would never forgive her if she tried again to leave without her.

"Bodies die, but souls reincarnate, endlessly, endlessly," the General continued. "In the meantime, we make better and more beautiful the flesh here. The living flesh. ¿Me entiendes?"

Improve the flesh that is still living by making it more beautiful. He was talking about shedding our bodies, our india bodies, from our bright souls—some part of her must have understood this.

"Yes," she said, as she always did. The work was not hard.

On Sundays, the General released Graciela from her duties, and Ninfa would go home to her village, leaving Graciela alone, free to wander into Consuelo's orbit. Consuelo circled Luis and the other graduate students at the art school. Perlita had halted her studies, but Consuelo hung around by the thread of her relationship to Luis, desperate to remain relevant, waiting for him to finish his studies and then elope with her somewhere far away. Las hermanas found Violeta, Maite, Claudia, Luis, and the others by the fountain, and then eventually they'd wander over to one of the cafés near the university: La Lágrima, or El Espejo, or even The Drunken City. They'd settle there for hours, letting their cups of coffee get cool during the rainy part of the day, watching students walking from the library. They remarked on how old they all felt, most of them now in their early twenties, still waiting for some great love or inner genius to reveal itself, deferring to the advice of La Claudia, who was now the art school secretary, unhappily married, a secret poet, and who seemed ancient at thirty-two. They called out to classmates of Luis's, wrote poems together, smoked, and picked at a stale torta one of them would have ordered so as not to get kicked out. Graciela and Consuelo would not return to the Estate until late, giggly and lightheaded, delighted that their small lives could feel so limitless during those long Sunday afternoons. Perlita never asked where they'd been.

One Sunday, they wandered the halls of the art school with Luis. All the gallery doors were locked, but Consuelo pressed her nose against the glass of one.

"This is the one I wanted to show you," she said to Graciela, tapping on the glass. Luis pointed at the long, narrow oil painting resting on an easel inside: a rose emerging from a pile of sparkling white skulls, and a little girl, an india with Graciela's face, pointing at a crescent moon. The girl in the painting was the version of Graciela that had arrived in the capital years earlier—long dark hair in two braids, round brown cheeks, dusty knees beneath a too-tight borrowed dress, and shiny beetle eyes— her little-girl self.

(How the Ladinos always see us. They insist upon this version of us. Why?)

"Is this your painting?" Graciela asked Luis.

"No," he replied. "That's Consuelo's. She's next week's lesson."

Consuelo grinned like she'd lost her mind. La loca, as if she were so different than we were.

A week later, early enough that the heat hadn't yet descended on the hills, Consuelo and Graciela ended up at Luis's studio, giddy with an entire day their own, before them and limitless. Here was the room where Luis worked and slept. Along one wall of the studio were a series of six soft-pencil drawings of a woman's nude body seated at the edge of a tub, a smudge instead of a face. At his desk, just beside the front door, were tools for drawing, sharpening, carving, cutting, shading, and painting, each in a special compartment. In one corner of the room a mattress lay on the floor, a tangle of grayish sheets tossed over it. He had a tiny stove and a kettle for heating water, and an old tub with a plastic curtain around it. Inside this room, Luis had everything a person needed.

Luis was inside when they arrived, setting a rectangular metal box onto a tripod. He turned a crank on the back of the stand and wheeled the metal box to the center of his room. Graciela startled when he spoke.

"You're looking at an object that will transform—no, revolutionize—the world!" Luis said. "Because of this"—he jabbed his finger at the metal box on its stand—"everything in the world is going to change. Art! Politics! Science! Love!"

"Where did you get this thing?" Consuelo said as Luis kissed her on the cheek.

"It's on loan from the university. So we can't break it, all right? Or else Juanmi will have me executed." He grinned. "It's like the ones they use for making films in Hollywood. But this is the first one they've made for rich gringos to use at home."

Luis motioned Graciela and Consuelo over and ran his fingertips over the top of the machine. A glossy black plaque read CINÉ-KODAK in gold letters at the front of the machine, and the same word had been pressed into a wide leather handle at the top. It could be carried like a suitcase. The metal box had three glass circles at the back, a coin-size one for looking through, a medium one that Luis said was the lens, and, beneath that, against the side, the widest circle, which looked to count down the seconds. At the left side of the machine was a lever, which Luis said needed to be turned constantly in order to capture light and movement as the film wound inside.

"It's fantastic," Consuelo said.

"Do you want to see how it works?" Luis asked. "Consuelo, go stand beneath the lights." Consuelo set her purse down on Luis's work desk, opened it, and took out her mother-of-pearl compact and lipstick. She fluffed the front of her hair in the mirror and freshened her blood-colored lips, then minced across the room to pose beneath the lights.

Consuelo knew just what to do. She turned a cartwheel and landed on splayed knees. She clutched her heart with one hand, held her other to her ear, eyes incredulous and wide at the sounds she pretended to hear. Whatever she was listening to, it was getting louder, approaching. A train, and she was tied to the tracks. A monster. An enraged lover. Luis turned the crank.

"You want to try?" Luis said. "Look into this." He pulled Graciela up onto a wooden step stool in front of the Ciné-Kodak and positioned her head in front of the viewfinder. She blinked a few times, catching her eyelashes in the glass, and watched Consuelo, who'd flipped upside down in the machine's eye.

Upside down, Consuelo mouthed horror, screamed silently, clawed at her hair, dissolved into tears, kicked and fought against the floor. Luis took Graciela's hand and, together, they turned the crank.

"Count," Luis said. "It's like dancing. Turn it twice for every second. One two, one two, one two. Got it?" Graciela watched upside-down Consuelo blow kisses. Through the glass, she seemed so far away.

"Okay!" Luis said. "Your turn." Consuelo blew a final kiss and Graciela went dutifully beneath the lights.

"Let me see! Let me see!" Consuelo shouted. She got behind the machine, winked one eye, set the other against the glass, and cranked the wheel.

Graciela squatted like the statue of Simón Bolívar on his horse in the plaza. She winked one eye, and then the other, but she was no good at her left. She played with her hair and stuck out her tongue.

Perlita had taken Graciela to the most boring movie in the world that week. It was five hours long, about a crazy man in Germany who loved to trick people into playing cards with him, full of trains and piles of money. Perlita had hated it and fell asleep almost as soon as it began. But Graciela had watched intently: a beautiful woman was crying into the camera. Words appeared between long, quiet moments of her sad face, and Graciela committed them to memory. The lady was angry with someone very powerful and could not stop talking. Her monologue finally done, she took poison alone in jail, and died.

That night Graciela had gone home and written down all the words of her speech. Now, for Luis's camera, Graciela recalled every word that she'd written in her notebook, replicated every one of the actress's faces during her speech. Trompuda, encachimbada, this was something beyond the familiar pleasure of Graciela's perfect memory, her guayabear.

This was time travel, explosion—the space before her vision went blank as she transformed.

When she was done, Luis removed the machine from the podium and opened it like a book. From its heart he unspooled the film, which shone a coppery gray in his hands. The three of them sat on the nest of blankets in the corner of the room, and Luis turned off the lamps. And then they watched themselves, written in light on the wall, right side up and flickering. Graciela sucked in her breath and clutched Consuelo's warm hand as another Consuelo, all air and pale-gray light, appeared. This Consuelo danced and bowed and winked and flirted, little sparks exploding around her as the film crinkled and popped. She trembled, as she always did.

Then Graciela appeared, widening her eyes and closing them. Luis had brought the camera close up to her face, capturing the shadows there.

"Who he is, nobody knows! He is there! He lives! He stands over the city—huge like a tower! He is damnation and eternal bliss! He is the greatest man who ever lived! And he loved me!"

Consuelo and Luis broke into screams of laughter, but Graciela applauded for herself. Watching her own face on film, well, it pleased her. She beamed inwardly. She was good at this.

The movie over, Luis turned on the lights and Consuelo sent Graciela home. "All right, chérie, you remember your way back to the Estate? Perlita will be expecting you."

Graciela nodded and made her way outside, unable to resist the temptation of standing and listening just outside the window. It was too high off the ground for her to peer inside, but the sounds told her enough to imagine what she might have seen had she been tall enough to look in the room.

She heard the wet sounds of Consuelo and Luis kissing, and the soft sounds their clothing made as the buttons of Consuelo's dress were undone and her bra hit the floor and Luis slipped out of his shoes, and unbuckled his belt and dropped his pants, and she heard all the noises that Lourdes had told us about, noises Lourdes claimed she heard all the time coming from her mother's bed whenever she had a visitor, and sometimes even when there was no man there at all. They were quiet, and then louder, and then very loud, and then quiet again.

Graciela ducked when Consuelo's little hand with its glossy red nails appeared and placed her delicate gold watch on the windowsill. Then Graciela stepped on her tiptoes, reached up, and slid the watch off, ran her thumb over its smooth, pearly face. She dropped it into her pocket. She needed something to hold on to, an opalescent eye to protect her. She could feel it, the world shifting, whatever safety she had in this place slipping away.

15

BY THE END OF 1930, WE WERE ALL JUST NEARLY GROWN. WHEN Cora's blood didn't come when ours did, and then her tetas puffed up and she started complaining of getting tired before the sun was even down, too tired to watch her precious flock of púchica birds return to the ceiba in the evenings, we weren't surprised. She and Héctor fucked about three times a day.

Héctor was delighted by the news—he wanted to get married immediately.

"Vaya, pues. Girl. Just the one plátano for the rest of your life? You're fine with that?" Lucía asked.

"Of course I am," Corita said. But, really, she wasn't sure. She loved Héctor, she wanted this baby, but she also thought about the dozens— who knew, maybe hundreds—of other plátanos that she'd never have the chance to inspect, what it meant for her world to narrow in this way. She'd thought she'd have more time. We all thought we'd have more time.

For María, the news of Corita's pregnancy was a balm. She loved babies, and now another would join us. And she'd no longer be the baby of the group herself; she'd be an auntie. She seized on the news with joy and hope, perhaps especially because she was freshly brokenhearted. The woman from the other side of the volcano was married, and to avoid her husband's suspicions, she had forbidden María, after only two miraculous romps, from ever returning to see her.

"Promise me that you will never call me by name," she'd said. María left and only let herself cry later that night when Lourdes was asleep. But she couldn't stay away from the other side of the volcano, and so lingered at night by Prudencia's fruit stall, took long walks in the forest, aching for this woman.

She spoke to her only once more, after she'd written her a letter and brought it to her door. It was foolish of her, but still she wrote about the woman's tetas, about her pretty eyes, about the moonlight on her skin when they made love. She wrote in the sweeping calligraphy that the nuns had taught her before she was made to leave school to work in the fields, that she practiced after she had left school for exactly this kind of letter. It was stupid of her. She was fifteen.

"Are you crazy?" The woman appeared at the door, seething. She ripped the paper from María's hands. "Get out of here! Do you want to get us both killed?" María reached for her. The woman recoiled, disgusted. She spat on the ground.

María was a few paces away when she heard her spit again and mutter, "Besides, I can't even fucking read!" and María understood that she'd barely known this woman, that she never would. She returned to our side of the volcano, this time unable to hold back her tears.

We were changing, and so was the country. The election was just a couple of weeks away. La Loca Prudencia was in the race, and so was the General, as second-in-command to the president, his old friend El Wimpy Guy.

"Why bother running in the election with him? You already live at the palace," Graciela asked the General, smiling with her mouth soft and open, so that he'd know she was joking.

"Close your eyes," Graciela told El Gran Pendejo. They were sitting at the long table in the palace library; Graciela was about to read the General's cards. She'd stolen Consuelo's tarot deck when she'd sensed the General was hungry for new tricks. He was fond of the readings she gave at the Society, and fonder still when she gave him private readings at the palace.

His fingers trembled over the cards, and she caught him peeking for the Chariot, or the Sun, or his favorite, the Emperor. She knew better than to scold him. She prepared to recite his good fortune, no matter what he drew, but she was impatient, tired of working so hard to pretend, of working so hard when she wasn't pretending. She wanted romance— sex and love and poetry and dancing like La Consuelito—all the things that weren't available to her as she shuttled between jobs.

El Gran Pendejo let his left eyelid flutter and flicked the corner of the top card with his fingernail. The Star. Better than the púchica Pentacles, or the Tower. He'd take it. Graciela whistled out of the side of her mouth, feigning distraction so he could flip it over.

"The Star . . ." Graciela began. "This is an auspicious card," she said, drawing out the word as he liked to hear it.

She'd been tap-dancing for years. She was ready for her life to begin.

We would have freed Graciela if we could. As the election approached, we got most of our information from Héctor. We didn't trust El Wimpy Guy; he was too closely aligned with the General. He did claim that if he won, and if the General won alongside him, he would return our ejidos to us. We'd have our land back. We'd be able to leave the fincas and the colonato, grow our own food again. But it seemed too good to be true. The ricos would never go for it, even the Ladinos, who thought themselves charitable.

Graciela had heard the General speak on the matter herself, at the Society. He'd begun the meeting with an epigram, as was his custom. "It stands to reason that my reason for unreason is certainty!"

Graciela recognized an echo of *Don Quixote* in the General's nonsense. He continued on: "It stands to reason, with certainty, that the campesino is starving, physically, mentally, spiritually, intellectually, economically, globally, culturally, critically, with certainty, he is starving." He rose and paced the room, the casta painting behind him. "How do we bring him into the light, I ask of the brightest minds of nuestro pulgarcito, los patrones del mundo cósmico, I ask of you." The General genuflected, not without great effort, before a trim man in a ruby-red velvet suit and matching beret who was seated at the long oval table beside Graciela.

Aguardiente shone in a crystal decanter. This was unusual. The General never drank, not even in the company of those who did. He never offered the stuff to his guests; he considered it poison. Graciela watched him now, sloshing his drink in the glass. Something was wrong. The General was drunk, seemed to float on another plane. He chattered on, aping El Wimpy Guy's platform for show, talking about the starving campesino and what must be done to save him. Bah! As if he wanted to save a single one of us.

"Communists are infecting the hills!" he said. "Something has to be done."

And what, the General thought, does the idiot president know about that? He shook his head. He was the one in charge in everything but name.

"Have some imagination, some depth!" he whispered urgently, seemingly unaware he was speaking aloud. "Human eyesight is never to be trusted." He finished his drink and glanced at his watch. He laughed to himself, then leaned over and whispered in Graciela's ear. "The moon will be enormous and pink with a golden haze, like a jellyfish. That is when the nation will rise from its slumber," he said.

She stood and repeated the General's words aloud, adding the coda they had practiced earlier: "That is when your star will rise in the waiting sky." The words shook in her mouth.

Back in the village, we lit up the sky with our rage. Someone, some fucking ass-kissing, jealous colono, or the bitch of the finca, or some fucking shithead, had noticed that we weren't starving to death, that we weren't using those púchica tokens at the finca shop. Whoever that comemierda was set the milpa on fire, punishing us for healing our land.

Cora woke up to the smoke in the middle of the night, sore tetas and all, and hiked to the other side of the volcano. She got there at dawn. Our crops were charred to the ground. It was a warning, no doubt. We were supposed to understand the meaning of this act: nothing belongs to you. We were supposed to be afraid, but we were too angry—the fresh-shit stink of the rotten cherries, our milpa up in smoke, María's shattered heart, all of our hungry bellies, and now Cora's baby inside her—our anger choked us.

After the milpa was burned, Lourdes begged Prudencia to use her powers to tell us who did it.

"I wish I could," Prudencia said. "But I see only the future. I can't make any sense of the past." We believed her.

LOURDES: But, listen. The moment I heard Prudencia say those words was the only time I thought she was a fool. At this moment I decided to make myself a student of history, to bridge the past that Prudencia could not make sense of with the future we all dreamed together. A pity that I was murdered just a year later.

At home Cora climbed down the volcano, returning to our village after bringing a bundle of food for Héctor. The path down was easier. Lighter without the delivery of food, and lighter because she had lost the baby. Cora had only just stopped bleeding, and she held her belly with care over the rutted path. They would try again—that's what she and Héctor told each other. There had been no explanation. Rosario, Alba, and Yoli had watched over her from the beginning. Everything was normal, they said, listening to her body, taking a look. And then she woke up with cramping and thick blood that shuddered as it left her.

There were so many rumors of what happened, a year later, after the election, after the coup, when the small rebellion Héctor and his men had been planning began with their descent from the volcano, when Izalco rumbled and smoked. That Héctor and his men had drunk aguardiente until they were blind, then descended into the fincas waving their machetes. That they'd rounded up the women and selected the virgins for a night of ritualistic rape. That at first they'd killed only finqueros, but that then they grew more indiscriminate—animals, children, one another. It's ugly, isn't it? And none of it is true.

All we know is that Héctor did not drink aguardiente ever. And he hadn't read any communist tracts—as far as we know, he didn't know how to read. He'd quit school long before we had. Corita told us that Héctor and the men had planned to raid the finca's company store. They'd planned to take the bulk of the grain that was in storage and use it as leverage to make their demands to el patrón. They would stop work until the ejidos were returned to us, until they received adequate pay for their labor—no more púchica wooden tokens! Until then they'd take the maíz and plant their own food. But by the time they'd descended the volcano, the General's plans had taken root in the capital. He had his parrots in the field, always listening. Invisible eyes everywhere. When El Gran Pendejo got word that the workers' agitation had transformed into action, he would send his men to destroy us.

16

AFTER THE ELECTION, THE GENERAL TOOK GRACIELA TO THE Society of Sacred Letters and Objects again. He was exhausted, he told her, as they walked over. He couldn't sleep. At the end of January 1931, the rich men of the capital had quietly voted for the new president. The votes were being tallied now, but twice that week the election had been ruled a miscount by an accord of the ministries. The General considered himself the only viable candidate, though he was merely the running mate of El Wimpy Guy. "I'm not worried," he said. "The people know what's best." El Wimpy Guy was somewhere—Guatemala, maybe?

Weeks passed without a certain declaration of election results. But that wasn't the cause of the General's insomnia. When he lay down to rest at night, he heard women screaming with laughter. They were mocking him, he was certain of it.

"La Cigua," he said, nodding at Graciela and pointing his lips, as though she were at fault. "There's only one thing to be done about it."

They were alone then, inside the Society. Graciela sat in her place and waited for instruction as the General lit the candles and pulled out a map of their nation and its neighbors.

"What rots here," he said, marking our western coffee lands with an X, "also rots here, and here." He circled the country to our north, and a long thin island in the Caribbean.

"Are you talking about coffee again?" Graciela asked. "Are you worried about the election?" She was prepared to reassure him, hand him the line about his rising star and the moon like a jellyfish.

"No," he snapped, turning on her harshly. "Shut up already about the election. I'm talking about our color. I'm talking about our minds. My friends from Los Yunais say that we're on the precipice of total communist domination, but I know that the future of our blood is safe with me. Have you learned nothing? Are you stupid? The final stages are on the horizon. All there is for me to do is rest. What matters is El Wimpy Guy will be safe in his little castle, and the future of our blood is safe with me."

Graciela hadn't felt his cruelty directed toward her for a long time. *What little castle?* she wanted to ask, but thought better of it, and shut her mouth.

She watched him mash his hands together, flinched as though he were squeezing her between his thumbs.

Weeks later, the election was finally called in favor of El Wimpy Guy. The news was relatively unceremonious, after the long wait. There was a perfunctory radio announcement, followed by a brief, smug uproar of victory from the General's camp.

El Wimpy Guy still had not returned to the country. The General continued to hold court in the palace. Graciela quietly turned eighteen. Her days at the palace had become long, quiet, irritating.

Months passed in stillness, long days in which the library was empty but for Graciela. She had read all of the books that the room contained, some of them twice.

One evening, when the library had grown completely dark, Lidia appeared and told Graciela that the General needed her. Graciela's throat cracked open like a swollen door; she'd been silent all day.

But now, late as it was, the General had been granted a vision, and it couldn't wait until morning.

When she arrived in his chambers, she found him lying on the floor, palms to heaven, belly rising and falling with his breath. This was his posture of receiving.

"Everything is changing," he said from the floor. Graciela nodded her head, waiting to hear what he meant. "My star continues to rise," he said. "And with it, our nation!"

He closed his eyes, searched for the right words. "Do you know where the beauty of this palace is grown? Where our gold is mined? It's the berries. Berry by berry, we become rich. Each berry dies when it's plucked, but it rises again in glory. Each berry contains a memory, a soul, a purpose—to sanctify this house with its noble sacrifice, to resurrect in the palace. Colón by colón, our Palace of Coffee ascends in glory. You know this. You know how coffee is made."

She did, of course. Coffee was made por las nenas—by us—pulling coffee berries from their branches, filling the baskets, carrying them through las faldas of Izalco. Those berries were making somebody rich, sure, but it wasn't us.

"We need to celebrate these treasures of our nation, to honor how beautifully we transform our native resources into glory—and what better way to honor beauty than with a beauty pageant?" he said, opening his eyes and meeting hers. "I'm going to host a pageant and you, Graciela, will compete in it. Arrayed in coffee cherries like a goddess, you will win." Graciela smiled, careful not to betray her smirk.

The General continued: "You will win because you will be the symbol of our future, of what makes this country great: you are the new india, our rising mestiza star. You are our native resource, transformed into glory." He sat up and rubbed his eyes with excitement.

Graciela struggled to find the right words. She'd heard it all before— she was indita, but not too dark, the future of the nation that the General desired. But it was one thing to sit quietly beside the General while he blathered incoherently about cosmic destiny and another to present herself to the whole country as a symbol of his great vision of change. She wanted no part in turning our native resources into glory.

"It can't just be a pageant, though," the General mused, before she could say a word. "We need to spread this message to all—to all of our people, to Los Yunais, to anyone with a stake in the future of our nation's cosmic race! And there's only one way to do that—we'll have to make it into a movie."

LOURDES: And so our Gracielita would star in her first propaganda film.

In the film, the General explained, once the pageant was over, Graciela, La Diosa de Café, would be murdered by a gang of communists, angry, on behalf of all indios, that she'd demeaned herself in this competition. They'd call her a whore, stone her to death on the steps of the presidential palace. Graciela's blood would stain the marble.

"We have to show everyone what these people are like," the General said, his voice shaking as he rose from the floor. "This is where the country rises up to snuff out the pestilent disease of communism. I seize my rightful glory and the fight begins, with your face painted on every shield of our noble army."

"I die?" Graciela asked. "You kill me?"

"You die," the General answered. "But listen carefully: I do not kill you. I set you free. After the election and the film, you'll have completed your transformation. You'll begin a new life," he said.

After all that, what was Graciela to do? She smiled blankly, hating herself for it. The effort she exerted to appear meek and obliging—the blank smile—seemed essential to her survival, but it was a poison too, destroying her. She did dream of a new life, but she wanted it to be entirely her own. She needed to separate her destiny from the General's.

"We begin this week," El Gran Pendejo said. And finally, he dismissed her.

They filmed in the ballroom of the palace, a dusty, windowless cavern trimmed in gold leaf. Graciela had never been inside it before. The General appeared to float off the ground, existing in his own kingdom, or in the land of imagination, his eyes misting and his nose running into his mustache.

Three students were taken out of the university at gunpoint to play the communists. They were about our age, only one of them slightly handsome. But the communists didn't appear until after the beauty contest. While that was being filmed, one of the students managed the camera, which had also been taken from the university, one played the judge, and one, the slightly handsome one, was coaxed into a dress to play one of Graciela's competitors.

In the film, Graciela wore un refajo and a necklace of red beads. The judge, a fishmonger bribed with a bottle of aguardiente, frowned as he announced the victory of La India Bonita Graciela. The other beauty contestants, women lured from their stalls in the marketplace with the promise of a good meal, cursed her scrawny ugliness as the General handed her a bouquet of roses and lilies.

The following day, in the ballroom, the three communists made their big entrance. They ran onstage in those wrinkly white pants, and the handsome one slit Graciela's throat with a machete. The General pulled a machine gun out of his pants and the three communists' hearts exploded. An old-fashioned bloodbath. Graciela played dead all afternoon. The General stumbled on the marble steps as he lifted her limp body, slipped on fake blood, and pitched them both to the ground.

When the film was complete, the students were invited to a celebratory dinner at the palace. Graciela watched their faces across the table, her eyes lingering on one, the handsome one, as their confusion danced into graciousness and then drunkenness over candlelight.

After the film, the General remained in the palace, and the president remained in Guatemala. Graciela listened politely to Ninfa's chatter while they cleaned together, and on other days, she sat, still and flat as a painting in the presidential library.

Late one night at the Estate, Consuelo burst into Graciela's room, crying, waking her sister.

Luis hadn't arrived to meet her the night before, and he hadn't been at the university to teach his class. She was sure he was angry with her because she'd flirted with his friend Juanmi. She pouted.

Graciela had no patience for her sister's bayunquería.

"Please just let me go to sleep! I promise to listen to you in the morning," she said. "There's nothing we can do about this right now."

Graciela fell back into bed. But Consuelo didn't sleep. She sat on the floor of Graciela's bedroom all night, rocking her pale shoulders back and forth, silent and shivering. Something was wrong—she knew it.

Consuelo worried over Luis's disappearance for the next two weeks. At night she'd lay down beside Graciela and smoke through the early morning, building mounds of ash on the pillow. Graciela stayed awake too. She told Consuelo that Luis had probably just returned home to his village to see his parents. Maybe he was sick. Maybe he'd quit his job at the university and simply didn't want to tell anyone. She didn't really believe any of this. Something felt wrong, but she wanted to remain hopeful for Consuelo's sake. (Had Consuelo asked the others—Las Rositas, Juanmi? *Of course I did, don't be stupid.*)

"There must be something I'm forgetting. Some clue, some message, some way to find him," Consuelo said.

Graciela watched Consuelo's distress grow and felt el susto pounding in her chest, that sense that she'd slipped from one reality into another but was far from knowing how to navigate this new world safely.

17

GRACIELA WAS WORKING WITH NINFA TO SCRUB THE TILES OF the kitchen floor. Perlita's childhood friend La Lindita Domínguez would be arriving for a visit the following day, and Perlita wanted the house to be immaculate. As she and Graciela cleaned, Ninfa sang along with the radio, the same heavy hum for every song.

Luis was still nowhere, and Consuelo was in a foul mood, out most days and nights. Perlita had told Graciela to make herself scarce too, once Lindita was there—Lindita didn't know she existed, and Perlita intended to keep it that way. If Graciela was seen by Lindita, she was to pretend to be a servant.

LOURDES: And yes, this is that Domínguez, the wife of my papi, the mother of the half sisters María and I never met. A country this small, we're all connected.

And then the music stopped, and the General's voice came onto the radio. Graciela and Ninfa stopped to listen. Serenely, he announced his victory, his sudden ascent to the presidency:

"In the utter darkness of last night, El Wimpy Guy was proven a traitor. He was swiftly expelled by our dauntless militia. I am here. You are now hearing the voice of your president. All prophecies have been fulfilled. I have stepped in to right the wrongs, to undo the deceptions and betrayals, to reinvigorate the land and its blessed people. I am the only one who can protect you in this delicate time. The forces around me have signaled their blessing. I sign off, with eternal tenderness, as your president."

Graciela's body went cold; her teeth began to clack in her mouth. Reflexively, she began to mutter a repetition of the General's words, then stopped herself. She was a malfunctioning machine.

"El Gran Pendejo," Ninfa hissed. She glanced over at Graciela and, seeing her terror, placed a hand on her back. "Don't tell me you're surprised?" she said, smirking. "It's not like anything will change."

No, Graciela wasn't surprised that the General had seized the presidency. He'd been at work on that for so long, it seemed. But this was only the beginning. Harm was coming, she was certain of it.

LOURDES: It was a quiet little coup, this one. In case it wasn't clear already, El Gran Pendejo believed El Wimpy Guy was on the wrong track. He'd promised to return the land to us, for one. And anyway, El Gran Pendejo was never going to be content as vice president. So he rallied the national army to assembled his theater of war outside the palace. El Wimpy Guy, visiting for a dinner that weekend, slipped out through the courtyard in his piyamas. He hadn't been planning on staying long anyway. He and his wife much preferred their home in Guatemala. They would remain there. If he fought the General on this one, he knew he'd only inflame his wild imagination. Bah, let the baby have its bottle! El Wimpy Guy was an old man. There were no principles or positions more important to him than his own safety.

MARÍA: El Gran Pendejo's only problem now was his old friend Los Yunais. They refused to legitimize his presidency, because he'd taken the role by force, and he determined to change their minds.

CORA: He felt, of course, that the coup was just a technicality. He'd been the freely elected vice president, and in the absence of the president, he had every right to assume the role. It would have happened anyway. "My reign was foretold by the ancients," he whispered, alone in the palace.

LOURDES: It didn't matter what he thought. El Gran Pendejo was illegitimate, a bastard without the recognition of Daddy Yanqui he so dearly craved.

LUCÍA: The only solution was to do a little tap dance for them, prove himself to them, someway, somehow. And what did they have in common? They all hated the communists.

LOURDES: La Prudencia never had a chance!

It wasn't long after the General's coup that Graciela returned from a day at the palace to find the front door of the Estate shattered. Sparkling frosted glass, like flakes of bone, all over the marble of the foyer. Perlita sat in the courtyard.

"You should know something," Perlita said without meeting Graciela's eyes. "Consuelo's painting teacher had an accident and was found dead today. Luis." She paused over his name, as if trying to remember it. "He was a communist, and his comrades pulled him out of Lago Coatepeque." She fiddled with her bracelets, still looking over Graciela's shoulder. "And also: Consuelo will be leaving us soon. She's lost her soul and is no longer welcome in this home."

Graciela begged Perlita to tell her what she meant—where was Consuelo going? But Perlita just waved her hand, said only that she wanted nothing to do with a communist sympathizer. She wanted nothing to do with a violent, classless whore. According to Perlita, when she'd told Consuelo that Luis was dead, Consuelo had gone mad.

"You remember that vase? That table?" she asked Graciela, who nodded politely. "She destroyed them when she lost her mind. She's lucky that I stopped her from killing herself. She owes me."

La Lindita had arrived by then for her visit and now was napping in an upstairs bedroom. Perlita was furious, mortified, that Consuelo had made this terrible scene in front of her friend, as if to spite her.

Upstairs, Graciela found Consuelo in her room. She ran to her, but

Consuelo stiffened, shook, growled like a panther, and pushed Graciela to the ground.

That night, and for most of the few remaining days before she left the Estate, Consuelo did not speak. There was a bandage on her arm, blood-soaked white cotton, a map of red tracing the length of her inner arm, wrist to elbow; there was a cut beneath her eye. Graciela brought her food that she silently refused to eat. She also refused to leave the room, and the air filled with the soft, wet stink of her wound and her misery.

Luis's parents came down to the capital from el campo, chewing coca leaf, with square, wrinkled faces and dusty clothes. They arrived at Luis's studio and began to collect his things—each fine tool that once had belonged to Luis's art strange in their old, tiny hands. We recognized the rough purple of his mother's fingers as the mark of someone who'd spent the early part of her life working indigo, making her ancient.

The viejitos made arrangements for Luis's body to be cremated, despite Catholic rites, and they left town immediately after he'd been transformed into ash.

La Claudia, meanwhile, wrote a poem to honor him, with lines about blind hovering angels and an endless flow of blood.

Consuelo, jealous that Claudia had the words for a loss that she felt belonged to her, was enraged when Maite used the university's letterpress to set and print the poem to share with their circle after Luis's death.

"If you see any of those amateur poems around, taped to bus stops or what have you, do me a favor and tear them to tiny shreds," Consuelo hissed at Graciela, the first words she'd spoken in days.

Consuelo was Chasca now, the princess who drowned herself after her lover's death. She looked and looked for water to take her. But while the water didn't take her then, someone else did. Consuelo was disappeared from the Estate in the middle of the night, by someone—no one seemed to know who.

CORA: Lindita and Perlita sipped tea in the courtyard the morning
       after Consuelo was taken, chattering beside the birds. The

ocelot snored in a circle of sunlight. Graciela greeted them on her way to the palace, not knowing her sister was gone. But that evening, when she returned to the Estate, she realized that Consuelo wasn't there.

"She's left for her trip abroad," Perlita said. "I told you about this!" She smiled and pointed her lips for Graciela to refill Lindita's glass of sherry. The women were sprawled now on the couches inside the house, a mess of discarded food around them on the floor. Perlita had told Graciela that Consuelo was no longer welcome and would be leaving—this was true. But where was she? Why hadn't she said goodbye? Would she ever return?

"Studying painting—the lucky girl!" Lindita smiled.

Graciela looked to Perlita, who said nothing, merely shrugged. She wouldn't meet Graciela's eyes.

LUCÍA: The susto that had been emerging within her became the beating of her chacalele. She tasted it with every breath. Where was her sister?

18

THE GENERAL'S CHAUFFEUR, JOSÉ, RAN OFF FOR GOOD WHEN he received the order to take the girl from the Estate. He couldn't stomach it. He'd come to terms with driving women out of the palace and back to their whorehouses or their concrete block rooms on the edge of town, once the General was done with them. But those women, at least, had entered the palace on their own two legs. He'd never been summoned to apply any force. And the General planned to keep this girl. So, after receiving the order, José had washed and polished the car, left the keys in the ignition, and begun the journey to his village on foot.

The heat of the day rose as he walked, the streets swelling with the morning crush of workers. He told himself that he'd find another job. He'd return to the coffee fields. He'd work as a night watchman at his cousin's bar. In the days after the General had taken the palace, the air in the capital had shifted. Working as his man felt dangerous to José; despite what he'd stolen, the General wasn't satisfied. He seemed more insecure than ever, awaiting recognition from Los Yunais, demanding constant vigilance from his small staff. José hadn't been given leave to go home in over a month. Now he could take care of his grandfather, whose eyes had filmed over with cataracts, whose remaining teeth clattered in his mouth as he spoke.

José was replaced the morning he left, by a man whom the General plucked out of the crowd in the plaza. The man sold ruffled newspapers, days old—weeks old, sometimes. He looked both pliable and strong—his weak jaw, his eyes that lacked a precise focus, his broad back.

El Gran Pendejo approached him and began to describe the position. The man shoved one of his old papers at him reflexively, without looking up to see who was speaking to him, and El Gran Pendejo batted it away like a cat.

"Listen to me," he said. If he was willing, the old-newspaper man could become the new president's go-to man. He would drive a long, polished car. He would take all orders without question, secure the bodies of necessary subjects for questioning, or for what-have-you, with discretion. He was to think of himself as Helios and his chariot, faithfully bringing light to the world. He would be paid richly for his efforts.

"Are you willing?" El Gran Pendejo asked, producing a small medal from his pants pocket—a throwaway thing, made of nickel and cheap satin; it had belonged to El Wimpy Guy. "Will you earn my devotion with your honor?" he asked.

The man shuffled to his feet, dropping the rest of his papers. "My Lord," he said, saluting the heavens as the General pinned the medal to his sweaty cotton shirt.

That night, the new man had entered the Estate through the front door, which Perlita had left unlocked for him, and retrieved the girl inside, as he'd been told to. She was light in his arms, dirty and bedraggled. She struggled against him, but weakly, kicking barefoot, shouting with barely any voice at all. No one would hear her. No one would help her.

The new man looked at Consuelo, at the bandage on her arm, at her wide nose, at the hatred in her eyes. What was a prieta like this, darker than him, doing here? Shoving her into the backseat of the car, he watched her open her mouth to bite him like a dog and he slapped her across the face, hard. She put up no fight after that.

LOURDES: Ay, buzo, Yina. Cuando vos vas, yo ya vengo. This is where we refuse to tap-dance. To entertain.

MARÍA: But we won't turn away either. Silence is for cobardes, hermana.

CORA: As the car entered the center of the capital, Consuelo wondered if she was being taken to the train station, if she was finally going home. But then they stopped in front of the palace, where the General was now the official Gran Pendejo, and she felt herself being dragged out of the car by her wrists and ankles. A little bit of fire caught within her again, and she kicked and screamed, hoping her sister might be inside and hear her.

LUCÍA: But Graciela was asleep back at the Estate. The new man carried Consuelo up the stairs, then tied one end of a rope around her waist, the other around the doorknob of El Gran Pendejo's bedroom. Consuelo tried to run for it, but because of the rope, she just swung the door open. The rope burned her belly and sides as it tethered her in place. She bled all along her ribs. The wound on her arm had reopened under the bandage. She screamed, swinging open the door, letting it slam against the wall, punishing her middle with the rope, raining plaster. She kicked her legs against the wall.

MARÍA: The new man left Consuelo there, afraid that he'd summoned the devil with his obedience. In his new room in the servants' quarters, his hands shook. He lit a candle and prayed. He had a daughter around Consuelo's age, but still . . . He knew he wouldn't leave this job. He was a coward, and he no longer recognized his ugly face.

CORA: There was just enough give in the rope for Consuelo to lie down on the floor outside El Gran Pendejo's bedroom door. Eventually she stopped screaming. There was no reason for it.

MARÍA: That's how the fucker found her. Asleep in the hallway until she heard his footsteps. She knew she wouldn't be able to escape so she played dead, slowing her breathing until her

chest didn't move. But she was his reward. He squatted down
and whispered in her ear:

"The petals of your lips are fine, but no rose your legs entwine." The
very epigram he'd used to insult her father, Germán, years earlier.

He knew Consuelo was alive; of course he did. He could see the life
in the body of any small animal. He knew what it was to die. Este baboso.

LOURDES: Not just an idiot, a púchica monstruo.

LUCÍA: I don't want to, but I'll tell what happened next. He fucked
her there in the hallway with his hand over her mouth.
"You're filthy," he said into her ear. She tried to bite down on
his hand, but he held her jaw open. "Not even a virgin. I can
tell," he said. And indeed Consuelo was not a virgin, but still
what he was doing hurt, it hurt in a way that Luis never had,
like fire pressing into her stomach. She shut her eyes.

LOURDES: When he was done El Gran Pendejo took from his waistcoat
the knife that he'd begun carrying with him at all times. He
sawed the rope off the doorknob, holding on to the side that
was tied to Consuelo's body. He stood and dragged her, still
on the ground, across the hallway and into the bathroom.
The moon hung heavy in the window. On a shelf above the
tub were bottles containing his sacred waters, and their glass
shifted and chimed when he slammed the door closed. He
locked her inside.

Later, Consuelo awoke in the tub. Time had stopped. She didn't know if
it was day or night. She didn't eat, drink water, or register the urge to pee
or shit.

Earlier, she'd vomited on the floor. Enough time had passed for it to
dry, for the smell to have become an unremarkable note in the stale air
she breathed.

She considered climbing out the window, not to escape her circumstances, to enter a life of her choosing, as she'd been doing at the Estate for years, but to leap toward the end of all circumstances. How beautiful that would be, she thought, to have no earthly tether—no mother, no Gran Pendejo torturer, no dead love to mourn forever. To be a particle of dust. To be nothing.

But even this, even lifting her head and climbing out of the tub, opening the window and gathering the scattered parts of herself on the sill, rocking back and forth on her heels until she'd collected the solidity and momentum to allow herself to fall—this seemed an impossible amount of effort.

She remained in the tub. Perhaps instead she could die this way.

MARÍA: At some point, maybe the next day, maybe later that night, El Gran Pendejo returned with a key, and it happened again. This is when Consuelo left her body.

LOURDES: Let me explain. Each time that he returned, Consuelo suffered. She cried for Luis, for Graciela, for her mother, for someone to find her. It was too painful for her to stay inside her body, so she floated to the corner of the room above the window and looked down. But seeing herself, her torturer, this was torture too. Her spirit left the dark bathroom where her body lay beneath El Gran Pendejo, went through the opening at the center of her misery, to the dark forest of our childhood.

Consuelo drifted between worlds—this is how she survived.

In the other world the light behind the trees swelled and then dimmed. Her great-grandmother beat the shuttle of her loom twice. Three-year-old Consuelo sat on the ground, between las faldas of the ceiba, watching. "It's getting late," her great-grandmother said, standing on tiptoe to unfasten the lasso cords wrapped around the ceiba's thick trunk with two deep-purple fingers, holding the rest of the loom taut in the other hand. She gathered the palitos, the chocoy, and la aguja—the long wooden needle—then lined up each thread on the bottom stick and rolled the loom toward her body, tucking it into the cincho at her waist, patting it to make sure everything was there.

The old woman squatted at the base of the tree and rubbed Consuelo's cheek. "You're tired," she said, as if she could tell by the child's softness. "Come here."

She lifted Consuelo up from under her arms. Consuelo rested her cheek on her great-grandmother's shoulder and allowed her eyes to close, lulled by la viejita's soft footfalls as she made her way through the forest in the dark. There was no path, but she knew each step by heart. The old woman hummed and rubbed her back with her fingertips.

She was right: Consuelo was tired.

She woke again in the tub, back in this world, her body pulsing with pain, a band of fire around her belly where the rope was still tied. She focused her eyes on a spider dropping her silks down from the ceiling. The spider wove a trap and then curled her legs around a shiny black ant, squeezing until she was satisfied. Consuelo shifted in the tub to rest her cheek against the porcelain. She was cold, freezing cold.

She returned again to the forest of her childhood. She returned to its soft opening, entering the canopy between the heavy trees. She watched the muscles of her great-grandmother's back beat in time with the chocoy of the loom. Her great-grandmother handed her the threads, bright-blue cotton. Here, she said, guiding Consuelo's little fingers to the weft. Under and through, she said. Her great-grandmother's hands were so soft, despite their years of indigo. Consuelo missed her own softness, wondered if she might ever find it again.

19

EARLY IN THE MORNING, ON THE SECOND DAY AFTER CONSUELO had disappeared, Perlita got into a car. A hired chauffeur carried two large suitcases and loaded them into the trunk. Lindita was already inside, smoking. By the time Graciela came downstairs to work with Ninfa, the car had driven away from the Estate, vanishing as it descended the hills into the capital's center.

Ninfa sat waiting for Graciela at the dining table, a burlap sack beside her, bulging with everything she cared to take with her from the servants' quarters, where she'd spent most of her adult life. She'd made café de olla from yesterday's leftover.

"I have something to tell you," Ninfa said. Graciela prepared to hear that her sister was dead. What else could it be? This heaviness, this terror that she'd been living inside of? She gripped the edge of the table to steady herself.

"Perlita sold your sister to El Gran Pendejo to pay off a debt. She got herself a ticket to Costa Rica too."

"Consuelo's at the palace?" Graciela asked. She sat. She'd been at the palace all day yesterday, sitting in the library in silence until she was dismissed. She hadn't even seen the General, who'd been mopey and short-tempered since becoming president. "Is she alive?" she asked.

"I made her tell me where she sent her," Ninfa said, ignoring Graciela's question. "Late last night. Perlita cried like a little girl, and I almost wanted to comfort her. But she sold that nenita to El Brujo like a piece of furniture." Maybe because for much of Perlita's life, Ninfa had been the closest thing she had for a mother, Ninfa had believed that Perlita, at her core, was not capable of forsaking a child the way she had Consuelo. "I'm done with this fucking fufurufo bullshit. I quit. I'm going home to be with my family."

"I'm going to get her from the palace," Graciela said.

"Don't," Ninfa cautioned. One dead girl, she believed, was better than two. "You haven't seen what that man does to his enemies."

"I have to. And besides, he's probably still asleep—he's perezoso, pero perezoso." Graciela stood. She needed to find her shoes. If she left now she could be there in an hour, forty-five minutes if she ran. What else? Her toothbrush, stupidly. Consuelo's tiny gold watch. A knife, if she could find one.

"Listen to me," Ninfa said. "You're bien smart. Smart enough to know that if you go, and if you find her, you don't come back here. You can't come back here."

Graciela knew that Ninfa was right. There was no safety for her in the capital if she defied both Perlita and the General.

"And if you're going to leave, you're going to need money."

Graciela shook her head. Money? She wasn't going to take Ninfa's money. But Ninfa reached into the burlap sack and took out a pair of silk stockings. She held them up to the light and pointed her lips—each leg was clotted with pisto, rolls of bills buckling the transparent fabric.

Graciela cackled. "No me jodas, Ninfa. Did you rob a púchica bank?"

Ninfa gave a sideways smile and removed a knife from her belt. "These are Perlita's stockings," she said. She began slicing them in half, splitting the legs. "And this is Perlita's pisto." Ninfa tossed a leg of cash across the table to Graciela, who gathered it in both hands.

"Impressive, no? I've been saving up." Now Ninfa cackled. "It's not her money, really. It came from the land. From the people who work on it. And the rest she borrowed," Ninfa said. "So I borrowed it back. It only took me a few months, poco a poco, you see. You know how she never trusted the banks." She swept the runner off of the table and expertly folded the leg of cash inside it, then wrapped la tela around Graciela's shoulders and back, tying the ends tight like a rebozo.

"You won't see me again," Ninfa said to Graciela, her cheeks wet with tears.

"I hope I do," Graciela said. She embraced la maitra. Another life was being born in this moment; her stomach, her chacalele, her eternal, memorious mind, they shifted and crashed within her like the ocean and mountains remaking the world.

"Diocuarde, cherita," Ninfa said. "Go now, before I lose my mind. I've got to find my way out of this monstrous place too. Diocuarde." The old woman passed Graciela her knife to take with her.

Graciela left the Estate. She couldn't bear to turn around and say goodbye again to Ninfa. She walked stiff with terror. The leg of cash had taken on its own heat and gravity as it pressed against her body, a pressure like a deepening body of water. When she arrived at the end of the street, she patted the waist of her refajo: toothbrush, watch, knife. She gave a little scream, a necessary release, because she had no tears. And then she took off running.

The door to the General's quarters was open, and despite the fact that it was midmorning, the room was swimming in candlelight, a hot haze of queasy golden flames and hundreds of candles, their clustered bodies dripping over each surface, wax pooling on the carpet. The General was awake, sitting at his desk, which faced the doorway where she stood. He'd covered the mirrors behind him with black cloth that shone transparent and indigo in the firelight.

"The communists have given me a great gift," the General said, showing his eyeteeth like a movie vampire. "Their little revolt has forced me to retaliate! And now I get to show everyone I mean business. I get to show my friends in Los Yunais just how strong I am." He slapped his desk. Graciela hadn't seen him so energized for months. She wasn't sure she'd ever seen him so happy.

"Where is she?" she said. "Where's my sister?"

"Tomorrow we begin the victory lap!" the General said. He looked over her shoulder, into the distance. "My men have been given their orders. Tomorrow we clean our beautiful volcanoes! We rid them of the traitors."

He studied Graciela's beautiful face, as if seeing it for the first time.

"Don't misunderstand me, though. I won't hurt you, of course. I'd never hurt you," he said. "But the dark ones, the filthy ones, you know those indios. We'll wipe those traitors away, wipe those communists away like dust."

Graciela understood then that when she left this place, she'd need to run fast, not just from him, but to us. We were the traitors; we would be dust. "Is she alive?" she asked.

"But those ants, they will reincarnate—lighter, brighter," the General said, rising from his desk, ignoring her. As he walked toward her, raising his arms like the lamb of god, revulsion filled Graciela's chest. Where was her sister?

"Did you kill her, hijueputa?" Graciela said. She'd never spoken to the General in this way. She'd never spoken to anyone in this way. Rage crowded out her fear.

The General's open hand landed on the cavern of her left eye, knocking her to the ground. Small, colorful lights crowded her vision. Dizzy, bright souls. She nearly laughed. Her cheekbone and temple throbbed; a screeching sound rose in both her ears. From the floor, Graciela looked up at his stunned, soft face, his wet-petal eyes. His smile was jubilant now.

Both of her caites had slipped off her feet. She held her hot face with one hand and grabbed a shoe with the other, brought herself to standing again. With tremendous effort, she threw the caite at El Gran Pendejo, right in the huevos. He buckled, folding in two, and moaned.

She'd bought some time, but only a moment, just enough for El Gran Pendejo to mourn his wounded balls while she escaped to the long hallway outside. Door after blank door, she called her sister's name as she ran.

Consuelo, that little cloud of ajuate. Agárrala al suave, Consuelo had been telling herself. Al suave. Maybe he'd kill her soon and it would be over. Al suave. But then she heard Graciela's voice. And pues, buzooooo, that broken little chacalele of hers started up again. She climbed out of the tub and pounded on the bathroom door.

The key was still in the lock, above the rattling handle. In the hallway, Graciela's hands shook as she turned the key and opened the door, and Consuelo, looking like a sack of utter shit, fell into her arms. Graciela propped her up and they ran toward the door, out to the plaza.

The mosquitoes hummed, ascending into the humid sky. Graciela and Consuelo ran barefoot through the capital, devising a rough plan as they darted through the streets, through the gathering crowd of workers selling fruit, polished knives, and newspapers. They'd find the train station, go to the village, and then they'd disappear, to Los Yunais. Los Angeles, San Francisco, somewhere. Wherever the next boat was going.

"I have enough money for us all to get out," Graciela told Consuelo.

Consuelo didn't ask how. Nothing made sense to her anymore; she wasn't even sure how she was still alive. Was she alive? Or was she dreaming again? She drifted, floating away from her bruised body.

The sky had turned a thick black with coming rain. Neither of them knew where they were. The clouds cracked open, and they were soaked in minutes. The streets had begun to flood with rainwater, garbage skimming the surface, and they slowed, desperate and aimless now, their lungs aching, holding hands like niñas. Around any corner one of the General's men could be waiting to throw them into the back of a car. But just as Graciela began to cry, a dog, a cadejo, darted in front of them, a flash of white fur. Graciela yelped and pulled her sister's arm, and the sisters followed the cadejo down a narrow alleyway, let it lead them right to the train station.

20

L AS HERMANAS RETURNED TO THE VILLAGE FILTHY, EN GUIN-
da. We were in the fields, finishing up for the day. We saw Graciela
come running to us, calling our names, dragging behind her a tall girl
who looked like maybe she was a skeleton.

It had been nine years since we'd seen Graciela, and her hair was still
tangled in all the same places as before. We screamed and embraced her,
uncertain she was real. On her cheek a fresh bruise was ripening. The
skeleton-girl stood beside her, half-useless, staring—at us, at the finca
house, at the volcano and the field, at the winding paths along the
horizon.

"Mi hermana mayor," she told us. "La Consuelo."

The skeleton-girl grinned and started to cry. Loud whoops and
whines, her eyes shifting crazily around in her head. She rocked back and
forth on her bare heels and hummed some deranged melody. What was
wrong with her, this wannabe-chelita in a torn lace dress? We didn't yet
know all that she'd run from.

We didn't laugh, though, tender bichas that we are—Lucía ran to find
Corita and Lourdes, and María took Consuelo by the hand, walked her
and Graciela to the shade of the ceiba, where they sat and waited for the
others to arrive. María took her tobacco out of the front pocket of her
striped overalls and rolled three cigarettes. She drew circles on Consuelo's back, and Consuelo seemed to settle. Our mothers had comforted us
this way when we were babies.

Soon, Lourdes, Corita, and Lucía arrived, screaming, en carcajadas, throwing their arms around Graciela and la calavera Consuelo. Above us, the branches filled with birds. All that love from when we were girls was back, surging around us, deepening the color in our cheeks. But happy as we were, seeing them in such a state—we knew something was wrong.

Graciela exhaled smoke and explained what was coming next, why we needed to gather our mamis and leave immediately.

"Aren't you hungry?"

"You two want a bath?"

"What the fuck?"

These are the questions we asked of them.

La calavera said again and again, "She's right. Mi hermanita is right."

Graciela told us that she had enough money to take us north, money for all of us.

"But we've got to leave tonight," she kept saying. We'd go to Hollywood. Apparently this was Consuelo's idea. We snorted. Hollywood? ¡Qué glamour! Couldn't we go somewhere closer? Tegucigalpa? Mexico City, even? Consuelo, this mystery before us. Consuelo, who hardly spoke, who refused to eat the food we offered her. She drank coffee, smiling with chattering teeth, then stood to go throw up under the ceiba, barely wiping her mouth afterward.

"Tell your mamis," Graciela said. "Help them pack."

"They won't go—those cachimbonas will hide in the trees with machetes, slice the head right off any fool who comes to the door," we told her. We sat and studied her face. "Miren que," we told her. "We won't be able to go anywhere tonight. Look, it's dark already. Let's get some rest. We can leave in the morning." These are the things we said.

"Gather your things," she said.

"Rich girl, you're dreaming—you know we don't have shit," we said, laughing.

"Say your goodbyes."

"Goodbye to who? We'll go together. Become güerita movie stars en el norte. Tear us out of this life, please. My hero! My prince!"

"Fine. Tomorrow, then," she said.

"Tomorrow," we said. An adventure, we thought. We couldn't understand that Graciela was telling us to run for our lives.

That evening our mamis—Yoli, Rosario, and Alba—circled around Graciela and her skeleton-sister. We could see how much they'd aged in Graciela's eyes.

They remembered Consuelo, even if we did not. "You were just a baby," they kept saying, and Consuelo softened. She let Alba and Rosario comb out her hair.

None of them had seen Socorrito for days, and as for Graciela's plan to leave and take us all with her, they just laughed. They asked if she'd lost her mind in the capital, drinking all that colorful water the General talked about on the radio.

"Bolsheviks?" Rosario made a face like we'd spat on her. "Like a little old Russian man?"

"We're a bunch of old women. What the fuck do they want with us? I'm not a spy!" Yoli clapped her hands and cackled.

"I don't have the energy to go to Hollywood," Alba said. "My back will finally give out and I'll die in transit, like a fucking beetle." More carcajadas.

"Seriously, though, Graciela. What's going on? Did you lose your mind?"

We took Graciela by the hand and left, tried to look for her mother, whom we'd seen just a few days before, in the market, or on her patio, or something. We took Graciela to the huge house on the hill where Socorrito lived with her new gringo husband. We knocked on the door, looked in the windows, pushed one open, and climbed inside from the patio. The house was empty.

We looked to Graciela's face for her reaction, but she was blank as paper. She told us again that there was no time to waste. Fine. We had no reason not to believe her, despite how crazy she sounded. We'd go with her. Enough of el colonato. What did we have here to lose? We descended the hill to rest. We would leave first thing in the morning.

.   .   .

That night Graciela and Consuelo stayed with Cora. Graciela told Cora
again that El Gran Pendejo was as serious as he was crazy, that we needed
to believe him when he said he'd wipe us away like dust. Lately, Corita
had been lying awake all night, her head spinning with grief for her child,
wondering where her husband was. She'd fall asleep at dawn and be awoken moments later to begin the day of cleaning and praying and lighting
candles. She was glad now for the company.

"So they'll kill us all to get to you. Is that right?"

Graciela was quiet.

"They know where you're from. Won't they just come here looking
for you? Have you thought about leaving?" Cora was rubbing her belly,
though her baby was already gone.

"He'll kill us all to kill us all. It's not just me they're after," Graciela
finally said.

Cora began to cry then. How much more would be taken from her?

Graciela reached for her hands. "We'll find our own safety," she said.
"We'll be able to start over, all together."

Above us, Izalco was awake, hissing, ash choking the volcano's throat,
filling our eyelashes, our hair, flaking on our hands, through the final
hours of our lives, claiming us.

21

LOURDES: The plan had been to leave on the first train the next day. Lucía and I stayed up late into the night. La Güerita del Norte was on the radio in the sorting room, singing a new song about a wild woman. January was the planting season, but the rot of last summer's ripe cherries lingered in the building, smelled up my hair all the time. When this song came on the radio, Lucía and I started dancing, kicking up our legs, laughing and shrieking like bichitas. It didn't matter how much noise we made, we figured—the patrón was passed out inside la finca house, and his bitch of a wife never came down here.

When those men burst in the door, we were still dancing, Lucía and me. Gray uniforms, about our age. They didn't know shit, I could tell just by looking at them, their soft baby chins and hard stupid eyes.

"Are you lost?" I said. I wanted to get us all in trouble, all the time. I could never shut my mouth. Why was that? Why did I touch the balls of the tiger every chance I got? Was I an idiot or brave? Or punishing myself for something I couldn't remember? "Turn up the radio, Lucía," I called to her, but I didn't dare shift my gaze from the men back her way. My voice was shaking, I could hear it. "These boys are here for the party!" I said, trying to pin my voice to a laugh. What the

fuck did they want with a pile of rotting fruit and a couple of
inditas, anyway?

"Can I get you a café con leche?" I said, pointing my lips
at la güerita Lucía. They didn't answer me, and Lucía was silent, back in her dark corner. They raised their guns.

"Bang. Bang-bang, you're dead!" I said, firing with my
fingers. The men held their guns steady, one pointed at me,
and the other in the corner where the radio played "La Llo-
rona." "Two guns, no dicks," I heard myself say, and then I
started to laugh, helplessly, my breath coming hard.

An angry noise, smoke. I watched Lucía fall backward
from the corner of the sorting room into the light, right onto
the mat of unripe, discarded berries. Blood soaking out of
her scalp like long red hair.

And I must have been dreaming then, because I grabbed
the shirt collar of the one still pointing a gun in my face,
pulled him to me, and said, "Dance with me, pendejo!"

LUCÍA: Just before I went, I saw her. Out the window, La Consuelo,
la calavera, standing outside the convent. Her eyes met mine.
She saw the men surrounding us, and then she looked away,
ran down the stairs of the convent into the basement.

I knew it would be painful. I closed my eyes and there I
was in the lines of the song, drowning, hopeless, lost.

The men chose me first.

MARÍA: Before it happened, I watched the horizon, preparing myself
to leave, trying to decide if I cared to join el bayunco of my
sister and La Lucía in the sorting room. I watched our volcano and I saw the shape of the men, coming over the hills. I
didn't hear them; I saw them through a dark veil of night,
moving through the hills in formation, switching direction,
getting closer. The pattern like rain beating over a lake's surface. Specks in the distance, grit at the bottom of a cup, and

then, when they got closer, an army of stiff-backed men carrying guns. They approached, their darkness clustering and filing, fanning out, moving tightly toward la finca.

But what would they want with me? I wasn't a communist. Everyone was talking about communists those days, on the radio, in the market, but I kept my head down. Cora's man—he was somewhere out in the hills, king of the Indios. I always told her to shush about the revolution when we were in the market. She, of all people, smart as she was, should have known better.

The dark shape got closer, and one body broke off, started up the hill where I was standing. I dove into the chicken coop to hide.

The man who was about to shoot me stood outside the coop, waiting. I watched his fingers tapping, one by one, against the dingy gray cotton of his right pant leg, counting five, ten, fifteen. He squatted down and crawled on his hands into the coop. The chickens flapped their wings and sent hay and shit and feathers into the air. He took a long look at me with his wet green eyes. This was a mistake; he'd been given the wrong orders. The shape of his bullet as it entered my body was the shape of his eyes and the shape of the tears inside of them, and the same shape of the egg forgotten in the coop, which opened and spilled its golden cloud. As I died, I watched the shape of his body: bent in half, hands on knees, heaving bile into the straw, sweating through the gray cotton back of his uniform shirt. How he cried.

I was sixteen years old.

CORA: I never meant to be a nun, but after I lost the baby, Sister Iris invited me to spend some time at the convent. They paid me what they could, and I was happy for the meals, the quiet of their company. I cooked for them and shopped for them. Feed the body, feed the spirit. That's what Sister Iris used to mutter when I'd return from the market, heaving a basket of masa, or when she'd slurp rum before dinner, chewing cacao seeds whole and spitting the flaky shells between swigs.

I told myself that I was getting stronger. But I felt like shit, and I was still deciding if I would end up staying. Sister Iris listened to the radio late at night and sent packages off with that boy who hung around. I recognized him from when I was living with Héctor, before he left for Izalco. Sister Iris had always been kind to me, and though we never talked about it, I think part of the reason she took me in was that she and Héctor were part of the same secret movement. She had pamphlets in her room and everything, tucked inside the hymnal beneath her pillow—I found them when I was changing the bed linens. They were the same ones that Héctor had shown me, about reclaiming the land for the people. I loved Sister Iris even more after that.

Then, Graciela arrived like a ghost, and her presence comforted me. She'd brought her sister, Consuelo, skinny and crazy-eyed. We all sat together, sipping chicha. Too much to say. I figured Graciela would tell me all about the capital when she was ready, and I'd get to know Consuelo then too, during our journey north.

That night I woke up a few times as I always did, crying, missing Héctor and the baby, wanting so badly to wake Graciela up too and tell her sleeping face. But I just watched her and Consuelo snore, let them rest. The last time I woke up, I saw Graciela sitting straight up, her eyes open but glazed over and moving, like she was dreaming. After a little while she slumped over and closed her eyes slowly, then snapped them open again and took in her breath fast. She looked as scared as I felt.

I knew I wouldn't fall back asleep, so I got up. Graciela was still asleep, but beside her, Consuelo was gone. I figured I might as well look for her and start in on the work I wouldn't be able to do the next day. I wanted to leave the convent beautiful for the nuns.

I held a brush in my hand and was on my knees, scrubbing each of the eighteen wooden steps one by one, when I heard him approach. I couldn't see a thing when I looked up, not even a shadow. But then he was on me, and something like fire tore across the center of my body. I saw that I was bleeding, and for the first time I was glad that the baby was gone from me. My eyes had stopped working, but I knew my legs were being pulled apart, my body ripped open. I felt myself hit the air, move through the ashy sky like a bird, and then I fell, and my neck snapped, and I kept falling. The flesh of my belly broke open like a torn bag, and I fell until I hit the bottom of the stairs, and there my body emptied.

22

L IKE THE REST OF US, GRACIELA HAD BEEN LEFT FOR DEAD.
Before she lost consciousness, she stood in front of a tower,
screaming our names, but by then we were gone.

The tower was made of waxen parts, all gray in the moon. Someone
had stacked our bodies like wood in a stove. Here was a child's broken
hand, and here a stilled face. Here, a wet ear, a backward knee. Here am I
and I and I and I.

The tower rose as tall as the chapel's steeple. The men's footsteps beat
over the sacristy's platform.

There was a darkness inside the mass, and Graciela watched as it fell
open like a door beneath a broken jaw. Tinny music began to play. And
then a camera's slow flash, and the bright bloom of a struck match.

A tiny man appeared in the glow, dancing in a spotlight upon a tiny
stage. El duende. His brightness was the spell. Graciela stood, rapt, before
him, his perfect audience. He wore a silk top hat, tilted askance on his
head, black shiny shoes that tapped a fast, metallic dance. He carried a
gleaming gold-tipped cane, which he tossed in the air, let wildly spin, and
caught in a tight fist; he tapped his shoes over the polished wood of the
stage, the patent leather reflecting the bodies revealed by the light. The
men moved inside the church, and smoke rose from the flames of the lit
pews, filling Graciela's nose. El duende gave a turn, a low bow, and then
beckoned her inside the tower with a wave of his cane. She fell to her

knees and felt her way in, pushing stiff limbs up to open the door wider. Once she was in, she closed it behind her.

El duendito's tap dance was our opening too. He made us a door so we could walk right through. Miren que: imagine us a kickline, el duendito's big finish. When Graciela crawled into the tower, we caught in the corner of her eyes like sand. The ceiba's long roots absorbed our blood, and we soaked into the soles of Graciela's bare feet. She inhaled us, her breaths shallow and ragged, one lung collapsing.

Blood sealed Graciela's mouth closed. She was fading into death, she thought. To the soldiers, her body was empty. The things they did to her they did to us. But she lived. And we found her breath and entered, floating on her air for those days she spent in that sweltering pile, our souls gathering, braiding with hers. We cartwheeled into her ears. Dead as we were, we sparked as we transformed into ghosts. Bright fucking souls indeed. It hurt, a terrible fire.

And Consuelo? She lived too.

When the men arrived, Consuelo threw herself down the stairs of the schoolroom and hid in a dark corner, behind a painting. Yes, the one with the chelitas and the indias, all those calculations. Consuelo had the ability to twist her mind into shapes, and she was good at being silent. In her mind she was back in the General's bathtub. Would it have been better to be murdered in that porcelain embrace or beneath the dark wood of the sacristy? She lived.

We gathered in her as we did Graciela, feeling our edges burn as we burrowed into her reddish-gold hair. We braided our souls to hers and felt that terrible fire again.

Consuelo waited for two days in the convent basement, until she was sure that the men were gone. She must have slept, moved, peed during these days, but the hours blurred, splitting her mind from any conscious acts of her body. When she tried to stand, when the stretch of silence seemed long enough, her knees buckled and she fell to the cool concrete, finally pissing herself. She crawled out of the basement and found our bodies stacked and mutilated. She pissed herself again. Graciela's body lay in our pile. Consuelo touched her sister's face and wondered aloud if she was dead too. No one answered her, not even the birds.

She and Graciela had talked about Hollywood, but now Graciela appeared as dead as the rest of us. Her mouth was sealed with fresh blood, her eyes dull glass. Consuelo shook Graciela's shoulders and tried to shout her awake. Her skin was cold. Consuelo's heart snapped, a kite on wind.

She carried us with her as she ran to the train station. She sat wide awake on the platform until the morning's first train. When had she last eaten? Her belly was full of angry snakes.

By the time she reached the port, Consuelo had stopped crying. Now she couldn't stop smiling. She was hysterical, delirious. Her teeth chattered. She hadn't truly slept in days, but she was alert, vigilant, revising her plan in her mind with a sharpness that surprised her. Maybe it was us, our bright souls coursing through her body of bones. She found the ticket booth and stood in line. She had to decide where to go before she got to the front. Her sister was dead. And she knew that she couldn't be alone. She needed to find someone who would help her.

Loath as she was to admit it, the only person she knew in el norte was Lindita Domínguez. Consuelo knew that if she went to San Francisco, where Lindita lived, and said all the right things, that Lindita would feel that she had no choice but to help Perlita's daughter.

At the booth Consuelo realized she had no money. The woman in the booth widened her dull eyes as Consuelo pulled a pearl earring off her earlobe and handed it over as payment. She was covered in blood, what more did that sallow woman with her lazy eye want from her for a goddamn ticket to San Francisco? Consuelo misjudged the woman, who handed Consuelo a ticket, as well as two rolled tortillas from her own lunch. Consuelo, idiot girl, was too stunned to even thank the woman.

Consuelo stood on the dock with her ticket and her plan, filthy, the tortillas sitting like stones in her belly, cackling to herself like a madwoman. Someone else's blood cracked and peeled from her ankle. She caught her face in the reflection of a woman's sunglasses, pitiful, a mask of puffy, unmatched parts, her sorrowful hair mashed.

People are ugly in a crowd. Their smell is one thing. But the grime of their fingernails, the collages of gruesome handbags, the mass airing of toenails, the unwanted view of the waxy whorls of a strange ear, the mutually sanctioned open-mouthed chewing in every filthy canteen, the idle picking of skin, the nibbling of mucus, the animal scrambling and pushing and opportunistic theft and petty outrages and assertions of being first in line. They're ugly like this, in every train station, waiting room, bus stop, and ship's hull in every port of the world. And here was Consuelo inching down into the ship's belly, breathing in all that skin. She found her cabin door, unlocked it with the light-copper key she'd been handed in exchange for her ticket. Seeing that the bed had not yet been made, its two-inch mattress bare, Consuelo lay on her back on the floor and felt the ocean push against her spine. All she could think to do was sleep.

Back in the village, Graciela still lay asleep beside our bodies. When she finally awoke, hours after Consuelo had left, she was broken and aching, unsure whether she was alive or in hell. And she'd lost her knife.

She crawled out of the pile and she carried us with her, our voices and our echoes. We rattled inside her, souls beating like wings, howling against her bruises. Somehow, she had lived. We should have lived too. Instead our bodies were filling with worms.

The village was burning. She found each of our empty bodies, the bodies of our mothers. She didn't find the body of her own mother, nor did she find Consuelo's body. She allowed herself to believe that maybe Consuelo's absence meant that she had escaped, that she was alive. She didn't know what her mother's absence meant.

Graciela moved on hands and knees, tasting the choking sky of our Middleworld, pulling herself up and away. The ceiba tree stood alone on the hill beside the coffee field, all of the birds asleep in its branches, all of the trees around our ceiba scorched to the ground, scattered black flakes of ash.

All was still.

Graciela could not run. Instead, she crawled beneath the smoke, two miles down the volcano to Don Patricio's train station, which was nothing but a wooden bench on a platform. She'd missed the day's first train, the very train that Consuelo had taken, smiling at no one with a mouth full of blood. The next port-bound train came at midday. From there, Graciela would make her way to Los Angeles.

The tickets for the ship in the harbor, bound first for Los Angeles, and then for San Francisco, were completely sold out. Inside her cabin, Consuelo lay screaming into her arm.

Another boat would leave in two days. But Graciela could not stay here. She watched the captain draw up the bridge. Below, men were loading coffee in heavy burlap bags into the cargo hold.

"Fuck it," we told Graciela. "What are you going to do? Wait? Go back to the village and get killed? Go back to the capital and really get fucking killed? No. Get the fuck out."

In that moment, Graciela didn't know that the voice guiding her was us. She was hearing all kinds of things—cicadas, the howling of dogs, the cries of the people in our village who awoke that day alive. She trusted nothing but that voice.

So Graciela did exactly what we would have done together, had we lived. She ran down the concrete steps to the loading dock, slipping on the algae and salt water, falling down three or four steps at a time. She crept like a cat behind the tower of pallets that held sacks of coffee and began feeling the bags in the back, closest to the dock, searching for the right one, lightly packed and low, a bag that would be loaded last and thus end up on top of the pile. She untied the one she wanted with her teeth, let the beans overflow and spill onto the dock, into the murky water beneath her.

And then she crawled into the bag, displacing more beans to make space for her body. Inside was a smooth and familiar darkness, heavier than the weight of water. The metallic, acrid scents of her skin and our blood blended with the oils of the beans, which were especially oily, in the arabica style that the gringos in California loved so much. But she didn't suffocate; she didn't drown in the beans. "I'm still alive!" Graciela nearly blurted out inside the bag, before clamping a hand over her mouth. Nothing about this was funny, but she laughed anyway.

Graciela was carried, with three or four other bags beneath her, through the air and into the cargo hold. "¡Milagrosa!" she said aloud, that she was not crushed, that she'd been set on top of the pile.

Below, the water carried Graciela. Above, the water carried Consuelo. We swam along with them, like the owls that had carried Blood Woman's hair in their beaks, soaring through the knotted roots of Xibalba's occluded sky when she too escaped into another world. Together, apart, the sisters traveled north on the water, parallel to the Royal Road, up the great continent's coast. Their nostrils and throats filled with the scent of the beans, with five hundred years of death.

Somehow, las hermanas lived to see another world. They clawed the dirt between their broken bodies and the sky, swallowing fistfuls and spitting it out, as we pulled them up and through. When Blood Woman first glimpsed the underbelly of Middleworld, it was only a pinprick of sky.

And here, we continue on too. Vamos a la vuelta.

23

SOMETIME AFTER THE MASSACRE, WHILE GRACIELA AND CON-suelo sailed away, we awoke in the capital.

Of course, we had no idea where we were. None of us had been to the capital in life. This was our first time, our first of many times, returning here as fantasmas. This time, we knew only that we were not in our village, that it was night, and while our bodies had rotted away in our village, we were still together.

We found ourselves on a patch of wet grass beside a fountain. All around us were large buildings—municipal buildings, ministries of health, education, and agriculture, and the Archives. It was the middle of the night, and two men in suits ran down the street, their shiny shoes clopping on the wet pavement.

We began to receive information. After the massacre, we learned, the people were afraid, and it had become very easy for El Gran Pendejo to hire any number of men to do his will. He'd hired two men, for instance, a taxi driver and a baker, to light the National Archives ablaze. And so, as they ran off, fire swam through the windows of the building.

We, eyeless ghosts, read each piece of paper as it transformed to ash. We absorbed the knowledge that they contained, that was being destroyed by executive order. Marriage records. Church records. Birth certificates. Death certificates. Yearly sales reports from fincas all over the west. Who knows who read this kind of thing or cared enough to count our names, but us? We watched until the building itself crumbled and sank, and only the Archives' bones remained, charred and bare.

Viejitos, angelitos, those with the blood fresh on their necks, and those who had been dead for years, they all rose up as a scattering of dark sparks. Polillas in reverse, they traveled to us on their black wings, away from the light of the fire. Their souls met ours and filled us with noise.

Remember us, they said.

We won't be forgotten, they told us.

We had no choice.

Later, with the sun sinking orange into the volcanoes, the General's men drove beside papery hibiscus trailing the city walls, sky bright even as it began to go dark, and the ballast of the volcanoes, slick black stone carved like sculpture. They drove high into the deep-green hills above the center, past wide, painted castles in luminous pink, peach, iridescent blue. Each one had a courtyard of fruit trees, mold-plagued English roses, and marble angels. Each estate was framed by a wall topped with the pale glass of shattered beer bottles.

The houses grew larger as they neared the Estate. They kicked down the front door when they got there and found it had been abandoned. Perlita had not returned.

As the years passed, mosquitoes thickened over the glass. Mold collected in the plaster and streaked the walls green, purple, and gray. The cabinets in the kitchen were torn out, the rugs and furniture gone. The ocelot wandered the hills. Too lazy to hunt, she begged the neighbors for food.

Downtown, the capital was brilliant again, white sun flashing off the metal carts pushed through the courtyard by indio food vendors. The city center had been washed clean by the rain—the presidential palace, the National Library, the ministries, and the sooty, hollowed-out Archives all encircling the grassy courtyard like sentries.

Just outside of town was un comedor that the General's men liked to visit for a meal and a pilsener in the widening days after the massacre. It was a simple bright-green block with an unpainted concrete floor. A woman crouched in the doorway. You remember her: Ninfa.

Ninfa rocked against the concrete, a paper cup between her knees, eyes like scratched glass. She looked ancient now. Perlita probably wouldn't have recognized her, the woman who had nursed her when she was a baby, except for the mole beneath her right eye, her softly sloping nose, the trio of saints' medals around her neck.

Like us, Ninfa was from one of those tiny volcano towns in the west. That's where she'd gone after leaving the Estate with her leg of pisto. By the time she'd arrived at her daughters' place, the killings had begun. She had nearly escaped with her daughters and grandchildren, but they were apprehended at the Guatemalan border. The soldiers called them communists, and then offered them a bargain. "Swear you're a communist," they said, "and we won't hurt you. We'll see that you get justice."

"Of course I'll swear I'm a communist. I'll swear I'm the King of Spain if you want me to," Ninfa said.

But the soldiers lined them up anyway. Ninfa watched them shoot both of her daughters, her three grandsons, her granddaughter, her sister, and her sister's husband. But when they got to her, they put their guns away and pulled out a machete.

Ninfa had prayed that she'd bleed out after the soldiers sliced into her—there were two of them, just a few years older than her youngest grandson—but she didn't die. Now her left hand was missing, cut freshly through the bone.

We die again each time we remember her like this.

The poets of the Society of Sacred Letters and Objects didn't write about us after the massacre. They wrote surreal poetry about making love to women with white skin and hair like clouds. They wrote bloodlessly, stylishly, afraid to denounce the General, to lose their patronage or worse.

The bravest of them all would only ever have the nerve to write a sly little short story about a cart driven through town by a skeleton that carries a pile of rotting corpses. It's an old story, a myth, la carreta chillona, rewritten with the teeth taken out.

That's the problem with a myth or story. It's what we're always trying to warn La Yinita about. If you don't tell it properly, if you say it too quietly, you erase everyone's face as you go.

So, the poets of the Society of Sacred Letters and Objects pretended not to know what had happened to us. They praised our great-grandmothers' backstrap loom weavings, they thanked El Gran Pendejo (a man of letters, they called him, a sculptor of nations) for funding their poetry salons. They talked about Cuzcatlán in the same breath that they praised the nation's emancipation from the "sad slavery of communism." They wrote colorless lines about our skin matching the soil where we worked, and never once mentioned our deaths.

Much later, from the distance of exile in Costa Rica or Mexico City, they'd speak out about us timidly, belatedly. But in the days and years after the massacre, they looked away.

And yes, reluctantly, we went to see him.

We watched El Gran Pendejo in his palace in the capital, pruning in that marble bathtub, spouting his nonsense like a whale. A few times, he invoked us with his thoughts, his vague fantasies of our "supple flesh" and our "beautiful dark eyes," the same eyes he wouldn't dare look directly into. We sang into his ears at bedtime, hoping to frighten him to his death.

He had no problem hiring an old dishwasher to be his new oracle, hiring a paletero to light his candles and hum over incense, to color the waters with bottles of food dye. He filled the presidential library with paid spiritualists and sycophants and held his séances there, at the long oval table where our Graciela had once sat and read books.

It was at that table, after the worms had been feasting on us for two years, that El Gran Pendejo celebrated the official recognition of his presidency by his very good friends Los Yunais. And it was there, the following year, bolstered by his very good friends, that he signed a law banning Black people from entering the country, and restricting the freedom of Arab people, Chinese people, people from India. This was not a surprise to anyone.

At this table El Gran Pendejo officially recognized the regime of Franco, beating his other very good friends Mussolini and Hitler to the task. He wrote letters at this table, in his halting, deliberate cursive, to all of them. El Gran Pendejo wrote love letters to the Japanese puppet state in Manchuria, and he brought in a Prussian colonel to direct the military academy, then sent Germany a plan for landing troops on the coast of Los Yunais.

Perhaps that last letter went a stroke too far; even El Gran Pendejo would have to admit that.

Indeed, when he finally entered the Second World War, it was not on the side of his beloved Fascists, but with the Allies, a sensible chess move, perhaps fearing Los Yunais would revoke their neighborliness and the legitimacy that they'd bestowed upon him if he declared his loyalty to the Axis. Besides, Los Yunais bought more coffee than anyone in the world—certainly more than Germany. He had to consider coffee and not simply the desires of his soul. Gleefully, he used the declaration of war as a perfect excuse to strip Japanese, German, and Italian citizens in our country of their land and property and send them to work camps.

And all along, outside the palace, the capital raged for all the familiar reasons—pay, food, education, land.

Later, once we'd been engusanadas for twelve years, after the strikes and the executions, the bans, and the curfews, the endless reappointments of himself through fair and democratic elections in which he was the only candidate; after telling the archbishop that he, El Gran Pendejo, was god; after transforming the primary-school moral curriculum into a manifesto of reincarnation; after he insisted, in his admiration of Los Fascistas, that schoolchildren be taught the Roman salute; after arguing on the radio, from the auditorium of the national university, that urination, defecation, and procreation should all be officially categorized as biological senses of perception; after the revolts at the university; after insisting upon his successes—*I built the banks! I built the Pan-American Highway! The Panama Canal!*—to the resounding applause of the few who still loved him; after finally pissing off the fufurufo coffee families by increasing export taxes; after the executions of military officers; after the accidental execution of a teenage boy from Los Yunais; after the executions of one hundred civilians; after an airstrike; after a nonviolent student strike; and then after a general strike—after all that, El Gran Pendejo finally fled. He ran for his life to Guatemala, where he was received nervously by El Otro Pendejo, and then left for Honduras, where he ultimately remained.

And when El Gran Pendejo's chauffeur stabbed him during his lush Honduran exile, avenging the murder of his father in our massacre after decades of polite service, shattering El Gran Pendejo's twilight years of guayabera shirts and teenage concubines—we had been twenty-four years engusanadas then, and, yes, we hissed and cackled into his ears. Yes, we watched it all.

PART II

∞

1932-1938

24

IN HOLLYWOOD, GRACIELA WAS REBORN, SMALL AND ALONE. A tiny shooting star, hot and bright, velvety black all around her—that's how she'd imagined her broken body inside the boat that had carried her through the dark waters north. She'd wanted to sleep straight through, but she couldn't, with the boards creaking over her head from the men above, rodents scratching and darting in the dark corners of the hull. The ocean rocked her insides until she coughed bile from her empty belly. And we woke her up too. We wrapped our voices around her, growing stronger as we sang.

The Los Angeles shipyards were full of rough men in those days. Half-conscious on a bag of púchica Folgers, Graciela was Venus on the half-shell, feet caked in our blood. The men whooped and hollered when she emerged from her sack of coffee. She scrambled off the dock and ran like a starved rat into the streets, terrified, giddy to be alive.

She exchanged her colones for dollars at a place nearby. A square-shouldered man behind a pane of glass with a circle cut out made the exchange. A woman dozed behind him. The man's hands shook as he handed over the cash, stacking it up between them in plump envelopes. Graciela took it, moved a few paces out of his line of sight, and then slid it back into the stocking leg, which was still bound to her chest by the tela.

The Los Angeles she had imagined shone blurry, a distance away from where she stood in the dimming harbor. She gathered herself, cracked heels, swollen ankles, every joint of her body stiff and sore. But it felt good to move, to walk the strange, darkening streets on her two bare feet. The air was wet, chillier than she'd expected. Above her, palms waved. Construction sites stalled for the night around wide-open pits, and ahead she saw low-slung buildings, houses of concrete block or adobe, modest and sleepy.

An hour or so later, she arrived on a street crowded with wide automobiles, walked past a bank with letters as long as her legs raised in mosaic tile on its side, a green glass pinnacle stretching against the darkening sky, the red velvet glow of a movie theater in a building tiled in green and gold, and so many gas stations, one after another. She glimpsed her reflection in the dark glass of a department store window and gave a little yelp. She was La Siguanaba, filthy, knotted hair thatched over half of her face, torn dress, and bleeding toes.

An enormous black top hat stood at the corner—a building unlike any she'd ever seen. Graciela read the words FINE FOOD painted in a crimson cursive script along the hat's band, though she didn't know then what they meant. Beside the words were a series of appealing icons: a sturdy sandwich ruffled with meats and cheeses, a winking lobster, and an enormous corncob. Her hunger had reached an unbearable state. Ravenous and dizzy, she found the door that led inside the hat and pushed through a brocade curtain.

"Oh, dear!" An elderly gringo stood behind a podium, wearing a faded bow tie and a stained vest, a lace handkerchief over his face. The laces of his shoes were rubbed bare, cord revealing itself like bone. The place was full, with orange leather booths along the round walls. A single table occupied the center of the room. Some of the diners turned to look at Graciela standing in the entrance, but they quickly returned their attention to their companions, unfazed, each one dressed as strangely as her, injuries that Graciela could tell had been applied with paint— a wolflike monster, a clown, a vampire, and a woman powdered white, with blood on her neck. It was possible, Graciela reasoned, that they might mistake her appearance for a costume as well, though hers was more convincing than all the others'.

And Graciela smelled like death, she was certain of it now, but the old gringo just kept his handkerchief to his nose and brought her to the small table in the middle of the room.

When the waiter, a stringy man with perfectly round glasses, arrived, Graciela pointed chaotically at the menu, selecting items that seemed large and filling from the cartoonish illustrations, the English words a blurred and boxy jumble to her eyes. A few minutes later her food arrived: a baked potato the length of her forearm, smothered in cream and cheese, a turgid gray slop that the waiter called a chocolate milkshake, and an entire chicken.

Halfway through the feast, Graciela felt her stomach drop and churn—the food had shocked her system. She rushed to the ladies' room, walls paneled in a red velour and gold-trimmed mirrors, which reminded her of El Gran Pendejo's palace and sickened her further. She vomited in the toilet. She felt better afterward, lighter. She rinsed her mouth and then washed her face at a garish tap painted gold, filling the sink with black soil, old blood, a ribbon of ceiba leaf that had been plastered to her forehead for days. She found a sliver of pink bar soap on the edge of the sink, and made bubbles, scrubbing her face, her neck, her hands and arms, gently. She balanced on one bare foot and then the other, scrubbing her feet and legs. Tiny strips of skin peeled off into her hands. Every part of her awoke in pain.

She was still filthy even after she'd finished, mud dripping in rivulets down her legs and arms. But there was her face, familiar, if damaged, in the scratched mirror. Her shiny black eyes, one lid swollen and tender. The bruise where the General had struck her had spread and swelled. And there were fresher bruises on her neck and forehead, filthy cuts spidered all over her face. She didn't remember receiving these injuries. A strange feeling, terrifying for Graciela, not to remember something. Later, it would return to her, the massacre, in jagged flashes and sounds. But for now, a blank.

Yes. She could see it now. Her dead face. She could understand how she'd been left for dead. Graciela dried herself with a damp towel hanging on a hook beside the sink. She was starving again. She returned to her table and devoured the rest of the chicken.

She was sucking the bones when el viejito gringo arrived, his handkerchief back in his dingy vest.

"We're closed, Toots," he said.

Graciela blinked at him as if she could will the words he'd uttered to make some púchica sense to her. She couldn't, but she reached into the stocking between her tetas and pulled out a fistful of cash—she'd be extravagant and reckless just this once, in her gratitude to the old gringo, the scrawny, bespectacled waiter, the bounty of this púchica top hat— and left it on the table without counting it. Then she got up and began her search for a place to rest.

Fortified by the chicken, Graciela walked deep into the hills of this new city, where the buildings appeared shabbier, with dirty curtains flapping in the windows. A woman—Margaret, Graciela soon learned—six months pregnant, who had stepped out for some fresh air and found herself retching instead, spotted her silhouette creeping along the sidewalk. Wiping her mouth with the back of her hand, Margaret noted Graciela's careful steps, her head alert and searching, the fatigue radiating from her spine. She saw in Graciela's shadow a girl in trouble. And the thing was, the timing of her appearance was perfect. Margaret's roommate, a thin-lipped girl from Iowa, had left town without warning, leaving her with double the boarding fees if her bunk didn't get filled before the end of the month.

"Hey, you!" Margaret called out to Graciela. "You need help? A place to stay?" As soon as she got the words out of her mouth, Margaret heaved into the street.

Graciela stood beneath a lamppost, steadying her feet, and reached for a knife that wasn't there. Always, nos falta el cuchillo. The gringa came toward her, into the light, and Graciela saw that she was pregnant. She didn't seem to notice that she'd frightened Graciela. She just kept talking.

"I'm Margaret," she said, sticking out a stiff hand to Graciela. "And this here is Roger junior," she said, patting her big belly with the other hand. "Or Thomasina, if it winds up being a girl. But I'm pretty sure it's a boy, because, you know, he did it to me from behind." Margaret's face reddened and she coughed out a rough burst of laughter. Graciela didn't understand a púchica thing that she had said, besides something about a baby named Roger or Thomasina, but she cackled too—joining a carcajada felt good.

Margaret's freckles looked like tiny flecks of ash from the volcano. Graciela smiled weakly at her and gave her name. She seemed harmless. Graciela let her words wash over her, trying to pick out the familiar ones.

"What are you, one of those Mexicans? Filipino?" Margaret shouted at her. Graciela understood that and she shook her head.

"You're not from here, though. Better that you get inside. It's not safe for the ones who look like you," she said. Graciela looked at her blankly.

"Damn," Margaret breathed, looking Graciela over. "You're tired, aren't you? Had a rough night?" Margaret made a pillow with her arms and lay her broad forehead down on the tops of her hands. Graciela smiled. She was exhausted. She let her eyes close, and Margaret grabbed her hand.

"C'mon," she said, leading her through a wrought-iron gate and down a narrow stone alley. "This place is clean, at least, and they run the hot water twice a week."

All Graciela knew was that soon she'd be asleep in a bed. She surrendered.

The next morning, her first in Los Angeles, she woke and found that the silk stocking stuffed with Perlita's cash was no longer pinned to her chest. The rebozo hung slack around her waist. Before bed, she'd stood at that desk and paid for a full month. She slapped her own forehead like a loca and slid to the floor. Anyone here could have robbed her, everyone was a suspect.

And then—for the first time since the massacre, since fleeing the General's palace with Consuelo, since her mother had been taken from her years before—Graciela lost her púchica shit. She had no money, no words, no sister, no mother, not even a púchica knife. She began to cry, and then to howl, kicking her bruised legs on the floor and beating the walls with her fists.

A girl with a scar near her throat brushed past her, smirking. Graciela lunged at her, grabbing at the untied lace of her boot, and then at the raggedy trenza that brushed her waist like a mule's tail. The girl tried to throw a punch, but she faltered and fell, and Graciela, bien encachimbada, pinned her to the ground. ¡Qué onda, Graciela! But Graciela's victory was brief. The sallow girl screamed and spat in Graciela's face, and then the others rushed in—nameless girls, a blur of reddened cheeks and grimy fists, all of them her enemies. Graciela collapsed beneath the rain of their bodies. They kicked her and tugged at her hair, shouting insults that Graciela didn't understand, that we won't dignify by repeating here. She could endure this too. Just one more fucking pesadilla. The women were crushing her—the breath began leaving Graciela's lungs, and she was back inside the tower of our bodies. She couldn't scream. Maybe she wouldn't survive this beating—was this how she would die, on the dirty floor of a boardinghouse in Hollywood, beaten to death by hungry women? She heard a familiar voice—Margaret was shouting for the girls to stop.

"Quit it! Lay off her, you stupid bitches." Margaret was not being kind; she was afraid. Remember—she needed Graciela's bunk full or else next month she'd pay double.

The girls, fat and scrawny, scowling and grinning, stilled their fists and turned to Margaret.

"Whatever it is, it doesn't matter," she said. Graciela sat up, encachimbada, but hollowed out. She shivered. Margaret held an empty, torn silk stocking up to the light: the only secret language that would ever pass between them. Graciela opened her mouth to scream. Margaret tossed the stocking, and it drifted down beside her.

"Our girl was rich!" Margaret shouted to the girls. "I took the finder's fee, but the rest is yours. Christmas gifts under your mattresses, see if you got one and fight each other if you didn't, you filthy sluts! Get to it." The girls took off running.

Graciela clenched her fist, but she was out of strength. She held her head in her hands and tried to shake the long nightmare from it.

But she couldn't hit a pregnant lady. And wouldn't she have taken the cash if she'd been the one to find it? What an idiot she was.

"Listen," Margaret said. "Your room and board are covered for the month. What the hell else do you need?" Again, Margaret was shouting at her in her loud voice, and Graciela didn't understand a word. But she knew that she was now outnumbered. She couldn't fight the whole boardinghouse.

Graciela pointed at a pair of shoes that lay on the floor beside the bunk bed. Damp canvas, with brown rubber soles. That's what she wanted, a pair of dirty shoes too big for her feet. She'd run out of our country barefoot, but the sidewalk burned here, and she needed a job— there was no escaping this place without shoes. Margaret made a big show of handing them over—but even she knew it was the least she could do.

Later, Graciela tried to plead her case in a frantic pantomime with the landlady, but it was useless. The landlady was a kind-enough drunk, nervous, with frizzy hair and pink lines threading over her nose and above her lips, and she stayed out of boarders' disputes on principle. She held up her hands as if in a bank robbery. She took a paper map from the pocket of her apron and handed it over to Graciela, slowly.

"Bring it back to me, when you come back," she said, pointing first at the door and then at her chest and patting her pocket. She looked at Graciela to be sure she understood. How familiar it all was to Graciela, alone, hungry, afraid, not understanding the words hurled at her, being stared at as if she were a misbehaving child.

But Graciela needed out, as urgently as she needed the cash that survival would cost here. She took the map and began walking the hills and wide, sidewalk-less streets of Los Angeles, looking for work. The city was the future she'd seen in *Metropolis,* but four times the size, brighter, with silver towers that seemed to swirl and shimmer in the heat. Somewhere was the water that had brought her here, but it seemed hidden in this massive desert place.

That afternoon, sudden rain snatched the landlady's map from her hands, and it was devoured by a gutter. Graciela ran into a glass-and-steel building to escape the storm, animated by her terror of what the landlady would do to her if she returned to the boardinghouse without the map.

She found herself inside of a slender, sturdy branch of the Los Angeles public library. She took in the walls of books, each spine labeled neatly and mysteriously. A gray-haired woman sat at the front desk, a wall of tiny wooden drawers behind her. At the sight of Graciela she brightened, as though she'd been expecting her, and motioned her up a flight of stairs to her left.

"Hurry," the woman whispered. "It's starting."

Upstairs, Graciela entered a room and saw people who looked like us, seated around an oval wooden table the length of the one in the General's library. There was a teacher, and here was a class for learning the language. Graciela found her place among them, the broad-faced men in overalls, and the women, some of whom reminded her of our mothers. They went around in a circle, speaking their names. They practiced the words for where they were from, and then they described their families and the weather.

After the class, Graciela explored the library. She pawed her way through the newspapers on their wooden dowels, looking for news of home. In today's world news from a place called Cincinnati, collaged with portraits of debutantes and a British submarine sinking in the English Channel, she found the name of our country.

There was a photograph out of a cowboy movie, of horses and their riders crossing a pale beach that, in black and white, looked like a dusty plain. The caption read: LIGHT FIELD ARTILLERY, DETACHMENT OF THE TROOPS. Above it was another picture in the capital, a busy, narrow street: THE SCENE OF RIOTOUS DEMONSTRATIONS AGAINST COM-

MUNISM. AMERICAN AND CANADIAN DESTROYERS HAVE ANCHORED
IN THE HARBOR.

At another table Graciela found a translation dictionary, English to
Spanish, and she worked, word by word, to understand the articles. The
news from home traveled slowly through her mind on this path of tran-
scription and translation. Faraway, slow—this was the only way that she
could bear it. Tired as she was, the class and the time she'd spent reading
restored some vital electricity to her brain, returning some of her mind's
old powers to her. Night was creeping along the horizon of the city. She
left the library and began the long walk back to the boardinghouse.

Graciela made a habit of returning to the library after that. She was safe
there. It was quiet during the hottest part of the day and she could rest or
fall asleep in a chair, and it cost nothing. She attended the weekly English
class and then wandered, looking for news from home, pulling her favor-
ites from the shelves and studying them with the fresh, slow eyes of a new
language. Her ability to guayabear returned as she healed. She began to
speak the language of this new place with the kind of ease we recognized
as hers alone. Soon, she'd gathered enough new words to talk with the
librarian, who helped her find work cleaning the library bathrooms.
Ninfa had trained her well, but the quantity of piss, blood, and shit at
this library was a hundredfold the mess that Graciela had cleaned at the
Estate.

When she'd been in Los Angeles about a month, Graciela saw a poster
taped to a kiosk at the bus station—twenty legs, pointed and raised per-
pendicular to the ground, twenty beaded skirts flouncing at the top of
each thigh, no faces—and she knew she could do that too. She put one
hand on the glass of the kiosk and extended her leg, as straight as she
could hold it, away from her body. She liked the way it looked. Hard,
apart from her. She took down the address in her notebook.

On the morning of the call, Graciela left the boardinghouse in a wispy
early morning. She'd gotten directions from the landlady the night
before. The woman had even drawn her a new map.

"It's a very long walk," she said, looking Graciela up and down, clicking her tongue. "At least two hours on foot."

If Graciela's mother was alive, if the flesh of her bones was not rotting, or being eaten by dogs, or cooking in the sun, she might be walking underneath the same sun as Graciela, over hills that perhaps were not so different from the ones Graciela walked now.

The sky was just turning pink when Graciela arrived at the studio, and the doors were still locked, but she was the first in line. When they finally let her in, she found the place slippery with bodies, like an aquarium. A blond woman stood on a platform in the back of the room in wide pants, facing away from Graciela. She was familiar—the movement of the bracelet around her wrist as she tapped on the shoulder of the man beside her, the arc of her neck. Graciela knew she'd seen her but couldn't place her name. The woman began to address the group with sharp, high little words. Graciela remembered her voice from the movies as a soft animal locked deep inside the throat, but now a disarming squeak came from that familiar face. She introduced herself as Rosie Swan. She was the star, and the director was letting her choose the girls who would dance behind her.

"Bodies," the director kept saying. "We just need to fill the space with bodies. A pretty face is nice, but good legs and arms are better."

Rosie waved him off. She found Graciela in the crowd and pulled her out by her arm. She'd seen her full name on the sign-in sheet.

"I think we're from the same place," she said to her, and Graciela was relieved to hear our language, for the first time in weeks. Those seafoam eyes, so close. Rosie hugged Graciela, startling her a little, and said that she believed their mothers had been friends for a time.

Her mother—Perlita. Graciela didn't know where to begin. "She's my aunt, I guess you could say," she finally stammered.

Rosie screamed and embraced Graciela again. "Listen, I gotta run," she said. "But your timing couldn't be more perfect. Meet me for lunch in fifteen? There's something I want to talk to you about."

. . .

Later, Rosie found Graciela at the door of the studio cafeteria and signed her in as her guest.

"So, when did you get here?" Rosie asked once they'd found a table. "What's your plan?"

They faced each other across the cafeteria table, identical plastic trays before them. A yellowish blob, our maíz transformed and made into creamy, uniform mush, alongside some kind of meat that Graciela was stunned to see floated slightly at the surface of a pool of gravy, shimmering with oily rainbows.

"Before, I did a little acting. Some dancing," Graciela said. "I have a job here already, but I need to make more money. And it's not what I love to do." It was all true, sort of, and Graciela held the words in her mouth with extra care, as if she were testing them, her creation of an altered reality.

"Yeah, yeah," Rosie said, "you and every other pretty girl in this town. But seriously, you got papers? It can be tricky without the right papers."

Papers? Graciela tried to understand what kinds of paper would secure her success in this place, but before she could respond, Rosie continued.

"Look, here's the thing. My mother's worried about me," Rosie said. "I'm all alone here, and there's lots of men. My parents live in New York now. I've been in L.A. full-time since I was in *Our Dancing Daughters*. My mom comes to stay every two months to check up on me, and now she's threatening to get a place out here if I don't get another girl to live with me. I really don't want her to move here." Rosie eyed Graciela again, considering her next words. "She'd love that you're from the colonia. It'd make her so happy that I'd be living with an old friend, kind of. I know this is sort of crazy, we don't really know each other, but I think maybe we can help each other out. Do you need a place to stay?"

Graciela nodded, terrified and delighted. "I'd love to stay with you," she said.

She was the luckiest girl, she supposed. The girl who could not be killed.

. . .

She moved in the next day. Rosie's mother, Isabel, met her at the door of the apartment. They sat on a white sofa in a bright room, looking out an uncurtained window shaped like an arch. Outside, there was the green curvature of hills, combed through with orange trees. Here was a familiar place, a place like the Estate, a place where she could hide.

"I knew your family," Isabel said. "We all did." Graciela braced herself for questions—what if Isabel wondered why she'd never heard of Perlita's niece? What if she'd heard what was happening in our country and asked where Perlita was now?—but none came. It seemed that Isabel didn't know Perlita beyond admiring her dress from across the room at parties, and either did not know or did not care to know more about the massacre that had occurred in her home.

When the conversation ended and Graciela stood for Isabel's embrace, she was enveloped by lavender, the scent that had been Perlita's, that had been her mother's.

LUCÍA: Ours is a small country, el pulgarcito. With so few of us, the same smells waft up all the time. Fantastic coincidence, improbable luck—these things happen constantly. Fucking exhausting.

That night, once her mother had fallen asleep on the couch, Rosie lent Graciela a nightgown and they brushed their teeth together. Rosie wore her feathery blond hair pinned close to the scalp in tiny pale-green rollers and was dressed in a quilted satin bathrobe the color of a tongue. After she rinsed her mouth, she opened the mirror and removed a jar of cold cream from the cabinet behind it. She dipped her hand into the jar, closed her eyes, and rubbed white into her cheeks, her forehead, her temples, her chin, down her neck. Graciela moved her toothbrush, carried all this way in her refajo, around the hard surfaces of her mouth in slow circles.

Done with her cream, Rosie glanced over at Graciela and noticed the toothbrush in her mouth, its wooden handle split and rotting, and opened a slender drawer between them. Inside, lined up like cash, like infinity, were pearl-handled toothbrushes, bristles stiff and immaculate, at the ready. Rosie reached into the drawer and pulled one out. Graciela spat, and Rosie took the old toothbrush out of her hand and threw it in the trash beneath the sink. Graciela picked up the new one, heavier, smooth, like some jewel, thanked Rosie, and began brushing all over again. Rosie winked at her in the mirror. Their first routine.

From the bedroom, the phone began to ring. Rosie, face and neck still white, ran out of the bathroom to answer it.

"Oh, shit, shit, shit, shit, shit," she said just before picking up the receiver and dropping her voice into the low coo that she'd been trained to make for the talkies. "My lion," she said now. She lay herself down on the carpet and wrapped the cord around her wrists, murmuring like a sleeping dove.

"You're so big and strong," she said. "I can't stand it!"

Graciela suppressed una carcajada and made her way to her twin bed and shut her eyes. Púchica, this day, this life. When Rosie's murmurs stopped, there was a click, a breath, and then the ringing began again until she answered. It went on like this, all night long, one man, and then another.

In the morning Graciela found Rosie sprawled on the carpet beneath her twin bed, wrapped in a sheet, like a little girl. Graciela worried about her for a moment, as she imagined Rosie's mother did. But soon Rosie was awake, the chatty older sister again, who knew everything and everyone in this town. Just catching up with old friends, Rosie said, explaining the phone calls. It's the only time I have—my days are booked! "Booked"—Graciela hadn't heard that one yet. And in the coming days Rosie taught Graciela more of the phrases that made up this new language through the bright promises she made to her: she'd take Graciela under her wing; Graciela was welcome; Graciela was to make herself at home here.

25

TWO DAYS AFTER GRACIELA WAS TOSSED ONTO THE DOCKS IN Los Angeles, Consuelo went onshore in San Francisco. She stumbled around until she found a place with a phone book, then called Lindita. She figured she would have returned from her trip by now.

Consuelo wasn't sure how much Lindita knew, how much she had seen or been told by Perlita, in the days before Consuelo had been taken to the General. All she knew was that the last thing Perlita needed was a rich family in el norte to know that Consuelo was a bastard, that Perlita, barren, had stolen her, raised her as her own, and then sold her to the General. She had a feeling that somehow Perlita had kept this information from reaching Linda's ears, even amid the mayhem of her last visit.

That was the nature of their relationship—they both knew too much and too little about each other. Perlita had told Consuelo stories about Mamá Domínguez. That her own mother had been murdered by a finca worker who had jumped the fence, like a lion at the zoo. That her brother had shot himself in the head shortly after his eighteenth birthday, and everyone had blamed Lindita for goading him into it. He'd always been melancholy, and she should have known better than to be such a tiresome bitch.

"How can a suicide be anyone else's fault?" Consuelo would ask whenever Perlita puzzled over the loss of Lindita's handsome younger brother.

"Don't call it that," Perlita would say.

She and Lindita were the best of friends.

And indeed, when Consuelo called, Lindita was delighted to hear from her and sent a car for her immediately. She embraced Consuelo on the steps of her house, a pair of neatly stacked flats in the inner Richmond. Lindita smiled, ignoring the chajazo on Consuelo's leg, her dim halo of grime and stench, nearly visible against the white midmorning fog. Consuelo returned the smile as graciously as possible, the corners of her lips cracking painfully.

"You must be exhausted from your travels," cherita Lindita said, inviting Consuelo to the upstairs flat, which she kept for guests, to sink into the bubble bath she'd drawn for her as soon as the girl had called.

Afterward, they sat together at a table beside a window box of geraniums and succulents, in the downstairs flat, where Lindita and her family lived, sipping té de manzanilla. Consuelo, her hair wrapped in a peachy pink towel, wore one of Lindita's satin bathrobes. She knew some of the lies that Perlita had told Lindita, so she worked with them. She told the woman that she'd gone to stay with friends at their beach house in La Libertad, and that while she was there, the revolts had begun. She hadn't known how to get in touch with Perlita, and so she'd fled, in accordance with the original plan, to study painting abroad. And the only place she could get to was San Francisco.

It wasn't a true story, but it was a story that Lindita would believe, one that saved just enough face for Perlita that she'd be obliged to back up Consuelo's account. Consuelo imagined that Lindita would be reassured by the notion that she was the kind of young woman who had friends who would invite her to stay at a beach house, and indeed, she could tell by the slight lift in the corners of Lindita's red mouth at the mention of the beach house that the detail had, in fact, reassured her.

"I had no idea," Lindita said again and again. "A mess, an utter mess. It's a miracle you're still alive," Lindita clucked. She stroked Consuelo's little hands with her vermillion nails. "I'll call her now. She must be worried sick."

Lindita called Perlita at her new Costa Rican home in the suburbs of San José. While Perlita had taken the money that the General had given her in exchange for Consuelo and left our country in search of a new and untethered life, this was not to be. "I'm so sorry," Consuelo could hear her say to Linda, clearly apologizing for Consuelo's presence in her friend's home.

But quickly, Perlita assumed a cheery optimism, promising to wire money for Consuelo to continue studying art in San Francisco. It was just as Consuelo suspected—she'd rather sacrifice a little more money than her reputation.

Consuelo spent the next two nights with Los Domínguez in their flat in the Avenues, and then, when a one-armed man arrived to take some aide-to-the-consulate's secretary kind of job, Consuelo—only because she was practically family, Mamá Domínguez said—went to stay in the family's apartment downtown, though she returned once a week for dinner and to practice English with Mamá Domínguez's children. Twin girls, twelve years old, one dark, one light. They'd attended the Star of Sea grammar school from kindergarten, and spoke and read English fluently, better than the language they spoke at home with their parents.

Sitting at Lindita's white lacy table with María and Lourdes's half sisters, these polite little girls who were so much older than we were at twelve—did Consuelo see our faces in theirs? Did she remember us in the village when she stared blank-faced at the darker one's profile, as she reached for another oval-shaped cookie to dip into her café cremoso, as she turned the squarish rocks of this language over on her tongue? Did she even remember our faces from that one brief day we'd spent together before the massacre?

In the new city, Consuelo knew almost no one. She avoided the students who gathered after art classes to gossip and smoke, before walking together in graceful formation, sometimes having persuaded the instructor—a rosy man who had a spray of reddish hair and always wore a cravat—to join them at a loud bar in Chinatown that served crab and squid late into the night. One or two of the students in the class would take their leave from the group by declaring they must get home to paint. ("I can't work when I drink; I have no constitution for it," or "I'm not as talented as the rest of you; I have to put the hours in!" or "Ah, today was an utter breakthrough for my work. I'll meander home by the sea to really make sense of it!")—all to the effect that they were serious and dedicated, stirred by the events of the class and the guidance of the red-faced instructor. But Consuelo wouldn't even say goodbye, barely acknowledging the instructor as she brushed past him. More often than not after class, Consuelo just hurried back downtown and stayed up late smoking, pacing the hall of her new apartment, eventually settling by a windowsill like a cat to watch the dawn, the slow construction of a sky-scraper in Union Square, people below filing like insects onto the street-car, underground, in and out of cars and alleys. She felt almost free, in a way, sitting by the window in violet light, her brain raw and shimmering.

The city had rebuilt itself from the ruins of its earthquake, and the floods and fires afterward. People who had lived in this city all their lives told Consuelo that the traces of the damage were gone, but that the force had cracked downtown in half, turned buildings to powder. Every once in a while, Consuelo felt a shake, just enough to slide a glass off the edge of a table, like a subtle sorcery. Those were the kinds of earthquakes that she'd known in our country. She'd forgotten the feeling of the big ones.

The class itself was just fine. Consuelo struggled to bring the lessons back with her to the apartment, to implement them. Alone, her brain went sideways; she was unmoored, convinced she was incapable of even the most rudimentary artistic expression. Staring at her own hand, she'd remember that the instructor had told her on the first day that she was holding the brush incorrectly. She hadn't understood him, and he showed her, adjusting her grip on the wood as if she were a toddler. So she threw the brush on the floor, remaining mute, as though she'd dropped it by accident.

"The practice of this form is very rote, really," the instructor would say, again and again. Or, "Imagine yourself a camera." After several weeks of this, Consuelo finally began to understand the meaning of these words, and she loathed him all the more. But it was fine, really it was. The class was called "Painting Reality," and they began with the typical still-life exercises—jauntier interpretations of old Dutch masters' fruit bowls—before progressing to anatomy, then self-portrait, all in oils. Consuelo had wanted to impress, and early in the term she presented a self-portrait that she'd completed hastily, during those initial weeks when they were still working on dappled apples and wet, sleeping knives.

"But that's not how hands work," the instructor had said, as if startled, his words incomprehensible to Consuelo, with a nervous smile that made her want to murder him. That twitchy embarrassment of his, seemingly on her behalf—she was encachimbada. He had refused to give any more notes during class that day; there was too much material to get through. Afterward, though, she appeared at his desk with the portrait. He sighed heavily.

"All right," he said. (Was she so hopeless?) He refused to rise from his chair, and offered a dull note, barely raising an arm to point. "Look at your arm," he said. "Notice the path that the veins take along the road of your inner arm. Notice before you paint."

Consuelo scowled at him. She wanted more from this pitiful man. She wanted to be seen, to be recognized. Her disdain seemed to energize him.

"Also, there's no sense of proportion here," he said, drawing tiny circles in the air around the portrait's face, as if he could erase Consuelo's work with the tip of his finger. "You have to be willing to learn how to see, to really see."

So now Consuelo was the one who couldn't see.

On her way back downtown that day, Consuelo had scurried east to the docks. Fat sea lions lay sunning, piled on the algae-slick wood planks, barking in the late orange light. She closed her eyes and threw the portrait into the stinking bay, where it bobbed and rested amid the ropes of brown seaweed, the garbage, shattered crabshells, and torn fishing lines.

Painting Reality. It was fine, all fine. But seemingly impossible, and not what she wanted to do anyway. It was achingly, tediously, annoyingly precise. Sure, she could do it—she wasn't actually blind, she knew how to fucking see—but she wanted to paint something that made her feel unordinary and small. Whatever the opposite of rote was, the opposite of proportion—not a bowl of fruit, but an atom containing all destined life, a cosmic landscape, a soul in detailed ecstasy. Something that existed that could not be seen. Of course she didn't have the words in this language to communicate any of this, and even if she did, what a fucking babosa she'd sound like, what a self-important, grandiose fool. Who did she think she was? She hated herself for even thinking this way, for being bored and ungrateful in the class that Perlita had paid for, for ignoring the instructor's stern reminders that she was incapable of doing something as simple as seeing, for having lived.

Outside of class, Consuelo never painted. In the new city, what she enjoyed most was filling her ears with salt water, savoring the long, silent distance it put between her and everything else. On days when she had the energy to do something more than hide at home after class, she'd walk west to the sea to admire the retaining wall they were building there. The wall was slick with moss, and aimed to hold the entire Pacific, its six-thousand-mile force, against the beach, though it stood unfinished, just rocks suspended in metal braces. Dutch windmills turned behind her, and she made her way through the Outside Lands to the Sutro Baths.

Halfway to ruin, the baths were still free to the public when Consuelo visited them; their waters moved with the Pacific tides. No one in this city seemed to visit the baths anymore. If they wanted to go swimming, they went to Fleishhacker Pool out on Lincoln. But the Sutro Baths were different—opulent and deserted, perched beneath a cliff at the edge of the world. When Consuelo went to the Sutro Baths she became a Roman goddess, or a consumptive Victorian heiress in one of the books that Graciela had recited to her from memory. Was this the water cure, taking to the sea, for health and for pleasure? The baths cleared Consuelo's head, quieted the loneliness that buzzed in her ears all day long, muffled our wails. We can't say we didn't envy her a little, resent her, even.

Consuelo liked to arrive an hour or so before sunset. During a few moments in the late afternoon, the baths' three glassine arcs became interlocking prisms. The space was originally built to hold thirty thousand.

Inside, Consuelo was alone, dazzled and dizzy.

It was almost always just her and the girl inside the frosted glass booth, who handed her a bathing suit worn by girls who won swimming medals at the turn of the century and hysterical women seeking the water cure. Black, with a floppy skirt, a white stripe around the hem. The girl would pass Consuelo a plastic cap and some soap wrapped in paper, and a thin white towel with the phrase *The Octopus Must Be Destroyed* embroidered along the edge in pale-blue cursive letters, words that, Consuelo had learned by asking, referred to the lost aspirations of the baths' founder: of defeating the tyranny of the Southern Pacific Railroad through the Roman vision of heated indoor public waters. Consuelo could barely speak this new language, but she tried. She asked questions every chance she got.

Pulling back the heavy copper-green door to the changing rooms, Consuelo listened to the way the glass rooms held the syllables of her polite exchange with the girl in the booth, pulling them into long echoes, bouncing them off the stained glass and over the water. Glamour girls lined the walls, with their porcelain doll-eyes, their golden-waved bobs. In her cap and suit, Consuelo struck a flapper-ish pose, flounced her skirt. She slapped her own ass for the joy of it, and the happy sound echoed over the ruins.

She had an hour and a half before dinner at Los Domínguez. She'd need to make her way through the baths en guinda. Dinner obligations, the strain of socializing when she would rather disappear—these were the sorts of things for which she should have been grateful, Consuelo scolded herself each week.

Inside the thick glass, there were six saltwater baths and a freshwater plunge pool, and Consuelo visited them all, beginning with the hottest and ending in the coolest oval of ocean water. Three trapezes, two rusted over. Seven slides. Each time Consuelo visited the baths she dared herself to climb the ladder to the slide, screaming as she plunged into the main pool, kidney-shaped, heated to eighty degrees by live steam piped in from the pump lodge. She stared at the work of the old pumps through the glass. Some windows were cracked, fine lines spidering through thick yellow panes. Some were the color of a bottle. One window, high above all the others, reflected rose light. Consuelo dove underwater and surfaced, again and again. She floated on her back and looked out beyond the empty bathhouse bleachers, to the ocean.

"Luis," Consuelo called into the ancient glass, high above her. "Luis, Luis, Luis." The name bounced from the cathedral ceiling, reverberating through the heavy stained-glass walls, echoing like a prayer. This was the only place in the new city where Consuelo said his name.

After the salt baths, Consuelo walked the room's steamy, palm-lined perimeter, slapping the tile floor in wet bare feet, teeth chattering, to admire the exploits of Sutro's travels. A glass box of stuffed cats: cheetahs, leopards, and a tiny tiger. A diorama of shrunken heads, a hall of gems, Chinese swords, and best of all, or worst, depending on the day, on her mood: the rotting mummy, small behind another panel of glass.

Then the tide pool shaped like a crescent moon, a murky turquoise color, filled with sea life. Here, Consuelo took off her cap and shook her hair, let it pick up the air's salt. This pool was decorative, but she dove in anyway, opened her eyes to nothing but a dark swirl, and pulled to the surface with green algae flooding her vision, tangled in her hair, which she'd let grow long down her back to spite the fashions. Where was her famous vanity?

For the first time in her life, Consuelo wanted to be touched by no one. She went days upon days without washing her face or her body at home—her visits to the Sutro Baths staved off visible filth. Afterward, her hair fuzzed and tangled painfully.

When Consuelo was done, she returned to the dressing room, where she showered with an ancient cake of soap imprinted with Sutro's name, then dried her body, dressed it, and realized that she had just seventeen minutes to arrive at the Domínguez home, clear on the other side of the Avenues. Still, she stopped and took a long look at the wall of golden-haired starlets, before returning her suit and towel.

Outside Sutro's garden gates the following words were inscribed in bronze:

THESE WESTERN SHORES SHOULD BECOME THE LANDS OF CULTURED GROVES AND ARTISTIC GARDENS, THE HOME OF A POWERFUL AND REFINED RACE. TO REACH THIS HAPPY CON-SUMMATION A TASTE FOR THE BEAUTIFUL IN NATURE MUST BE ENGENDERED AMONG THE MASSES.

Consuelo had learned the words by heart, copied them into her note-book her first week in the new city, like a promise. She stopped to read them as she left, out of habit. They reminded her of the words that Gra-ciela had to memorize, and of Perlita's garden. Our country had seemed to want the same thing—to be the home of a powerful and refined race, a land of cultured groves and artistic gardens. Whatever "powerful and refined" was, though, Consuelo now felt the opposite.

Last week at dinner, Mamá Domínguez had told Consuelo about the man who, years before, had tried to sue when the baths wouldn't rent him a bathing suit, how Sutro had said if he let those people, Black peo-ple, into his water, then he'd have to allow everyone. His business would be driven into the ground. But Sutro would sell the man a ticket to watch from the bleachers, if he'd take that.

Mamá Domínguez's story made Consuelo wonder what exactly her face meant here. Perlita had always told her to be careful. With her curly hair, if she spent just a bit more time in the sun, she might be mistaken for another kind of child. All this rain and fog here, and still her skin was darker than it had been at home. In the capital, Consuelo had carried a parasol on walks and wore a wide-brimmed hat with a satin sash tied under her chin, but here that sort of thing would feel old-fashioned. Chela is as chela does.

In that basement, during the massacre, Consuelo had memorized the casta painting, the one Lucía had found years before. Ladinos, a man and a woman, their heads large and central on the canvas, the contours of their faces tracing the outline of nothing. A mestiza woman branched out behind them, and then a rich gradient of other faces, in white lace collars, in rags.

The sky was white and the wind unwound Consuelo's hair from its wet bun, whipping the curls around her face. Twelve minutes until dinner. Consuelo would be late no matter what. The thought of sitting at the table, practicing her English with the children, was more than she could bear that night. These days, more often than not, Consuelo felt drowned. She decided to go back downtown to her apartment and call to apologize, say she was sick. She dreaded their disappointment, their concern, which she knew would be sincere.

In San Francisco, Papá Domínguez was a lovely family man, a Consul-General. He doted on his twin daughters, praised their accomplishments at school, and smiled like a man who had never committed an act of violence, not even against the members of his own family. The week before, he'd opened his wallet at the table, taken out a bill from his last trip back to the capital, and laughed until tears pearled in the corners of his eyes.

"The General's new whore!" he said, holding up a five-colón note. At the words, Consuelo was immediately ashamed. She had been the General's whore.

On the bill was the face of an ancient india, line-drawn in iridescent blue, her eyes like the backs of beetles. "She told his future the right way and he, el indito, rewards her by putting her face on the money. It's embarrassing, but what a story! She could have asked for anything, and he's nuts enough to have given it. And what does she ask for? Not water for her little shit town in Izalco, not a new road, or a school, or even some money for her grandchildren. No, la bruja doesn't want money—she wants to be on the money."

Consuelo wondered if he knew about her father, that he'd once been the General's fortune teller, if Domínguez knew any more than she did about his mysterious death. He'd probably sat around this table talking

about Germán in the same way. He wouldn't have known anything about
Graciela, whom Perlita had kept a secret—but was this how he'd spoken
about the husband of his wife's best friend?

Papá Domínguez passed the bill around, and Consuelo laughed too,
to be polite, when it came to her. Consuelo studied la vieja's face until she
could put the money away and reproduce her features in her notebook.
Their broad noses were just the same. Perlita had always told her, when
she was a child, that she would grow into her nose one day. She'd say this
out of nowhere, with a smirking smile that cut Consuelo's insides—here
was a periodic reminder that she was so ugly that her nose startled the
people around her, even the ones who may have loved her, and that they
couldn't help but comment, laugh. From the side, Consuelo's nose was a
beak; head-on, a pear. On la india, it was unremarkable. On Consuelo—
Consuelo stared at herself in the mirror, as she was wont to do—well, it
was a nose. It wasn't so terrible, really. Sheesh.

LOURDES: Yinita, don't forget, you have the same nose.
LUCÍA: Of course she does. Simón, it's bien cute. Consuelo's off her
rocker.

Consuelo walked to the train that would take her home, considering
what lie to give as an excuse for refusing the hospitality of Los Domínguez. The train got crowded early each evening, and the feeling was unbearable, pressed against so much skin, breathing the cigar breath and
baby bottles of everyone with five cents to ride the train from the ocean
to the bay. When the streetcar was too crowded, Consuelo would step off
early and walk through the lemon light of downtown and up the hills to
her apartment. She knew what to say now to the doorman wringing his
white gloves outside her building. "Thank you." "Good evening." As she
went upstairs, she repeated any new words she'd learned that day: *I remember, I remembered, I will remember. I fight, I fought, I will fight. I find,
I found, I will find. I leave, I left, I will leave.*

Inside, Consuelo took off her shoes and stockings, unbuttoned her
dress, unpinned her wet hair, and put on her nightgown. At dusk, from

her window, she could see out to Nob Hill, to Market Street, full of Slavic girls dressed like angels, selling flowers out of carts. Tiger lilies, birds-of-paradise, fuchsias, calla lilies, forget-me-nots, peach-roses, and carnations dyed green and blue and violet.

She decided she would paint la india. She hadn't really painted outside of class in months. She took the cloth off the easel that Perlita had paid for and dragged it across the floor. She began unwrapping the brushes from their soft case, taking the paints out of a low drawer, and the drowned feeling lifted a little. She mixed the egg in with the tempera and tried to see, before committing a stroke. She stirred and conjured vision, searching for that golden ratio that the instructor loved to dissect, a proportion she had once thought was natural, innate, obvious, but now understood, because she was dull and unseeing, insensitive to it as she was insensitive to all geometry, that she must hunt for it.

The phone shrilled, and Consuelo dropped the palette to the ground. She picked up the receiver, knowing Mamá Domínguez was on the other end of the line. Consuelo heard the older woman's ragged breath and knew that she'd worried her; she told Mamá Domínguez that she'd fallen asleep, that she'd be over soon. Had Perlita been there, she would have slapped Consuelo's face, called her rude and selfish.

Consuelo hung up the phone and dressed: her stockings and shoes, her blue lace gown, the pearls, all things that had been delivered in a large box to the apartment downtown, shortly after Consuelo arrived in San Francisco. (At the bottom of the box was small card on which a dashed-off line and single word were written: "—Perlita.")

Consuelo pinned up her hair, still wet, and put on a boiled wool coat for the fog. In the elevator's mirror, the skin of her face was pale gray. Heavy bags under her eyes. A bit of lipstick helps, but only so much.

Mamá Domínguez embraced Consuelo at the door and took her inside. Around the table, the men were playing chess and drinking. The children had been put to bed. Mamá Domínguez tapped the maid on the shoulder and told her to heat a plate on the stove, and then introduced Consuelo to a man who spoke Spanish with a Mexican accent. He was staying in the new city for three weeks, with Los Domínguez. When the maid placed the plate on the table, it occurred to Consuelo that she'd had nothing to eat all day except a boiled egg for breakfast. Careless. Stupid.

Mole enchiladas, made in honor of the guest. Consuelo ate with purpose. The Mexican checkmated his host, and the air filled with soft congratulations. Consuelo ate so quickly that she spilled mole down the front of her dress. She didn't look up from her plate until the food was gone. The man was too handsome: black, wavy hair, smiling lines around his eyes, a nose like a knife. And Consuelo was suddenly very tired. She'd stuffed herself like a wild beast, and she felt dizzy and drunk, too afraid to meet the Mexican's eyes. She was the only one at the dark wood table, until he left his chess game and sat down beside her.

"Why are you late?" he said. Consuelo decided to take his question as a joke and laugh. Laughing was what she did when she found she could not speak. After a beat, Consuelo told him that Los Domínguez were friends of her family, which did not answer his question, but, thankfully, he seemed satisfied with her response. He asked about Consuelo's studies, and she told him that she was learning English.

"I heard that you're a better painter than you are a speaker of English," he said, and Consuelo nodded, silent, trying not to laugh into the quiet. "I've heard about your paintings," he said. "Would you let me see them?" Consuelo listened carefully, as if tuning into a radio station, to Mamá Domínguez laughing from the living room. They were on to cards now, and the strange reason the Mexican had for not joining them was to remain in Consuelo's company.

"Are you all right?" the Mexican asked.

She was not.

Consuelo hadn't slept in days. She couldn't steady her hands. Oh, Painting Reality, that stupid instructor. This was all fine. But she couldn't steady her hands to paint or see or do anything else, really, because at night we crawled in her blood. When she did that self-portrait, early on, we watched her mix the egg into the powder, imagine a mineral-pink sky, a gradation to angelic blue, like the silk of La Virgencita's shawl, deepening into indigo. We crept in, into her blood, into the flecks of paint undiluted by egg or water, into her ears to hum, crept as delicate fingers into the hollow of her throat, into her mind. We reminded her that once we'd lived.

Consuelo had noticed her shaking hands and remembered that apparently she did not know how to hold a paintbrush. Strangely, she hadn't had a good cry since she'd first arrived in the city. No, she was not all right. She walked across the city three or four times in one day, trying to exhaust herself. She floated in salt water for hours. She felt weak, and inwardly agitated, nothing like the woman she'd thought she might eventually become.

Consuelo felt the Mexican studying her.

"A pleasure to meet you," he said, when Consuelo failed to respond to his question. He kissed her hand. Consuelo watched his reflection in the stylish, oval mirrors hanging on either end of the dining table as he got up and left the room. She caught her own face too—red, sweating, as if she were ill. She sat alone in the dining room and listened to the Mexican make his gracious good nights. Next to the door, La Virgencita, in blue, hung in a golden frame above the cocktail bar. Consuelo swore that, for a minute, La Virgen raised one of her pious, downcast lids and winked. Her stomach lurched.

"Fuck me," she whispered to her crazy head, the demon in her belly, the black smears that materialized suddenly in front of her eyes. She walked half-blind to the bathroom, where she collapsed on the floor. "Shhh," she said to the closed door.

Later, before the driver took Consuelo home, Mamá Domínguez embraced her at the door and told her that the Mexican would like to take her to see some fish in Golden Gate Park, but that she must be very careful, because of all the animals. In the Outside Lands, bison ran wild. Some crazy gringo kept filling the place with all sorts of creatures— zebras and emus and koalas, maybe even a tiger.

Linda sounded as if she were speaking underwater. Consuelo was too tired to ask what she meant, too dazed by a churn of nausea to worry about the details of the message. Mamá Domínguez kissed Consuelo on both cheeks, and Consuelo stumbled into the waiting car. She nodded off in the backseat and, when she got to her building, someone helped her into the elevator up to the third floor. Inside the apartment she tripped over her easel and crawled into bed, dizzy and feverish behind the eyes, belly bloated and stretched like a drum.

She awoke in the morning in her mole-stained dress, shoes still on her feet, and spent the day retching into the porcelain toilet. She sweated and stuck her head beneath the faucet, opened all the windows, then shivered. Her brain felt lacerated, useless. Dark-gray fog settled in the sky. It must have been late afternoon. She vomited more.

That evening, Lindita called to gossip about the Mexican, and hearing Consuelo's broken voice, arrived in a car to take Consuelo to the hospital, where a doctor bound off her arm and counted the dark marks that had risen from beneath the surface of her skin. He drew her blood and announced that Consuelo would spend the night. After sleeping all day, Consuelo lay awake in the hospital bed until dawn lightened the windows, blinding her with its glare, so that when the doctor re-entered the room and told her she had dengue fever, Consuelo could not see his face. The doctor asked her to sit up, and then laid his fingers over the skin of her back, which had just begun to itch, and described the lacy rash that had spread there.

"When did you arrive in this country?"

Consuelo ticked the weeks off on her fingers. Four. A month.

"A jungle mosquito must have bitten you just before you boarded. A little memento from home." The doctor laughed. "You're very lucky. A few years ago we would've had to quarantine you, Jungle Girl. After the earthquake, the plague was all over downtown. Diseased rats crawling out of crumbling buildings. Rats on the ships moved right into Chinatown. Wouldn't even have drawn your blood," said the doctor. "You people infest our country." He smiled good-naturedly.

When Consuelo was a little girl, a friend of Perlita's had gone to visit her husband's finca in the west and returned with dengue fever. Perlita whispered about the illness as if it were a terrible secret. "Horrible," she said, shaking her head, as if the woman had contracted the disease after seducing an indio disguised as a mosquito.

When Consuelo was finally allowed to return to her apartment, a bouquet of flowers in a green frosted-glass vase was wilting at the door to her unit. She picked up the note from the mat; they were from the Mexican, and she didn't have the energy to read the expanse of his handwriting, too long, too many optimistic cursive flourishes for a woman he'd only just met. Consuelo felt a slow choking as she struggled with her key. Inside, she stuck the limp flowers in the sink, and let the water run over the flowers and his letter, bleeding the ink.

Consuelo wrapped herself up in a blanket and sat on the floor in front of her easel. She laid out all of the sketches of la india that she'd worked on in the hospital. As she began to paint, Consuelo sang softly to herself, her body still and warm and calm, as it hadn't been in weeks. She sang a part of a song she remembered from her early days in our village. We sang with her. *My mother is the volcano, my sister's in the sky. Who am I, who am I, who am I? My mother the volcano, my sister the sky. Who am I, who am I, who am I.*

26

IN HOLLYWOOD, ROSIE TOOK GRACIELA OUT AT NIGHT TO MEET short men with bulging eyes, movie producers. Rosie fawned over these feo men in a way that she understood to be purely in her own self-interest as an actress on the rise. We thought she was acting like an idiot, and so did Graciela.

One night on the way to dinner Rosie tumbled on the sidewalk and told her date something jodida like, "Your heart really is made of pure gold," when he did nothing more than hold out his fat little hand to her. Grinning like an idiot, she lay on the filthy ground in a silk gown the exact color of her hair, the fabric sopping up the blood on both her knees. Graciela gritted her teeth and looked down the street for a way for them to make an escape.

Rosie's date gripped her elbow at a right angle and folded his lips in thin parallel lines, a smirk. Graciela stood behind her, picking up the train of her gown like a bridesmaid, and like that they made their way to the restaurant.

Graciela's date wasn't much better, boring and loud with a waxy pink face. He talked like a distant train horn, blaring at no one, staring far beyond the table where they sat, as if he wanted to make everyone in his presence fall silent and then fall asleep. Rosie drank too much and passed out with her head on the table.

Graciela's date stared at her chichis in the gown that Rosie had chosen for her. He boomed right into Rosie's date's ear, "I'm going to fuck her into the ground." Rosie's date revealed his lower teeth unpleasantly and choked out a ha or two.

Graciela tried to lift Rosie's head from the table. Her date nudged Graciela's in the ribs, maybe to hint that, despite Graciela's stony silence, she might understand English.

"Look at her," he said. "Even if she understands a word of what we're saying, I don't think she talks. She's a dummy."

It was a new country and here Graciela was new too. Without thinking about it too much, she threw the contents of her drink in her date's face, breaking the glass on the other guy's head like cracking an egg. Hollywood slapstick!

She lifted Rosie from the table and hoisted her over her shoulder to go home. The men didn't dare follow. The crowd went wild with applause.

A few weeks later, with a less gruesome pair, Rosie led the group back to their apartment. She sat at the edge of her twin bed and untied the fur around her neck, let it dawdle to the carpet. Her date hiked his trousers up from the pockets, sat beside her on the bed, and patted her knee. She crawled onto his lap and he shoved his flat face into the base of her neck, made a series of wet noises, opening and closing his eyes as if slowly waking up from a nap.

Across from them, Graciela's date sat on her twin bed, gawking like a fucking idiot. Graciela stood in the doorway. She watched too. Rosie's date's head glistened reddish. The two of them folded onto their sides.

Graciela's date turned to her, and she joined him on the bed. He looked at her with the urgency of someone holding a knife. Fuck it. Graciela wasn't sure that she wanted him, but she knew she wanted something. He held on to her, pressed his lips against hers, unzipped Rosie's dress from Graciela's body. He tasted of the whiskey they'd drunk, of cigars—not unpleasant—but his tongue was a slug, everywhere at once. He shut his eyes tight. If Graciela closed hers too, the feeling of his skinny arms, the way they tightened around her like ropes—well, it wasn't awful. Graciela, like anyone, was curious, and she knew what would likely happen next. Her date unzipped himself and his cock flopped out like a guy

waiting behind a door, more youthful and startled than any of us would
have imagined from the lines around the man's eyes. It pulsed, asserting
its life, its veins pompous and bright. We screamed. Lucía nearly peed her
pants.

Graciela's date gripped her shoulders and lowered her backward onto
the bed, parted her legs with his still-trousered knee, and to his surprise,
he slipped himself inside her easily enough. He gasped. We knew the
beginning of this feeling and we knew the way it was supposed to finish—
with a wild, noisy brightness. But the exertions of this tripudo producer
weren't going to get there. This, once Graciela's date found a rhythm
inside of her, was more like someone else brushing a knot out of her hair.
He punctuated his efforts with grunting coughs. Graciela imagined a
small lake, drying in the sun.

When it was over, when the man had dragged himself out of her and
rolled onto his back, she felt something inside of her opening up and lifting off. Not exactly pleasure. The air around her head grew lighter. And
that was it. She thought she could do this again if she needed to; maybe
it would be better next time.

From the other side of the room, Rosie exhaled a soft puffy cloud of a
snore. She was pretending. She feigned sleep sometimes, we guessed to
be alone with the few thoughts she chose not to share with Graciela
throughout the day. Everyone had to keep certain things to themselves.
Rosie was beneath her bed now, a sheet wrapped around her, like on the
first night Graciela had met her.

Rosie always looked beautiful, but as Graciela had gotten to know her
better, she'd learned how chuca Rosie secretly was. She rarely bathed,
maybe once a week, and at night she hardly bothered to wash the pan-
cake makeup and mascara from her face. That first night, the cold
cream and the pin curls, was a rare occurrence, a habit imposed by her
mother's presence, maybe. Most mornings Rosie's pillow was smeared
with lipstick and powder and black crinkles of eye makeup that looked
like little ants. At the start of each day she just put more makeup on over
the face she'd worn to bed. She'd spill coffee and lick the table. She fell
asleep in her clothes, drooling into the sheets. All those pearl-handled

toothbrushes—she hardly used her own. But knowing about Rosie's personal habits made Graciela love her more tenderly. Her messy little sister, no matter that Rosie was older.

In Hollywood Graciela's life still felt like make-believe. But here she wasn't playing the part of the General's brujita, or an orphan india. She was a "Spanish" girl. What does that mean? Lots of things. In one movie: a red dress, layers of ruffles, a basket of fruit perched on her head. Everyone assumed that she knew how to dance. She learned as best as she could and found she was pretty good at it. She'd studied this kind of movement at the movies with Perlita. Sitting in dark theaters all those years, she'd watched the bodies, those rows of kicking legs, arms supple as lengths of silk, haughty chins, eyes downcast and peaceful as the Virgin's. She'd committed their gestures to memory.

She had a professional shot now too, a picture with her hands raised in dove wings above her head. She wore a bow tie, a top hat, and jacket, her body bare underneath a pair of sequined bloomers that, later on, left silvery scales on her most private skin. In the films in which Graciela first appears, you can read her name in the credits, along with First Chinese Girl, Second Eskimo Girl, Third Squaw, or Island Girl 4. But more often, during her early years in Hollywood, she wasn't named or even numbered, just one of many figures moving in formation, barely distinct, a veiled face in a sultan's harem. We followed her face from film to film. It was wider than others, those black eyes that directors said made her "a perfect Oriental." In profile her nose was straight-boned, and wide at the bottom when you looked at it head-on. Her skin was the color of the cardboard that held the dish soap in the studio's cafeteria, where she also worked.

Along with her work in the studio and its cafeteria, Graciela kept her custodial job at the library. She knew that alliances could shift and that life wasn't cheap; she'd need enough money to be able to move quickly, to change her plans, to disappear, if ever that were necessary.

Girls disappeared here too. The girls she worked with at the cafeteria, gone suddenly in the middle of the week. There were raids, she heard, sometimes right there at the studio. All the more reason to stick with me, Rosie told her. They tend to go after girls with a certain look, she said, wrinkling her nose.

Graciela understood: *girls who look like my mother, girls who look like my friends, like my sister, like me.*

Sometimes she worked for twenty hours straight in huge rooms illuminated with shining machines, bright-white bulbs, the sharp ticking of clocks in the background. If the General's palace, its long, dark rooms, dripping candles, and swathes of velvet guarding the sun, if that place had been a cocoon, well, here she was something else. A fucking calaceada butterfly. If you went to the movies those days, you saw her face.

Eventually, Graciela began collapsing out of physical exhaustion from working long, dazzling days on outdoor sets, in sunlight she breathed like air. Calaceada, pero calaceada. When she had to, she rested, panting in the shade with other girls, fanning herself with folded paper. It was the only way to forget.

Rosie, meanwhile, had decided that Graciela was going to make it big; obviously she would, why else would they be friends? Morris, Rosie's agent, another barrel-shaped man, took Graciela on as a personal favor to Rosie.

"I'm the biggest girl—by miles—on Morris's list now. But I bet you could take Dolores's place," Rosie said, after Graciela signed herself over to the man.

Dolores, Rosie said, used to be a big star before talkies, but now the only roles she could get were in the background.

"Because of the way she talked?" Graciela had never met Dolores, but knew of her—Rosie's ex–best friend.

"Yeah, and she's a little morenita. But not even as dark as you," Rosie said. "You're bien lucky—you're darker than her, but just as pretty. You speak better English, and you dance like a fucking dream!"

Graciela thought that Rosie might simply be jealous of Dolores. Dolores was beautiful—as soon as Rosie mentioned that she knew her,

Graciela started seeing Dolores's image everywhere, on theater marquees and billboards above the highway. Graciela could tell that something had happened between the two. It was clear in the stiff way that Rosie began brushing her hair, or plucking her eyebrows, whenever Dolores was mentioned—the way she sat upright in her seat and stopped eating when Isabel, in town for the weekend, as she so often was, had asked about "that cherita little Mexican girl." Rosie tersely replied that Graciela was her best friend now.

"Dolores has disgraced herself, dressing in feathers and talking nonsense," Isabel began saying soon after, quickly aligning herself with her daughter's feelings. "Tawdry." She creased the newspaper along the middle of Dolores's face—an article about her latest affair, with some married genius—and set the paper aside.

But Rosie used Dolores's story as a point of reference for Graciela's career, about which Rosie seemed foolishly, buoyantly, optimistic.

"You want the biggest roles you can get. No more small stuff. No more Oriental dancing girls," Rosie said. "You know, Dolores started out with big roles, played Brazilian queens, before she opened her mouth and swallowed all those shitty little parts. She didn't have to do that." She sounded almost sorry for her old friend.

Rosie paused, studied Graciela's face, frowned. "You need a new name. No one here can even say yours," she said. "Think about it."

And she did. Of all people, she could see the appeal of a new name. "Graciela del Norte," she offered slyly, a week later. "La India del Norte. Cielita del Norte."

"Come on!" Rosie said. "Ma ve. What about Linda? How about Carol or Betty? What about Grace North? You don't have to be güerita to take a name like that. You get to be new here."

Graciela wanted to be new here. She wanted to glide on the edge of others' perception, give no one the satisfaction of knowing exactly who she was at first glance. She wanted to be smart and mouthy like Lourdes, brave like María, tender and protective like Cora, as mysterious as Lucía.

Finally, she found her new name in the trash after mopping up the bathroom floor. Lux toilet soap. A glamorous woman smiling on a curl of cardboard paper: Grace Lux. The name was light, bright, holy.

> LUCÍA: And with this soap she became clean? In some ways. When she spoke the new name aloud, shared it to the smug satisfaction of La Rosie, Graciela invoked a spell to erase the memories of her old life.
>
> MARÍA: But damn that memorious mind, the moments of our death surfacing so often in its deep waters. Of course she could never clean us away, try as she might.

As Grace Lux, most nights Graciela drank whatever Rosie had at the apartment. When they went out together, Rosie dressed her in a dirty gown she'd grown tired of and called her beautiful, and older men would send bottles of Champagne across dark rooms to them, would order songs to be played just for them on the pianos and light their cigarettes.

Graciela liked being drunk, feeling as if her body moved beneath a volume of warm rushing water. Sometimes she woke up like Rosie, with her shoes still on her feet, beneath her twin bed, on the couch. Or outside—sometimes she found her way to the beach. She'd take off her shoes and walk out to where the sand was flat and traced with foam. The soles of her feet picked up tar, and she didn't go home until morning. She'd wake up with a dry mouth and seaweed wrapped around her ankles.

Sometimes she drank so much that she'd wake up in a strange bed, in the dark, and she'd crouch to the floor to dress, and then tiptoe out into the California light, emerging like Judy Garland in *The Wizard of Oz*. She'd jog along the shore in a long evening gown, scanning the bleary morning for a cab to take her home. Once she was back at the apartment she shared with Rosie, Graciela would shake the sand out of the chiffon and hang the gown in the bathroom to steam while she drew the hot water for soaking herself in the tub. Rosie slept those long mornings into afternoons, napping on the couch, vomiting into a salad bowl, complaining of her head.

Most mornings, Graciela lay awake in darkness that had a taste—

rough and wild and sour—listened to our rabbit heartbeats, negotiated with our wails, until the room glowed gray. Soon it would be time to work. She was dazed, fuzzy, but never threw up. She would prune in the bathtub with no memory of the night before. How did she find herself in this place, soaping tar off her bare soles? She wouldn't know. Her mind's contents were erased, as if stolen, the night before a blank page. But the black soles of her feet would conjure a tactile memory of El Gran Pendejo's proclamations about the transmission of healing energy through the soles of unshod feet and of longer ago, on the volcano, the earth's radiance entering her body as she ran with us, kicking off her caites.

Throughout the day, as her mind cleared and the alcohol's powers were diluted, our faces would return to her.

When she did sleep, that night returned to her. Graciela would crawl, on her hands and knees, looking for bodies she recognized. A woman facedown beside a stream she remembered from our childhood. Graciela was certain she saw her back rising and falling with breath. She would shake her shoulders, and call out for her mother, for Consuelo, for us.

But then the woman's face would swivel to meet Graciela's, her neck breaking in Graciela's hands. Her eye sockets writhed with maggots. A scorpion crawled out of her mouth. Who was she—La Cigua? Or was that her own face, her own wide nose?

Graciela would wake from these dreams pressed against a cold window, standing in front of that tower. We would guide her back through the dark to her bed, and then lie down and wait. We sang to her. "Arráncame la Vida," "Sisters of the Stars," "Vamos a la Vuelta." We felt her mind fraying with each dream, each memory. Her ability to guayabear, the way she held on to everything—it was not always a gift.

Champagne, Graciela decided, really worked for her. She didn't dream when she drank. It wiped her mind clean like a fizzy mop.

27

LUCÍA: In San Francisco, the Mexican doted on Consuelo. He kept
sending her flowers, and after receiving one perfunctory
thank-you note from her, he hired a friend to serenade her
outside her window. *Why?* Consuelo wanted to shout down
to the friend the first time this happened. *Are you sure you
have the right address?* Instead, she pretended to be asleep.
But the next time it happened, she stood on the balcony and
waved politely. She remembered how alone she was and
she blew two kisses, one for the singer and one for the
man who paid him. *Tell him I'm charmed,* she called down to
the friend, who wasn't any more or less handsome than the
Mexican.

Consuelo told herself that she didn't have a choice.
She had no money, and the Mexican did. She let herself be
cared for. Inside of her apartment, he offered to brush her
hair. It was curious. He began riding the streetcar across
town to her in the middle of the day, with a big pot of soup
that sloshed all over his lap, to help her recover.

All she wanted was everything—quiet, adoration, new
boar's-hair paintbrushes, a silk dressing gown the color of
salt water, sparkling wine, financial ease, a mother, a sister, a
faceless patron to whom she owed nothing, to walk through

a gallery in Paris wearing a fur coat with nothing underneath. Luis had promised to take her to Paris one day.

But sometimes, all that Consuelo really wanted was nothing. She wanted to die, and she thought of it constantly.
Visions of her death intruded on her dreams, her waking
hours. Why hadn't she died in the massacre? Or, better, why
hadn't she died before the massacre? Why didn't she die
now? Walking in front of the streetcar, she could pretend to
slip on the tracks. Who would know? Who would care?
And there was the whole ocean, waiting, oblivious. The edge
of a knife, a bottle of pills. Who would miss her? Death sent
inviting spirals to mesmerize her. But we kept her away. We
wanted Consuelo to live.

CORA: The Mexican took her to the Outside Lands, steering the
lightness of her body like a balloon on a string. White fog
drifted over the shoulders of her black velvet coat; the air
changed and a chill moved right through her. Consuelo
shivered—in the hospital she'd lost eighteen pounds, and
now she never could seem to get warm.

It was just like Lindita had said—there were strange animals all over the park. There was a fat, furry creature, a bear,
dark gray and stout, in a eucalyptus tree above them. White
fog swirled around his shaggy ears, and he cuddled on his
branch, shoving pawfuls of narrow leaves into his mouth.
From where he sat, the bear could see an elephant mother
and her young son, splashing in a man-made lake. Ostriches
and peacocks trifled along a dark path that led to the sea. A
zebra muddied his hooves in the rose garden. And while
Consuelo didn't see him, she felt certain that the tiger was
there.

They made their way to the aquarium. Light poured in
from long slatted windows facing the sky, heels tapped and

circled on the marble floors, pausing before the gleaming tanks of coral and swimming creatures. A team of men in white were deployed with trays, offering snails dressed and oiled to the people gathering now in the aquarium's foyer.

Consuelo knew that she needed to get out of this place, where she felt as though she were being watched at all times, by this nice man, by Lindita, and, from a distance, by Perlita. She needed to make her own way in a place where she knew no one, would depend upon no one, a place where she was certain that she knew how to hold a paintbrush. All those rich girls, Las Rositas, and their summers in Paris. That's where painting was shifting and exploding into new forms— why couldn't she go to Paris to become something new? She'd seen an exhibit of eternal spirals from a Paris group here in San Francisco that animated her with a sudden rush of oxygen. Afterward, Consuelo wanted to see, to live, for the first time in months. The paintings were a series of private galaxies; they felt interior, specific to her. She felt their geometry entering her, rearranging the atoms of her being.

And she'd taken one figure-sculpting class, paid for by the Mexican. She'd avoided clay up to this point. Or Perlita had steered her toward painting with the idea of Consuelo acquiring a refined and decorative skill. After scrutinizing the model's body—her heavy thighs spread flat on the stool, her asymmetrical breasts, the slope of her shoulders, comparing the model's stillness against her own clothed parts— Consuelo reveled in the slick weight of the material, sinking her fingers into the clay, earth crusting beneath her nails. Seeing was feeling, in clay. With some money the Mexican had given her for food, she bought a five-pound block of clay after the class, and wrapped it in her scarf as if she had stolen it, returning to her apartment to work with it alone. She was creating something for her dead novio Luis, and she wanted no one else to see it.

Later, she had changed the subject when the Mexican asked her about the class. Clay was private. She had to get out of here. She had to find a way to buy her own clay, to make her own secret eternal spirals. Paris—she wanted to go there and she wanted to go there alone.

MARÍA: Basically: If she could just get herself to Paris, then she thought she wouldn't have to rely on anyone else, for anything else. She thought she'd be able to make her own way, that her wild talent would be recognized and she would be free to live on her own and to make the art she wanted to make. I don't fucking blame the silly puta, as crazy as that sounds. If she stayed in San Francisco, what would the shape of her life be? She'd be struggling to see in her painting class. Eventually, her patrona, Perlita, would stop sending money, and she'd be forced to get married to this boring, nice man who had taken her to see fish.

"This whole place," the Mexican said, "is made up of a vast family of displaced fish." He pointed to a sallow gold fish with huge blue eyes, Seale's cardinalfish, according to the label. "This one came from the Philippines." It darted behind spiny coral like a child running into a dark forest.

When the aquarium had opened, they'd been moved across town—tiny frogfishes, fat, flat mola molas, a trio of giant squids—in boxes of glass, strapped top to bottom in steamy towers, sloshing down Market Street on a fleet of trucks that bore five thousand gallons of seawater. And of course, before that, they'd swum the Pacific from as far off as the warm waters of the Philippines; or some, like the squid brothers, had plunged beneath icy volumes off the coast of Alaska. In a dying town, the lusty sea lion had been trapped by the triangulated vectors of nets and muscles cast by a fisherman and two morose drunks, who were paid nothing for their efforts.

The Mexican chattered endlessly. Consuelo didn't mind—she let his facts fill her porous head like a light show.

Because otherwise, all she could think was: Luis would have loved to walk through these rooms of stolen fish and fossils.

He never left her. Sometimes, Consuelo hated him for haunting her. Had she never been taken to the capital, she wouldn't have had to suffer his loss. Had she never had to suffer his loss, she would never have been taken to the General.

But other times, she longed for him so vividly it was as if she could will him into returning. Fucking the Mexican the night before, she fumbled her way into dark halves, separating her mind from her body. She learned that this was the only way she could feel pleasure during sex, and that sometimes this was enough pleasure to summon Luis's memory. She did it like a spell.

LUCÍA: Now Consuelo turned up the fur collar of her coat—she hadn't given it up at the door, because she was always cold in this city, even inside. In front of a tank of barracuda arrayed like the rungs of a ladder, she brought her elbow against the inside of the Mexican's arm and placed her hand in his pocket.

LOURDES: Unless you're stupid, you can see where this is going! Placing her hand in his pocket. ¡Ma ve!

MARÍA: Bien stupid.

LUCÍA: She wasn't just fishing around for his dick, I'll tell you that.

CORA: Ahem. Meanwhile, outside, she was sure that the tiger was peering through the life-fogged window, at the people circling inside the aquarium. She felt his eyes. The autopsy had reported that Luis had simply drowned, though Consuelo didn't believe that bullshit for an instant.

LUCÍA: Something to know about Consuelo: At age twelve, she'd opened a mirrored bathroom cabinet inside the Estate, and a thermometer fell and shattered in a bathroom sink. She'd watched the mercury dart over the ridges of crystal with the same strange appetite she had now, standing before the final tank in the aquarium, a school of minor fish, tiny things, uniformly metallic. She imagined swallowing each and every one of their silvery bodies. She remembered the mercury in the bathroom. Had she swallowed it then, she wouldn't be here now. She would have died. She would not have met Luis, and she would not have seen his ashes, and she would not have been given to the General, and she would not have witnessed our massacre, and she would not have suffered the horror and guilt of her survival. She wouldn't have become so sick that she nearly died in a Yunais hospital, and she wouldn't have the nightmares that plagued her every day.

A shark dozed inside the tank, ignored. The Mexican was suitable. He had taken Consuelo to an elegant party at the Steinhart Aquarium. He wore medals.

But something had changed after the hospital. She had begun painting every day. One tiny canvas done. All she wanted was to fill a silent room with her paintings, examine what was the same among them, discern in them the patterns that she couldn't make sense of in life. Try to untangle the tortured noises inside her head—voices that screamed, that begged for mercy. Could she silence them?

She wasn't seeing any more clearly and she hated every single thing she painted, but she was making something every day. Painting, working that lump of clay. The exertion exhausted her, but the daily effort felt healthy, sane. She wished she could tell Luis. Luis's dead eyes were the only ones she wanted on her paintings. He'd be proud of her vigor.

But maybe some of this vigor had to do with the Mexican, Consuelo reasoned. He was not exhausted by life. His childhood seemed to contain nothing worth hiding. Meanwhile Consuelo darted around his gentlest questions about her own life. What did your father do for a living? Are you close with your mother? She stuttered and tried to be unspecific—encountering the details as they flashed into her mind, she wanted to do herself violence.

When I was four I was kidnapped.

My boyfriend was murdered.

Just a couple of months ago, I was kidnapped again, tortured by a maniac, and then I watched a massacre in my childhood home.

These were the raw facts of her existence, the things she couldn't tell the Mexican. She told him things like, "My father worked in the Ministry of Health," which was not an outright lie. And when the Mexican then asked if her father had been a doctor, she merely shook her head and mentioned how cold it was here in this gray city.

She wanted to run from the Mexican, to tear herself out of this life. Was it possible for her to make herself despise this mild, handsome man? He would get sick of her anyway, she told herself. Why was he torturing her with his politeness? What good could Consuelo possibly offer him? Standing beside him, she felt made of torn paper and old glue, blood, pus, and metal pins. And look how whole he was, how strong! His skin had that rich-person glow. He would be just fine without her! She wanted to tell him to go fuck himself, to take his money and run. Arráncame la vida.

MARÍA: The Mexican suggested that they leave San Francisco at the end of the year for a long vacation at his family home in

Mexico City. There, Consuelo could continue her study of painting. And in the spring, they'd return to the States and settle in Los Angeles. Better weather, was all he had to say about that. Consuelo considered Los Angeles, along with the idea of becoming someone's wife. And why not? The fish had survived their relocation; why couldn't she? He'd pay her way, claro. But Consuelo knew: she wanted to relocate even farther from here, and alone.

LOURDES: With that sinister little flicker behind her eyes, with her hand in his pocket.

MARÍA: She glimpsed the roiling ugliness inside her, her heart's stampede of galloping horses. What kind of woman thinks of hurting a good man like this? Taking his money, running away to Paris? Who would even consider this? The horses inside her said, *You're a bad, bad, bad girl. Run, run, run, bad girl.*

LUCÍA: Half believing she could make herself stay, she told herself that she'd make a good wife. She said yes, of course, her hand still in his pocket.

LOURDES: She didn't love him and she never would. She was hungry. She sold the furs he bought her, later pawned the ring he proposed with. He'd known enough of her situation to offer her help. She took it all and spent it on a ticket to Paris. It was that or climb the rocks to the cliff overlooking the Sutro Baths at Lands End and throw herself into this ocean. Who could blame her for the choice she made? Not me.

28

T WO YEARS AFTER ARRIVING IN PARIS, CONSUELO BEGAN LIV-
ing in an apartment on rue de Castellane. It belonged to someone
else, a friend of a man she'd slept with once or twice, a lazy-eyed man who
rented it to her at a bargain, unfurnished. She didn't have the money to
fill its bare corners. The living room held her landlord's old brown-and-
pink-striped couch, a wide, copper-engraved Moroccan plate that balanced atop a stool, making a table, and her easel. She spent her mornings
walking the hill to the Sacré-Coeur, or wandering through the Luxem-
bourg Gardens, or going to as many galleries and museums as she could
before collapsing. She let the sun burn her, let herself become soaked and
shivering in the driving rain. Sometimes the galleries offered a compli-
mentary coffee, and this seemed to be how she sustained herself. Consuelo had a theory that exposing herself to the elements would toughen
her constitution, and that satiating her visual appetite for beauty would
satiate her hunger.

It didn't work.

Often, having worn her constitution out, in the middle of the night,
painting, Consuelo's body attacked itself. When this happened, Consuelo could not breathe without the feeling that her ribs were breaking.
She knew that the next few hours of her life would be determined by a
large and hungry fear, el susto.

In the green room in rue de Castellane she painted through most nights. She was getting better, she told herself. Or if not better, less afraid. She wasted less time talking herself out of painting. Her hands shook less. At least here she knew that she could see, how to hold her paintbrush.

The shining cocks of the Surrealist circle treated her like she was a moron but invited her to all of their parties. Going home from those parties, if she could walk swiftly enough, listening to her heels striking the ground, she could cut through the giddy fog of the men's bombast. Their work wasn't all that good, all that smart. Hers, she bitched to the moon, was better. She resented that one of them had started a tropical series. He was from Bruges.

Around this time María began haunting Consuelo. She hadn't thought she'd return as a seven-year-old child. As a teenager, the youngest of us, sixteen when she died, but still more woman than child, María had felt that she was becoming more her own self with each passing year. She'd eased into her body, grown to love the square of her shoulders. She enjoyed making the people around her scream with laughter. She had accepted that she loved women, and she was casually pleased to learn that neither she, nor any of the rest of us, seemed to care. So the scrawny child's afterbody surprised all of us. This little-girl María had filthy black hair, the texture of a broom, cut jaggedly above her shoulders, and a ruffly pale-pink dress, dusted in dark soil, too short on long, skinny legs. A rag sling held one of her thin arms.

María hated this fucking dress. She always had. She preferred the denim overalls Sister Iris had given her a few years after she'd outgrown the dress. And yet, here she was.

María appeared to Consuelo late at night, briefly at first, a reflection in the bathroom mirror, a familiar hallucination when Consuelo was on a familiar edge: painting days into nights without eating, drinking only wine, heart-ravaged. Before taking her Benzedrine. Sometimes in the calm after.

Actually, Consuelo had seen a lot of María over the last several weeks of manic preparation for a group show at a gallery. Though she may have recognized María vaguely from the day she spent in our village before the massacre, Consuelo certainly couldn't place her. The ghost could have been four years old, six, seven. Hard to know: she was small, indita.

Maybe because she seemed benign and anonymous, Consuelo was consoled by María's presence instead of frightened. La consolación para la consolación—was that what María was? A light came on inside Consuelo's mind when the girl appeared to her. She was inspired. She began thinking of her as her "divine lamp."

A gift bestowed by the Nine Muses, affirming Consuelo's latent genius, an angel of inspiration, a buried vision of home, whatever that meant; Consuelo had even tried to paint her as she'd once painted Graciela.

Anyway. Now tiny María sat on the old couch in the living room of Consuelo's green room, dangling her scabbed legs. The rising sun filled the room with a harsh red glare. María stayed for as long as she could. Consuelo had never seen her so whole.

Consuelo genuflected before the little girl. She reached into her pocket for a box of matches and lit a candle.

The little girl scrambled up from the couch and pinched the flame between two dirty fingers, snuffing it out. She giggled. Consuelo felt the fire enter her body, and she whispered to herself that she wasn't afraid. María's afterbody vanished with the light.

A couple of years earlier, in San Francisco, just before she'd left the Mexican, a palm reader had told Consuelo that she would lead a double life. She'd been charmed by the idea. Each painting, each day, each dress, each man, offered a delicate sampling of another life. She was trying very hard in this life, to laugh easily and contentedly, to push las pesadillas to the very edges of her mind.

Right after María vanished, Consuelo found herself gasping for air. Her lungs were being compressed, then beaten. Recognizing el susto, she pitied herself generously, clawing her way across the carpet like an animal, like a monster, indulging in a growl in between the helpless pulls of breath. She climbed hand over hand up the velvet curtains, raising herself to her feet. But the noose around her throat tightened, and the pain in her chest became jagged, and all the while Consuelo told herself a story: that she knew how to breathe, that breathing was simple, really. Her head became light as she stood, as if it were a thing unattached to her body, and her vision blurred and she hit her chest.

Usually, Consuelo could listen for a rhythm to beat through the chaotic rigor of her attacks and find her breath inside of it. But this attack was worse than the others. She bore her fingernails into the flesh of her palms and tugged at the handle of her balcony window, opening the heavy glass to the noise and light. She found the Benzedrine inhaler she was supposed to use, jammed it against her teeth with violence, but el susto would not be treated or reasoned with, and besides, it had already knocked her body to the floor.

She gasped, tore at her hair, clawed her throat, felt the promising beginnings of respiration blooming. It was a beautiful apartment. Yes. Consuelo wheezed in and out, pounding on her chest again to move air through the lungs. The spots on her vision faded. She clutched the balcony, sucking air until her wheezing subsided and she began to breathe heavy, labored breaths, but breaths all the same. She told herself she was probably just excited for her group show, for her life.

Outside the balcony, on the narrow street below, it was ten in the morning, a clear-skied Wednesday. A kid hawked papers. Two fine ladies walked arm in arm, gossiping. A cat stretched in a triangle of sun on the sidewalk, and Consuelo listened to church bells, and then the approach of a train. An hour. Two. Her body became very cold and she crawled back inside, pulled an afghan off the bed, wrapped the blanket around her shoulders like an old woman, and returned, blinking, back into the sun, to sit on the balcony. Her breathing quieted and she began to feel once more like a creature made of solid material. Her lungs ached.

She had no time for this shit. For the hours lost, hours stolen from her art. She lived, you see. The gallery show was in a couple of weeks, and she needed to get to work.

Consuelo opened a bottle of wine, lit every candle in the house, although it was still morning, and painted until dark fell and the wax puddled and flames blackened the walls with their dance. She was Artemis: the hunter, her warrior heart, and her hot arrow.

On the afternoon before her gallery show, she cooked lunch, broiled trout as she'd seen it done in our country, with lime and lemon, oregano, and thyme. The trout would be her first meal in days. She didn't want to stop working, but when smoke billowed into her room, she put aside her paints and brought the fish outside to eat on the balcony.

The week before she'd met a man, an aviator. An unhandsome, rich man, who'd declared his love for her forcefully, within minutes of their meeting. He terrified her, but Consuelo fixated on him, like a sore. He'd taken her in a cab to see his airplane with the enthusiasm of a child. Inside the plane, he'd sat her on his lap, his dick hard beneath her. Consuelo had pretended to ignore it, pretended not to be afraid. This guy, though. He started crying as soon as they were up in the air, cutting through clouds. The motor was loud. So loud he had to scream:

"Kiss me!"

"I never kiss men I've only just met!" Consuelo screamed back, her ass riding his sorrowful erection. She was lying, of course. She just found him bien feo. When he turned his wet face to her, his hands shook on the wheel, and the plane rattled and bucked like a body in deep water.

"Please," he said. "Please." Consuelo shook her head. "Please," he cried again. "Please, or I'll send this thing down into the sea." Consuelo laughed and rubbed herself against him, teasing out his hardness. What was attractive in him was his desire.

"Please kiss me," he said. "Please." Consuelo shook her head again. With a long, slow sigh, he turned the wheel, hand over hand, in a full circle, and her stomach dropped, and she fell against the side of the pit and she realized she was screaming.

"Please!" he bellowed. "Please kiss me! Do you think I'm ugly? Is that it? If you don't kiss me I have no reason to live. If you don't kiss me I'd rather die than live. Do you hear me? I'd rather die. Please. Please, I tell you."

Consuelo lunged for the crying aviator, looped her arms around his thick neck, and pulled his mouth into her own. Fine, okay, una mordida. She let his tongue explore her lips, let him groan into her neck and then the floor sprang up and her knees buckled and she fell against the wall of the pit, and she puked out everything inside of her as the world corrected itself.

The aviator continued righting the plane, sobbing into the wheel. After a moment he said, "It's just that I love you so much already. It's crazy! I know! This whole thing is crazy!" He laughed. "You're making me lose my mind, you know," he said softly, the crying having stopped at last. "You don't even know the damage you're capable of," he said.

Consuelo covered her ears with her hands and shut her eyes and kissed this man. Oh, she'd fucked uglier men, though in far less dire circumstances. She cursed herself for being so stupid as to flatter this maniac in the first place by getting onto his plane.

The aviator rubbed Consuelo's back with one hand, making the soft breathy noises one uses to comfort a baby. She slapped his hand away and buried her face in her knees, covered her head with her arms. He cursed in French in gentle whispers and shook his head side to side as if embarrassed for her, easing the vessel to the ground, where his crew stood in a line of applause.

That night the aviator read Consuelo his poems. She nodded tersely at the ones that weren't terrible. He gave her a bath and an oily kind of massage that he said he'd learned in the souk. His hands were big and veiny, much darker than Consuelo's. He lay down on the carpet and mumbled prayers to her, offering a large porcelain bowl of Champagne for soaking her feet. Consuelo told him that was a stupid waste. He told her about being lost in the desert for days, claimed he'd hallucinated her face. "I loved you before I even laid eyes on you," he said. She snorted, cackled. He said he would fly Consuelo to her volcanoes and marry her there so her mother could attend the wedding. She told him her mother was dead. Long after midnight, he cried into his glass of wine and begged her forgiveness for his reckless behavior in the airplane. *I love near to the wild heart,* he told her. He asked if Consuelo would like a pet jaguar of her own.

At that she finally relented. She told him yes.

They had demeaning sex, which was both boring and slightly brutal. She bled, and her mouth felt dry afterward. He told her he loved her again, pleaded with her a little, and Consuelo wondered why she didn't simply dismiss him from her green room. And why she was still thinking of him now, considering his proposal of marriage?

If she did marry the aviator, she could be assured a different kind of life. He was rich, and not just an aviator but also a painter and a poet, and he ran in the right circles. Consuelo found his writing pompous and boring, and his art overly simple, but he knew all of the artists she admired and orbited. He moved through rooms with the grace of a more handsome man, as if he himself were some kind of currency. Marrying him would ensure stability. What was an invisible patrón, anyway? They didn't exist. She could keep painting, get better. But still—why did he frighten her? Didn't everyone say that flying was wonderful? Maybe it could suit her. And! He had fucked so many beautiful women. Consuelo studied their faces at parties. Maybe she was missing something outrageously gorgeous about him, and if she could find a way to adore him as he claimed to adore her, a virtue and depth would be revealed in her character.

Luis's face, staring down at her from the emerald-green wall, did not soothe her mind, but rather inflamed it.

Consuelo had sculpted Luis's death mask in San Francisco. It wasn't a true death mask—his body had been burned before she'd even thought of making this—but she'd sculpted it from memory.

Now Consuelo studied his placid face, and considered bringing it to the gallery this evening to sell. Already in the gallery were the three oil paintings that she'd completed to enter the show. Yes, she'd take the mask also. She was tired of looking at his dead face and missing it, of imagining his judgments of her failings.

She heard a soft, mechanical whirring from inside the apartment. She strained to understand the noise. Like an urgent, rhythmic rustling. A neighbor? She pressed her ear to the wall, and then to the floor. No. She was inside the noise. Consuelo studied the ceiling. Maybe her condition was worsening. The attacks never began like this.

A silk nightgown draped over the arm of the couch suddenly sprang to life. A little bird flew out from the pile of cloth, beating its wings furiously. It smashed its body against the glass of the balcony door. The feathered body thudded to the floor, and Consuelo was certain it was dead. The apartment was silent. And then the bird flew up again, smashed its body against the same glass. And then flew up once more. Each time Consuelo stifled a scream.

Consuelo wondered if the bird saw an enemy in its own reflection. She grabbed her nightgown from the couch, found it was full of shit and downy underbelly feathers, and draped it over the balcony door, tucking the silk around the handle to cover up the glass. She opened the doors again to give the bird a path of escape. It careened into the glass again and panicked. Consuelo ran to the bathroom, took a towel, and then emptied her black beaded purse on the hallway floor. If she could approach the bird without frightening it, she could ease it into her purse with the towel, nurse it back to health, and set it free.

The bird lay panting for a minute. Consuelo lay down next to it. Him. She felt it was a him. He puffed into a brief fit of action, then panted and wheezed. He bled from his beak, shat frantic drips. Then the bird stopped panting. Consuelo halted her breathing too and made her eyes hard and still to attune to the life leaving the bird that she could not save, and the little bird slowly dulled, as if transforming into a thatch of straw. Consuelo cradled the towel around the bird's body and reached for the beaded purse. She would bury him in the courtyard downstairs.

She rose to her feet, her joints aching from lying on the floor. Immediately, the bird flew from its nest in the black silk lining of her purse out the balcony doors and into the wide gray sky. His wings knew exactly how to carry him.

Consuelo drew the curtains, turned to face the living room, and gasped. With the departure of the bird, the little girl had returned.

"Tell me what you want from me." Consuelo reached for her, and her hand passed through a weightless veil of cobwebs. The little girl babbled in our old language, Nawat, but Consuelo didn't remember it, couldn't understand.

"Thank you for visiting me, for providing me with a divine lamp by which to paint my art." Consuelo forced the words out of her belly, slowly.

The little girl snorted, laughed, and switched to Spanish. "I am not your lamp!" she shouted. "I'm a cipota!"

She climbed onto the copper Moroccan table at the center of the room, put her hand on her heart, and began to sing: "Vamos a la vuelta, de toro-torogil." Broken arm and all, she stomped her feet and held her balance on the copper plate as it tipped. Each tiny toenail was crusted in black dirt. She screamed the next verse of the song, "¡A ver a Doña Ana, comiendo perejil! Cortando una rosa, sembrando un clavel."

Consuelo knew this song. She had a feeling she'd heard it as a child, on the volcano. Sung in a round with children. Let's go in a circle around the bull, though there were no bulls in this country, no bison or buffalo either. Something about watching an old lady, Doña Ana, eating parsley, cutting a rose, planting a hibiscus. The parsley was good for her.

Now she clapped her hands and screamed along, losing her breath. Consuelo and María leaned back into the couch. Consuelo was exhausted; her ears vibrated with pressure, as if she'd been plunged underwater. She was not afraid of this little girl in the filthy pink dress. She knew her—but how?

She sang the next line with her: "¿Dónde está Doña Ana? Doña Ana se murió." Where is Doña Ana? Doña Ana has died.

La cipota shouted the next line: "¡Engusanada!" Full of worms—just like us.

"Where are you from?" Consuelo asked, but then she knew. On the day before the massacre, she'd seen her, like this, but older, tougher, in men's pants and short hair. She'd shared a cigarette with her. Consuelo had admired the drama of her thick eyebrows. Consuelo's hands had been trembling, and she remembered how they'd steadied around this girl. How she'd greeted her with an easy smile. *Qué onda.*

"I'm from Izalco," the little girl said.

"I thought so," Consuelo said. She wanted to cradle her—feed her, scrub her clean with the last of her hot water in the yellowed bathtub. Why was she here? What was her name?

"I came back. So you won't forget us," the little girl said to Consuelo, reading her mind. "I'm María. María-Malía."

María! Of course. That was her name. She couldn't have been older than sixteen when they'd met, but she'd already had a little streak of silver hairs growing along the temple of her choppy man's haircut. Consuelo could see them now, sprouts of silver shining in the late-afternoon light, the birds returning to their ceiba, the volcano's smoke, the terror and urgency of that day, y a la vez, her feeling of heavy death, a slow collapse inside of her.

Consuelo turned to her again, but the little ghost girl had disappeared. She was alone again.

Consuelo slept fitfully after that, on the floor. When she woke it was dark. She plunged into a cold bath to revive her spirit, and then stood naked, dripping, shivering before the mirror as she painted her face extravagantly. She dotted her cheeks with a lipstick the color of hibiscus flowers.

It was difficult to know how to dress sumptuously for the weather here. Consuelo wanted to show her skin, but it was so fucking cold. She put on the same silk nightgown that she'd fallen asleep in, and a men's thick wool overcoat that she'd found in the closet, a little musty. She pulled a blanket from the closet also, a vibrant Stewart plaid wool with moth-eaten tassels, which she wrapped around her shoulders like a rebozo. Costume jewelry. Giant pink rhinestone earrings in the shape of fans. Then she closed one eye, and the other, painted a shimmering black pupil and thick lashes on each lid. She gathered the death mask beneath an arm. She was ornate and lumpy and dilapidated, startling.

The gallery was already full when Consuelo arrived, panting, with the death mask damp beneath her arm. She hadn't expected this crowd, and folded her body into its waves, breathing in all those living smells, savoring her own powders and musk. Usually, Consuelo panicked in the thick of a crowd. But tonight her heart quickened, just for a moment. This was different. This mass of bodies was alluring. The crowd had gathered for her. She held up a trembling hand and shouted, "Et voilà. She's here!" The crowd parted and rained a gentle applause down on her.

Near the end of the night, a man wanted to buy the death mask. He was from Marseille and spoke French like an Italian. He introduced himself to her as Lucien. Consuelo's lipstick was slick as blood and she put on her charms for him. She stroked the mask with one sharp red fingernail.

"He watches me. He growls and moans when I'm in a bad mood, or if I pick up the telephone to flirt," she said. The mask was a dull, pale gray, the clay rough in a way that seemed barely dry. Consuelo had found that once she began talking, even after arduous, silent days of painting in her apartment, she had a hard time stopping.

In the corner of her vision María appeared again. She was the same girl, but no longer una cipota. Her afterbody was older now, teenage, short and stocky, with that thick black hair cut jagged. She stood beside a table laden with bottles of wine and cried tears of blood. Consuelo's sight began to blur as she recognized the María-Malía that she'd met those last days in the village—the men, Graciela's lifeless body, the ash of the volcano and the ash of the burning bodies. She was freezing cold and sensed an attack coming, and she knew that she had to leave.

"So, do you want it or not? The mask," Consuelo spat out.

Lucien smiled nervously. "It's a little more than I'd planned to spend tonight." But he'd just started as a law clerk for Laval's practice; he'd received his first paycheck only the day before; Laval had aligned France with the gold standard; if you weren't an optimist now, you were an idiot.

If he was being honest, Lucien intended to spend as much as he liked tonight.

LOURDES: Laval, if you don't know, was another jodido fascista. Also, he was rich. He began as an idealistic lawyer, and then he went Nazi. He hardly practiced law by the time Lucien had started working for his firm, and in the years to come, he'd be appointed to the Vichy government as minister of state, meet with Hitler, and make promises to the Germans about Belgian mines filled with gold. Of course Lucien couldn't know all of these things about the phantom founder of the firm where he'd just begun to work.

LUCÍA: But, really, wherever you looked those days—you'd find a púchica Fascist.

"What if—well, if I buy the mask, can I see you again?" Lucien asked Consuelo. Consuelo was nauseated by the suggestion, and by the return of the ghost girl, but she needed the money, and who was she to have ethics about this kind of thing? Plenty of men wanted to see her again. Too bad. The ghost girl vanished from beside the refreshment table. Consuelo scanned the crowd for her face, feeling the walls of the gallery closing in on her. Lucien waited expectantly for her reply. She looked into her wineglass and all she could see was blood.

"Fine, yes, I'd do anything to see you again, Lucien. You're so charming. You have exquisite taste in art. I'd love to see your collection sometime." The right phrases fell out of her mouth as Lucien handed over his pay, in cash, for the mask. Consuelo scribbled a false phone number on one of his remaining bills, then pushed through the crowd, and left the gallery with the money in her bag. The death mask crackled and whirred like a broken machine, hissing curses at her. Consuelo ran home with her heart in her throat.

After meeting the artist and buying the mask—which he later regretted when he had to pay his rent; he was in no position to spend the majority of his first paycheck on art—Lucien went into the bookstore three streets down from his apartment. He was broke but infatuated. He climbed a ladder to retrieve an atlas from a high shelf, cradled the heavy, glossy book that he'd never be able to afford, and sat on a stool in the back room poring over a map of the Americas, tracing his finger to the tiny kernel of a nation where Consuelo had come from. Like so many before him, he was surprised to find it was not an island.

Meanwhile, Luis's death mask lay facedown on his desk, accumulating dust for a brief handful of years. Work consumed Lucien, and he was nervous about hammering into his landlord's wall. When it came time for him to flee Paris, years later, he found the mask again, but decided against taking it with him over the Pyrenees. He could carry only what fit on his back. In any case, Lucien did not survive the war to come.

29

EVERY SUNDAY GRACIELA ATTENDED MASS JUST TO HEAR THE Latin. Rosie had stopped speaking Spanish to her—*For your own good,* she'd said—and the English Graciela learned, day by day, in the studio and cafeteria and library, was rough, but improving, in rapid blocks of shaggy speech. She understood English better than she could speak it, and she read it better than either. On set, the cameramen taught her new words: *cut, roll, goddammit.* In the studio cafeteria, where she worked scouring industrial steel, the hours compressed tidily, her hands turned a pure and beating red, and the other nenas shouted to one another over the water, in our language, in this country's, in their own. And in the library Graciela scrubbed toilets and tile grout and caught the whispers of women tending to their bodies.

But, strangely, dead as Latin might be, Graciela understood it all. The words must have been stitched into her brain during childhood. The dark ribs of the church reminded Graciela of her lost life, of her mother, nodding off beside her in the pew every Sunday.

Socorrito hadn't been religious, but the nuns had required that anyone in their school attend Mass at least once a week. So Socorrito would take Graciela to the eight o'clock Sunday service. Once, she'd asked her daughter how she'd liked it. Graciela had said that she liked the occasional use of incense and watching the candles get snuffed out by the golden cone, the way the stained glass was heavier at the bottom of each

window, how it carried blue and red and green light across the room, settling on her friends' faces. She'd been excited to take Communion after
she turned seven but was disappointed by how stale and transparent the
wafer was. It tasted of tears.

The church in Hollywood had the kindling smell of incense and the
host. Water hummed and rolled down the stained-glass face of the Virgin, glowing amber and blue in the window beside Graciela's pew. She
didn't believe any of it—not the host, not absolution, not the Resurrec-
tion. She never had. Well, maybe the Virgin—Graciela craved the softness in her closed eyelids.

One Sunday, Graciela left the church at the end of Mass and felt the
warm sun on the concrete steps. Hollywood had been her home for
almost two years—time enough to have given birth to another self. The
General had believed in reincarnation—it lessened his worries, he said.
But reincarnation had never soothed Graciela's worries, especially after
witnessing our deaths. What soul could survive that kind of death, what
soul in that pile would ever ache to come back to this world?

There was a wide soil path nearby that she sometimes followed into
the hills, into the woods gleaming with evergreen and eucalyptus. Today
the leaves blinked like eyes in the breeze. Graciela walked toward them.

She walked uphill for a time before she came upon an abandoned
picnic: a red blanket, an overturned wicker basket, an empty bottle of
wine. Graciela took off her shoes and sat on the blanket, unrolling her
stockings. The ground was wet from morning rain and it soaked through
the blanket, through the skirt of her dress. She lay on her back and stared
up at the Hollywood sign, each letter wide and rust-streaked, like a row
of dirty teeth. It was so near she could have reached for a smooth rock in
the grass, thrown it into the sky, and hit a letter.

Graciela often couldn't believe that she lived here. It certainly didn't
feel like home. "How does it feel to be truly at home?" the General had
asked her, after she'd been stolen from her mother. She'd escaped from
that home on a river of blood and she still hadn't found a new one.

Her watch, which had once belonged to Consuelo, read ten a.m.
She'd stop by the library; today was her day off from cleaning bathrooms,

and she could sit and read for a few hours. After that, she'd drink her way to bed.

In the square pocket of Graciela's cotton coat was a flask that one of Rosie's dates had engraved with her initials. He, a small, sweaty man with surprisingly thick fingers and a hazy puff of fine hair that seemed to have been scooped onto the top of his head with a shovel, had presented the flask as a gift and then spent the night panting nervously in their bedroom while Graciela slept on the couch in the living room. His patent-leather shoes squeaked out the front door before dawn. Graciela knew by Rosie's quiet that morning that she wanted to forget all about this date, so Graciela had taken the flask from under Rosie's bed, filled it with bourbon, and begun carrying it around with her. Now she reached for its smoothness in her pocket, twisted its cap open with her teeth, and let the warmth inside settle onto her tongue like another sun.

From the hills above came a long, low scream, and a bright movement swept across the sky. Graciela sat up, rubbed her eyes clear. Red trails flashed over her vision. A body had fallen through the blue. The light swelled—Graciela must have drifted asleep. She saw, again, and again, the eerie trace of a heavy body falling as if thrown. Not a bird. A part of the sign? No, something had fallen off of the sign. Something with weight, but no volition of its own. She put on her shoes and stockings and climbed up to it.

Behind the letter *H* leaned a splintered wooden stepladder. Graciela scrambled up the brush to meet it. On the bottom step of the ladder sat a glossy, cream-colored patent-leather purse, the length and width of a book. Its latch was undone. Graciela's heart beat too fast, trying to tell her she should be afraid. She wasn't. She seized the purse like a prize. Inside was a roll of bills, fives and tens, and a silk coin bag filled with a lipstick and a tiny mirror. Graciela opened a handkerchief embroidered with the initials "P.A.E." and found a pair of plastic-framed sunglasses, one lens scratched, a set of keys to the Hotel Arcade, and a note on paper from the same hotel, folded into thirds. It read:

I am afraid. I am a coward. I am sorry for everything. If I had done this a long time ago, it would have saved a lot of pain. P.E.

Graciela slid her wrist through the handle of the purse and climbed to the top of the ladder, step by step. The ladder was sturdy, built to hold a workman twice her size. When she arrived at the top, she looked down at the hills, and her eye found the answer. A woman lay on her side, in a mint-green suit, at the bottom of the ravine. Graciela's brain understood, and her body swayed; the ladder moved like the generous bough of a tree. We held her.

Beneath Mount Lee, Hollywood was waking up late. Streams of traffic and a gray-gold haze softened the skyline. Graciela read the note again. *I am afraid. I am a coward. I am sorry for everything. If I had done this a long time ago, it would have saved a lot of pain.*

And what about her pain? Graciela tried to imagine just one piece of it, the landing, tried to light up the flesh of her own body with that sensation, and found that she couldn't. How long after that kind of fall does a body stay alive? How soon before death does the brain stop? When does pain end? Below was a red diamond, the blanket where Graciela had been sitting. Had the bright shape that held Graciela entered that woman's sight as she fell?

That old song on the radio: *Tear me out of this life by the roots. Take me out of this world.* The desire had entered Graciela's mind too sometimes, but she hid from the impulse. She told herself then, in her old life, that wanting to die and wanting to leave her country were parts of the same impossible action. But here she was, still alive, and everyone she'd known gone. Graciela considered if she'd been even more afraid, even more a coward, than P.A.E. during all those years inside the palace. She tucked the note back into her purse and climbed down the ladder. Even if her mother were alive on the volcano, she must have thought, like Consuelo, like all the others, that Graciela was dead. Graciela wondered if she could have saved us. Had she been willing to die a little earlier, to let Consuelo die, would that have been enough blood, enough souls, to appease the General? Probably not.

. . .

At the police station Graciela waited in a long line to speak with a woman who looked about sixty and sat at a desk behind a screen window. When it was her turn, she slid the purse across the ledge and told the woman that there was a suicide note inside. The woman took the purse, slid her window closed, opened the latch, and dumped all of the contents onto her desk, the cash, the coin bag, the note, the handkerchief, the hotel key, the sunglasses.

"Where did you find this?" the woman asked Graciela, without looking up from the form on her desk. She was making a list of the purse's contents, estimating the price of each item in cursive script. Handkerchief: one dollar. Coin bag: twenty-five cents. Lipstick: fifty cents. Sunglasses: five dollars. She unrolled the bills: thirty-five dollars. The top of her hair was thinning, the rest a wiry, metallic gray.

"I was walking in the Hollywood hills," Graciela said.

"Where, exactly?"

"Up by the sign. The *H*." The woman raised her sparse eyebrows. She licked her left forefinger and opened the folded note, reading it with a blank face.

"People leave notes like this all the time, darling. She's probably just trying to upset a man who loves her, don't you think?"

"I'm not sure," Graciela said. "I don't know why someone would do that."

The woman put her head down and wrote "Lady's White Purse Found in Hollywood Hills" across the top of the form. She waited for Graciela to step aside, and called the woman behind her in line, who we watched bite each one of her fingernails at the corner until the flesh opened, and then press the bloody patch of skin onto her tongue, sucking it like candy.

Graciela was hoping she wouldn't have to talk about the body, that the police would find the woman themselves. That's what happened in the movies. Detectives took an object like that purse and used it as a key, unlocking door after door, making discoveries on their own. They were the professionals; Graciela was just a girl from out of town.

"It's a nice purse," said the woman behind the screen. "I'd carry this,"

she said, balancing the handle over her wrist and holding it out. Behind
Graciela, the line of people with secrets to report—murders, rapes, rob-
beries, fraud—was long and growing. We had to intervene.

LOURDES: Graciela, if you don't tell her what you saw, the purse will sit
in this office and become the possession of this woman, and
the detectives will never drive up into the hills to climb the
ladder. They'll never look out over the hills and find the
woman in the green suit.

CORA: Her body will rot and soften into the ground. Her people
will find only her bones.

MARÍA: Or no one will find her at all.

"I saw the woman's body," Graciela finally said, letting our voices
guide her. "At the bottom of the hill." The woman behind the screen
stared back at her, dull-eyed, like a cat walking into the light.

"Whose body?"

"The woman who owned this purse, I think. The note. I saw her."

"You saw her jump or you saw the body?" The woman clicked her
tongue twice.

"The body," Graciela said. She checked her memory against the bright
contrails of movement replaying in her mind.

"Well, geez-maneez, why didn't you say so in the first place?" The
woman shook her head with a violent little twitch and opened a drawer
in her desk, pawed the papers for another form. "Are you sure she was
dead?"

Graciela nodded, and followed the woman into a smaller room,
where she was submitted to a grim questioning.

The detectives Graciela had seen in the movies were nothing like the
mild, ordinary pair of men she was faced with now. But they needed her
help. And telling them helped her too: each time she told the story it
became a little more like an object, something apart from her. A seg-
mented thing, with an arc. The ladder, the note, the pale smudge of mint
surrounded by brighter, more living, green grass.

Officer Stern was young and fine-boned, with a slick flop of blond hair that he flipped off his brow with quick upward juts of his small chin. Blue veins mapped the territory beneath his eyes; he seemed not to have had enough sleep the night before. He had both hands wrapped around his cup and took long, desperate pulls of his coffee. Periodically he sprang to his feet, walked to the window, placed an ankle in the palm of one hand, and stretched out his back. When he spoke, which was far less often than his partner and superior, Officer Roberts, his voice arrived surprisingly dense, dark, and deep.

Officer Roberts was old, crackle-skinned, and gentle. He was the oldest detective on the force, valued for his experience.

"I'll never retire," Roberts told Graciela. "No wife, no kids, no pets, no hobbies, no friends. I'd die out there."

His laugh was a silent, elliptical mouth, black fillings, spittle. He was stout, boxy, but strangely frail. His dust-gray hands shook over the papers that Graciela signed, securing the truth of her statements, and when she walked with the detectives back into the hills to retrace her story, Roberts stopped before the peak of the first slope, his figure stooped into halves, and he wheezed into his thighs. Stern averted his eyes from his superior's buckled body. He handed Graciela a cigarette from his pack, lit hers and then his own, cupping the match with a nervous dignity. The tobacco of these cigarettes wasn't quite the match of the ones our mothers had rolled, but Graciela took in the light greedily. She flicked the ash and watched it spark on the ground. Roberts quietly regained his composure.

They made their way slowly, stopping every few minutes to rest. The body wasn't where Graciela had left it. This troubled her, but the men took their time. During one stop, Stern spotted birds as Roberts panted beside them, pointed at the sky, naming each one. Red-tailed hawk. Rock dove. Bushtit.

Cora, were you helping him?

Roberts slowly got moving again. They were Laurel and Hardy, but sadder.

"You're our golden girl," Roberts rasped later on, in the office, after the fruitless search. "No wonder you're set to become a movie star." Stern's hair flopped over his eyes as he nodded quickly and made a note on his pad.

"But I haven't done anything," Graciela said.

"You came forward with that purse, didn't you?" Roberts said. He swirled the tip of his pencil around in the grime of the ashtray on his desk. "Some girls would have taken the cash and run without looking back."

Some girls would have. Graciela had, when she'd left the Estate. She'd do it again. She held Roberts's gaze until he looked away.

Not long after that, the police found the body, facedown, in the mint-green suit, on the other side of the field from where Graciela had seen her. No one could understand why, or how, the body had migrated. The coroner examined it for bruises. Not the ones from the impact of the fall, but more intimate ones: traces of fingers gripping the soft flesh of her upper arm or throat, a wound from a blunt object that could have been held in a hand, anything that indicated a rape. He didn't find anything, aside from the bruise that traced her broken spine, widening it like a swollen river.

Graciela met the girl's parents at a press conference. They sat together at a long table placed on a platform in front of the police station. At the beginning of the conference, before she'd spoken to them and told them her name, a photograph had been taken of her and them. They'd stood behind her, each with a hand on one of her shoulders. Graciela brought her hands to their backs and felt fire moving through their bodies. Her hair was hanging in stringy black ropes. She'd just left work in the cafeteria and unpinned her long, braided hair, shaken it out.

After the story hit the newspapers, after Graciela had given an interview on the radio, after the press conference, after the invitations to audition for bigger roles started coming in, the girls in the cafeteria started to look at her differently. In the middle of the shifts they'd stop their work and stare. Graciela just put her head down and scrubbed.

Then Morris called and told her she was a genius for this publicity stunt. Did she know that his phone was still ringing off the hook? On the phone with him, she opened a bottle of wine and drank it down. Morris chattered about vision, magnetism, more than just a pair of legs or a cute mug. Her brain stopped listening. She was so tired.

Outside the window, birds moved through the sky like a fistful of ash let go in the wind. Black specks, their bodies a wise whole, growing broad, narrowing with a pulsing swiftness. The sky went bloody and then softened into violet, and still the dazzling cloud filled the atmosphere with their shape-shifting, scattered like loose tobacco dancing in the palm of a hand, returned to form: fluted, round, hourglass, trapezoid, star.

Murmuration. Graciela would learn the word for this leaderless dance and its reason—to escape predation—many years later, inside the San Francisco Public Library on Bartlett Street. But that night in Hollywood, after she'd found the body, those dark birds—hundreds of them? Thousands?—moved namelessly, reminding us of the birds that gathered in the ceiba each evening. Their shape was something of home, of our life before Graciela went to the capital and met the General, a shape we'd seen during the only years she was ever a child, a child and nothing more.

Soon, Graciela was offered a big role in a jungle movie, as the princess of a tribe of warriors, charged with inventing her own indecipherable language, just like Dolores. And Rosie, probably a little jealous, sniffed that a role like that was beneath Graciela, but Graciela didn't care. The role meant no more small parts, no more kicking in a line of legs meant to look identical, no more sultans' harem scenes.

Quickly, the patterns of her life shifted again.

30

OF COURSE CONSUELO MARRIED THE AVIATOR, AND YES, AR-
rived at a different kind of life for herself. He was rich, an heir, but
for some reason, he moved into her green apartment on rue de Castellane, and brought no furniture of his own. He was bad with money, he
told her, and also he didn't need furniture, with all the travel he did.
Consuelo had hoped he would furnish the place with even just a long
plush couch for her to nap on in the afternoons. She knew that he could
have afforded to.

Now it'd been almost five years since their first meeting, when the
aviator had nearly killed them both. Consuelo told herself that she loved
flying as a way of rationalizing her marriage. She whispered it to herself
to soothe el susto. She didn't say aloud that she didn't love the aviator.
Maybe this—a new life—was enough.

And he did introduce Consuelo to the one person in Paris she'd most
wanted to meet, an English painter named Helena. Helena made the
kind of work that Consuelo had wanted to make when she was in San
Francisco—her paintings were delicate and defiant, with monkey-faced
women stirring cauldrons overlaid by tarot cards painted in a sacred
geometry. Eerie green smoke, crystals, ships, holy processions, tigers,
birds, and horses, horses, horses.

Being an idiot, the aviator introduced Helena to Consuelo not as a
painter, but as someone who'd slept with a married friend of his. But
Consuelo knew Helena's work, admired her paintings so ferociously she

often thought about tasting their colors. Lately, though, Helena couldn't seem to get a gallery show anywhere. Likely, this was because of the married man.

From a distance, Helena gave the impression of having wide, muscular shoulders, ribs that tapered only slightly to a square set of hips, hardly any breasts. She'd spent several months in a sanatorium and was rumored to be writing a novel about the experience. In her spare time, she rode horses. In a true version of Consuelo's origin myth, Helena had grown up rich and run off to Paris to escape her family and become an artist. Once there, she'd nearly become a muse instead, but she wasn't the kind of woman or artist who listened to all those old men who took themselves so seriously, and, from where Consuelo sat, observing her, it seemed that Helena's freedom to openly defy and denigrate these men had saved her. Or at the very least, preserved her art.

Up close she was softer than she seemed from afar, with long, dark curls and broad cheekbones cut like quartz. Her face wasn't sharp, but structured, architectural. Her cheeks flushed pink, an unexpected soft flush. Helena was like that—younger in years than she behaved, tiny pearl earrings edged in crystals making the shape of a flower on each earlobe.

When they met, Helena, in a purple silk gown and muddy men's riding boots, squeezed Consuelo's hand perfunctorily. She bared her teeth. Consuelo made small talk over the din and Helena grew visibly bored and then went out to the patio to get some air. Consuelo traced her purple gown across the room, studying Helena's feral nature, as if searching her own wild heart in a mirror.

Consuelo believed that a friendship with Helena would cure the loneliness she felt here. She wanted Helena to study her the way she studied Helena. She wanted to live as a hyena or a swan in one of Helena's paintings, wanted Helena to write a story dedicated to her, wanted jokes that only they understood to weave themselves into their work. She wanted Helena to look her in the eyes and recognize her as a fellow great artistic mind, and then confide in her. Consuelo invited her over for tea, and Helena accepted, but the afternoon in Consuelo's apartment was formal, both of them relying upon the stiff graces that had been imposed on their gawky teenage selves in finishing schools on opposite sides of the world.

Consuelo finally mentioned, after Helena abruptly stood to leave, that she loved her work, and that she herself was interested in art, that she'd love to apprentice under her, or something like that. Helena flushed red.

"I hardly paint anymore," she said. "It's become more of a hobby that I've set down, lately."

"I saw you in a group show last year," Consuelo said, maybe too insistently.

"I'm on a break. I just need to get better," Helena said. Since the married man had refused to leave his wife, and since Helena had been in the sanatorium again, she'd convinced herself that she needed to start over. Study others' work, take notes, draw in charcoal. "No sense in wasting canvas. You know what I mean?" Helena pulled a men's silk top hat over her curls and made for the door.

Consuelo nodded, not wanting to keep Helena and incite fatigue or boredom or resentment in her. But she was devastated.

Helena seemed uninterested in friendship, at least in a friendship with Consuelo. But why? Consuelo kept trying, waving at Helena when she saw her on the street, certain that if they could bind together, they'd both be taken more seriously as artists in this circle of loud men. But Helena was impassive, numb inside the vortex of the married man, who said her work was mediocre and that she shouldn't be painting like some two-bit medium.

Soon after, the aviator took Consuelo to a birthday party—really more of a séance. The birthday girl, a dancer from Nantes, knew that her career was practically finished now that she'd reached thirty, and her only wish was for the spirit of Anna Pavlova to guide her into her next act.

All of the women were dressed beautifully, long, narrow torsos in chocolate-colored velvet, rosy pearls, and funereal black lace veils. Consuelo had worn her veil, but terrified of not being seen, of disappearing, had also chosen a velvet gown in scarlet. They were all seated around a long table, a goateed Russian writer of political tracts beside the birthday girl in the event translation with the spirit might be necessary.

The lights were dimmed, the candles lit, and the cards laid out on the table—the atmosphere was set. But the mood was broken by a thumping entrance—a late guest. A salty-eyed, unclean man, with wide thumbs like the heel of stale bread. The other men in attendance weren't as extravagantly dressed as the ladies, but they were neater, appeared more completely assembled than this man did, in their plain white shirts and wool trousers, their mustaches waxed, their faces, even if gaunt from too much wine and nicotine, smooth as paper. Their eccentricities appeared curated. A one-eyed poet wore a jeweler's glass screwed into his dead eye socket as a false, telescoping monocle, for example. Among these men, this new guest gave the impression of a golden retriever, the hank of his tongue, the dirt of his oversize paws, delightful and disruptive.

Consuelo eventually discovered that the clothes the man—León— was wearing constituted the one outfit he possessed: canvas pants that had once been white and were now smeared with decades of grime and paint, and a rough, gray linen shirt of the kind Italian fishermen wore in Marseille, as filthy as the pants. Jute sandals, even in winter. He'd made a habit of arriving at dinner parties with pink roses, as he did this one. He plucked them from old women's flower stands and tucked them into the bib of his shirt. But up close, he smelled as if he awoke each morning floating on his back in the Seine.

"Trompe l'oeil," the aviator whispered in Consuelo's ear. A trick. "León's from one of the oldest, richest families in Paris," the aviator said. "His grandmother spent her youth eating bonbons in the Palace of Versailles. He and his ex-wife had a gorgeous house in Nice too, and one in the Italian Alps."

"What happened?" Consuelo asked.

"What do you mean? To his marriage?"

"No, how did he lose the family fortune?"

"Oh, come on! Don't be so naïve. He hasn't lost a thing. As far as his family's concerned, he just hasn't grown up yet," the aviator said. "Look how he eats, if you need any more proof. As crude as he pleases, but hardly in a hurry. You have to start noticing these details, Consuelo, if you ever want to understand people."

León was an artist. He painted headless women with perfect tits and sad blue vulvas. Indeed, he was rich, had grown up in grander homes even than the Estate, but Consuelo would never have guessed from the roughness of his face, or from his politics. He was an aspirational revolutionary, had even heard about the massacre in Consuelo's tiny country—he was the only one in all of Paris, it seemed to her. León tuned into secret radio stations, kept boxes of pamphlets in his apartment that he handed out at parties.

Squinting, Consuelo imagined he could be a version of Luis. But even Luis's ghost would have thought León was a pendejo.

León was seated across the table from Consuelo, his elbows bent, wrinkling the linen, and his napkin fallen to the floor. But he ate slowly, considering each bite, temples pulsing in the flickering candlelight as he chewed. He wasn't hungry at all, not that night, not ever.

Consuelo thought León was the only one of his kind, but he was just the first she had happened to meet; Paris was crawling with his breed.

From then on, whenever Consuelo saw León at a party or a gallery, she tried to speak with him. Something about him drew her in, but he always seemed bored by her, almost offended by her presence. Consuelo asked him one night if she'd done something to upset him. He looked right through her and put his cigarette out in her glass of gin. From then on, she knew better.

Nobody in Paris, it seemed, wanted to hear about how Consuelo had studied painting in San Francisco, how she'd learned French as a teenager. They wanted to know about the Maya. About temples, about Nawat, about mangoes and cryptograms and jaguars. That Consuelo had already told them about her family's station in society, the home in the country, the Estate in the capital, the crazy General, Consuelo supposed, was interesting from the outset, but when she told them she'd had an affair with her private art teacher, that she'd worn clothing her mother hadn't approved of, about Las Rositas, she became just as boring as the rest of them. If the paintings and sculptures she worked on early in the morning while the aviator was still asleep were ever to be taken seriously by this crowd, she had to distinguish herself. She needed to alter her approach. Put on new airs. What they wanted to know about her past had more to do with color, shape, and taste than pedigree. By imagining herself a little bit more like the way she'd once imagined Graciela, Consuelo would make them fall in love with her. She'd tell them what they wanted to hear.

"Darling," they said at parties—the photographer and his wife, a Russian dancer, a poet who was developing his own private language. "Tell us about the volcanoes. Tell us about the fruit that grows on the trees."

So Consuelo told them that the mother who'd birthed her was a volcano, that the stubborn early stars of the dawn sky were her sisters. She told them that she loved the jungle, that just after her breasts had appeared, she'd covered herself in honey and disappeared for three days, running into the forest with the hope that the most beautiful insects would find her, cover her in iridescence, an image of the artist's body that would later find its way into Consuelo's paintings. Paintings she hadn't yet finished, of course.

She talked about gigantic butterflies dragging their spindly legs across her honeyed body, and dragonflies, and gold-flaked beetles. Once, when she was very drunk, she told them that she'd lost her virginity in the jungle, snakes watching from the vines, and that the man turned into a jaguar as soon as they both came. She laughed the whole time. They could choose to believe her or not.

The wife of a painter whom the aviator said was a joke, but must be deferred to with delicacy, blinked slowly and sniffed when Consuelo told her about the jaguar, disturbing the wine in her glass. But her blithe little game didn't fool Consuelo; she and all the others were fascinated, hooked, beholden.

"I want to take your picture," a very important surrealist photographer, the most important one of all, said to her one night at a party. He'd heard all of Consuelo's stories. "Put you in a silver light." Yes, he would, Consuelo thought to herself. Yes, he would, yes, finally, at last. She looked around the room, saw that Helena was listening, seemed intrigued. Consuelo nodded, and then, to assure the photographer of her promisingly mercurial nature, she contorted her face, doing her best to look deranged.

Soon Consuelo was posing for him, going to his studio and playacting, wearing African headdresses, smoking opium.

LOURDES: In Paris, African masks were still the thing. These cheles—it's almost as if they can't come up with anything on their own, no? This famous photographer, a genius with a fake name who called himself a citizen of the world instead of just admitting he was from some little pueblo outside of Philadelphia.

LUCÍA: He wasn't a total idiot. He did that thing with the sunlight and springs and screws and stuff.

LOURDES: And? So? Noticing the sun makes this man a genius?

CORA: Anyway. The night before Consuelo first went to pose for him was a rough one. You see, the aviator's mother despised her. Consuelo had lied and said that her father was a captain in the army and that her entire family were devout Catholics and even that she'd once considered taking the vows and becoming a monja—she thought these lies, with her charm, would smooth things over between herself and her new mother-in-law, but they didn't. The old bitch hated her the second Consuelo said the name of our country aloud. "All I can see is the Indian. No wonder she's always hysterical," she said.

MARÍA: But that's exactly why the photographer liked Consuelo so much. Because she was hysterical.

LOURDES: Hysterical! Most of the time she was too depressed to even raise her voice properly. He'd have shit his pants if he could hear our jelengue!

LUCÍA: Yeah, so she showed up at the photographer's studio the morning after the aviator's birthday dinner at his mother's home, when his mother called the marriage a disgrace. What did the old puta say? "It's a greater shame to marry a foreigner than a Jew!" And the aviator didn't do a thing. He just sat there, refilling his wineglass, while his mother called his wife a whore. Then she stopped talking to Consuelo altogether and just addressed her son, that enormous drunk baby.

"Why did you have to marry an aborigène?" He smiled with his lips slightly parted, like he thought the whole thing was funny. Consuelo tried to remember a moment when she hadn't despised him.

CORA: She excused herself to the old bitch's bathroom and locked herself inside. She reached into her chonis for a handful of blood and smeared it on the walls. Handprints and smears at first, and then, over the bidet, she gathered more blood and took her time. A row of pigs, each one larger than the one before.

MARÍA: The next morning, the surrealist photographer gave Consuelo a straw basket that he wanted her to wear as a hat, and another hat with coconut fibers that went straight up in the air, and a mask decorated with cowrie shells, which he instructed her to embrace like a lover.

"Stare into the eyes of the face, listen for its hollow river-melody," he said. *That doesn't make any fucking sense,* Consuelo snorted to herself. But she lit a cigarette and stared at the mask.

He put the coconut-fiber hat on her head and asked her to imagine her face as a white linen sheet drying in the sun. She made the blank face of Ninfa. He begged her to turn her head.

"I must feast upon your aristocratic nose, in profile!" he screamed. Consuelo's vanity was fed, though she hated her nose. She gave it to him, and he made disgusting slurping noises.

"And now you are Saint Thérèse and you transmit your electricity to me through the ecstasy that you feel. It will be visible inside both nostrils. Your very eyelashes will grow. Okay? Are you with me or is this just over your head? Make yourself come? Can you do that for me?"

"I can do that without even touching myself," Consuelo said. This was not true.

The genius's mouth fell open. "Do you pray?"

Consuelo shook her head and conjured a false earthquake. Afterward she put out her cigarette by kissing the lit end. For him. If she could frighten the photographer a little, he might consider her interesting enough not to abandon her after this shoot.

"You," he said. "You are all that is marvelous and troubling in this world!"

And he didn't even come up with that line himself; his buddy did.

If Consuelo had just wanted to fuck around with an artist, she could have slept with the photographer—but the risks were too high; she was getting work out of this precarious arrangement, and he seemed content simply to observe Consuelo lose herself through his lens. She needed the opportunity to be seen.

But as soon as the other artists took notice of her, León suddenly was happy not just to talk to her, but to fuck her too. It was like his dick was the greatest artistic compliment he could offer.

The first time all he had to do was follow Consuelo home, walking three paces behind her on a night that he knew the aviator was flying over the Sahara and that she'd had too much to drink. He wasn't even a very good painter. But his flat, mute hatred made her weak in the knees. Or so she told herself. At the very least, his derision spurred her to look for a crack in his hatred, an opening that she might fill with light to change his mind about who she was.

Consuelo was smarter than he was and a better painter, and she knew it, but León had never once asked her about her work. Consuelo wasn't alone in this uneven kind of desire. The women in her circle, Helena, all of them, fucked self-important male artists, lesser artists who depended upon their women's imaginations like parasites. They had to if they wanted to remain relevant. Fucking these men, stroking the egos in their dicks—well, it was like some kind of tax.

That first morning in bed with León, at the apartment she shared with the aviator, Consuelo told León that she was a painter too—would he like to see her work? Oh, baby, he said, and pulled Consuelo to his chest, stroked her hair until he fell back asleep. When he'd been snoring for a while, Consuelo untangled her hair from his big, dry hands and went to the bathroom to wash. It was nine in the morning; she dressed for a moonlit garden dinner party and made up her eyes. In the bedroom, León was still asleep. Consuelo turned the key in the lock and crept downstairs to the bakery, and bought, with a handful of her husband's money, pastries of a size and richness that León pretended to be too poor to enjoy, but that she knew he loved. He was still asleep when she returned.

Consuelo set to work in the kitchen, heating water for coffee. She had a plan. When León awoke, she'd call him into the kitchen. They'd sit together, letting morning light warm their feet on the parquet. They'd have breakfast, and she would show him her work. Maybe just one painting, a tiny one on a four-by-four-inch canvas, in different shades of gold metallic paint. The back of her mother's—Perlita's—neck. The palms of her mother's—Socorrito's—hands. My mother the volcano, my sister in the stars. He'd scrunch up his nose and give her some notes. The kind of notes he'd give any other artist. He'd take his time. He'd tell Consuelo, slowly, with precision, exactly where she'd gone wrong. The part he hated most, and why.

Consuelo craved the nourishment of those words. Even if she was a better painter than he was. To be seen by someone else who at least had the vocabulary, the strata of taste, to address her as a peer. And perhaps he'd get better, and one day she'd respect his work! And what had begun as a fuck would evolve into love, artistic companionship, a secret partnership. At parties, people would whisper about them. But León would be as much Consuelo's muse as she would be his.

She knew she was getting carried away—the sensation of balloons carrying her off the kitchen parquet. The wild motor of her heart thrummed, all those hummingbirds inside. When Consuelo sensed León's figure in the doorway of the kitchen, she pretended not to notice, turned slowly to face him with an easy smile. His face was blank.

"Where the hell's my coat?" León said, to Consuelo or to himself, she wasn't sure. The night before, he'd thrown his filthy coat on the floor on their way to the bedroom. This morning, Consuelo had picked it up, shaken its dirt out the window, and hung it up. She went to get it for him.

"I'm just having a little breakfast," Consuelo said. "Care to join me?" She lifted the carafe of coffee and poured a cup.

León tilted his head to the left side, a slow half-shake, as if turning his head to the right and back again would have been too much trouble.

"I have work to do," León said, moving to the door. She set down her coffee cup and dried her hands on a towel, following him across the kitchen for a kiss, but he was already gone.

At another time in her life, Consuelo would have made the more satisfying choice of throwing the platter of croissants after him. But today, she sat still on the balcony for the rest of the morning. She ate six pastries, smoking cigarette after cigarette, the golden holder getting hot and singeing her fingertips. Consuelo, missing the fire that had once lit her from within, savored the burn.

She knew the aviator had slept with other women since they'd been married. Some she'd even been introduced to at parties. She wanted to ask them why, to learn what they saw in him, so she could try to see it also. He wouldn't be home for weeks.

There were reasons Consuelo hadn't left him yet that had nothing to do with money. For one, she liked watching him take off in the plane when she was riding in the cockpit with him. He was sedate and prayerful, even when drunk, and he never tried that crazy shit again. He could barely get it up at all, and so the memory of him nearly crashing the plane for a kiss the first time they flew together was a dissonant, faint dream. And what else? Once he'd vowed that his careless drawings, which she also didn't particularly admire, were only for her, could only exist because of her. She was his rose, he said. She liked that, the part about being a rose.

. . .

One evening Consuelo drew a bath and let the water spill over the lip of the tub. The aviator was still somewhere else, flying over the desert. Consuelo sank into the water and thought of Lago Coatepeque, where Luis's body had been found.

Once, Socorrito and the other women had taken Consuelo to Lago Coatepeque. She'd been three then—none of the rest of us had been born yet—and the women had cuddled her, fed her sour mangoes with alguashte, and danced her feet through the cold water of the caldera. That afternoon Consuelo had fallen asleep in her mother's arms beside the water, and she had awoken later that evening, as they bounced together in the back of a truck, riding back home up the volcano.

This is what she remembered. But the memory itself had grown threadbare. It was possible that she'd embroidered it over the years. Maybe it had been just Consuelo and her mother. Maybe there had been no mango with alguashte, no nap in the sun, no truck ride home.

Consuelo had a postcard of Lago Coatepeque that she'd slipped into her pocket from one of those tourist shops in the plaza when she was a teenager. As soon as she saw the postcard that day, she knew that she needed it to hold together the threads of that faint memory of her mother. Because this lake existed, she did too. Her mother existed, and beside the lake, her mother had once adored her. She'd glanced over at Maite, who was browsing magazines near the cash register. Maite would have lent Consuelo a few cents to pay for the postcard, but her need was immediate and secretive. She slipped the card into her lumpy velvet pouch. She didn't want to talk with anyone on earth about why she needed the postcard.

Now she kept it in a frame that hung on the wall of her apartment where Luis's death mask had once been. She bent her head to kiss the framed gray caldera whenever she entered or exited the emerald room.

The next afternoon, Consuelo decided she absolutely had to get out of her apartment, so she took herself to the movies. Sometimes she felt she was going mad, she was so lonely, and so it was perhaps no surprise when she saw her dead sister's face, enormous on the screen. Maybe she'd gone mad after all.

Up there, tall as a house in close-up, were Graciela's black eyes, her heavy, dark hair, the wide nose they shared. Graciela grew smaller as she gathered her hair into a bathing cap and made her way to the edge of a swimming pool, in a long line of other women. One by one, the women dove into the water headfirst. Graciela did it like the others, with both arms above her head, a glossy smile impermeable as her body cut through the surface. Only the slightest rippling wave followed her.

Where did she learn to do that? And was this a dream, or was her sister somehow alive?

Consuelo had found Graciela's body. She'd seen her sister's motionless face, unsmiling, slick with blood. Consuelo had blamed herself, of course. Why hadn't she found her before running, like a coward, into the basement, while there was still time to hide? She squinted now into the screen's tunnel of light. Everything in the movies was a trick. Trompe l'oeil.

THE PRINCESS: GRACE LUX. Consuelo wrote this name, and the name of the studio, on her arm in lipstick, as the credits rolled. She sank down into the seats and waited to watch the theater's next screening, just to be sure. She stayed until dark.

Each frame tricked Consuelo into believing that Graciela was searching for her. Watching her move her mouth to a dubbed script, Consuelo told herself that Graciela's huge black eyes were moving around the dark seats like searchlights, searching for her own. She swore that Graciela owed that slow, lash-fluttering wink to her, and she winked back.

Consuelo used to watch her little sister study her movements in the vanity mirror. When Graciela claimed that she couldn't raise one eyebrow independent of the other, Consuelo had pressed her thumbs against her sister's straight india brows and showed her the muscles to isolate. They practiced. The way she threw her coat over her shoulder at the end, that movement was Consuelo's too.

She went home and wrote a letter to Graciela. She imagined it had a fine chance of never arriving, drowning instead in the sea. *Mi hermanita preciosa, mi estrella, daughter of Socorrito*—Consuelo told her sister everything, as if they still shared a room in the Estate. She told her about the paintings she couldn't finish, the aviator, the loneliness, the Sutro Baths, Los Domínguez, Paris. She wrote about her desire for friendship, to be taken seriously, about León and Helena and the photographer, and all the stupid rules of her circle, which was so unlike the Rositas. She craved that ease, all that friendship, the freedom to finish work and then share it, in the mutual trust that eventually they'd get better. That was how Consuelo remembered it, anyway. They were babies then. She concluded the letter with the following baseless accusation:

> *You think I'm pathetic? Unimaginative? Lonely? Haven't you ever wanted to be carefree, understood, and fucked, all at the same time? Haven't you ever been curious enough to turn yourself inside out, to examine that other life like a photograph's negative?*

This was a lot to say to a little sister who was supposed to be dead, in our humble opinion.

The letter was twenty pages, and Consuelo mailed it to Grace Lux's studio in Hollywoodland, saying a prayer that Graciela really was alive, that she hadn't just completely lost her fucking mind, that this letter would somehow get to her sister.

Can you fucking believe it? It did.

31

WRITING TO CONSUELO, EVEN IF IT WAS MONTHS BEFORE Graciela ever received a reply, even if Consuelo wrote back with a riddle or a drawing of a conch shell and nothing else, felt like the greatest care Graciela could offer herself, a tending and combing out of her mind's knots. The letters she received from Consuelo measured time in a way that she felt incapable of doing in her life in Hollywood. And Consuelo was a fucking hoot. She was wild in a way that felt to Graciela unreal and bizarre. She was married to a púchica aviator? Was she faking this life? Was she writing a book? But Consuelo was still Consuelo, despite the fantastic stories she told her about men who thought they were extremely important. She described her secret paintings to Graciela, and confided her loneliness. She was the only being on this earth who knew la Graciela del volcán and the Graciela who had lived in the capital, both.

Cariña Cielita, remember that night we heard someone walking the halls of the Estate and were sure it was a ghost? And it was just Perlita's night watchman on his first night on the job after she got paranoid and thought she was being spied on?

Graciela's letters to Consuelo were often a ledger of her own failings, but always a reminder that she existed, despite all the reasons she should not.

Graciela wore Consuelo's watch on her wrist every day, and the tiny gold hands on its face continued to move, despite her blackouts, despite those long early mornings when she awoke in the sand and salt, despite the steam of the studio cafeteria. Before each shift, Graciela tucked the watch into the pocket of her apron, and afterward, she'd fish it out and its face would be a cloud.

Pretty soon, though, Graciela was finally able to quit that job. She'd started working in parallel production, making Spanish-language movies at night, and by that time, the tiny gold hands on Consuelo's watch didn't matter anymore.

LOURDES: Different forces governed time in parallel production, told her when to eat and when to fall into bed. Whether she was sweating under the white lights of the studio or not. Whether she was in a dance number or the scene's star, a goddess eight feet tall, or sitting off-camera filing her nails into sharp points.

At the studio, Rosie claimed not to speak a word of our language, the language Graciela spoke in parallel production, so sometimes, in the middle of the night, Graciela played her. Rosie with a black lace shawl, Rosie with a comb in her hair, Rosie with a crucifix between her breasts.

It was in parallel production that Graciela made a friend, Scooter, one of the few actors who spoke both our language and English. Sad-eyed Scooter pretended not to recognize her the first few times they worked together, but Graciela didn't take these things personally. He threw himself down ladders for a living and she'd never seen his elastic face move into a genuine smile. He was sad, and it had nothing to do with her. But he spoke a perfect kind of terrible Spanish—all the words in the right order, but misshapen, full of holes— and finally began talking with her when he understood that Graciela's beauty didn't make her unkind. She insisted that they speak in his language.

Scooter had grown up on the road, with his parents taking him from show to show. By his account, they were loving. His father braided his mother's hair at night. His mother sang songs about the bruises on the knuckles of his father's hands, bruises that seemed only to swell, darken, and break open, never fade. The three of them slept on park benches together, limbs folded and stacked. Early mornings, his father stood in the road and estimated how well they might fare if they were to drive in a chosen direction, how many would come to watch them hurl their bodies into brick, beat each other senseless.

Scooter demonstrated. He pulled a chair out from the table where he sat with Graciela and climbed the rungs of its back. At the top, he grinned and kicked up a heel. The chair remained still. He opened his arms wide. Behind him, Graciela watched the girls in the kitchen watching him. They rolled their eyes, impressed by nothing. Scooter lifted his leg behind him like a ballet dancer, and then swiftly brought it forward, kicking the chair over. Before the chair crashed to the cafeteria floor, he paused in the air, righted himself, and pumped his legs as if he were riding a bicycle. This was the second time the man had shown Graciela this trick, but she indulged him. After he'd landed soundlessly and folded his body into a low bow, Graciela clapped her hands. The girls in the kitchen smirked, at Graciela and at him. So did we. Graciela was too nice to these idiots.

"It's a special kind of love," Scooter said, "when a father throws his child down a flight of stairs." Inside the collar seam of every shirt he'd owned as a boy his mother had stitched a suitcase handle with fisherman's wire. His father would reach for the handle invisibly, swing him ten feet in the air, and throw him.

"Other little kids—they don't get close to their fathers the way I did. Every night on the road, my father took off his coat and wrapped it around me, and then put his arms around me too, held me like that until morning, when we'd hit the road for another show."

Above them, the fluorescent lights hummed. Three in the morning. Scooter ate a ham sandwich. In front of Graciela was a cup of coffee that tasted like clay. All those years on our mothers' backs in the fields, all those late mornings in the National Palace, Lidia bringing her cafecitos as she read in the library, and now Graciela couldn't remember what coffee was supposed to taste like, only this lukewarm substance in front of her. She dumped powdered milk into her cup until the liquid swirled gray.

In the beginning of their friendship, Graciela had a feeling Scooter was talking to her only because he loved Rosie, like every other man did. But Scooter was what Rosie called a trout. "There are two types," she'd told Graciela as they sat in the back of her car on their way to a party. "Trouts and buffoons. The buffoons are dumb and not particularly sweet, but they like to show off for you. You know, big shoulders, furry chests, loud voices." The trouts were like Scooter, who greeted them at the party—thin in the face, eyes that seemed too observant and large, an obvious tenderness. Weak and pleasing. He was Graciela's friend because he was a trout, and Rosie would never sleep with him for the same reason, wouldn't even puff her little lips in his direction. He seemed to know that Rosie would never love him, but he continued to seek Graciela's company, regardless.

At the party Rosie and Graciela attended a few nights later, buffoons fell to the ground, one after the next, and did push-ups. One removed his white bow tie and shirt, held his arms straight against the ground, his body a long, trembling line. Someone balanced a glass of wine on his back, just above the leather belt. A few minutes later somebody put another glass beside the first one. Graciela left the room to find a toilet, and when she returned, the circle around the man had hardened and hushed and spread wider. There were now four wineglasses standing along the man's spine. Graciela stood on her tiptoes to watch the liquid inside them bob on the sea of his breathing. Someone edged to the front and placed a bottle between the man's shoulder blades. There, the ribs of his undershirt had gone damply transparent, and just above the bottle, a muscle quivered like a gear. The man growled through his lower teeth. Sweat ran from his hairline into his eyes and he blinked furiously.

"Get a picnic basket and maybe a parasol!" somebody called from the kitchen. Rosie tittered, Graciela turned her head to wink, ice clinked in someone's glass, and the man lay bleeding in the center of the room, wine puddled under his fallen arms, crystal shards along the part of his hair. He rose, grinning, glass falling from his body, his thin mustache and top row of teeth a slick, deep red.

Later, when he was back in their bungalow, the man told Rosie that he hadn't cut his mouth with the glass when he finally collapsed beneath his own weight; he'd been biting his tongue to maintain his posture. Scooter stayed at the bungalow that night as well, but only because he was ill from too much Champagne. He borrowed one of Rosie's tooth-brushes and then draped his long body over the edge of the couch. Graciela slept on the porch, perplexed, a little pissed, that Scooter never tried anything with her.

The following afternoon, still on the porch, baking in the sun in Rosie's party dress, Graciela wrote to Consuelo, as she always did when she felt completely alone.

> Dear Consuelo:
>   I drank so much last night that I'm still drunk today. It's noon, and I woke up on the porch. Has this ever happened to you? My hands are shaking. Pray for me that I don't pickle my brain like curtido and become incapable of doing anything useful with this mind or body.

Later, through the middle of the night, Graciela played Rosie's mirror again, a girl on a train with her overbearing mother, on her way to fame and fortune.

32

GRACIELA LANDED A STARRING ROLE IN HER NEXT FILM: A woman in love, a woman who swims naked in a caldera, a woman who gets thrown into a volcano, a sacrifice. *This is the glory of your career,* Rosie said, and yet Graciela felt half-dead the moment she left the studio every day. The clock of her body was broken and could not be willed to sleep. Maybe she fell asleep for moments at a time on the streetcar. And often she hid inside during the day's swell of heat—surely she slept then too. Usually by late afternoon the throbbing in her head had evaporated into a kind of wobbly ease and Graciela drifted into the world and back to work. She ate less and saved her earnings.

She was certain that someone, a many-eyed, many-bodied beast, was following her. A man walking across the street from her at three in the morning, shuffling and glancing over at each streetlamp, darting into a liquor store and coming outside when she reached the corner. Cutting across the empty street to her side. Though the man looked different every night, his menace, his flashing dog eyes, remained the same. More than once, Graciela had taken off running back to her apartment. She could swear he was behind her, calling out to her, using her old name. Sometimes he was inside a dark car, slowing at a misty corner. Sometimes he met Graciela's eye on the streetcar and pushed through the crowd to get closer. When the train was empty, he sat beside her, grinning. Graciela made a habit of getting off the streetcar before or after her stop so he couldn't trace her.

When she finally got home, she'd shuffle out of her clothes and lie awake over her sheets for a few hours. This is when we'd appear to her, in the grayed light, gathered around her sleepless bed, following her from room to room. Sometimes the gringa who fell from the *H* did too, her face scrubbed clean, raw, and red, its smooth, bloody gleam the inverted core her parents' papery skins had been. A hallucination borne of sleepless mania, or guilt, a nightmare dragged into daylight, or simply: ghosts. You don't believe us? We grow annoyed, finding words for the inexplicable: believe us or don't.

Graciela still made time to read the news from home at the library and relied upon the dictionaries to translate less and less. She found tiny paragraphs about our earthquakes, and the villagers crushed to death as they slept. Sometimes she found El Gran Pendejo's name, and she stared at the letters on the paper until they caused her physical pain.

Every few months or so Graciela wondered if the General had seen any of her films. She told herself that if he'd wanted to find her, he would have tracked her down years ago. Sure, she had a new name. But no one really believed that she'd been born Grace Lux.

"Am I a Grace Lux in this?" Graciela would ask Rosie, trying on one of her blond wigs. "Am I La Güerita del Norte?"

"Do you honestly believe that anyone like us keeps her own name?" Rosie would say. "Who gives a shit?"

Despite Graciela's restlessness, she usually awoke eager to walk for hours, to exhaust herself. She'd walk the hills, find her way to the beach.

It was there one afternoon that she found herself talking to a stranger, a handsome man who immediately filled her with pity. He drank red wine from a bottle and told her that he'd lost everything. He burped and smiled without charm. He reached for her hand and squeezed. I have nothing left, he said. Something told her to give this man whatever he wanted—out of her own misery and exhaustion, her drunkenness, her fear that here he was, the many-eyed demon man who had been stalking her, and the delusion that this was the only way to be rid of him, she fucked him with the blind stubbornness of a sleepwalker. The tide came in, and Graciela left him there, sleeping. She stumbled over rocks and scrub until she reached the road. It was time to head to the studio.

Scooter was outside smoking when Graciela arrived. When he saw her, he moved out from under the streetlamp to block the door. She knocked gently on the top of his head with her knuckles and said, "Open, Sesame!"

Scooter frowned, and Graciela wondered for a moment if she'd said something to hurt him the last time they'd drunk together. She couldn't remember.

"There was a raid in the cafeteria this afternoon."

Graciela shook her head.

"Uniformed men with clubs hanging from their belts took four kitchen girls and shoved them into a van."

"What? Why?"

"Because they're like you. Mexicans with no papers."

"I'm not Mexican."

"Doesn't matter. Look in the mirror. Got any papers?"

Graciela had never told Scooter how she'd arrived in Hollywood. She'd never told Rosie either. Of course she didn't have papers. But that Scooter could detect desperation in her face frightened her.

"What's going to happen to those girls?" Graciela asked him.

"Hold them in jail until they can figure out which bus to put them on to send them back." Scooter tossed his cigarette to the curb, and Graciela watched the sparks dance. The girls in the cafeteria were young, teenagers some of them, a few of them mothers of tiny babies whom they sometimes tied to their backs as they worked.

"What about their families?"

"You know, they're trying to get rid of as many of you as possible right now. You need to be careful." None of the girls from the cafeteria had been drawing attention to themselves like Graciela was, as if letting her face show up on billboards were the only way to make a life.

Graciela pushed past Scooter, angry for reasons that she didn't at the time understand, and went to work. That night they filmed a scene in the mountains. Birds of paradise, stuffed and propped to resemble a flock.

Graciela's character was to be married to a leader of the opposing tribe, her marriage an offering of peace to both of their peoples. The only problem was that she didn't love him.

Graciela walked through the gray light to an all-night five-and-dime, where she bought a chicken sandwich and sat at the counter eating it, staring past her reflection into the case across from the counter. The glass held tiny bottles of liquor, aspirin, and knives, weapons for self-defense and for cooking. She pointed her lips at the knife case.

The sleepy old man at the register pouted a kiss at her and opened the glass door. The knife Graciela wanted lay on fake blue velvet over foam, its blade six inches and its handle curved and inlaid with iridescent shell. The old man slid the knife across the counter to her. He tapped on the handle and said, "Abalone." He showed her how it folded into itself. "For safety," he said. And there was a button she could press on the handle discreetly, by feel, to release the blade and stab anyone through the heart.

Graciela gulped the end of her sandwich and bought the knife. Walking the rest of the way home, she kept her hand inside her purse, her fingers wrapped around the abalone handle.

LUCÍA: It wasn't long after that a man in uniform came knocking on her door. La güera Rosie answered it. He asked for Graciela de los Ángeles, which no one here called her, so Rosie was suspicious, and even though Graciela was home, asleep in her twin bed after working all night, Rosie said, prim as can be, "There is no one living at this address by that name."

The man was pretty sure something wasn't right, but then again, why would this blond movie star be hiding a wetback anyway? So he left.

LOURDES: But he didn't really leave!

MARÍA: Right. He sat in his car with binoculars. He waited and we watched him as he watched for her. Rosie drew the blinds and locked the door. When Graciela got up, Rosie told her about the man, about his uniform, the car he'd arrived in. She told Graciela that she should be careful, and we could tell Graciela was afraid, but she just rolled her eyes. By now the car was gone. Graciela packed her knife in her purse and walked to work.

LOURDES: But the man was at the studio. He was the same uniformed pendejo from a few years before, when Graciela found the body of the girl. You know, the young one, the nice one who liked birds and would always talk about this and that. The other one, el viejito, had died. But a cop is a cop is a cop is a cop, no?

He came right onto the set with his gun in the air and he screamed, "Mexican nationals, line up against this wall!"

Graciela was already in costume—she had feathers in her hair and, in brown face paint, wearing necklaces made of sea-shells, was marrying a gringo. She recognized the cop. Looked, looked quickly away.

The director yelled, "Cut!"

The gringo actor rolled his eyes and asked, "How long is this going to fucking take?"

An indio dropped the screen he was holding. All around him were fake mountains, palm trees, monkeys in the trees, a river. A big fake volcano in the center of the room. The indio tried to run and tripped on a cord. The cop grabbed him by the back of his shirt and hit him with his stick. The sound made me sick, as sick as a ghost can be.

"Don't fuck with me!" the cop shouted, scanning the set with his gun in the air. "You and you and you." The cop pointed to a man carrying sandbags, a man with a spool of film, a man with a broom. "And you." He pointed to Graciela. He looked her body up and down with the dull eyes of any pendejo anywhere looking at a pair of tetas attached to some body. As if he'd never seen Graciela in his life.

The men lined up against the wall beside the man who had been beaten, who was lying on the floor. Graciela didn't move. The cop raised his gun at her. She walked toward him with her hand on her hip like a siren, like that silly pechita Consuelo.

Graciela pulled something from inside the waist of her skirt and bit her lip. She used both hands to hold what looked like the kind of knife los fufurufos use to eat their steaks. She aimed for the cop's solar plexus and stabbed.

When the cop fell, Graciela ran to the volcano. The men scattered out the back doors. One pulled the indio who'd been beaten up by his armpits and carried him out on his shoulder. The director was screaming and calling Graciela a maniac. She was at the base of the volcano, climbing the ladder that led to its little caldera. She jumped inside and the set came tumbling down—papier-mâché, and fake lava, and big painted foam rocks.

"You fucking bitch, you fucking wetback bitch!" the director was screaming. Dust and rubble and paint and feathers settled on Graciela, who sat like a glassy-eyed doll at the base of the broken volcano.

And that other sad-eyed gringo ran to her. Her friend, El Scooter. Yes, Scooter—ridiculous name. He grabbed her by the arm and pulled her outside.

CORA: But the man Graciela stabbed wasn't dead. She didn't stab him too well—just enough to nick the knuckles of his left hand, scrape the meat of his palm.

MARÍA: And then he'd started screaming at the top of his lungs, looking around the set for help, bleeding, dripping sticky blood all over the fake volcano and these stuffed birds—what are they called, Cora? I don't know, quetzales? Torogoces?

CORA: They looked like some storks and geese that someone painted bright colors.

LUCÍA: Outside, Graciela was shaking and sobbing while El Scooter talked to her.

"It's time to disappear now," he said. Graciela went pale. She was wiping her bloody knife on her skirt and folding it up to put back in her bag. "Leave," he told her. "Run for your life."

MARÍA: Oh, let me finish this part. I love a sappy fucking movie goodbye, all misty and shit.

"Give me that knife," Scooter kept saying. He looked straight ahead, his lips barely moving. He guided her down the street, his fingers wrapped around her upper arm, pushing her like she was a statue. And Graciela, her skin seemed to turn to wax; she gave no sign that she'd heard him at all.

"Give it to me. Just give it to me." But even I knew that we didn't have any time to spare. El Scooter had to make himself disappear too.

Just then, a shaggy white dog with red eyes came running down the sidewalk. It leapt into the air and knocked Graciela to the ground. Lourdes screamed. Graciela threw her arms around the dog's neck, and the dog licked her face with a long pink tongue, its tail thumping the wet sidewalk.

"What the hell are you doing?" El Scooter shouted.

Graciela blinked and stared into the dog's eyes. The dog laid his head on her chest. This cadejo loved Graciela, as if it had known her for a thousand years. And in a way it had— los cadejos always know where to find us.

El Scooter hailed Graciela a cab, cursing under his breath.

"I'm going to take him with me," she said, "This pink-eyed freak." She kissed the dog's long nose, the top of his head.

"What are you talking about? You've lost your goddamn mind," El Scooter said. "You're nuts." He looked around, seeing nothing.

He eased Graciela into the cab. The dog hopped into the backseat and turned three circles before settling down with a contented groan.

"Just give me the fucking knife before you go," El Scooter whispered. Graciela had her hand buried inside her bag, and she shook her head. She wouldn't, or couldn't, loosen her grip on the abalone handle of that knife.

He finally gave up and threw a roll of bills into the back-seat. The money bounced off her knee and onto the floor of the cab. Graciela sank into the dog's fur and closed her eyes.

"Get her to Central Station, and make sure she gets on the Daylight Limited," El Scooter said to the cab driver. The driver nodded. Graciela's skin went cold, and her teeth chat-tered. She sobbed into the dog's fur without making a sound. From the curb, El Scooter stared into the cab's backseat, at Graciela and the dog, with a look of longing in his eyes, and for a moment we were still on the set, actors in a movie. When the cab started moving, El Scooter ran down the dark street into an alleyway, where he vanished behind a dump-ster. The cadejo sniffed out the window and howled.

At the train station, we became something else. Moths. Graciela's life in Los Angeles was dying, she was out of her mind, and we had to show her what to do next. This was how we got her on the right train. We danced, darting in and out of the lamp that shone over the map of California on the platform, over its scroll of orange poppies, across a bridge made of gold. Four of us, polillas, spun out of the air. *You're going here,* we told her. *San Francisco.*

The train horn sounded as the car approached, and the dog, who'd been curled up, a majestic fluffy mountain on Graciela's lap, startled at the call and ran off through the crowd. Graciela chased the dog's flash of tail, despite our protests. *Let him go,* we said. She asked strangers: *Have you seen my dog? Did you see my dog run this way, white, with red eyes? He was just here.* Most didn't answer, or only shook their heads. Graciela had left her feather crown in the cab, but her dress was made of animal skin, and she wore shells that clinked musically around her bare ankles. The dog was nowhere. She boarded the train.

PART III

∽

1938-1942

33

I N THE BOOK OF THE PEOPLE, THE *POPOL VUH,* CREATION HAP-
pens at the end, after Blood Woman has discovered a field of maíz that
multiplies not by miracle, but by her own tending. When humans are finally formed, by hand, maíz, blood, bone, all of that, gota a gota, the
timeline goes haywire. The pages of the book scatter in the air and land
in the Eternal Now, where all time exists at once.

And so it is for us. After Graciela arrives in San Francisco, our souls
trailing her like polillas, we travel—into the past, into the future, into our
old homes, into flesh. We exist in all directions. As the waters swell, we
dream together, awakening in brief bodies. Here, time has collapsed, and
we fall through it. This is our Eternal Now.

We climb over ruins and ice plant overgrowth at the Sutro Baths. We
bathe in the wind, sand stinging our cheeks, a howling in our ears. The
water gathers us, and the salt draws out our stories. Here we find that way
of seeing clearly that comes from beside the sea.

We learn that our ocean has its own life underground. From the
Outer Richmond to the Mission, the waters travel, becoming a secret
lake, Dolores, that carries us together to the Mission District, where Graciela finds a home, snaking a path between Seventeenth and Eighteenth
Streets, winding under hills and graves. In the Mission, the marshes rise
and fall with the tides. Under the high school, beneath the windowless
brick armory, there are doors and drains, pumping the water out, carrying it away, emptying into China Basin, the bay's wide mouth.

Some say Dolores is neither creek nor lake nor marsh, but a miraculous spring. When the conquistadores discovered the water, they called it "ojo de agua" and named it after Our Lady of Sorrows. They tested the soil by planting maíz that they'd stolen from our lands and then laid claim to the place in the name of Christ.

More stories came later. Dolores was imagined into a lake that wails, carrying the grief of all who walk above her. Viejitos claimed to remember the traces of an underground dock when they were young. Others say there is no lake beneath the living feet of San Francisco, warping the sidewalks, draining West to East, despite what all the old maps claim. But who are we to blame anyone for inventing a myth? Maps are based on older maps.

Back in our bodies, we all pass the infinite time, in our own ways— we've told you before: sometimes we do our own thing. Lourdes, for example, when she's not haunting los comedores looking for shrimp and gossiping with us, she's visiting the fucking library.

LOURDES: Escúchame. One library leads to another. I like the library on Bartlett. But, if I stay there reading long enough, I'm bound to enter a púchica vortex. Puya, it's like being hit over the head with a rock. I wake up thirty years in the future, back in our country, breathing in a body as beautiful as I would have become, if I'd fucking lived. It's how I started working on my little project.

I really got going on it when I met this one gringo who was writing a book about the massacre. Let me tell you, he needed my fucking help.

I spotted him shuffling through the capital, with his Velcro sandals and his floppy blond hair. I thought he was another surfer on his way to La Libertad. Or worse, one of those Jesus-complex guys—a Mormon Jesus guy or a Peace Corps guy who thinks he's Jesus. In 1969, a lot of idiots came through our country, and a lot of them thought they were Jesus.

This one seemed to have a different purpose, though, a púchica quest, like Indiana Jones or a private eye. I kept bumping into him in my hauntings of the National Library, where I liked to spend my midnights, floating above the rotting papers set into their shallow graves of milk crates. I found him serious, a little too earnest, and easily frustrated. I followed him around for a bit after that, spent time listening to him, his polite, stiff exchanges with the jicama vendor outside his hotel, observed his easy smile, and, once I decided that I liked him, I made him listen to me.

Tom was his name. Tom, an intrepid fucking gringo who loved to read about "our chronic unhappiness," our recurring nightmares. But I digress. Que Dios lo bendiga.

The thing is, whatever Tom was reading in our moldy library wasn't adding up. He was frustrated, couldn't find what he seemed to be looking for. Paper fell apart in his sweaty red fingers. Reading so much longhand Spanish gave him a headache, and he was always polishing the steam from his glasses and mashing his temples with a dusty hankie. Pobrecito.

"Happy countries have no history," Tom said one night, thinking he was alone. He drew out the words with such smug conviction, like a detective cracking the case or some shit, so much that I had to laugh and frighten him a little.

"Yeah, yeah. Well, let me tell you, cipote, we have plenty of fucking history. Despite what you've referred to as 'the disturbing paucity of this municipal archive' in your little notebook there."

Tom rubbed his eyes and scribbled an ancient glyph on the notebook in front of him. I pushed it off the table like a cat. "I don't speak Mayan, pendejo!"

He jumped beneath the table and let out a tiny moan.

"What, you've never seen such a pretty guanaca?" I watched him cower. Maybe I'd gone too far. "Ay, I'm not going to hurt you. Do I look like Siguanaba to you?"

Tom bit his chapped little knuckles.

"She's not that bad, actually," I said.

"I'm sorry—it's just that you startled me," Tom said. "I don't think I've talked to another soul all day." His breathing slowed to normal. He had an excellent constitution. He'd invented his own kind of yoga, which he practiced upside down, like a bat.

"Listen," I said. "You might learn something from me. Did you know that Salvadorans were voted by UNESCO or some shit to be the second most emotional people in the world?"

"I didn't know that," Tom conceded. "Second to whom?"

"The Filipinos," I said.

Tom nodded and stroked his silly little blond goatee.

"My point is that we're happy. And we're also a fucking mess. The saddest sad poets. The greatest lovers. The eternally undocumented! And we're the finest artisans in the world—haven't you read Roque fucking Dalton?"

Tom began scribbling notes in ballpoint pen all over his pink forearm, as if he didn't have a notebook right there on the floor in front of him.

" 'Happy countries have no history.' Thank god we have ours! Do you know about our long-lost golden age? Back in the day of the Federal Republic of Central America. That was how we broke free of the Spanish, then broke free of the Mexicans. It was supposed to solve all of the problems of imperialist rule—the land disputes, our one-crop bullshit, and the malnourishment we suffered because we had to export las tres hermanas—corn, squash, beans, in case that isn't in any of the archives either—all over the world instead of feeding our own people."

Tom indulged me, sat up like a chuchito and listened—once I'd convinced him that a Black guanaca was worth paying attention to. (It couldn't have hurt how outrageously beautiful I am in this body. My tetas alone should be UNESCO World Heritage sites!) But I speak with authority. I've amassed and ordered a collection of books, documents, and photographs from libraries all over the world—I don't trust our púchica National Library one bit.

"So you see, we decided to unite—Costa Rica, ¡presente! Guatemala, ¡presente! El Salvador, ¡presente! Nicaragua, ¡presente! Honduras, ¡presente! Chiapas, even, that rogue state of Mexico, ¡presente! United we were stronger. We would not be swallowed by Spain. And after Spain spat us out, we would not allow Mexico to swallow us either! We declared our independence."

"So why didn't it stick?" Tom asked.

"The vague answer, the one you don't want, is 'civil war.' That means something different to you norteamericanos, no?" I said. "Everyone dropped out but El Salvador. And then what else could we do? The cheese stood alone, as you people like to say."

"But what does this have to do with the . . . the massacre?" Tommy asked. He whispered that last word, as if I might get him in trouble for saying it.

"Listen, you baby. This is your first lesson. There's a lot for us to get to, but trust me when I tell you: I'll give you the story like it really happened." I ruffled his hair. Tommy saw my hand land on his head but felt nothing. He told himself that he was dissociating, losing his mind.

Some eras are better than others, though. I nearly lost my mind in the 1990s. I found this book in the library on Bartlett that gave me a terrible headache. This lady, a little norteamericana with a sour face, tufosa, pero bien tufosa, she spent a week in our country smoking cigarettes and drinking at the Sheraton, and then she had the fucking balls to write about how we don't understand scientific facts, that our only subject is our own misery. She went to some village

fair and got mal de mayo from bad meat, then wrote a fucking essay about that, finding time to call the dance performance and all the fucking knickknacks that were for sale
ugly and made unskillfully. Ay, how can a person be so bored
by everything that surrounds her? "Desultory!" Everything,
"desultory!"

But the thing that bothered me the most wasn't the book
itself. La viejita was a decent writer, not terrible. What really
pissed me off was the quote on the cover: "No one has interpreted the place better." I made that book fly off its shelf and
across the room. It thudded off a cork bulletin board and
landed on top of a stack of *SF Weekly* papers.

But ay, you see? All this poetry that I've been gathering
is evidence, testimony. Some of these hijueputas wrote
that we never existed. Black women, Indigenous women—
I've read every book in the library, swum through those
microfiches, surfeado la red, looking for us, and none of
these hijueseismilputas, not one, has even heard of La Prudencia Ayala. Maps are based on older maps and books are
based on older books. So, along with the pleasure of being
able to admire my own beautiful ass once again, I don't mind
the fucking exhaustion and ache of re-entering my body in
short bursts.

I refuse to be invisible.

Meanwhile, María, mi hermanita, she tells our stories her
own way, paints like the hand of god works through her, sits
in the hard orange plastic booths of a doughnut shop en la
Misión, makes everyone fall in love with her. Te juro—the
old lady refilling the coffee, los viejitos doing dirty deals, the
teenagers with floppy hair—they all fall in love with her.

She paints outside too, on filthy walls, in narrow alleys
lined with fungal trees and flowering rosemary. She carries a
ladder, with a pie-tin palette resting under her arm. Her

black-and-silver hair is shaved into a fade. Friends bring her
water, cigarettes, or pan dulce from around the corner.
There's something soft and angelic about María's face, wrinkled now. She paints Our Lady of Sorrows in the alleyway.
Later, she paints seven teenage boys from our country, who
were accused of a crime they did not commit. She paints a
field of lettuce doused in poison, the poison polluting a river,
and women with faces that she remembers from when we
were all children. These women cry into the river.

Businesses roll white primer over María's paintings,
sometimes just hours after they are completed. Photogra-
phers start trying to capture them before they disappear.

Ay, but it's a relief for María to return to this body, instead of to the body in which she was a child. She's glad not
to be mistaken for anyone's lamp, but to make her own art.
And, it's a relief, a pleasure, to be desired. Women fall in love
with her when they catch a glimpse of her on her ladder,
knowing it might be weeks or months before they see her
again.

She always comes back.

Corita, when she comes back, she's old. Wrinkled and
grumpy as hell. Her body hurts. The joints of her fingers are
swollen and purplish. She tends the rose gardens in el parque
Golden Gate, muttering and growling. She scares people.

A while back, must be en los ochenta, she was taking a
nap in one of the meadows en el parque, where the bison still
stomp around, and this gringa in a long skirt carrying a
bongo drum approached her. She wore a curious pouch,
bulging with blown glass, on a filthy cord around her neck.

"Mother," she called out to Cora, waking her. "Mother,
the buffalo gotta roam. This is their territory," she said.

"¿Qué demonio es?" Cora awoke with a start, furious.
She has no more tenderness these days, she tells us. All gone.

She says that she's tired of living—the terrors of her life return in this body, and her only escapes are sleep and the
roses. That first time her body returned, beside the ocean,
she was delighted, like the rest of us. She wiggled her fingers
and dipped them into the cold, salty water. But now she returns older, her mind like string, pulled more brittle each
time. Her knees ache, and the hours are too long. Her back is
hunched with growths on the bone.

Anyway, the gringa hippie closed her eyes, began beating
her drum, twisting her voice in a series of toots and honks.
"Buffalo! Gotta roam roam roam, can't fence them in, desire's too strong! Buffalo, let them roam roam, roam, Mother
oh oh oh!"

This stupid fucking song, it filled Cora with rage. Mother.
She was not this woman's mother. Her baby had died, and all
further opportunities to be a mother had been stolen from
her. She charged the fence on her arthritic knees and swatted
the bongo drum out of the gringa's hand.

"Mother, you must be the tiger that got loose in the park
all those years ago. Blessed be," the woman said. She gathered
her bongo from the dusty path and continued on her way.

Cora did like that comparison, to the tiger. It felt deeply,
surprisingly, correct to her. She was the tiger that got loose
en el parque. Stunned, she growled. It was good to be recognized. Inwardly, she forgave the gringa for bothering her,
and let her growl bloom into a roar. She turned to the buffalo, who was emerging from stillness, swaying and shaking
its blocky forelock. She sang our song to it, majestic beast, the
closest thing to toro any of us would ever see. "¡Vamos a la
vuelta, de torotorogil, a ver a Doña Ana, comiendo perejil!"

When Lucía returns she's a teenage güerita. Mystery lights
her face; her skin tone is similar to Rosie Swan's, to that of
the ladies in all the yogurt ads and telenovelas.

When she's in this body, walking down misty streets without a sweater, hair puffing out at her temples, glasses tucked into the pocket of her low-rise jeans, or worse, left on Muni, out too late flirting with older boys, nervous and giggly when they ask her, "What are you?" She's never enough of anything for them; her mother's white, or maybe her grandfather is—well, she's a perfect, unsuspecting detective, a very natural ghost, shape-shifting, relaying messages—she reminds me of you, Yinita.

But, for Graciela, time remained constant. 1938. She's just gotten to San Francisco, found a boardinghouse on Twentieth and Capp, along the southern rim of the mythical lake Dolores, and a job canning peaches at a factory perched on the bay called Half Moon. And she's just learned she's pregnant, by a man whose face she hardly saw.

In those early days in the city, she swore she could feel the ground swell, our waters pulling her. But that may have been the heavy nausea of those weeks. Our waters swelled and so did hers. Her lower back ached. She'd been tired for a very long time, and now, before she'd even left for work each morning, her limbs were heavier than she could bear, her back stiff and tender with el duendito sitting on her hips, filing down her bones with cruel delight. She cursed herself for throwing up food that she'd paid for with her first week of work. She was starving, exhausted, and angry.

All she wanted was for someone to hold on to her hips, to pull up and back, to relieve the weight and tension that accumulated from hours on her feet. Who would do this fucking thing for her? Nobody. She was alone. And then there was the agony of her feet. Stuffing them in shoes in the mornings with the awareness that she'd be walking up Van Ness to Aquatic Park and then down to the Half Moon cannery, and then standing on them all day, and then, walking

back down Van Ness to the boardinghouse in the Mission—
it was enough to make her weep a little. But she laughed at
herself instead. Por la gran puta. These fat little feet had carried her up and down Izalco. On these feet she'd run for her
life, crawled out of a pile of death; her broken body had run
afraid on these feet. She'd been a barefoot stowaway, and in
Hollywood she'd danced all night after working on them all
day. And now, this, this was the only time her battered feet
had moved her to tears. At the boardinghouse she slept with
them resting on her pillow; it barely helped.

Away from her mother, away from us, there was so much
she didn't know—what to do when everything she ate caused
heartburn, when she couldn't sleep at night because her
joints felt shredded. Why was she so fucking thirsty? Y, para
más joder—what was she going to do when this baby arrived?

Qué onda, Gracielita. Vamos a la vuelta.

34

I N THE LATE DAYS OF HER PREGNANCY, GRACIELA STARTED RID-
ing the bus to work, sneaking in the back door when she could, to save
a few cents. The route took her, daily, by the local firehouse.

"You know you can leave the baby there if you need to," a girl across
the aisle said to her. Graciela wasn't sure she understood. The girl looked
her up and down, her mouth a mean line. "You're about to pop, aren't
you? They take babies at that firehouse, no questions asked. As long as
you drop the kid off before it's three days old. You just leave it outside the
door." Graciela stared back at the girl blankly, letting her believe that she
didn't speak English, until she finally rang the bell and stood to exit.

Now that Graciela had heard this sinister fairy tale about the firehouse, she couldn't rinse it from her mind. Back in Hollywood, she
would have gotten off the bus a stop early and found a bottle of wine to
drink before work. But here, now, even the smell of alcohol made her
sick. Probably the pregnancy, but she'd found it was a relief not to be
drunk all the time. Besides, at the cannery she had to be sharp, auto-
mated; otherwise she'd cut off all her fingers.

Instead Graciela considered the information in small pieces throughout the day, allowed herself to imagine what it might feel like to wrap a
newborn in cloth and carry it in her arms to the firehouse, to pull the
bell, to leave the baby in the morning fog, waiting for someone to find it.
Would she choose words to say goodbye, would she whisper a promise—
would it matter?

That evening Graciela held her belly. She was cold, and she wondered if the baby was too. She'd missed the bus and would need to walk a while. Of course she wouldn't leave the baby at the firehouse. How cruel, how cold. How could she ever forgive herself?

But then again, maybe both she and the child would be better off that way. And how would she ever know?

A few mornings later, a new woman appeared beside Graciela on the canning line. She was older than the other girls on the line, and Graciela noted an incongruous soft halo of inherited wealth around her face. She moved quickly, as though she'd done the job before. Graciela knew this woman. She had worked at the art school. This one, what was her name? La Claudia, daughter of Don Patricio. She was rich. No, it couldn't be her. What was she doing here?

Graciela looked into her face and was transported to our country. She was a child again, staring through the dark beside a fountain in the presidential plaza, at a grown poet with ojos claros, a woman her sister wanted to be so much that she hated her a little. "You wrote the poem after Luis's death," she said. "Do you remember me?"

La Claudia, daughter of the railroad, dropped her can of peaches on the concrete floor.

That evening, the women walked to the bus together. In our country, despite her despised husband, Claudia had fallen in love with some communist, and her father had lost his mind. He'd sent her to Los Yunais to get away from the communist, but when he found out that she'd been living with him, he'd disowned her for a couple of years. Now, though, her father was sick. He'd forgive her, she knew, so long as she repented. This job at the factory was temporary, just for spending money while her father finalized the arrangements to bring her back. She didn't mind it too terribly.

Claudia would turn forty this year, and was somehow less bitter than she had been in our country, when Graciela remembered her smoking by the fountain, dispensing advice as she tapped out the ash, her face a sour line.

They had missed the last bus, and were walking together up Van Ness's steep dregs, when Graciela felt a burst of water exit her body and flood the inside of her legs. Claudia was the one who whistled for a cab, who took Graciela to St. Luke's Hospital on Twenty-seventh and Army, and who paid the bill for Graciela's delivery of a healthy baby boy. Before Graciela had been discharged from the hospital, Claudia was on her way back to our country.

A few days later, Graciela was back at the boardinghouse with her baby. She'd nearly bled to death in the hospital.

Graciela was crushed under the weight of birth. Leave the baby on the steps of the firehouse within three days! Ha! Those first three days passed without rest, each a door closing in her face. She let them close. Her body was wide open, gaping and tender. There would be no firehouse. Even if she could have gathered herself and the baby to leave the boardinghouse and travel across town, and even though the child's screams filled her with rage and terror and she was menaced by strange, persistent thoughts that spiked into frantic urges, commands she sometimes heard chanted in a sinister whisper—*Throw yourself down the stairs. Take a knife from the kitchen and peel off the skin of your inner arm. Why poison this sweet baby with the milk from your breasts?*—she also knew that she couldn't give him up at a firehouse. She simply could not. He was hers. Salvador. His fat, round-at-the-bottom feet, the ripe red of his cheeks, his long eyelashes. My god, she loved him, and whatever goodness she possessed was now in service to his. She would knife anyone in the heart who tried to take him from her.

Survival was a shape-shifter. It was as if her body had been cut into quarters and scattered—her arms were in different rooms than her legs. Oh, she adored him, this small rabbit, downy cheeks and hands curled up like buds. When he cried, a hot wave of susto surged inside of her and she went nearly blind with panic. When he cried, she remembered the cries of thirty thousand of us, that living nightmare returned like a visitor. Her shape had shifted. Every bone of her own body was wrong, every opening raw and broken, except for the spigot of her breasts. Chapped nipples and aching with weight, but they worked. The baby latched without incident and Graciela lay wet and bleeding, in shapeless, racing hours that were neither night nor day.

Three women, Josefina, Clara, and Silvia, had all arrived at the boardinghouse the week that Graciela was discharged from the hospital. Josefina and Clara had grown up in the same village in our country, and like Graciela, Silvia had arrived in San Francisco alone. Graciela didn't believe that she or the baby would have survived those early days after birth without them. They established their patterns of care with ease, and in the space of a few days they had become her comadres.

When Silvia came into the room, Graciela, sitting with Salvador by the window, was startled. Silvia offered her a bowl of atol, and a jar of hot tea from manzanilla that she'd picked in the neighborhood.

"Fuck," Graciela said, and then, "Thank you!" Silvia smiled warmly as she handed Graciela the tea, ignoring her incoherence.

"I didn't know that so many of our plants would be here too," Silvia said. Graciela hadn't noticed it until she mentioned it. Bugambilia, jamaica, manzanilla, artemisia, jacaranda, flor de amate—they all grew in this neighborhood.

"Let me take him for a minute," her friend offered. "Just so you can get back into the bed." She had two children that she'd left behind in our country. Graciela suspected, from the way that she talked about them, that both were dead, but since the birth Graciela didn't trust her memory and was afraid to ask more questions about Silvia's life. Asking certain questions right now felt like begging for a curse.

Graciela handed her Salvador to hold. Silvia clucked and cooed, charming the baby's eyelids to close, rocking him back and forth on her bare heels. She pointed her lips at Graciela's bed. "Just rest a moment," she said.

"He'll need to feed soon," Graciela said in protest.

"I'll wake you," Silvia said. "Shush shush shush," she said to them both.

Clara burst into the room as Graciela settled into bed.

"You don't want your womb getting cold right now," she said. She was brash, loud, and certain. She closed the window and drew the shade. "This is the warmest thing I have." Clara unrolled a rebozo that Josefina had woven for her when they were girls and laid it across Graciela's destroyed middle on the bed.

"Ay, give her a moment—she's just going to sleep," Silvia said.

Clara waved her off. "This will be quick," she said. Clara's mother had been a partera in our country, and Clara had received some midwife training from her. Graciela let Clara wrap the rebozo tightly around her body, resting in her expertise, though the other woman was still practically a stranger to her.

The baby didn't yowl or arch his back in Silvia's arms. Why was that? Graciela wondered what awful things he must know and fear about his mother. Messages in the milk, or all of those months, simmering inside of her core. Clara's hands were on her belly now.

"It's yuca like this for every new mother. I remember," she said. She massaged the twinge in Graciela's hip. "First we warm la matriz," she said. "Then we start shifting you back into place. This shouldn't hurt, okay?"

Everything hurt. The bones around her eyes, the tendons of her ankles. Her crazed mind and its nest of hallucinations and terrors. Everything had been wrong since the birth. But she was warmer now. She drank the tea and let her eyes close again.

Earlier, she'd screamed at the baby. She'd fed him, changed his runny diaper, and soaked the cloth in soapy water in a bowl in the tub, meaning to grab it before another girl complained, but of course forgetting about it, because the baby had begun to cry and wouldn't stop. She'd rocked him, hugged him close to her, hummed to him, rubbed the dense wrinkles of his tiny back. He screamed and wouldn't stop. She'd lose her room in this boardinghouse—so far, the landlady had let her stay but Graciela knew she wasn't happy about it—and of course, just then Graciela remembered the shitty diaper soaking in the bowl in the tub, and she heard one of the girls getting home from work and heading into the bathroom, and there was no point in racing in now with a screaming baby, or even calling down the hall. No one could hear her over the baby's cries. The baby's face had become a red fist and then Graciela had screamed back: *What do you want? What do you want from me?*

The baby stopped crying just for a second, then hiccupped and wailed again. Graciela's heart stilled with shame. What kind of terrible mother was she, unable to soothe this little baby, who until a week ago had been part of her own flesh?

She went to sit by the window. Some fresh air for them both. Let me do something right; the doctor says he needs the sun for his jaundice. She sat, she rocked him, and he began to still and grow heavier in her arms. And then her mind settled upon something disturbing, una pesadilla: if she let him go, no one on the street below would doubt it had been an accident.

That was when Silvia came into the room. Probably saving them both.

Clara was rubbing Graciela's hands now, to improve their circulation, she said. These women in the room beside her, at least in this moment, made her less afraid of her own raw brain, made the idea of remaining in this life, of surrendering to its terror, more possible. Graciela felt, for the first time in days, that she was still alive. And the baby, with his murky blue-black eyes, alert and then drowsy, hungry or inscrutable; he was still alive too.

35

LATER, IN THE SPACE OF THE BRIGHT, STRANGE DAYS WHEN the Occupation of Paris shifted into the bones of the city, Consuelo finally received a letter from her sister. She hadn't heard from Graciela in months.

Mi Hermana Cherita Consuelo,

To answer the question in your last letter: "How do you sleep through the night without tethering your mind to the floorboards?" Well, I don't. Now that Salvador is nearly two, and I can't work with him strapped to my back anymore, the girls in the boardinghouse take turns watching him when they're off work and I'm at the cannery. And when I'm off work, I'm watching their kids. I never sleep. This baby wants to eat and play all night.

But I stopped drinking. Having Salvador rearranged my brain. My memory isn't as good as it used to be either. In Hollywood a bottle or two of Champagne would calm me, but now a drink only makes me sad and angry, and so sick I can barely move. I couldn't be that way around the baby. Also, if I were even the slightest bit drunk at the cannery, I'd likely lose a finger in an aluminum barrel of peaches.

Come see me!

Abrazos,

Graciela

Come see me! Graciela wrote at the close of her letter, as she always did. Reading those words now, in the strange shift that was happening outside her window in Paris, Consuelo missed her sister with a deep ache. She hadn't seen the aviator in weeks, and the idea of leaving Paris to go to sleep sober, in a bunk bed beneath her sister and a drooling baby, in a room full of chatty inditas—well, a part of it appealed to her. She folded the letter into her slip; she'd remember the invitation later, when she would be even more afraid and even more alone than she was now.

But before crossing any ocean, she'd need to get out of Paris.

In Paris, Consuelo was still a stranger. Once, she'd fainted on the street and strangers had stepped over her body; once, she ran through the filthy rain with one shoe. No one really cared. No one comforted her or reassured her that she was distinctly beloved or good or welcome. When had anyone, ever? Consuelo often told herself that she enjoyed the solitude of the life that she lived separate from her husband, but she admitted to herself, as she considered her sister, as she considered leaving her life in Paris, that this was a lie.

Since leaving Hollywood a couple of years before, Graciela had been living in San Francisco on a little street named Capp. Consuelo didn't remember Capp Street. She'd never been to the neighborhood that Graciela described in her letters, didn't even know that places like the boardinghouse where Graciela slept existed in the city that she'd once lived in years before. And not long after arriving there, Graciela had given birth to baby Salvador, making Consuelo an aunt. She didn't ever write about his father, and Consuelo didn't ask.

Graciela had arrived in San Francisco alone, but she'd managed to build a life. She'd found hermanas. She'd made her own way because she'd had no other choice. Maybe, Consuelo thought, that was the difference between them. That was Consuelo's failing.

Yesterday, France had signed the armistice. It needed Los Yunais to jump in, but they held back. Paris was emptying, but loneliness had slowed her efforts to leave, for several weeks now.

Consuelo locked the mailbox and came out into the street to stand in the sun. A tank blocked the sidewalk. A Nazi soldier sitting atop it removed his glasses and whistled at her.

She had to leave Paris. The aviator had been gone for weeks; he claimed to be in the United States, but Consuelo didn't believe him. He said shit like that all the time, and really he was just across town with some other woman. Consuelo had no idea when he was going to return to the apartment, but she knew that she'd rather leave Paris than wait for him to come back while the city filled with Nazis.

She went back upstairs and filled a bag with a silk nightgown and Graciela's latest letter. What else? She couldn't remember the last time she'd painted. She'd married this man thinking she'd become a great artist with his support, but she was stifled and stilled, looking at the art of others through aquarium glass, once again unable to hold her paintbrush properly. How much of the blame was her own? A good deal, she admitted, though it was also true that her husband got sharp-tongued and sulked when she painted on any canvas larger than the palm of her hand, furious if she introduced herself as an artist. *She's my muse,* he'd say, as if embarrassed for her. In the beginning he'd at least pretended to admire her work.

Another silk nightgown went into the bag. She pulled the postcard of Lago Coatepeque off the emerald wall and put it in the bag as well, before heading outside again.

She began walking to the train station. Another escape from another country. But this time, at least, she wasn't already half-dead.

Two poets whom Consuelo recognized from a party a year or so ago appeared on the next street, walking at a clip. Consuelo, forgetting their names, ran to them.

"You're still here!" She was out of breath by the time she caught up with them. One carried a bulging leather bag on his shoulder and blinked with annoyance as he shifted it to the ground to face her.

"Have we met?" said the other, smiling tightly.

Consuelo gave her name. "Enchanted to meet you—I'm the painter." She bit the inside of her lip in hatred of her vanity.

"Forgive me," said the one with the big leather bag. "I'm unacquainted with your work."

"Oh, I see," said the other. "I've heard your name before. Didn't your husband leave for the States last month? What are you still doing here?"

Consuelo clutched her stomach in surprise. This is how she learned that her husband really was gone. That he didn't intend to return for her. Many years later, she'd say that she was as surprised that he'd left Paris without her as that he'd managed to pack his own suitcase. But now, she bit even deeper into her lip, until the blood sharpened her senses. Her brain ticked more slowly, her lungs heavy, as though drowned—she indulged a sudden ache for watery death. Who would search for her? Who would mourn her? No one.

The poets continued speaking over the din of her mind, and Consuelo tried to pay attention: a group of them had fled to a house in Marseille. From there, they might be able to continue on to the States, or maybe to Mexico or Spain or Morocco. They'd go where it felt safest, and of course it depended on what papers they could get and if anyone could help them. They were leaving this afternoon.

In order to keep living, Consuelo startled herself into saying that she'd join them.

"You will?" The one smiled at the other, the one with the heavy leather bag; he just looked away.

"I mean, may I? May I join you?" Consuelo said, unable to tame the panic that crept into her words. "Please take me with you."

They looked through her, lids heavy as with sleep. Why wouldn't they look at her? she wanted to know. Why couldn't they see her? She was alive, at least, we reminded her. Be grateful for that, we told her, as her mouth filled with the taste of ashes.

36

OUTSIDE THE BACK DOOR OF GRACIELA'S BOARDINGHOUSE was a splintering set of stairs that creaked and snaked up the back of the building. Graciela climbed up them with Salvador in her arms, and sat on the top step, outside of a stranger's door. Beside her on the landing was a ceramic bowl of cigarette butts floating in clouded water and a few green glass bottles, also plugged with cigarettes and rainwater. Wooden clothespins floated in another bowl. Downstairs, a cat explored the modest square of concrete and leapt a fence. Salvador was two now, no longer a baby, but lately he needed to be carried before sleep, and so Graciela sat rocking him on the edge of the step.

Clotheslines crisscrossed the box of the yard with clothing that had been left to stiffen after last night's rain, and a skeletal bougainvillea vined over the wet wood and inserted its spines and blooms into Graciela's view of the sky. If she had the time, or the energy, she'd cut the plant back before it tugged the building down like an enormous hand, and let it bloom bright and pillowy elsewhere. If she had time, she'd fill the cement square with pots of flowers, places to sit and enjoy the breeze. Like at Perlita's house, she supposed.

But she had no time.

The sky was pink and tangled with telephone wires. Crows settled on them, gossiping. The line dipped with their weight as they hopped and filled the softening air with their carcajadas. Like women, like us.

By the time Salvador was asleep at last, his fat cheeks flushed, the sky was black and we watched Graciela carry him back down the stairs, one hand humming on his back, the other hovering over the splintered banister until she reached her door.

With her boy's sleeping cheek on her shoulder, Graciela used the last few minutes of her own waking hours to write down everything she could remember. She fought her mind's desire to forget, cutting a path through the wilds of her memory as she wrote. Most nights, she didn't get very far. Salvador would wake again or she'd fall asleep with the pencil in her hand, her cheek pressed against the notebook on her pillow. She wrote down what she remembered of her life before the General, about her mother, the volcanoes, and us. What exactly the General had said to her before she fled the palace. When a woman's laugh sounded like a scream, or a car horn honked too close, or ravens cut too low across the sky, sometimes a door inside her mind would fall open and memories of the massacre flooded in. But her perfect memory wasn't what it once was; she figured that the years of drinking must have worn some holes.

As a refuge from the past, she tried to chronicle her days in San Francisco too. Salvador's new tooth breaking through his gums. His fat feet in the foam of the bay at Aquatic Park. The luscious hemispheres of the peaches at Half Moon, after she'd dug the spoon in for the pit, sliced the fruit in two. They came from some dusty valley an hour or so away, and were transformed by her labors, made slick, unreal, a uniform bright orange in their aluminum baths.

When Salvador had still been small enough that Graciela had been able to keep him strapped to her back most of the day at work, she'd sometimes take them the long way back to the boardinghouse, through Japantown. Here, she could sit for a moment and Salvador could stretch his legs before bedtime. There was a teahouse in a courtyard run by a woman, Miyuki, who had a little girl almost Salvador's age exactly. Miyuki would bring a blanket and spread it out over the mossy square stones of the courtyard, and once or twice the women laid their toddlers down on the blanket together, and watched, cheering, as they patted each other with round hands and gurgled, happy to tumble together and play after sleeping most of the day on their mothers' backs. Miyuki's mother lived in Nara, and she'd knitted the blanket of wool dyed and spun on their island, then mailed it to the other side of the world when Miyuki was pregnant.

Meanwhile, the boardinghouse filled with babies. Silvia had another, and then Clara gave birth six months later—a tiny girl, whom she named Dorinda. And then Josefina had a daughter.

Right around the time Dorinda was born, the cannery went south. Clara had lost so much blood during the birth that for weeks after, she barely had the strength to hold the baby, much less feed her. She had no idea when she'd be able to work again. The father was nowhere. And they all knew that the cannery was set to collapse soon anyway; none of the mamis could count on it to feed their babies.

"Rest," Graciela had said while Clara was still pregnant, enjoying the opportunity to be stern with her loud friend. "I'll pit peaches for the both of us tomorrow."

But one morning not long after Dorinda made her way into the world, Graciela, Josefina, and Silvia arrived at the cannery to find a note taped to the door. Closed indefinitely. None of them were surprised. Graciela was afraid, sure, but also relieved. She was sick of carving peaches open with a spoon, sealing them into tin cans. She wanted to feed herself and her comadres, their children. She had an idea about what they needed to do next, and she'd been saving her money.

That night, Graciela, Josefina, and Silvia cooked for the new mother, as they had every night since she'd returned home from the hospital. Clara needed iron for her blood, and atol with avena for her milk. They kept her warm, wrapping her body as she'd once done for Graciela, using every blanket they had in the boardinghouse.

Graciela sat with the new mother and rocked her child until both Clara and Dorinda were asleep. Her own son was sleeping on his cot a few feet away, on the other side of a sheet, but Graciela was dreaming awake.

Graciela often took evening walks down Twenty-fourth Street and through their neighborhood. She felt large and safe under the pink sky, entirely her own. She knew she and las comadres couldn't stay at the boardinghouse forever, but it'd be nice to stay in this neighborhood, if they could, where more people from our country were arriving every day.

As the lights went on in the windows of the houses she passed, Graciela would look inside and feel a physical desire. Her muscles tightened at the warmth and security that she saw there. Food on a table, a family gathered. Music and laughter drifting out and down the sidewalk. She copied down the addresses of places with FOR RENT signs in the window. Even when she visited those places and her rental applications were turned away—she was always too much of something, too india, too much an unmarried mother, too poor, too foreign—Graciela kept in her possession the dream of a free life.

Now, with the cannery closed, with Dorinda heavy on her shoulder and purring, she knew that life had to come soon. She settled the baby with her mother, pleased by the sight of her fattening arms. And then she returned to her notebook. She ticked through the list of addresses, calculating for each one the possibilities of space and light, re-counting the cash she kept sewn on the inside of her dress. Space and light—with that, she felt sure they could do this.

37

IN MARSEILLE THE SURREALIST PHOTOGRAPHER PRETENDED not to know Consuelo's name. He didn't ask for it either. She sat on the dock all day with the poets and sculptors and painters and strangers and sycophants and played cards until they were beaded in sweat that smelled like wine. And then they jumped off the dock into the filthy water. "No matter!" they said. When the bottles slipped out of their hands onto the splintering wood and shattered green glass underfoot: "No matter!" Even when night fell and their shoes filled with blood. When they all ended up fucking one another in that terrible closet, taking turns, the sweat from the last fuck reviving with the lank heat of the next body's—no matter. They saw no reason to complain, to do anything but rejoice. They were out of Paris. They were alive.

Consuelo slept in a room with eleven other people whom she'd vaguely known in Paris, but whose snores and phlegm-clearing coughs and tantrums while waiting for the bathroom she assimilated into her brain like a song. They slept with all the windows open, their bodies arranged like the fish laid out in the stalls of the souk downstairs.

Sometimes Consuelo woke up in the dark, hot room and considered leaving, but no one wanted to be alone—not one of them. And eventually, the south would be occupied. Maybe they should cross the Pyrenees, one suggested soon after they first arrived. But they couldn't conjure the energy, or sustain the frenetic, sober state of mind, necessary for leaving

France. They'd as soon swim to Morocco as they would cross the Pyrenees.

They looked at one another, at the souk, the filthy dock, the walls papered with stupid coded games, the deck of tarot cards a small woman with long red hair had painted. Marseille, sun-drunk in shades of fuchsia and terra-cotta, was a beautiful pit of quicksand. Frequently, Consuelo was asleep by six in the evening, and awake by three in the morning.

Often, as she lay awake in the middle of the night on her rag-stuffed pillow on the floor, she thought of her sister. A can of glistening peaches! And Salvador! How strange to think of Graciela as a mother. Consuelo still thought of her as a little girl. Graciela, in San Francisco, working in a cannery, Salvador strapped to her back. Salvador. Her little nephew. She'd probably never meet him, Consuelo decided. She'd scare him, wine pulsing brightly through her veins at four in the morning, sickening her mouth. She was unsuitable for children.

She heard León out in the hall, fucking the woman with the long red hair. There were no doors here, only silk curtains separating the sleeping room from the hallway from the bathroom. So the hallway, at night, seemed private.

Everyone wanted to know why Consuelo wasn't in New York with her husband—it was one of the only things anyone ever wanted to talk to her about. She didn't know if they were just curious about the nature of her marriage, or sick of her.

Consuelo had been to New York a few times. Never for more than three or four days at once. Just a flight with her husband, a night or two of parties, and a return. Her first time there, they'd gone straight from the landing strip to a party hosted by some actress. Consuelo had been starving and exhausted when they'd arrived, and she'd needed a bath. The aviator had a white tuxedo waiting for him in a hallway closet. Around two in the morning, Consuelo had begged him to take her back to the hotel—or at least somewhere for some food. Without looking up from where he sat, identical blondes on either side of him—what shape was their desire?—he tossed her the key to their hotel room. It skidded to her feet, and she watched it spin until its golden finger pointed in her direction. Slowly, carefully, Consuelo bent to remove her shoe and then she threw it, heel flying in circles like a dagger, across the room with all her might, shattering an ugly Kandinsky rip-off in a glass frame above the aviator's head. Take me home, she said.

Another time, at a famous movie star's house, Consuelo had found a quiet room and crawled into the bed she found there when the aviator refused to take her home. Someone came in and took a photograph, but she didn't mind. Consuelo liked having a lens trained on her face, and the restful sensation of pretending to sleep, softening the lines of the face. Now, in Marseille, Consuelo carried the image of the bed with her in mind, always seeking rest. At four in the morning, she'd recall every detail of that bed: the headboard, padded in leather and brass-pinned, six feet tall, the four satin pillows beneath her head, the flat heaviness of the mattress like a sea.

Consuelo had received the photograph in the mail sometime after they'd returned to Paris. She'd given it to her husband, written a note on the back: *Don't lose yourself, don't lose me.* Her face is away from the camera, and a silk sheet covers her breasts like a gown. He carried the picture with him every day after that. Maybe he did love her. Maybe he just liked showing people he'd just met a photograph of a beautiful woman, exotic and fair and fiery and strange and mysterious and rich-looking—she was all of these things and none of them. Either way, Consuelo didn't care. She loved her face in that photograph.

Soon, an architect named Felix arrived in Marseille. He was golden-skinned and charming, and he smelled clean. The others deferred to him with a detached politeness. He was known for designing an alabaster temple surrounded by water. Inside was a spiral staircase that led to an astronomical tower. It was for a child.

"I respect his work, I suppose. I just don't particularly like it."

"It's very—hmmm—sincere."

Felix had come to recruit them. He'd come into some luck, he said, and he was forming an artists' colony in some Roman ruins not far from Avignon.

LOURDES: Some luck, ha. Who do you think paid for that shit? It's
1941. It's France. Obviously the motherfucking Vichy paid
for this shit. The Nazis. This was a Nazi-funded artist colony.
Because they wanted to keep Paris pretty for themselves.
They wanted to go to the theater and look at the Arc de Tri-
omphe after their shit was all over. They wanted compliance
and order. Yeah, they wanted those artists to keep making
their pretty art. The quieter and more inscrutable, the better.
Don't worry, they said. We'll find you a scenic fucking cave
so you can pretend that you're on the run! Or better yet, that
you're the only people left on earth, tasked with creating a
new world with the dust.

But, of course, this lucky artist told Consuelo that she'd
be perfect for the colony. He said that he'd heard about her
work. It pleased her that he said this while the others were
still at the table, even if she knew he was lying. Why would
he lie to her? What did he need from her? Was he trying
to fill a space? Did he catch a whiff of her estranged husband's money?

But still, she was flattered. Probably his lie was rooted in
physical desire. He'd bothered to flirt with her: it had been a
long time since anyone had told Consuelo that she and her
art were perfect for anything. She knew she couldn't turn
down the invitation. She'd go to the colony and stay until
she got word about her chances of getting to the States.
What else could she do? The aviator seemed to have forgotten that she existed.

Ultimately Consuelo lived in Oppède, in her "kingdom of rocks," for
nearly a year. Once a week she walked into town to the market in Cavaillon. Twice each month she took her turn on the kingdom's radio station,
signaling to the Resistance in a code she struggled to understand.

Over the course of the year, she wrote two hundred letters to her sister's new address in San Francisco, sliding the pages beneath a smooth

slab in her cave until she could take them to the post office. One day she drew her family tree with borrowed charcoal on the back of her old postcard of Lago Coatepeque: what she remembered of Socorrito's face, her own face, and Graciela's. She tucked it in an envelope to send to her.

In Oppède there were four children too, all Felix's. Gap-toothed Eliane, chubby Renaud, freckled Magali, and Lorène, with the long face. They'd come here ahead of their father, up the ancient rocks, with beehives strapped to their backs. They believed that honey brought good fortune. They starved for that sticky golden light. They poured it over sad garden potatoes, drizzled it on unripe figs, and every morning Consuelo stirred a thumbnail of it right into the shitty sludge the people in this kingdom of rocks called maize-coffee.

Felix was usually already up when she woke, perched like a cat on the old rampart rocks overtaken by vines, soaking up the sun. She'd smile at him and then head to the cave where she worked.

Here, artists didn't sign their names, hardly showed their work to anyone else. But they all seemed to be working in furious solitude, like the bees. Every day they retreated from the light, crawled into the shade of themselves, and worked on their art.

Days were spent digging, smelling the soil beneath the sun for disappointing potatoes. And then digging to plant. And then digging for clay. What they made, and the hours they spent making, were supposed to be egoless, necessary. But Consuelo had never worked with anything resembling diligence, and her ego didn't disappear just because the kingdom of rocks considered each of its members part of a guild. She was quieter here, though. Her rage settled. If she began a sculpture, she intended to complete it. She wasn't half as wine-drunk in Oppède as she'd been in Marseille or in Paris. Her loneliness remained, but it didn't feel like a knife.

Sometimes Consuelo imagined returning to Paris when the war was over to receive a degree from the École des Beaux Arts, sculpting a lifetime of lasting art, making her name. The clay of this region was like ropes in her hands and her fingers and wrists ached at the end of each day in a way that pleased her. As she slept, she worked out shapes and the story of how she'd bring them into existence. While she drank more coffee, scrubbed potatoes, and complained about the mistral, she was building towers in her mind.

And who knows—perhaps the ruins were only the beginning, and the Reich would vanish into dust. Perhaps the work made here in the ancient stones would last. One hundred years from now, pilgrims would hike the Luberon to touch relics formed by Consuelo's hands. And so, morning after morning, she took her coffee and honey, while manic silhouettes of birds filled the rosy sky as if shaken from a bag, the mountains edged in moss, and Felix would return her smile with his own, finish his own coffee, and then make his way along a path of jagged rocks, sometimes crawling on all fours, to his cave studio, where he'd work in a devoted, productive silence of which Consuelo was unspeakably jealous.

Usually he'd pass by her station a few times over the course of the day. Sometimes he'd smile and venture to ask her about her work. The chain of girls being born inside the volcano—what about them? What about the woman in her cloak of butterfly wings? What about the eyeless lady walking a jungle cat on a leash? He never asked her about the sculpture that she'd started and still hadn't finished of her husband, flying on the back of a bird.

Often, toward the end of the day, Felix and Consuelo drew together as the sun set. Felix would draw something on a piece of paper, then fold it and pass it to Consuelo. She'd shield her eyes with her hand while she contemplated her response.

You're beautiful, Felix wrote one day, then passed it across the table to her.

I know, Consuelo scribbled underneath.

Felix wrote another: *I want to know you.*

Consuelo hadn't known what to write in response, so she'd invited Felix to her cave that evening.

That night, Consuelo crushed melon-colored rose petals into her bucket, filled it with water, and bathed. She combed out her hair and braided it, tying it in knots around her head. She put on a silk nightgown that her husband had bought her in Paris. Rosettes were embroidered on the shoulders, and the nightgown trailed through the dust of her room of rocks. Consuelo's heart beat in her cheeks. She was sweating through her gown, and hot wind swept through her room. She listened to Felix's footsteps coming up the path, to his cheery whistle, and she cursed again. Only an idiot, an idiot whore, would do what she was doing. She prayed he would miss her room, find himself lost, concede to the darkness, and head down the rocks. She held her breath and fanned at damp half-moons beneath her underarms. Some women were cool and smooth as stones; Consuelo wasn't one of them. She heard Felix's feet outside her door, heard him call, "Bonne nuit!" into the windy night. Already she felt his heat, his breath on her skin, and she lost her balance for a moment. Clinging to a smooth cool slab of rock, she paused before pulling the curtain open for her guest.

When she did, her stone room filled up with his eyes. She looked up to meet his gaze and found his mouth instead. Consuelo pulled him inside the room, onto her scratchy wool blanket on the floor. His hair filled her nose, she felt his lips on her shoulders, his hands all over the silk of her gown. Her body glowed with the rock-warmed heat of his. They fit together, perfectly matched, filling each other, and Consuelo knew there would be no words, no stopping, and she held as much of him as she could at once, kissing his eyes, his bumpy nose, the golden span of his solar plexus. Somewhere far away Consuelo heard the fabric of her gown tearing, and she pulled him on top of her, holding his eyes with her own, and then he was inside of her, sank deeper, and she kissed him hard until she felt the scream rise up through her chest.

The next morning she stirred honey into her maize-coffee again and watched the dawn come up over the haze. Felix drew the Luberon. She watched him capture a stand of pines, an ocher crevasse, the outline of the old castle's ridged rampart.

She would not tell him that she loved him.

Later that month, an uneasy week passed—Consuelo's blood never came. Unfazed, delirious, she made love to Felix every day. Then another week began and she lost track of time. She watched as Eliane lost both her front teeth, and then as saw-edged bunny teeth slowly replaced them. Renaud's voice deepened an octave and squeaked. One night, someone broke into the studio and made off with supplies and finished work. None of Consuelo's art was taken, which lit a fire of envy in her nervous little head.

Meanwhile, Felix sent her more drawings: A celestial tower built into the trees, one wall made entirely of crystal. A house carved into the top of a cliff overlooking the sea, with stairs inside leading down to an underground artists' studio. A Provençal cottage of ocher stone, an enormous greenhouse containing birds-of-paradise and Venus flytraps and vines and papayas on the second floor and a ceiling of glass on the first. Piles of ocher rocks lined the garden, and Felix had watercolored heliotropic arcs of lavender, dark-orange roses, fig trees and cherry, honeysuckle and vine, and a studio for drawing, painting, and sculpture. In each of his plans, Felix would draw a woman who looked just like Consuelo in one of the rooms. Sleeping with shoes on her feet in one house, casting clay into a mold in a dirty smock in another. Consuelo and a dog, standing inside the greenhouse, amid statues of her own creation.

The others had begun to notice what was between Consuelo and Felix and passed them both with smiles, but few words. Everyone knew that Consuelo was married.

And then finally, after nine weeks, Consuelo had to admit to herself, and to Felix, that she was pregnant.

From the beginning, the people of the kingdom were prepared to abandon everything if they needed to. They'd tear down the radio tower and its mess of wires. They'd destroy the gardens and let the fountains dry up. And everything in the studios—the cakes of paint, the scraps of canvas, the favorite paintings kept on display, the half-hard sculptures—would have to disappear entirely. If they had to leave in a hurry, they knew they couldn't leave a trace. And of course there were the ones who had escaped the death camps and climbed the mountains to find refuge in the kingdom. The half-dead ones, tattooed and silent, who scaled the rocks and came back to life inside the stone caves. They'd all make themselves disappear in the woods, if the day came. When the day came.

In Cavaillon, just below them, the Vichy burned farmers' fields. They were wending their way deeper into the hills. A man with a briefcase had appeared in the kingdom of rocks, taking pictures, stealing sketches he'd torn out of someone's notebook in the studio.

More finished paintings disappeared from the studio, and the artists began bringing the work they loved best, along with their documents, into their beds at night. An American man was issuing visas, and there were rumors that he would be in Cavaillon soon. In the kingdom, the artists began planning their next moves.

Consuelo, though, had a path out.

After a year of silence, the aviator wanted her back. She'd long stopped hoping he would remember her, would chase or even desire her, but one day, while she was at the open-air market, a man had approached her and told her that a message was waiting for her at the post office—it had been delivered bearing only her name.

In his letter, the aviator had apologized briefly for leaving for the States without her. He would send airfare and money immediately to bring her to New York. They could try it all again. She only had to say the word. Consuelo felt very little after reading the letter. He was bored, lonely, frustrated—she could practically smell it—and she felt certain that his request for her to join him had nothing to do with her.

And besides, Consuelo felt no great longing to leave Oppède. She called herself an ungrateful whore as she fell asleep at night—no one else in the kingdom of rocks had a way out—but she'd never been happier than she was here. She was too embarrassed to even say the words aloud, though.

Weeks later, she finally wrote back, with one hand on her growing belly, asking for a divorce.

He wrote back immediately: *I refuse to grant this outrageous whim.*

She asked again.

The aviator sent an envelope containing train tickets, plane tickets, a velvet glove filled with money, and a brief note: *I refuse.* Consuelo told herself she was insane. It was insane not to leave. *Why are you even here in the first place?* everyone had been asking her since she'd arrived.

Of course Consuelo knew that the colony received a subsidy from the Vichy, like a compromise. Everyone else worked the shrubby garden, cursing other surrealists, the art world, and New York City, which went on without them. If they did know, they pretended not to know that Nazis, the same ones burning the farmland beneath them in order to starve the French villagers, had made room for art and culture in this space for them. Their world went on. They worried aloud that they'd never be missed, that they'd never re-enter the Paris scene, that out here they'd die. They kept their happiness, and their relief, to themselves.

Meanwhile, Consuelo kept working too. She loved the evenings. She molded clay and painted. Little unfinished pieces. Poco a poco. In the mornings she returned to the pieces that she'd worked out before sleep, and, slowly, her little unfinished shapes assumed a logic—she herself seemed to have assumed a logic. She was stripped down, golden-armed and sharp-toothed. She finished her paintings and ordered them against a wall in her cave. She worked for hours without looking for another soul to distract her. Filthy bare feet and hair she trimmed with a knife, late-afternoon headaches from malnutrition and chronic sunburn, Felix at work in his own space, his baby inside her, their friends working like bees, the honey children, soft mountains, and bright old rocks.

No one knew exactly how old the archway was at the base of the ruins, but some said that it had been built during the Roman Empire. Consuelo chose the broad keystone rock at the top of the arch, unaware that this would be her last work in Oppède. She dragged a ladder down the rocks to the archway and then went back for her sculpting tools. She was nine months pregnant. The face that Consuelo carved into the rocks was intended to be her sister's, to sit as guardian of the kingdom.

The face had a broad nose, nostrils that flared a little, and high, wide cheekbones. The eyes were open. In the sun, the rock sparkled with flecks of mica.

"Is it you?" Felix asked Consuelo, after she climbed down from the ladder.

"My sister," she said. Someday, she hoped, long after Consuelo was dead, a stranger might find Graciela's face in the rocks and restore their kingdom.

The world was burning just beneath them, another farm gone to ash in the village, but here—she felt she could stay here forever.

38

LAS COMADRES WAS BORN WHOLE, CREATED OUT OF NECESsity. Is that how the dicho goes? Mothers are the invention of necessity. Necessity is the mother of invention. Guateber.

After the cannery closed, Graciela and her friends were full of need. They needed care for their growing children. They needed a place to rest that was their own. They needed money to pay rent on the building, to buy their kids shoes. They needed one another.

So by the time Graciela found the place, just off la calle Veinticuatro, and an old landlady who, mean as she was, was willing to rent to four inditas and their kids, their plan was in motion. Las Comadres had been mapped on paper; she'd whispered through its mechanics with Clara, Josefina, and Silvia while their babies slept. They were ready.

The ground level of their new home was a storefront, soon to be the center of their business, a café with thick, wide windows, a few rusty keys gathering dust on their sills. The landlady's dead husband had been a locksmith.

Upstairs was a long, narrow hallway, with two bedrooms branching off on either side. At the end of the hall was a bathroom with a clawfoot tub. A toilet in a separate room, tiny as a closet. Graciela sewed long curtains to hang at the back of the storefront to separate the café from the stairs to the living area, where the babies were bathed together in the tub, where the mothers lay down beside their children to dream. A luxury, this dreaming. Their little hands curled above their heads.

Las Comadres rotated responsibilities and pleasures: childcare, running the café, and their own quiet hours of rest and creation. These
were shitty hours of rest and creation—enough time to bathe, to fold
laundry, or to fall asleep after opening a book. To be a mother is to be
interrupted constantly. But this is how they survived it—the interrup-
tions, yes, but also the cost of food, the rent, the utility bills, the necessity of work and thus of childcare, the sleep deprivation that necessitated
collapse, the noise that had no remedy. As the children grew, Graciela
traded English classes to the other women in exchange for a few
extra hours of babysitting. And on the mornings that Graciela took the
kids while the others tended to their work or the café, or slept an extra
hour, she'd walk with the smallest baby on her back, and the bigger
kids holding both of her hands, through an alley filled with jacaranda
to the library on Bartlett Street, where she sat on the cool marble
floor with three or four babies piled on her lap. She read to them in a
whisper. When they started losing their minds, she took them to Dolores Park and raced them to the top. They turned somersaults down
the hill. After the business started doing well, they sometimes got ice
cream.

They began by serving tea—no coffee—to customers out of their
yellow-tiled kitchen. Coffee, of course, had boomed again after the massacre. Because the ones who survived were half-dead, our work was
cheaper than ever for los patrones, and as a result, cheaper than ever for
Los Yunais. Pacific Mail shipped two-hundred-pound bags of it for free
to the San Francisco shipyards, where men from our country unloaded
the bags and processed the beans into red cans with a willowy Arab man
in a long, starry tunic on the label. Graciela couldn't stand the sight of
those red cans. Instead she walked her neighborhood with a basket and
harvested plants for infusions: manzanilla, bugambilia, and jamaica, all
the plantitas that had once mothered her. For her favorite regular customers, she served her friend Miyuki's tea.

The last time Graciela had seen Miyuki, the woman had given her
three large canisters of tea, wrapped in her mother's blanket, to take back
to the new house with her. Graciela had looked at Miyuki like she was

crazy and shook her head. The tea smelled beautiful, and it must have been worth a fortune.

For the business, Miyuki said to her. That's when Graciela noticed that Miyuki was fighting tears.

Graciela tried to ask what was wrong, but Miyuki shook her head and cried. She didn't want to talk about it. Graciela hugged her for the first and last time as Miyuki pressed the bundle of fabric and tea into Graciela's arms.

When Graciela returned to Japantown to look for Miyuki later that week, she found the windows of the teahouse, and of the other businesses in the courtyard, boarded over.

Graciela didn't see Miyuki again. Japantown's people were made to disappear simply for existing, for calling the place their own.

As Las Comadres settled into their home, they had the space, time, and light to return to the treasures of their lives before—rooting them into the neighborhood. This was their living Eternal Now.

Josefina was one of the lucky ones who remembered how her grandmother used to weave using a backstrap loom, and she made telitas and cositas to decorate the storefront and sell in the café.

And Clara, when she'd been a child in our country, had wanted to become an artist. Now she had a space of her own and two hours every other morning to sit at the window and paint. In the middle of the night sometimes, she could be found running down the street with that loud voice of hers to attend a birth, bringing light into the world.

Silvia wanted to make the foods she remembered from the time before her mother had died and her father had taken her to the new city to work at the shipyards, but there was no one left whom she could call for the recipes. There were no cookbooks, and she couldn't find everything she needed at the market in the Mission, which seemed only to stock food for the thick-legged, freckled police wives in the neighborhood. So she did the best she could. She bought white bread and powdered milk and worked to transform it into queso patachuca.

Soon a series of whispers from a few viejas sent her to Chinatown, to the Richmond, where she gathered ajonjolí, masa harina, queso blando, and, like a chemist, she experimented, ruining pans, cursing herself for wasting ingredients, until she began getting it right. Las Comadres began serving pastel de piña, jugo de tamarindo, and quesadilla—and listen, we're not talking about a flour tortilla with shredded cheese or whatever desmadre you have in your mind; this is a golden cake covered in ajonjolí, batter beaten for an hour, fluffy and delicate, a little sweet, a little salty.

It was from Graciela that Silvia had learned how to listen to the viejitas, how to get the maitras to spill their recipes, the questions to ask to steer them back to the food. And the importance of writing it all down so it wouldn't be forgotten again. Best of all, they no longer went hungry.

Later, when their landlady got sick, she was entirely alone. Silvia brought sopa a couple of times a week—the decent thing to do. La viejita choked it down, smiling for the unremarkable kindness, after years of complaining about the stench of "Spanish food" coming out of her building.

When she died, never married, no kids, no relatives in this country, she left the building to Las Comadres. An inheritance, paid off in full. None of them could fucking believe it. Las Comadres belonged to them.

Other members of the neighborhood disagreed. They believed that the building that housed Graciela and her comadres, the street that they lived on, la calle Veinticuatro, even the tides of Dolores, the mythical lake beneath their feet, did not belong to Las Comadres, or to anyone that looked like them. They believed, as had the dead landlady—whose gift of the building didn't absolve her, in our minds, for talking loudly on the telephone about her "promiscuous Latin tenants"—that this place belonged only to their own kind. That old landlady, the neighbors said, was loony in the end—those Mexican girls must have pulled some witchcraft, some kind of dirty manipulation. They were certain that Las Comadres would be short-lived. Cops slowed their cars and leaned out their windows when Graciela and the kids walked down the street. The blonde behind the counter at the corner store where Silvia sometimes shopped for her ingredients refused to speak to her directly or meet her eye.

We stay close to Graciela, though, and we care for her comadres as our own. Take Corita, for example. She's calaceada, pero calaceada. Beaten down by life and angry to return to it. She shuffled into Las Comadres one morning, filthy with soil, a hummingbird floating above one hunched shoulder as though her long ear bore nectar. Josefina, with her little daughter napping on her chest, was reading tarot cards at the table by the window—Graciela had taught her, and they found it brought in good business.

"Tell my fortune," Cora said, settling herself in the chair across from Josefina. "I want to know everything good—love, sex, romance." The bird vibrated gently, and Josefina shuffled the cards. This would be easy, she thought. She knew exactly what to say to women who asked these questions; they wanted a journey, a quest, even an anciana like this one.

About Corita, though, Josefina was wrong. She wanted to hear about her past, not the future: Héctor, his smell, their baby, a life that could have been. Josefina handed her the cards to hold, directed her to choose three, then place them facedown in the center of the table.

"I sense a man, honest, hardworking, idealistic," Josefina began, preparing to turn over the first card. The baby stretched her tiny hand out of the swaddle at her mother's chest and let out a wail, piercing the air.

It was all too much for Corita.

"Ay, puya. I have to go," she said, and rose with difficulty. It was too painful to remain here in flesh. Earthquake of time, disaster of it—Cora saw too much at once.

"Here, take this," she said, handing Josefina a little bundle. Inside was a fistful of rich black soil. "Tell Graciela hello from Cora," she said. And then her body vanished. Josefina screamed. The bird hovered a beat and flew out the open window.

Las Comadres chose to interpret Corita's soil as a blessing. Soon after Corita's visit, the library on Bartlett needed someone who could speak

English and Spanish, who could lead the children's storytelling programs, who could bring order to the shelves, and Graciela got the job. She kept some of her café shifts, but the library job brought stability to Las Comadres. They would not be intimidated. They were home.

And as more people like us arrived in the neighborhood, Graciela and her friends welcomed them in, befriended their children, fed them, and let them rest at Las Comadres while the newcomers looked for a place to stay.

When a teenage racist threw a brick through their front window, Graciela went outside barefoot, her knife gleaming. The chickenshit ran into the night, pissing his pants.

The porter at the library knew a handyman who could help. The next evening he'd found Las Comadres a new window and soldered a grill of elegantly curving iron bars over both front windows. He asked only for Silvia to bake a quesadilla de oro for his family, and for his two cipotes to join the English classes that Graciela was teaching at the library.

"Those are free. Anyone can join those," she told him.

"Shit. Two more quesadillas, then, please."

At the library Graciela started a book club too, which became a poetry group as well. Something those fufurufos in France whom Consuelo hung out with would have called a "salon." Graciela's was spared a lot of hot air by inviting only women to join. She always took the time to read the newspapers of gringolandia that the library subscribed to as well, to keep tabs on what was going on in our country. *The Christian Science Monitor*—ay, who gave this holy scientist the job of monitoring the world?—particularly loved writing about nuestro pulgarcito in those days.

TRADITIONS OF EL SALVADOR TURN NATION AGAINST NAZISM described the customs of our people. "All is clean, verdant, tranquil, and bounteous," the reporter wrote. Practically a travel brochure, no? This Christian Scientist ended the article with the kind of anecdote that made Graciela flinch. El Gran Pendejo had entrusted a Nazi diplomat to be his oracle. *Oracle* was not the word the newspaper used, but they described his role, and Graciela recognized its duties. Hitler's official spokesman had worked closely with El Gran Pendejo, counseling him on what to do and when. But then, suddenly, the Nazi was fired, and later found dead. He'd killed himself, allegedly, and the General declared the suicide an unequivocal victory for his own good name.

It had only been very recently that El Gran Pendejo had turned against Nazism. And it wasn't because of clean, verdant, tranquil, bounteous us, that's for sure. We were already fucking dead, of course, thanks to him, Nazi warlock that he was. El Gran Pendejo supported the Nazis up until he absolutely had to side with his old friends Los Yunais and the Allies after Pearl Harbor, still hurt that it had taken his old friends so long to recognize him.

But enough of that. Graciela closed the newspaper and got back to work.

39

WHEN IT FINALLY CAME TIME TO LEAVE THE KINGDOM OF rocks, Consuelo gathered the tickets and the velvet glove of money and left Europe alone.

She made her way to Paris, to a tensely guarded airport. Her flight to New York was delayed. She unfolded a coat from inside her battered suitcase and prepared to lie down on the floor of the airport to sleep until her flight in the morning, when a woman with dark glasses approached her. Lucía.

To Consuelo's eyes, Lucía was a spy, without question: the sunglasses, the trench coat, the staring. Consuelo covered her face with the soft part of her inner arm and let her mind flit in and out of consciousness, a fly alighting on old fruit, hovering and rising. Lucía carried a notebook in her left coat pocket. Consuelo read her as American, with that boring, smooth kind of beauty that indicated a lifetime of whole milk, a long plain coat, sunglasses, hair side-parted and glossy.

In approach, Lucía knew to lean into flattery, to bribery. She told Consuelo that she looked like a Hollywood star.

"Which star?" Consuelo said. She really wanted to know. "I've been told I resemble a young Rosie Swan," Consuelo said.

"No, not her," Lucía said. "Another one. What's your name?" she asked.

Consuelo didn't care if the spy only wanted to scrutinize her passport, to line the inside of her suitcase with wire, that she probably suspected her a Vichy. She was exhausted.

Lucía tossed a box of Gauloises into Consuelo's lap. Consuelo squealed and held them aloft like the Eucharist.

"How the hell did you get these?" Consuelo asked the spy. They'd vanished during the Occupation; Consuelo had been hand-rolling and sharing cigarettes with three or four others anytime they lucked into a fistful of tobacco. The cigarettes! That detail made her certain—Consuelo almost chastised the spy for her sloppy façade.

Consuelo settled into the warmth of Lucía's voice. She knew her, though at the moment she wasn't sure how. The spy told her that she'd worked as a newspaper reporter, but what she really wanted to do for a living was write stories, that she loved hearing other people's stories, that whole books might be written about Consuelo's life.

"What do you know of my life?" Consuelo asked. Consuelo didn't buy it for a moment—the notebook, the sunglasses, that film noir coat, the placid gringa smile. Lucía was a spy.

"Tell me," Lucía said. She already knew the story but listening to Consuelo tell it herself was part of the alchemy. Consuelo, who hadn't spoken to anyone for days, had to form the words herself.

Consuelo began to talk, and then she could not stop. "My labor was too early, like a fire all over my body . . ."

We remember it. We were with her. When the soft dust kicked up around her feet in that cave, and Felix carried her over his shoulder down from the kingdom of rocks. When he flagged down a pickup truck full of melons and begged that the driver take them to Cavaillon—we were with her. When he lifted her into the back of the truck and she called out with a sharp pain, suddenly certain that everything was wrong, and he climbed up afterward, and she caught her breath with his hands steadying her knees—we were with her. We were with her when she rode in the back of that melon truck, after making a few jokes about the melon in her belly, thrust into early labor—before her breath changed, before the earth began tearing and quaking inside of her in rapid beats. We were with her, waiting for the horses to pass.

"A river of horses," Consuelo said now, her voice shaking as the words unfolded for Lucía. "A sea of horses, a freight train of horses."

"They're here for the melon parade," said the viejito driving the cart.

Horses shitting as they ran, horses with flies buzzing over the cha-jazos on their backs, horses stinking in the heat. Horses with frightened eyes like gibbous moons. Horses like the ones in Helena's paintings. Horses.

"How many more?" Felix asked the driver of the cart, as the dust swirled and crested above the cart in space. Felix held a handkerchief to Consuelo's face for her to cough into.

"How long have you lived here?" the driver said. "We do this every year."

Consuelo patted her breasts nervously then, thought to herself: *Maybe it would be better if after this baby is born, I leave her here with Felix. He could be both mother and father to her. Or he could find a better woman to be his wife, a better mother for this little jewel.* She had that ticket to New York, after all. That rich husband.

What Consuelo could not say now is that her labor came faster than the doctor in Cavaillon expected. He'd removed his glasses and set them on the table beside the cot where Consuelo lay, and scolded her for never once having come to visit him during her pregnancy, his finger in her face, and she told him to fucking shut up and help her now. We were with her then too.

We were there when Felix cheered for her. "Bravo, chérie," he said, and held her hands and she wept and screamed, and they took slow, deep breaths together. And when it was time to push, and the blood was every-where, and the nurses counted, and the doctor put his glasses back onto his face. "Slow down, not so fast, slow down," he whispered angrily to her. "She's a tigress," he said to no one in particular, and tied her wrists to the frame of the cot. Consuelo chewed the cord off of her right wrist, and then her left, and spat. We were there, relieved, when the doctor stood back to smoke a cigarette, and the head nurse took over. When Consuelo screamed, "I'm breaking I'm breaking I'm breaking"—we were there.

"The head, the head," the nurses said.

"Crowning, crowning, crowning," said the doctor. Consuelo lost consciousness then. We watched the nurse take the baby and exit the room, the raw, uncrying small body in her arms. The baby had come too quickly. Consuelo, inside of a darkness, knew something was wrong.

And, some time later, another nurse, a young one who reminded us of the youngest nun at our school, when she covered her mouth and gasped, we were there too. "It's gone," she said, and death slipped into the room through a door cracked open enough to let in the morning's light. And then, like birds trapped in a room, beating their feathers and delicate bones, all of the bodies rushed, all of the bodies stumbled and rattled their parts and looked for a way out.

"Shut the door," Consuelo screamed.

"No heartbeat," the doctor said.

And when the room was silent, a long, thick silence that filled the ears with the beating of blood, oh, that silence, that pitch-dark tunnel we carry inside us, and the child, dark rosebud, had been brought back into the room and was lain on the table beside Consuelo and Consuelo began to scream, "Take it away take it away from me get it the fuck away from me"—we were with her.

We watched them pull the dark blood-moon placenta out of her. And they stitched her body up and she screamed and screamed. And afterward she moaned and rocked, and they tied her to the cot again and told her to rest. Felix left the room to get some fresh air in the courtyard, and he stared up at the mountains. Consuelo waited, sobbing for some relief, and we remained there with her.

And then Felix left the hospital, and he walked half a mile until he saw the train station. We watched him. Cavaillon was waking up. Grocers were unfolding their tents and laying out their wares: new cherries, grapes, melon, cheese, chanterelles, asparagus. No river of horses. Felix sat on a bench at the train station as the sky turned from gold to blue. The first train pulled slowly into the station, and then he was gone, like the horses were gone. We watched him leave and we returned to Consuelo's side. She drifted in and out of sleep for hours; her eyes fluttered. She couldn't sit up. She screamed at the fire searing her body and mind and begged for water. The nurse brought morphine and left, shutting the door tight.

"Stillborn," Consuelo said to Lucía. The blood surged in her cheeks. "Write this down: Stillborn, like my life in art." Consuelo cackled. "No, don't. Erase that."

Consuelo took a few long pulls on her Gauloise and held it out until the ash grew and spilled to the carpet. Lucía the spy set her pen down on the top of her knee; on the placid lake of her face, her mouth twitched and fell.

"The baby was gone and I was bleeding out," Consuelo said. Like a confession. "Had she lived, I could have tried to be her mother, maybe." Consuelo's eyes widened, as if stunned by an explosion. She wailed the way she had when she was a child ripped from her mother's arms.

Lucía removed the tickets from her shiny little purse and placed them in Consuelo's hand, hot with susto. "Listen—it's time for you to listen to me. You should go to San Francisco. Go see your sister. New York and that husband you barely like—they won't disappear."

"Who's paying you to tell me what to do?" Consuelo asked.

"I've been sent to you," Lucía said. "That's true. But no one's paying me." She let her face open to Consuelo. "You know me. You know you do. I've been with you this whole time."

"I know you?" Consuelo searched la chelita's face, envied her pristine trench coat. She'd owned a shiny little purse like that at some point. And look at her now. Her shoes were made of rope, her feet filthy, the skin of her heels torn.

"Your mother is the volcano, Izalco," Lucía said. "Your sister is the star, Graciela."

How? How did this glossy-haired güerita know about that private little song of hers? She looked like Veronica Lake or Dolores del Río, nothing like the cipota fantasma María, who had visited her before. She'd been with her all along? Hardly. Consuelo was alone in this life.

"You watched me die," Lucía said. "In our village, you watched me die, and then you ran. I saw you."

Consuelo sucked in her breath.

"Here's the telegram," Lucía said. She took a small piece of paper from the pocket of her trench coat and held it up, her movements too quick and jerky for Consuelo to read anything aside from her name, her sister's name, and the word FINALLY.

"Graciela will receive it later today," Lucía continued, returning the telegram to her pocket. "She'll be expecting you."

"I'm sorry," Consuelo said. She had no other words.

"Oh," Lucía said, waving her away. "You'll need this too—fare for the cab to her place. You'll go there after you arrive. Don't lose it." Lucía pressed the stack of bills and a note with Graciela's address into Consuelo's hand, folding her dirty fingers over the pile. She shrugged, her hand still covering Consuelo's, meeting her eye. "What else could you have done? They would have just killed you too." She frowned, shook her head.

"Here," she said. "Take this too." She took the shiny purse off her shoulder and dumped the contents of Consuelo's small, shaking hand—the tickets, the money, the address—into it, then hung it on Consuelo's bony shoulder like a hat on a hook. "You lived—so live the life you want."

And with that, she turned and walked away, her body folding into the crowd and disappearing. Again, Consuelo watched her go.

40

C ONSUELO ARRIVED IN SAN FRANCISCO AROUND MIDNIGHT and took a taxi to Graciela's new home. When she got out of the car, she walked into the middle of the narrow street and examined the houses on the block where her sister lived. A streetlamp and una lunita llena revealed a row of low-slung buildings, economical replicas of the Victorian style that she remembered as being all over this city. Several mail slots gleamed beside the doors; each building appeared to house at least two or three families.

The one that was Graciela's house had metal grates on the windows and a low iron fence in front of a set of stairs that led to a narrow porch and front door. There were chalk scribblings on the concrete in front, woody roses, and laundry drying on a rope tied between the iron handrail of the front steps and a hook jutting out beneath one of the windows. A vine of bougainvillea spilled over the fence, its flowers waving like paper lanterns.

Most of the houses seemed to be painted in brown and gray, depressing colors, Consuelo thought, for houses with such ornate, extraordinary details. They demanded color. But Graciela's was painted a lime green that dazzled in the sun, which to Consuelo, in the moonlight, glowed the soft green of a cacao tree. The disorientation Consuelo felt at arriving in a strange place after dark had never faded for her, despite all of her travels over the years. Her senses swirled, lost in the frantic streetlamp-lit moths, the smell of piss and garbage, the cars and sirens, punctured by a cop's whistle two blocks away, on la calle Veinticuatro. For a moment, she forgot that she was here to see her sister, Graciela.

Late spring, 1942. Consuelo had experienced her thirty-fourth birthday in the sky, flying over the sea between worlds. Gray in San Francisco, buds open and scattered on the wet sidewalks. By fall, Oppède would be overtaken by Nazis. She'd gotten out just in time.

During the months that she'd lived in this city a decade earlier, Consuelo hadn't visited this neighborhood at all. Different neighborhoods held different weather patterns. The air here was softer than she remembered, but the misty fog was familiar.

Then, from behind a heavy curtain, Graciela's face appeared in the window of her little green house and Consuelo screamed, then clamped her hand over her mouth, fearing she'd woken up the neighborhood.

"Come in!" Graciela was saying now in the doorway, waving Consuelo inside and into her arms. Consuelo was la calavera, like the last time the sisters had been together. Graciela's long braid, still wet from the bath, had fallen from its coil down to her waist. Consuelo breathed in her little sister's soapy warmth. Graciela wore a bright yellow bathrobe and cotton pajamas with red flowers all over them. Her cheeks were round and red like the flowers, and Consuelo nearly collapsed with relief onto her sister's shoulder. Minutes passed like this; the sisters rejoiced without words.

Four round tables surrounded by scratched wooden chairs. A sign that read LAS COMADRES hung over a cash register at a bar with metal stools. Graciela lived inside a restaurant.

Behind a sweeping curtain, upstairs, was a long, narrow hallway with small rooms on either side. Graciela slept in the last one, with Salvador. She cracked open the door, and Consuelo squinted to see her nephew cuddling a stuffed bear on a low mattress. Another mother and child shared a bed in the same room.

Graciela presented Consuelo with a rolled towel and a bar of soap and led her to the bathroom at the end of the hallway. She fell asleep in the bath, forgetting where she was entirely. In this bathtub she could be anywhere. She slipped into the Eternal Now, bathtubs collapsing through the elevator shaft of her life's timeline: the tub at the Estate, Ninfa scrubbing her at four years old; the watery rooms of the Steinhart Aquarium; the Sutro Baths and their salty pools; the tub on rue de Castellane; El Gran Pendejo's bathtub; the princess Chasca embracing a stone and falling to the bottom of the lake in search of her lover's body. Consuelo let the water drain and there she slept until morning, the towel wrapped around her for warmth. Sometime in the night, Graciela peeked in on her, to make sure she hadn't drowned. Then she turned off the light.

When she woke up, Consuelo found Graciela in the kitchen. Graciela poured her some tea. She glowed again like an exploding star. The yellow linoleum tile chilly under her bare feet, the greasy ceiling, painted cerulean, the light and noises of this place—almost too bright, it was a marvel, a dream. Her sister was not only alive, but here in this room, in the kitchen of her café and home.

Consuelo began opening drawers and sticky wooden cabinets. She was terribly skinny, the bones of her spine sticking out like knobs through the bathrobe that she'd borrowed from Graciela. The night before, Graciela had noticed how skinny she was, her rope shoes and her filthy torn dress, saw that she'd come with nothing, and laid out clothes for her to wear during her stay. She'd be cold here. Graciela was always cold in this place.

"You must be starving," Graciela said. She began to prepare a plate with some of Silvia's pan dulces and fruit from the market. She began to spoon avena into a bowl for Consuelo.

"I want to see all of your stuff," Consuelo said. "All the things you use every day." She opened a drawer of utensils—spoons and knives in shining order—and stroked the stacks with one finger. "I'm jealous of your customers. They must know you better than I do." She turned to Graciela piteously, waiting for her reassurance. Why hadn't she come sooner? Consuelo hated herself for an instant. She'd missed so much.

"Come on, eat," Graciela said, placing the plate of fruit and pastries on the table. Maybe the food would soothe her sister's chaos. "Before we open up for the day and all this goes away."

Consuelo picked at the spread as Salvador appeared in the doorway, four years old in a week's time, his pajama shirt up over his belly, dragging the bear on its face over the linoleum. He startled at the sight of Consuelo, her wild eyes, her feet, standing in his mother's bathrobe, a bouquet of knives in her bony fist.

"Cielito lindo. My, what a little prince," Consuelo said. She knelt before him, and the boy ran behind his mother. Graciela took the knives from her sister's hands and placed them in the sink, one hand on Salvador's shoulder.

"This is your Auntie Consuelo." Graciela crouched beside the boy, holding the small of his back. "She's come to stay with us." Graciela chose her words carefully. "Stay" instead of "visit," because she hoped Consuelo would. She wanted to understand who her sister was, all over again.

The child was beautiful, with Graciela's black eyes and long lashes. He wiggled two fingers at Consuelo.

Graciela joined her sister at the table and tried to convince her to stay. Here Graciela had found a family. There was plenty of room for her. Can you believe that they owned this house? All of it was theirs. The old broken tiles in the bathroom, the bedroom window that wouldn't fully close upstairs, the faucet that dripped rusty water beneath the sink—one day they'd fix it all. But for now, they were good, stable. Their children were fed and happy. She had a job at the library and the café was doing well, and they had plenty of friends. She couldn't wait for Consuelo to meet the others—Silvia, Clara, Josefina, all of the children. The neighborhood itself reminded her a little of home too. There was a jacaranda tree right out there on the sidewalk—did Consuelo see it?

Consuelo was silent for a long time, trying to imagine Graciela's life, and herself in it. She didn't know what the fuck a jacaranda tree was. Had she ever seen a tree in her life? Did she even know how to see? That fucking teacher. Painting Reality! Learning how to see! And frankly, she dreaded meeting all of these friends, all of these hermanas who'd replaced her, who'd done a better job than she ever could at being family to Graciela. She needed a drink and four thousand cigarettes. She wanted to tame her nerves well enough to be able to cry and not stop crying for hours, to tell her sister everything that she'd told Lucía, la güerita ghost spy, about the horses and the baby, about waking up to Felix gone. But no, no, she couldn't speak that vortex of terror into being, not with this beautiful child right here, cowering from her eyes. Could she live here one day, learn how not to be terrifying, make some decent sculptures again, return to painting? Could she?

How spectacularly would she fail?

Consuelo opened her mouth and described the house in the country her husband had promised her. "Like a long white ship," she said, "on the very edge of New York." Graciela couldn't pretend to be impressed. She changed the subject.

"How about a magic trick?" she said, taking Consuelo's battered watch from her pocket and returning it to her sister, placing it beside the bowl of avena. Consuelo smiled, considering the inert, ticking watch for a moment before touching it, as if its scratched, clouded face, its delicate golden chain, its hook and eye, were aspects of a living specimen, a venomous snake. She dangled the watch over her left wrist and reached across the table for Graciela to clasp it closed.

Graciela had a few hours before she needed to be at the library, so she, Consuelo, and Salvador walked to Aquatic Park, where the wall between the bay and the land was studded with the gravestones from the Odd Fellows Cemetery. She pointed out the Half Moon cannery with her lips as they passed, the building's tower, the stupid fresco inside: a bunch of blue-eyed gringas picking fruit. Ha. The place was a museum now.

Consuelo caught her reflection in one of the windows. Always, when faced by herself, she met her own eye, glanced up and down her mirrored body, tightened her stomach, sucked in the flesh of her cheeks to examine the bones, scrutinized the parts of herself that she didn't see in photographs. She was empty-handed, malnourished from her year in the kingdom of rocks, not as strong as she'd imagined herself to be. She wore Graciela's long wool skirt and lumpy sweater, a pair of thick socks, and rubber boots that one of the women had hung on to from the cannery days. Graciela had thrown away the sandals made of rope.

"I can't believe you used to be a movie star," Consuelo said. She hadn't meant to be cruel, exactly, but she felt the need to speak the words aloud. She'd never seen a trace of anything glamorous in her little sister, and certainly didn't now.

Graciela looked annoyed. She was annoyed, having understood Consuelo's implication—an india, like you?—and fallen back into their old dynamic. Had she even written to Consuelo about the reason she left Hollywood? Stabbing the cop and all the rest? At the moment, uncharacteristically, she couldn't remember if she had. She'd tell Consuelo everything later that night, once Salvador was in bed, once the sparks of her sad passions had settled. Her big little sister. She needed some food and some rest. She looked crazed.

"Ay, there's really not much to it. Just a job like any other," Graciela finally said. "I was never really a star. More like a whole bunch of small parts. I was versatile, they said."

Consuelo shook her head. "I'm sorry. That was stupid. I don't know what I'm talking about."

"You must be exhausted," Graciela said. "Let's get you home."

They walked south on Van Ness, homeward on the Royal Road. At Market they shielded their eyes from the sun and crossed over the streetcar tracks to Gough, then Valencia, then they were back in the Mission, their path narrow and shaded again. A viejito indio came by with roses in a paint bucket, and Graciela bought some to commemorate the day: blood-red, wet with dew.

Una indita sat nearby on a green wooden bench.

Salvador grabbed the roses from his mother's hands. Graciela flinched, as she watched a thorn prick her son's finger, as a duende's teardrop of blood appeared, but he didn't seem to care. He ran to the woman on the bench.

"¡Abuela!" Salvador called out. He shook the roses like a rattle and petals rained down at her feet. Graciela realized that he thought he was looking at the woman he'd seen in the drawing Consuelo had sent them. He thought he was seeing his abuela's eyes.

"Mis hijas," la viejita said. "Mis hijas." She faced las hermanas. She wore a flowered scarf tied under her chin and leaned against a pair of shopping bags that were slumped next to her on the bench. Both of her eyes were clouded over with cataracts. The woman was ancient, much older than Socorrito would have been—old enough to be their great-grandmother, their great-great-grandmother.

Consuelo's breath stilled with susto, and she studied the old woman's face, wanting to believe, despite all reason, that this old woman was Socorrito.

Salvador reached to pat la vieja's hand, and Graciela picked him up and set him on her hip.

"I'm sorry, maitra," Graciela said. "We thought you were someone else." Salvador had been doing this lately—searching the faces of strangers, certain that he knew them.

La maitra whispered hoarsely, a prayer, maybe, looking nowhere. She cackled without a sound. Graciela tapped her sister on the shoulder, taking her out of the spell.

Consuelo couldn't believe her mind. It was scrambled, useless, damaged. Permanent heatstroke! Too much wine! Paint fumes! She wanted to scream. What was wrong with her that she couldn't tell her mother from a stranger? She began to sweat. Graciela took her by the elbow, and Salvador led them as they continued down the Royal Road.

We walked with them as they went, a few steps behind; they didn't see us. Lourdes carried her plastic bags of paper, the maps, the poems, the letters she'd found and printed in the middle of the night. La María-Malía swaggered in navy-blue Dickies, her silver hair shaved close on the sides and back, a long lock swooping over her beautiful broad forehead, her igneous eyes crinkling at the corners, winking and pointing her lips at all the pretty guatemaltecas crossing South Van Ness.

"She's too young for you, Malía," Lourdes told her, again and again.

"I'm too dead for her," María laughed back.

And la anciana Cora, hunched and muttering, her face smudged with dirt, leaning against a teenage Lucía, eyeliner smudged in moody circles and eucalyptus in her hair from soaking all day in the ruins of the Sutro Baths.

Together we walked past Lourdes's library. Past the bakery where Graciela would purchase Salvador's fourth birthday cake, chocolate with blue icing. The icing flowers would turn his tongue, his fingers, his cheeks a brilliant indigo blue. We continued down la calle Veinticuatro and walked past a brick wall that would one day serve as a canvas for one of María's disappearing murals, the story of La Siguanaba and her children. We walked past the newspaper office where Graciela would start a paper for the neighborhood. We carried them home to Las Comadres.

And then we returned to the Royal Road and walked north again to Geary, and then we turned west and walked to the edge of our world, the sun in our eyes, heavy over the sea. Tired now, we gathered ourselves beside the ocean. We stood together in the wind, let the shadows collect whispered accounts of our origins, and faced the sea, that place where we see the dawn of life. When the sun disappeared behind our world, our bodies did too. It hurt a little, but mostly, we felt relief at the unbraiding. We set down our weight. As always, we have no idea when we'll be back.

But listen to us—we call out to you now. You don't hear our soft voices, our wicked, beautiful laughter, our songs, do you?

We're still here. Listen.

ACKNOWLEDGMENTS

Many thanks for the brilliance and patience of my editor, Naomi Gibbs, whose incisive and generative magic fills me with awe and gratitude, and for my incredibly savvy-yet-tender, charm-bomb-genius agent, Stephanie Delman. To be read by you both, with such care, intelligence, confidence, attention, curiosity, and grace, is a tremendous honor, and you guided the transformation of this pile of pages into a book. May we cackle all together soon. Thank you to Lisa Lucas and the whole team at Pantheon, especially Josie Kals, Julianne Clancy, Altie Karper, Cat Courtade, and Natalia Berry, and to the gorgeous Trellis Literary Management for see-ing me and inviting me inside. Thank you to Allison Malecha, Niki Chang, Juliet Mabey, Planeta México, and Oneworld Publishing, for taking these ghost gals around the world.

Lemme pull a Lourdes here and tell you about the books, libraries, scholars, Life Springs of Knowledge that I've been enriched by through-out the process of writing this book, to which I'm forever indebted. Books are made of other books. These are some of the books that lit the path to my own: Ilan Stavans's translation of the *Popol Vuh,* as well as Michael Bazzett's divine version; Roberto Lovato's *Unforgetting;* Ingrid Rojas Contreras's *The Man Who Could Move Clouds; Women Artists and the Surrealist Movement,* by Whitney Chadwick; *The Cambridge History of Latina/o American Literature; Dictatorships in the Hispanic World,* by Patricia A. Swier and Julia Riordan-Goncalves; *Dividing the Isthmus: Central American Transnational Histories, Literatures, and Cultures,* by Ana Patricia Rodríguez; *Seeing Indians,* by Virginia Q. Tilley; *To Rise in Darkness,* by Jeffrey L. Gould and Aldo A. Lauria-Santiago; William Krehm's *Democracies and Tyrannies of the Caribbean; Remembering a Massacre in El Salvador,* by Héctor Lindo-Fuentes, Erik Ching, and Rafael A. Lara-Martínez; the articles "The Popol Vuh: Primordial Mother Participates in the Creation," by Bettina L. Knapp, and Claudia M. De La Cruz's "Can Art Represent a Country? In Search of Salvadoran Cultural and National Identities Through 20th Century Literature, Poetry, and Art"; *Miguel Mármol,* by Roque Dalton; Thomas P. Anderson's *Matanza; The Little Prince* and *Wind, Sand and Stars,* by Antoine de Saint-Exupéry; *Kingdom of Rocks* and *The Tale of the Rose,* by Consuelo de Saint-Exupéry; Leonora Carrington's fiction and tarot; so much Eduardo Galeano; and *Volcán,* a brilliant anthology of Central American poetry put out by City Lights. And more thanks to Carlos Henríquez Consalvi, and to a place that is like a book in its multitudes, El Museo de la Palabra y la Imagen, in San Salvador. Big shout-out to Tami Suzuki of the San Francisco Public Library and to Catherine Morse, Edras Rodriguez-Torres, and Charles G. Ransom of the University of Michigan library system. All of my admiration and gratitude to the work of artists Guadalupe Maravilla, Kiara Aileen Machado, and Lorena Molina. Thank you to Andrea Santiza, for the potent and the precious, to Karla T. Vasquez, for the nourishment, to Angelica García, mujer bendita, for the songs.

I'm grateful for the places and people who published my work, invited me to write with them, gave me time, space, and pisto, read my work with exquisite care, taught me, and supported me. Thank you to the Gould Center for the Humanities, for sending me to El Salvador. Thank you, Rackham Foundation, for a pair of travel grants that took me to France and to the Butler Library at Columbia University so I could investigate the historical footprints of one version of Consuelo's wild life. Thank you, Tyson Award, for helping me pay my rent. Thank you to

Marlee Grace and the Have Company Residency; Meghan Forbes and *Harlequin Creature;* to the *Boston Review,* especially Min Jin Lee; to *Pleiades,* especially Rosebud Ben-Oni; and to *Ploughshares,* and the special kindness of an editor. Thanks to *The Wandering Song* editors Leticia Hernández-Linares, Rubén Martínez, and Héctor Tobar, for publishing a version of the dream of indigo. Thank you to the Under the Volcano Sandra Cisneros Fellowship and to Magda Bogin, Nelly Rosario, Aysegul Savas, Adam Foulds, Tim MacGhabban, Keetje Kuipers, Radhiyah Ayobami, Robin Myers, and Emily Withnall, and especially my dear friend, hermana, and travel companion Lizzie Hutchins. You are *Perros Románticos,* all of you. Thank you to Tin House, for the time, space, and kindness, particularly to Lance Cleland; and to my residency neighbor and treasured balm/elixir buddy and cool-mom soulmate, Chelsea Bieker. Thank you to Aspen Words and Isa Catto. Thank you to Mike and Hilary Gustafson, and to the Literati Bookstore community, for covering my shifts when I absconded to write, and also to Brian Short and Katie Vloet for letting me skip town in the interest of this book. Thank you, Christin Lee and Room Project, and thank you, Good Hart Residency and Sue and Bill Klco. Thank you to the Periplus Collective, especially my dear friend and mentor Esmé Weijun Wang, Ash Huang, Vauhini Vara, and my 2021 Fellows cohort. All my gratitude to the life-changing Helen Zell Writers' Program at the University of Michigan, Ann Arbor, especially to my teachers Peter Ho Davies and Eileen Pollack, and to the inspiring writers I met in workshops there: A. L. Major, K. Rose Miller, Rebecca Scherm, Rachel Farrell, Meron Hadero, Airea D. Matthews, Claire Skinner, Camille Beckman, Gala Mukomolova, Megan Levad, Daniel DiStefano, John Ganiard, Eric McDowell, Daniel Hornsby, Matt Robison, Marcelo Hernández Castillo, Derrick Austin, Brit Bennett, Rebecca Fortes, Olujide Adebayo-Begun, Henry Leung, Chris McCormick, Dan Frazier, Dan Keane, Kendra Langford-Shaw, Maya West, Mairead Small Staid, Jia Tolentino, H. R. Webster, and so many others. The next platter of chicken tenders at Old Town is on me.

Thank you to so many dear friends, generous, smart readers, and inspiring writing companions over the years, you many-gendered comadres of my heart, and of this book: Alana DeRiggi, Julie Buntin, Jacinda Townsend, Lydia Conklin, Jaimien Delp, Aisha Sabatini Sloan, Ali Shapiro, Lillian Li, Patrick Martin Holian, Courtney Faye Taylor, Hyeseung Song, Sakinah Hofler, Elisa Wouk Almino, Lisa Low, and, for decades and millennia, mi hermana-maestra Leticia Hernández-Linares. Carcajadas of tenderness, joy, and appreciation, and all of my love to dear friends Natasha Varner, Meridith Hoover, Sylvia Nolasco, Julie Cadman-Kim, Annie Gaus, Maggie Guerra Marks, Heidi LaValle, Erica Brown, Liz Ferdon, Cristina Domínguez, Kate Duchowny, Jeanne Joesten, Amy Sacksteder, Crystal Flynt, Abi Celis, Andrea Lipsky-Karasz, Madison Cruz, Matthew David Flores, Jamie Vander Broek, Charlotte Bruell, Jon Yahalom, and Erin Upton-Cosulich. Thank you, Elianna Kan, Melissa Danaczko, Julia Ringo, and Nadxi Nieto, for believing in this book. Lequietta "Lala" Folk, Nicola Gherson, the Ann Arbor YMCA, Cheri Whitner, and Amanda Houston, thanks for taking care of my kid. Thank you, Christine Asidao, Andrew Ching-Hung, and Joel Rubenstein, for taking care of me.

Thank you, with everything I've got, to my beautiful family: Charles, Oliver, and Bella. I treasure you three. And to my roots: Miguel, Jean, Fran, Michael, René Alberto, Angel, Mario, Jules, the magical Em Dalmeyer, and my wonderful nieces and nephews, Brookie, Brandon, Donaven, Mila, Robbie, Ryan, Richie. Thank you to ur-comadres Iris Biblowitz and Ninfa Álvarez Pleites. And to Archer, Uncle Mario, and all the others who are with us, laughing through the veil.

A NOTE ABOUT THE AUTHOR

Gina María Balibrera earned an MFA in Prose from the University of Michigan's Helen Zell Writers' Program. She has received grants from Aspen Words, Tin House, the Rackham Foundation, and the Periplus Collective, as well as a Tyson Award, an Aura Estrada Prize, and Under the Volcano's Sandra Cisneros Fellowship. Her work has appeared in the *Boston Review, Latino Book Review, Pleiades, The Wandering Song: Central American Writing in the United States,* and elsewhere. She lives in Ann Arbor, Michigan, with her family.

A NOTE ABOUT THE TYPE

This book was set in Adobe Garamond. Designed for the Adobe Corporation by Robert Slimbach, the fonts are based on types first cut by Claude Garamond (ca. 1480–1561). Garamond was a pupil of Geoffroy Tory and is believed to have followed the Venetian models, although he introduced a number of important differences, and it is to him that we owe the letter we now know as "old style." He gave to his letters a certain elegance and feeling of movement that won their creator an immediate reputation and the patronage of Francis I of France.

Typeset by Scribe,
Philadelphia, Pennsylvania

Printed and bound by Berryville Graphics,
Berryville, Virginia

Designed by Casey Hampton